ANDEAN REBEL

Three Days in a Life

GREGORY ARTHUR SOLSRUD

ANDEAN REBEL
Three Days in a Life

Table of Contents

Dedication

To My Children,

To Whom every day I urge to live to their fullest potential. Study hard and master your undertaking. Dream big for dreams change the world.

Upon giving this advice, I realized that the best advice is the advice shown not told. For them and for all of us who have a dream, I have written and sent this book out to the world.

Hasta la Victoria siempre!

TO THE SUN

Oh the sweetest mistake! Oh Sun! You saw
Your innocent people
Under the merciless sword
Like amber wheat grieving before mowed
Vainly their dying eyes
For vengeance and protection looked up forever faithful to you
You neglected them,
As you followed your timeless path,
The bloody and the still died.

José María Heredia
Latin Revolutionary Poet
(1803-1839 - Al Sol, 1826)

Chapter One – Sunday Morning

Inside the cockpit of a small airplane, a young man with sharp eyes peered for his landmarks among the thick jungle foliage. High Andean ridges rose majestically above him, providing refuge to men who fought for life, liberty and the pursuit of happiness. The government feared them in their country of Colombia. These men awaited the plane's return; their success gave them time to rest before another foray.

With the small town of Santa Angelia beckoning in the distance, the young man looked below for the subtle color change, signaling where the hidden canyon began. He cut power, descending to where the plane's own turbulence fluttered the showy, red flowers atop the tall Ceiba trees. The stall horn cried in fear. A small slit in the verdure opened, and a dirt path appeared. The plane, heavy and slow, dropped in the dead air below the treetops. The young man pulled sharply back on the yoke, creating just enough lift to cheat gravity and land the plane softly.

He chopped the engines and pumped the brakes. The plane rolled swiftly, eating up the narrow trail, stopping finally under a green roof of interlacing tall trees. The young man wedged himself out of the side window and dropped clumsily to the ground. Men came up to him, smiling broadly, clapping him on his back like a long-lost brother while kissing the various medallions hung around their necks. An old man, with curly, dappled white hair and worn clothes, pushed through the crowd; he threw his arms around the young man and kissed his cheeks.

"You have been gone a long time," the old man said. "I am happy you are back safely."

"It has been your fault," the young man replied. "Because of the victories, the Air Force has been shooting at anything that moves. I have been playing hide and seek with them."

"Every time you come back to me, I know God has returned you, and our cause is just," the old man said with great feeling.

The young man, whose name was Anthony Wyatt, tall and broad-shouldered with sun-streaked light hair, wore an olive green shirt, stained with grease and sweat, and khaki paratrooper pants. He took off his aviator glasses and wiped them on the hem of his shirt. As he dusted himself off and ruffled his sweat-soaked shirt, he looked back down the road; the palm fronds cut evenly to allow the high wings of the plane to clear them, but barely. Even a haphazard helicopter could never believe a plane landed on such a path.

He felt good.

"Do you have anything for me?" the old man asked.

"Yes," Anthony answered. "It's in my pack, buckled in the co-pilot's seat. Let me crawl in and get it for you."

Anthony started towards the front of the plane.

"No, I will bring your pack to the tent," he called out, happy that the young man had remembered. "Come. Eat something and rest."

The other men, who had greeted Anthony, started opening up the cargo doors. Several boxes and duffel bags fell from the overstuffed plane. Anthony, although he knew it was foolish, never asked how much or what he was carrying. The supplies were needed; that was enough.

The old man, named Carlos, walked towards the tents hidden among the trees. Anthony started to follow, when the men shouted loudly. He turned around; the men were unloading several cases of scotch. In rapid Spanish, Carlos ordered several of them to follow him with the cases.

Anthony followed Carlos into a tent, stooping slightly to enter the doorway. He flopped onto the bed and exhaled.

"I'll bring you something to eat," Carlos said, leaving the tent.

Anthony Wyatt was extremely tired, hungry and relieved. He was back to the home he had made here in the mountains after being away and seeing the other camps and leaders of the various resistance movements. Now, he could eat without being poisoned, and sleep without being knifed.

"What a trip, I thought I'd never get back," he said aloud.

"Anthony, like the ancient cat of Egypt, you bring luck and bounty, every time you return," a voice said, in clean, crisp Castilian.

Anthony jumped up. The man who spoke walked in and embraced Anthony. He was tall and sinewy with tight set eyes and a hawk nose. His hair was long, wild and black etched with white, tied back with a silk bandana. Juan de la Valle was the leader of this band of rebels.

"You look none the worse," Juan said, as he held Anthony at arm's length and looked at him with piercing blue eyes.

"I don't care what I look like. I'm just happy to be here," Anthony said.

"War brings out the worst in men," Juan replied. "And in this constant war, men are constantly made worse."

Juan went over to a small, dirty footlocker, lifted the lid, and pulled out a bottle.

"This should help until Carlos brings us something to eat." He poured out two glasses of heavy, red wine. "I promised myself that I would drink no more until you returned," Juan said. "It's damn hard to find Spanish wine in the middle of this god forsaken jungle."

Like a connoisseur drinking his last glass, Juan swirled the wine, inhaled the fumes deeply and took a large drink, which he kept in his mouth for several moments. Finally, he swallowed and turned to Anthony.

"It is in small moments like this that I can remember I am human and for what I am fighting," Juan said.

Before Anthony answered, Juan jumped up.

"They followed you in," he shouted. "Help me. Hurry!"

Juan ran to the side of the tent and heaved an ammo case to the ground. Anthony lifted one end. It was heavy. Juan was throwing blankets and boxes aside.

"I've got the launcher," he yelled, pulling it out of a slim case.

Juan jerked up the other side of the ammo box. He dragged the box and Anthony out of the tent. Three helicopters swooped in tight formation over the camp, their wheels skimming the tops of the tall Ceiba trees.

"We still have time," Juan panted as he trotted. "They are searching for your plane. When they come back for their next pass, we must be ready."

The trees were alive with men scurrying in all directions. Juan sent branches whacking back at Anthony as they hurtled through the undergrowth. Anthony wanted both hands to cover his face. Juan, with his long legs, leapt through the jungle like a leopard, the rocket launcher in one hand and the other pulling the ammo box.

They ascended a slope where the trees and vegetation had been cut back. They came to a well-concealed bunker, made from the downed trees and brush. Juan dropped his end of the crate and leapt over the log wall.

"Lift it up to me," Juan commanded.

Anthony grasped each end of the crate, his arm stretched as far as he could reach. He squatted and threw his hips up, heaving the crate against the logs. He levered each end, slowly stepping the bulky crate higher.

"Hurry! I hear them returning," Juan yelled, adjusting the firing sights.

Anthony bulled the box to the top of the log wall and pushed an end towards Juan. He grabbed the free handle and pulled the box towards him, crashing it onto the floor of the bunker.

"Jump inside," Juan bellowed. "Load me quickly."

Anthony leapt over the wall into the concealed firing station. Anthony righted the case and wrenched it open. Two rows of red tips looked back at him. He seized one.

"Stick it in," Juan said quickly, bringing the launcher to his shoulder.

Anthony pushed the rocket into the back end of the launcher and heard it click into place. They waited.

The first helicopter appeared. Anthony heard the trigger click and the sharp whoosh of the rocket. As he bent down to grab another rocket, he heard the explosion. He looked out. Around the fiery ball, a second helicopter careened. Juan fired again. It exploded.

"Great shooting," Anthony screamed, watching the debris fall in front of them.

"Load me quick," Juan ordered. "Another flies behind."

The third helicopter tried to escape by flying vertically skyward. Anthony watched Juan tip the rocket launcher back leading the heaven bound target slightly. Anthony heard the click of the trigger. The third helicopter disintegrated into flame. Anthony shielded his eyes from the blinding light, feeling the heat on his face. The forward momentum of the helicopter flung debris at them. They ducked and flattened themselves against the logs as hot pieces of metal crashed down on top of them.

Juan whooped ecstatically, pulling Anthony up and hugging him. Anthony had mud and black ash all over him. Juan looked unscathed except for a small smudge on his left cheek.

"Welcome home," Juan said, squeezing Anthony on the shoulder.

"I didn't see anything following me," Anthony said.

"That'll teach those bastards to come chasing after you," Juan replied. "Load me up, in case there are more following behind."

Anthony picked up another rocket as Juan switched to the other side of the makeshift bunker looking out toward the mouth of the canyon.

"Hold still so I can push it in," Anthony said.

Juan settled the launcher against the top of the wall, and Anthony loaded it. They sat silently for several minutes.

"Damn! These American-made rocket launchers are good. Light and dead accurate," Juan said with a laugh. "Americans make the finest weapons."

"Juan, I'm sorry. I will be more careful in the future."

"It's not your fault, Anthony," Juan replied. "They keep rebuilding the radar installations. We blew up the one for this section last week, but they must have fixed it under the cover of the night."

"They have portable ones which they pull behind a truck," Anthony replied.

"Technology keeps marching ahead," Juan said. "That's how they followed you."

"The portable ones are not as powerful. It must be close," Anthony said.

"Do you know what they look like?" Juan asked.

"I've seen one," Anthony replied. "They all pretty much look the same."

"We have to knock it out," Juan said. "If they can use radar and defend with coordinated air support, we'll never push them out."

"I'll retrace my route in with Carlos. We'll find it," Anthony said.

They sat silently scanning the skies for more aircraft.

"I think it was only them," Juan said.

"They usually fly in packs of three," Anthony replied.

"We should return and see if they caused any damage," Juan said, sliding the launcher off his shoulder.

"You destroyed those helicopters," Anthony replied with a grin, "You damned near killed me running with these rockets."

"We downed all three," Juan said contentedly. "Young, bold pilots don't live too long."

"They were flying too slowly," Anthony agreed. "It allowed us to reload and down all three."

Juan unloaded and gave the rocket to Anthony to repack. Anthony closed the case and locked the lid. They worked together to carefully hoist the box up and over the wall, walking slowly back to camp.

A crowd of soldiers was waiting for them by Juan's tent.

"Where'd they come from?" several called out.

"*Antonio* returned with admirers, and I made them feel welcome," Juan replied, holding the launcher over his head and waving it.

The men laughed and clapped Anthony on the shoulder.

Juan stayed talking with his men for several minutes. His Castilian Spanish contrasted sharply with the course dialect spoken by his men, almost contrasting as sharply as his tall, lean figure against the squat, heavy indigenous stature of his men. Like the single-minded conquistadors who trampled this same ground, centuries ago, Juan de la Valle sallied forth with a maniacal panache, which inspired and awed his men. His men called him "*El Jefe*" -- "The Chief".

Anthony dragged the case and launcher inside the tent, straightening up where Juan had thrown everything around. When Juan came inside the tent, Anthony asked him how he heard those helicopters coming.

"Survival," Juan responded, "from many years of long survival. You are picking it up too. You weren't far behind me."

"One step can be the difference between being whole," Anthony said, "and being in pieces. I've learned that from you."

"The more success, the more trouble and these attacks," Juan said.

"You have the *federales* on the run," Anthony replied. "You are a target."

"Yes, like a sitting duck," Juan replied.

"You have more men than the army colonel in Santa Angelia. You are a general of an army," Anthony said.

"We are guerillas, not regular foot soldiers."

"Tito is hell bent on attacking Santa Angelia," Anthony said.

"Yes, Tito is readying his men. He wants to attack immediately."

"Excellent," Anthony replied without thinking. He saw Juan's jaw tighten.

"Excellent if you wish to die," Juan said.

"I heard Mono wants to join you," Anthony said quickly to change the subject.

"You did? From whom?" Juan responded, staring at Anthony.

"From Tito," Anthony replied. He had forgotten to hold his tongue; Juan was extremely paranoid, fearing betrayal from everyone.

"Tito thinks he can control Mono," Juan began slowly.

"Mono commands the largest force in the country. I've flown into a couple of airstrips he controls. They have tanks, artillery, everything."

"Yes, he is well-financed, I even hear his men call him *Capitán General,* but . . .," Juan threw back his wine in one swallow.

"But, what?" Anthony pressed. "It is what you have been talking about, a grand alliance of guerrillas. First, Tito came to you and now Mono will be with you. The *federales* will be on the defensive now."

"Yes, the resistance forces must work together, but it's too quick. We should wait."

"Why wait? The *federales* are in a general retreat in this section. Once we take the next valley, we can control the whole coast, Cartagena, Barranquilla," Anthony responded excited.

"If we lose?"

"We won't."

"What if we do?"

"We regroup," Anthony said.

"The Colombian army must win, or it loses. We are *guerrilleros,* we win if we do not lose. Think with your own head, not with someone else's," Juan said.

"I am," Anthony replied.

"And those helicopters? If they had been a little faster off the ground, you'd be the one up in flames," Juan responded vigorously, slamming his fist against the footlocker. ,

"Softly," Carlos said quickly as he entered the tent. In his gnarled hands, he carried two sandwiches and on his back, Anthony's heavy pack. "Save your fight for the *federales,* and leave the furniture at peace."

"Carlos," Juan chuckled, easing the tension, "you always have wise advice. What have you brought us to eat today? *El jamon serrano?*. Where have you been keeping this smoked ham?"

"If it were not for my advice and my food, both of you would be dead by now," Carlos replied, looking at Juan.

Carlos sorted through Anthony's pack, pulling out various packages and laying them aside. Finally, he held up a small, pink box.

"Thank you, *Señor*," Carlos said, smiling broadly, slipping it into his pocket, "this means a lot to me."

Anthony nodded. He looked at Juan, thinking whether he should bring up the attack again.

Carlos continued to rummage through the pack, pulling out a large brown bag.

"Very good! I see that you brought more ham. We will throw a small party," Carlos said.

"Tonight we will eat well," Juan answered.

"In three days, we will sleep even better in the nice soft beds of Santa Angelia," Anthony said, trying to make his words casual and light.

"We are going ahead with the attack, *Señor*?" Carlos asked.

"No," Juan said.

"Wait until Tito comes. He knows how to look at things," Anthony said.

"Tito talks of his 'Gran Colombia.' Well, now it will be here before he knows it," Carlos said.

Juan smiled, reached over and squeezed Anthony on the shoulder.

"Tito and you are becoming right good friends, and maybe with Mono, you do not need me anymore."

Carlos saw that Juan had not let go of Anthony's shoulder. He walked over to the table and stood in front of Juan.

"Finish up the sandwich. I need to clean up in here," Carlos said.

Juan eyed Carlos. He grabbed the sandwich in front of him with his two hands, wolfed it down and left the tent.

Anthony watched through the tent flaps as Juan walked over to a group of young men squatting on their haunches. The tightness in his shoulder slowly disappeared, as the strong wine absorbed into his bloodstream. The precious cargo of ammunition and supplies were here now. He remembered the hard, rough faces of the other rebel leaders. Regular rules did not apply. Only Juan's fierce reputation had kept them at bay. Trust was a strange commodity here. He knew how difficult it was, knowing who to trust as well as when. Anthony went out of the tent to hear what Juan was saying.

"Diego," Juan addressed the one with long arms and a dirty red bandanna tied around his neck, "I need you to lead a deceptive sortie. Are you up to it?"

"Most definitely, Jefe!" Diego stood up quickly. His clothes were a mishmash of different uniforms stained identical by the jungle mud.

"When I have finished telling you what to do, find thirty others who will not tire from a long night with no sleep."

"I already have thirty volunteers, Jefe!" Diego motioned to his group and some other boys lying under the trees. Juan looked at the group, all wide-eyed and soiled and young.

"Do you know where the trail cuts across the peak giving you a clear view of the town?" Juan asked.

"*Si*, Jefe!"

"Can you find it at night?"

"Of course, I have been there many times at night."

"Good," Juan added as he patted Diego on the shoulder. "Go and find the supply master and have him issue each of you a flashlight. Check to make sure each one works and take extra batteries."

"*Si, Jefe*," he replied solemnly.

"Go up to the pass at sunset and start walking across the peak in single file. When you are below the peak and out of sight of the town, double back and do it all over again and again until daybreak."

"You wish us to walk in circles all night long?"

"Yes, I want the army spotters to think there are a thousand men crossing over into the valley."

"We will run all night, Jefe," Diego said proudly, "When it is completely dark, we will save time by coming back along the trail with our flashlights off. They will think there are one hundred thousand men coming."

"You catch on quick, Diego," Juan smiled broadly. "When you are older, you will be *El Jefe*".

"It is an honor to learn from you, Jefe."

Diego saluted stiffly, turned sharply and whistled to his comrades. They quickly gathered up their meager possessions and followed him towards the central supply tent. When they had left, Juan turned to Anthony.

"Those orders are easy to give. Tomorrow, I might have to give orders that mean death. It is difficult to give such orders when looking into a face so young."

Anthony nodded.

"It is a simple ruse," Juan continued. "Simplicity usually works best in a complicated war."

"Your strategy works," Anthony replied, trying a different track. "Your victories make you much feared."

"Is that what they are saying about me in the street?" Juan asked.

"They say you are much respected by your men, but . . ."

"But, what?" Juan asked.

"The politicians fear your intentions."

"*Mis intenciones, Antonio?*" Juan looked at him closely. "My intentions are for peace. The people closest to me, my men, respect and trust me, yet the politicians for whom we fight, don't trust me?"

"I wouldn't put it so strongly," Anthony replied. "They don't trust what they can't control."

"What do they say about Mono?" Juan asked.

"Mono, he's a *paisano*. They trust him," Anthony said. "I don't mean to upset you; I'm telling what I hear."

"At least, they know my men respect me," Juan replied. "Do you know how many came to me today?"

"No."

"Over two hundred," Juan replied proudly. "I will lead them through this war alive. I have them training with some of the older men right now. And the group led by Diego, did you see them?"

"Yes, I saw them," Anthony replied.

"Most of them came to me over six months ago. They do everything I tell them or else I tell them to go. And do you know another thing about them?"

"What?"

"None of them have fathers," Juan said. "All of them killed by the people's politicians and their mistaken mistrust. Diego has been with me over a year. When he came, he was filled with revenge. I told him that revenge would burn him up and kill him. He had to fight for the living, for the men surrounding him. Now, he is a leader and the other boys look up to him."

"The army should be so lucky to have such dedicated soldiers," Anthony said.

"The army and the paramilitaries create an endless supply for me," Juan said. "They come hungry and fearful; I make them men again."

He studied Anthony's face. "Do you wish to sleep?" Juan asked.

"No," Anthony responded.

"Good. Tito is coming," Juan continued. "He will want to talk with you."

They saw Tito come striding through the men. He was a short man, stocky, with a shock of white hair that gave him the look of a learned judge. He was groomed neatly, and no matter how muddy, dusty, or thick the undergrowth, his uniform was spotless.

Tito's eyes lit up when he saw Anthony.

"My American son," he hailed Anthony in a large booming voice, "for too long have I not seen you. I have worried. And you are finally back safely, no?"

From the first moment Tito had met Anthony, he treated him like the son he never had. He encircled Anthony with his beefy hands and gave him a great hug. Anthony winced.

"What is wrong, son? Have you weakened since you left?"

Tito turned and saw Carlos.

"Carlos, have you been feeding our American hero?"

Carlos nodded affirmatively, but said nothing.

"No, I'm fine. I just hurt my arm," Anthony replied.

As soon as the words left his mouth, he regretted them. He saw the look in Tito's eyes.

"What happened?" Juan asked quickly. "You told me nothing about an injury."

"It's nothing. Your victories make you famous, and they want to find you. While looking for you, I took some ground fire and was hit in the arm."

Tito pulled up Anthony's shirtsleeve. He shook his head softly as he saw the temporary bandage.

"The shrapnel only scraped the side of my arm and did not go in," Anthony said.

"Who put this on you?" Tito asked.

"I did."

He shook his head softly from side to side and made clucking noises with his tongue as a gentle chastisement to Anthony. He removed the bandage and moved the skin with his fingers so he could have a better look inside the wound. Anthony grimaced.

"Just as I thought," Tito said. "Juan, the wound is infected."

"Have you had a tetanus shot?" Juan asked Anthony.

"Yes. In the States. Before I came here."

Juan nodded and called to Carlos. "How much time do you need to take him to the doctor in town?"

"I don't need to go to the doctor," Anthony interrupted. "I'll clean the wound better. It will be fine."

Juan ignored him, and continued to Carlos, "How much time, and keep in mind that you cannot be seen in town?"

"A few hours, Jefe. We could be back by midnight," Carlos replied quickly.

"Juan," Anthony insisted. "I'm fine. I'm sorry for not telling you about being shot, but I can take care of myself and do not need to be fussed over like a schoolboy."

Juan looked at him calmly. "You are under my command, correct?"

Anthony nodded.

"Then you will do as I ordered." He saw Anthony stiffen slightly and decided to explain himself.

"Anthony, I do not want to lose you for even a few hours. Here in the jungle, even a small wound can be serious. Bacteria grow rapidly here."

Tito tousled his hair with his thick hand and said, "Go see the doctor, Anthony and come back before we have time to put our pants on. We need you full of health."

Your wound is infected," Juan continued. "Either you did not clean it properly or the cloth was unclean. It needs to be cleaned professionally and possibly, antibiotics administered. You are no good to me with a raging fever or an infected, swollen arm."

Anthony started to say something, but seeing the serious look on both of their faces he nodded, "Yes, sir."

"We should leave immediately, Jefe?" Carlos asked, looking at Juan.

Juan nodded.

Carlos led Anthony out of the tent. They walked down the main trail, following a ridge away from the camp.

They had walked a considerable distance when Carlos stopped abruptly. They watched a distant figure come towards them. Carlos took off his cap, waved it vigorously, and shouted.

"Here is someone you must meet," Carlos said excitedly. "She is the doctor's daughter. She is beautiful."

"I can't see her well from here," Anthony replied.

"Wait," Carlos said quickly. "It will be worth it."

Carlos sat on a nearby rock, pulled out a comb and ran it through his unruly hair. Anthony sat down beside him.

"I become as excited as a schoolboy thinking about her," Carlos replied. "It is too bad I am an old man. It has been a long time since I saw her."

"Will she take you as her boyfriend?" Anthony teased.

"No," Carlos answered shaking his head vigorously. "You don't understand Colombian women, the good ones. They flirt with you, and with their eyes and lips, they make you feel sixteen. Any further, it's for one man."

"So, there's no hope for you," Anthony stated.

"I love to feel sixteen," Carlos replied with a devilish wink.

"I'm younger than you," Anthony replied. "I think I will be safe."

"You wait. She will put you in your place and the only thing you will think of is how you can be near her."

"I don't think . . ." Anthony started to say before Carlos waved him to be quiet.

"Shhh, be quiet now, here she comes, let me introduce you formally."

"Good Day, Senorita Sofia Maria De la Conception Matifino," Carlos called out, bowing formally as she approached.

"Thank you kindly, Señor Carlos Jesus Garcia Fernandez," the young woman responded. They embraced each other warmly.

"We are most honored by your unexpected visit. How have we received such fortune?" he continued in the same low respectful tone.

"I saw it was a pleasant day, and I wondered what my neighbors in the mountain were doing."

"How is your mother?" he asked.

"She is fine," she replied, clearly happy to see him. "How is your belly?"

"It is fat and fine."

"You have not visited us," she said coyly.

"El Jefe has kept me very busy. He gives me no time off."

"I will speak with him about it," she replied.

"If he listens to anyone, he will listen to you," Carlos replied. "Are you staying for dinner?"

"No, my mother expects me back. Don't look so downhearted. I can stay for a while. Unless you have other plans?"

"Serving you was our only plan for the day," Carlos said.

Carlos turned to Anthony and continued, "Let me present my comrade in arms, the chief pilot for the air force of the resistance, *Capitan* Antonio Wyatt."

"Antonio Wyatt?" she answered. "I think he needs a few more names."

Carlos laughed loudly. "You see, I told you she would put you in your place."

Anthony Wyatt never knew how to act when he was introduced to a young, beautiful woman. Her shiny black hair curved eloquently around her oval face highlighting her long, graceful nose, straight white teeth and her red, slightly rounded, full lips. But it was her eyes that held Anthony, dark and expressive surrounded by uplifted brown eyebrows and delicate high cheekbones tinted pink. Her olive colored neck and hands moved gracefully as she talked and smiled. Her cream-colored shirt and dark slacks covered her athletic, curved body. His Midwestern upbringing halted his displays of affection out of embarrassment. He stood there, not knowing whether to embrace her, shake her hand or eke out a weak wave.

Sofia leaned forward and kissed Anthony lightly on the cheek. She smelled sweet and clean.

"I saw your plane come up the valley. I wondered if I was to meet you. *El Jefe* Juan has talked of you often when he has come to visit my mother. Where did you land?"

"There is an airstrip beyond the hill behind us," he said. "It's difficult to see, even if you know where it is."

"*Señor* Wyatt is being modest. It's only a dirt road and no airstrip," Carlos remarked. "I fear for him every time he flies the plane."

"You look fresh from a long walk, was it pleasant?" Anthony inquired politely, trying to deflect the attention.

"I was looking for some wild cocoa beans that used to grow along the hillside," Sofia said.

"Cocoa is my favorite drink when it is cold," Carlos said.

"When I find some beans, I will make cocoa for you," Sofia said.

"I will wait for that moment with great anticipation," Carlos replied.

As Carlos finished his sentence, a man came running up.

"Carlos, I'm glad I caught up to you. El Jefe wants to talk to you," the man panted, breathing hard and holding his side.

"Excuse me, *Señor*, but we must start back," Carlos said. "It's probably important."

"What is it Carlos?" Sofia asked.

"I'm not sure," he replied quickly. "We need to return to speak with El Jefe."

"May I come with you?" Sofia asked.

"Yes, of course. We were on our way into town; most likely El Jefe wants me to pick something up or speak to someone."

"You were going into town? To visit me?" she asked teasingly.

"No, but I would have seen you," he replied happily. "We were coming into town to see your mother. *Señor* Wyatt has an injury that El Jefe wants your mother to examine."

She looked at Anthony.

"It can't be that serious because you are not carrying him. What is wrong?"

"I was shot in the arm, and Juan believes the wound is infected," Anthony replied.

Sofia turned to Carlos.

"You do know that the military is in town. It will be hard to explain how an American just happened to wander in. They will ask many questions. It could be dangerous for him."

"I was going to wait until it was dark before I came into town," Carlos replied.

"Good. After we see what El Jefe Juan wants, I will accompany you back, and I can learn all about the conquering *Yanqui*," Sofia said, smiling slyly to Anthony.

Carlos motioned the young soldier to lead ahead. They walked in single file until they came to Juan's tent. Carlos went in, while the others waited outside. Juan came out immediately with a wide smile on his face.

"Forgive Carlos' poor manners," Juan said smoothly. "He should have brought you inside immediately."

Without waiting for a reply, he opened up the front of the tent and motioned them in. When she came inside, she saw that they were all smiling.

"What makes you all smile?" she asked.

"Carlos," Juan said promptly. "He was planning on keeping you all to himself and not letting you visit with us."

She walked up to Carlos, bent over and kissed his stubbly cheeks. She put her arm around his waist and looked at them.

"Don't give too much trouble to Carlos, or I'll be mad at all of you," she replied.

"We are jealous of Carlos," Tito replied sincerely, "because he is the special one, and we are not."

"I love you all equally well, Tito," she replied. "But you are right, Carlos is my favorite. He takes very good care of me.

"He takes very good care of all of us," Juan replied.

"I've brought the medicines you asked for," Sofia said, walking over to Juan.

"Thank you," Juan responded, taking the medicines from her. "Did you have any problems bringing them?"

"No," Sofia replied, "the colonel does not strictly enforce the rules."

"The colonel does not enforce the rules for you," Juan replied.

Sofia looked at him and replied, "You have been talking to my mother?"

"Doctor Matifino and I are old friends," Juan replied.

"Well then you know that the colonel has been to our house many times. He respects my mother greatly."

"*Senorita* Sofia," Juan said, "have you met Captain Wyatt?"

Anthony heard her respond. Juan bragged about his acuity as a pilot and his appetite for adventure. Anthony wanted to reply glibly, but his tongue felt like it weighed a ton.

"Mr. Wyatt is our great hope for the future," Juan continued without a pause. "With his connections in the United States, he will make his government recognize its error in supporting the current, corrupt government."

"Mr. Wyatt must be a very important man in his own country," Sofia replied. "Very impressive for one so young."

"I'm not," Anthony stumbled on his words. "I'm not that important."

"I've known El Jefe Juan for three years, and rarely does he praise someone. You must have some abilities."

Anthony reddened and did not say anything.

"Captain Wyatt is becoming a fine leader. The men already look up to him. Isn't that true Tito?" Juan asked.

"Yes, Anthony is our good luck talisman," Tito replied heartily, tousling Anthony's hair.

Anthony managed a weak smile.

Both Juan and Tito spoke to Sofia with great attention. Tito offered her his seat, while Juan brought her a small glass of strong coffee. Each of them spoke at once, attempting to attract Sofia's attention. Sofia showed favoritism to neither man, responding politely to each. Anthony watched, relieved that the attention was no longer on him. He was mesmerized by Sofia. She was beautiful. The more Anthony watched, the more entranced he became by the slow rise and fall of her shapely breasts with each delicate breath.

"Anthony. Anthony." Juan's voice broke Anthony out of his reverie.

"Yes, the ..." he began hesitantly. He hoped that they had not noticed that he had been staring so intently at her.

"You see why I believe we must send him to your mother," Juan said. "He's already becoming delirious because of infection."

"No, I'm tired, that is all," Anthony replied, grateful that they had not noticed anything.

"My mother will help him as she helps everyone," Sofia said. "If you need Carlos, I can take him to her."

"Thank you for the offer. I need Carlos right now," Juan replied. "I will send him down later to receive your mother's report and guide Anthony back."

"My mother will be sorry that you will not be coming," she said with a smile.

"Yes," Juan replied. "Duty calls when life is starting to improve."

"Before we go, I need to grab something from my tent," Anthony said quickly. "I'll meet you at the trail head outside of camp."

She nodded. Anthony left the tent.

Juan, Tito, and Carlos accompanied Sofia out of the tent, embracing her cordially and wishing her a speedy return. Juan was the last to embrace her saying, "Until later, *Senorita* Sofia. I expect Anthony is in good hands."

"Look at her, Juan," said Tito, as they watched her walk back along the main trail. "She can't help the way she looks. All the men seem to know when she is coming and they line up along the trail to glimpse her."

"She's a beautiful woman," Juan added. "The men never call to her or make vulgar comments."

"Yes," Tito said. "Strange, in a country where we men enjoy making such comments and women are flattered by them."

"They do not call out to her because I would crack their skulls," Carlos said.

"Carlos," Tito said smiling, "I did not know you were in love with her. How many times have you asked her to marry you?"

Carlos glared at him.

"You are lucky that she is still within earshot, or I would hit you," he said vehemently.

"Carlos, don't take me seriously," Tito replied. "I have as much respect for a beautiful woman as you."

Chapter Two – Sunday Afternoon

"My father was murdered when a bomb exploded on a bus he was riding," Sofia said.

She stopped to face Anthony. They had been walking quickly, crossing from one rocky trail to another down towards town.

"I'm sorry," Anthony replied.

"So am I," she said. "They never found him, only parts of the bus all over the street, and they never knew who did it."

"You must be close to your mother."

"I am. She has accepted it better than me. She still believes in God," she replied bitterly.

Anthony kicked the rocky ground with his feet.

"You don't know what to say," she stated.

"No. I've never met someone and started talking about such things so quickly."

"We can stop talking," Sofia said.

"No."

"We can talk about something different."

"All right," Anthony said. "Are you thirsty?"

She nodded.

"We can stop here," he said. "It's too light to enter town now."

Anthony pointed at a large rock. Sofia crossed to it. He swept off the top of it and invited her to sit. She sat with her legs crossed, looking at him. He sat down next to her.

"How about flying? Are you as good as Juan says you are?" she asked.

To Anthony, flying was as natural as breathing.

"Flying is who I am," Anthony replied. "My first picture was me steering the yoke of an aircraft. I was three years old. My grandfather loved flying. My uncle was an aviator with the Navy. My dad flew in the Marines."

"You feel as if you could never die while flying through the air," she replied.

"Yes," he answered.

"You're lucky to have something which completes you," she said.

"Sometimes when I'm confused, I'll go flying," Anthony replied. "Things seem to sort themselves out up there."

"Will you take me up some time?" she asked.

"Yes," he responded. "Your mother is a doctor?"

"Yes, the best doctor in Colombia, or for that matter, the world," she replied.

They sat for a while without talking. Anthony couldn't pull his eyes from her face.

"Carlos said you would make me feel like I was sixteen," he said, "and now I feel like I'm sixteen. Every time I think of something to say, I think it will sound stupid, so I sit here and say nothing."

"Do you like looking at me?" she asked.

"Yes," he replied.

"Look at me for awhile," she said.

He turned to look at her; his heart raced.

"See, that wasn't so hard," she continued.

"Not for you."

"You're different," she said.

"Thank you," he replied. "It didn't sound like a compliment."

"It was," she said. "Everyone else I meet talks like a bird."

"How do I talk?" he asked.

"Like the cat that ate the canary," she replied.

"You think I'm arrogant?" he asked surprised.

"Your mere presence here suggests you are here because of some convoluted need to help," she replied.

"I didn't come here to help," he said. "I did not even know where Colombia was before I first came down here. All I wanted was action."

"Action?" She looked at him skeptically. "I don't know what you mean."

"It doesn't matter," he said, not wishing to reveal his thoughts to her. "Shouldn't we begin walking? I would like to get back to camp before midnight."

"No," she replied. "I would like to know why you are here. I want to understand why any of you foreigners are here."

"Why I am here, me personally, or any foreigner?"

"We never asked for your help; you forced it upon us," Sofia replied harshly.

"Maybe so, but somebody here is taking the money," he stated. "That's not why I'm here."

She looked at him. He could tell she was fuming.

She turned to him and said sarcastically, "I know why you're here. You're here to help us poor people in the Third World realize our full potential. We have a saying here that everything below the Rio Grande is in the Third World. But we don't believe we live in the Third World. I would trade anything here for life in your home up there in 'El Norte.'"

"So would I," Anthony responded strongly. "I was tired of my life in the States, the world of unlimited opportunity, but . . ." Without looking at her, he continued, "After high school, I went into the military, dreaming of adventure in far-off places."

"The military," she questioned. "I wouldn't expect anyone to go voluntarily into the military. What did your parents say?"

"My parents? My dad died when I was young. My mom always encouraged me to follow my dreams, to live life to the fullest. The military paid for my education."

"There are free military schools in the United States?"

"Well, as part of going into the service, they'll pay for your education," he replied. "The military taught me a lot."

"Why Colombia?" she asked.

"What?"

"Why did you come to Colombia?"

"When I was discharged, there were only dead end jobs staring me in the face. I grew restless and wanted to use my skills more. A security firm hired me to protect convoys, VIPs and munitions caches."

"Do you like to fight?" she asked.

"It's what I've been trained to do," Anthony replied. "I'm good at it."

"How many men have you killed?"

"I . . . I don't know," Anthony replied.

"Guess," Sofia said, her eyes narrowing, "One? Two? More than Ten?"

"I've never counted," Anthony mumbled.

"Wait until you've lost somebody that you love," she replied. "You won't, because you're a mercenary."

"No," he said with agitation. "I'm not a mercenary. I'm . . .," his voice trailed off.

Her words cut him to the core. He had never considered himself a mercenary. Mercenary sounded like such a violent term. All he wanted was something more exciting than he had. He had to explain himself to her.

"We need to go," she said sharply.

"Please," he began.

She stood up and started walking, calling out to him, "It is a long walk, especially for an injured mercenary."

"You lead, and I will try to keep up," he replied, the words coming out harder than he intended.

She turned and he followed her closely, keenly watching every move she made. He should not have said anything. It had been so long since he had spoken with someone like her. She, at first, seemed to want to understand him. He must be extremely careful from now on. He didn't believe she would betray Juan or Tito, or even Carlos, but what value did she place on his life, especially after he had lead her to believe he was willing to sell his for money. He would make her understand his good intentions.

Darkness fell quickly as they made their way down the narrow mountain path. They descended, half-walking and half-running when the slope became steep. She questioned Anthony no more, only pointing out different features of the surrounding mountains made more mysterious and forbidding in the light of the waning gibbous moon. They stopped occasionally to catch their breath and drink from the canteen. When they approached the edge of the town, Sofia stopped. Anthony could hear rushing water.

"Hold onto my hand and place your feet exactly where I put mine," she said breathlessly.

"I can make it alone," he said.

"It's deeper than it looks and if you fall in, you will be swept into the main current past the next bend," she warned. "Then the river will kill you."

She grabbed hold of his hand and pulled him down through the brambles and brush where they reached a wide creek bed. Anthony could hear the roar of the river downstream. She crossed from rock to rock, following ledges and a rocky outcropping, reaching the other side with only slightly wet shoes.

"I am going to climb up. Follow me in a minute," Sofia said in a low voice.

After they climbed up the steep slope, she stood silently, breathing in the atmosphere of the town. Everything was quiet. She turned towards Anthony, who came up behind her, indicating to stay quiet, as she took the silk scarf from around her neck and tied it around his head, obscuring his features. She took off his military jacket, reversed it and put it back on him, brusquely turning up the collars around his face. She instructed him to look down and to keep his arm interlocked with hers.

His head swam as she spoke to him up close, the smell of her sweet breath mingled with her scent from the scarf. He nodded when she finished speaking, only hearing the part of keeping his arm laced with hers.

A rifle shot in the distance brought him instantly back. He cursed silently for allowing himself to feel this way. It was not right. It was not expected. As she pulled him out of the safety of the jungle and into the danger of the open road, his senses became instantly alert. He could not afford to jeopardize himself, the other men, or Juan by being tempted. He had a duty. Keeping his head down to keep his face hid, his eyes moved constantly while his ears prickled to every sound. Soon, he felt her stop, he heard a key scrape in a lock and saw her push open a large door.

Once inside, he looked up. They were in a small garden. She was pulling him along a well-manicured walkway to a flight of steps. She led him into the back of the house. They entered a small kitchen.

"*Mami, Mami*, I'm home," she called.

Anthony closed the back door of the kitchen as he entered. A small indigenous woman was preparing food on a stone table. He heard voices through the doorway, as he walked through the kitchen. Sofia entered through the other door, her arms interlocked with her mother. Her hair was white and wavy, and she wore a doctor's coat.

"Here he is, Mami," Sofia said coolly. "Captain Antony Wyatt, chief pilot of the Air Force of the Resistance."

"A grand title for one so young," she came forward and shook hands with Anthony.

"I have no official title," Anthony replied.

"So much the better to have an important sounding unofficial title," Sofia's mother said with a smile. "We might need it to enter into some restaurants in town. Welcome to our home, I am Romona Matifino."

"It is my honor, Doctor," Anthony said, "El Jefe sends his regards."

"El Jefe Juan," she stopped, weighing her words, "how is the good commander?"

"Busy working towards his Gran Colombia," Sofia interjected. "He has sent Antonio to you. He was shot in the arm. The wound is infected. On our way here, I have been telling him that you are better than any American doctor."

"What a pleasure a wise daughter is," the Doctor said, moving close to her daughter and squeezing her arm. "If you will excuse us Sofia, a doctor's work is never done. I will finish quickly so we can eat. Follow me, Captain. I have a small office in the front of the house."

Anthony followed her warily into her office. He should not have been so open with Sofia; he must hold his tongue.

"Strip to the waist so I can look at your wound," she commanded as she washed her hands in a small basin. He quickly undid his jacket and shirt and stood bare-chested. She cut off the haphazard dressing. From the quick intake of her breath, he knew Juan was right.

"I will need to clean this wound vigorously. We are short of anesthetic," she stopped speaking, searching for the right words.

"I understand. It will hurt. Let me lie down while you clean, in case I pass out," he replied.

She nodded. She extended the headrest and footrest of the table on which he sat. He lay down. She slid a small pillow under his head. She prepared a small table of equipment, gauze and chemicals. She slid a stool close to his right arm and began cleaning.

At first, her movements only made his eyes water, but as she moved deeper and deeper into the wound, his head swam from the pain. He closed his eyes, determined not to scream or pass out.

"That should do it." Her voice seemed far away. He pulled himself back to her.

"Are you finished?" he croaked.

"Yes, for now. I will need to check it tomorrow."

She held up a pair of forceps; he could see something within its tongs.

"What is it?"

"Here is the reason your wound wouldn't heal, a small piece of metal. It stayed in your arm, causing the infection," she replied.

He nodded, feeling ill from the pain. He heard her tell him to rest there for a while. He felt the door shut, closing him in darkness. His arm hurt.

He hated to be alone in the dark. He was not scared; the dark made him think. Thinking pained him, thinking about what could have been. *Mercenary*. How could Sofia think he was a mercenary? A trained killer hired to murder her people. How could he explain to her that he came down here, not to kill, but to live? He was dying up there. The greatest country in the world with the greatest opportunities, and he could not find a decent job. It always came down to that, money. Here, he didn't have any money. He had more important things to worry about than money; here, he had to worry about survival.

He forced his eyes shut, trying to whitewash his mind of all thought. He wanted to fall asleep to stop thinking. A hand touched his shoulder; he opened his eyes. She was standing above him.

"Sofia," he said.

As Sofia and Anthony left the camp, Juan and Tito entered the tent. Tito cracked open a bottle of scotch, drank some, and pushed it towards Juan.

"I thought the scotch was for when we are successful," Juan said looking at the bottle.

"I feel lucky," Tito said.

"Those helicopters today made you feel lucky?" Juan asked, leaving the bottle untouched on the table.

"No, being perched over the town of Santa Angelia," Tito said slowly. "My sources tell me the military will pull out and leave us this town."

"You mean Mono's sources," Juan said. "He's the one who told you that."

"Mono's information has been reliable in the past," Tito said.

"We will follow them out as they leave, right?" Juan said. "Move right into the wide open valley, exposing us to air attack?"

"Mono has anti-aircraft weapons," Tito said.

"If the army doesn't leave?" Juan asked.

"We force them out, seize their weapons and use the soldiers as bargaining chips when we sit down with the government negotiators," Tito replied.

"Why do we need Mono?" Juan asked.

"Mono wants to join you because of your reputation. The politicians and papers talk about you more than him."

"I don't see why the politicians talk about me. Once we are united against them, their life of entitlements and greed will change radically," Juan stated.

"It's coming to an end," Tito said. "Once you unite the other resistance groups, peace is just around the corner."

"I wish I could believe it. Something's not right," Juan replied. "Mono once told me that he fights alone. Why has he changed now?"

"You can ask him yourself," Tito replied. "He is coming."

"He is? When?"

"At dusk. When he comes, I want you to tell him we are going forward with the attack," Tito said.

"W are not," Juan replied.

"Juan, we have talked about this. It is our time. If we can take the next valley, we will control much of Colombia and bring this war to a halt."

"You and Mono do the fighting; he seems to love war," Juan replied.

"Is that so bad for a guerrilla fighter?" Tito snorted.

"Maybe not for a guerrilla fighting every day as a soldier. For its leader, it is a crime, worse than that, it is sinful. The only enjoyable part of war is in its end."

"Strange coming from you. You have been fighting for years."

"What has it accomplished?" Juan replied bitterly.

"We need to attack now. Christ, what's holding you back? It's your plan, not mine."

Carlos entered the tent with several of Tito's men. He saw Juan's tight face, the grinding of his teeth and the jutting of his jaw. Juan stared intently at the table.

"What is the feel of the town?" Juan demanded without looking up.

"Jefe?" Carlos asked.

"What did you hear?" Juan asked.

"The town was unusually quiet. The soldiers were not out in the cafes and walking around. One soldier I knew told me they had been ordered to stay in the barracks; only official visits in the town were allowed."

"That is what I've been hearing," Juan said in a soft voice. "It has me worried."

"You're reading too much into it," Tito replied. He ignored Juan's shaking head and continued. "The army does not know what to do. They have been defeated so many times they are afraid to come out and fight us."

"I do not think so," Juan replied. "Were you ever afraid to leave base?"

"It is a new military, Juan. How many times have you worried in the days leading up to a major engagement, only to realize later that the worry was wasted?"

"This is different, Tito. Before I worried about how we will execute our plan. This time I am worried about the plan itself. It is especially bold."

"It is not risky," Tito said vehemently. "We will have Mono with us, supporting us from the south."

"I do not believe that the military is evacuating this town."

"Mono's sources are excellent," Tito replied. "They've never been wrong before."

"Every other time I could validate the rumors with what was happening before my eyes. This time it is not so."

"We have seen a lot of movement along the road," Checo responded. Checo acted as Tito's second-in-command.

"Movement does not mean retreat," Juan replied. "A battalion that is preparing to evacuate does not sit around hunkered inside its compound. Soldiers should be busy packing up the equipment of war. Others should be sneaking in to town, trying to see their girlfriends one last time before they go."

"There seems to be fewer soldiers in the town," Checo added.

"Fewer soldiers walking around town. We do not know how many are inside the base. I see movement and changes, and I do not have a sense of where it is going," Juan responded.

"We do not need to know," Tito replied. "We have a very good plan. We execute our plan, and we will control central Colombia."

"You cannot put butter on your bread until you milk the cow," Juan replied.

"You and your idioms," Tito replied exasperatedly.

"You understand my point clearly," Juan said in a hard voice. "We cannot claim to control this area of Colombia, until we control this valley, and we do not control this valley."

"Yes, we can," Checo replied. "We will link up with Mono's forces in the south and rout the retreating *federales* from this area."

Juan stood and went over to the table. He looked carefully at the varied charts.

"We fought this same colonel and his men in Calica," Juan mused.

"Yes, we kicked their asses," Tito said proudly.

"He is now here defending this valley of Santa Angelia. He ran in Calica," Juan said.

"He'll run again," Checo said.

"He is not running. He has the chance. He could pull his troops out, but he stays," Juan replied.

"He has been issued an ultimatum by his superiors," Checo replied.

"He is a rational man with options," Juan responded. "There is no rational calculation to cause an individual to lay down his life."

"He doesn't think he is going to die," one of the other lieutenants replied.

"In all armed conflict, there is the chance of death," Juan replied. "The chance is greatly enhanced in the mind of a rational man. War is an affair of the heart."

"We will rip out his heart and be done with him," Checo said.

"We cannot rip out his heart if we cannot ensnare him," Juan said, then paused to think, "If the colonel isn't fighting, who will we be fighting?"

"We will fight whomever engages us," Tito said.

"We cannot win against an unknown foe," Juan said. "That is suicide, not courage. We must know who we are fighting."

"It doesn't matter. We have more firepower than in Calica," Checo bragged. "We can overwhelm them more than we did there."

"In Calica, this colonel thought he could win because he had superior firepower," Juan said.

"He's an idiot," Checo scoffed.

Quick as a flash, Juan pulled out his knife and held it to the neck of Checo.

The room fell quiet; Checo eyed him tensely.

"You have a gun, Checo, I don't. You have superior firepower, but in a flick, this knife severs your head from your body."

"Juan, let Checo alone," Tito said, standing up slowly.

"He wants me to kill him by sending him into a battle unprepared. Why not send him now to the Elysian Fields?"

"Juan, I need him," Tito said.

"Each of our weapons has advantages and limitations," Juan said, slowly. "My opponent cannot rely on simple superiority of better weapons. The greatest victories I have won come from initiating my advantages against the army's weaknesses, gaining a battlefield advantage, winning and then retreating before their withering and superior firepower can overwhelm us."

Tito stood up and walked closer.

"Jefe, take your knife away," Tito said, moving closer to Juan.

"My knife?" Juan whispered. "Good for close work, but impossible to stop a tank."

Several of Tito's men fingered their weapons.

"Tito, why do you rely on Checo?" Juan asked.

"Checo?" Tito replied. "He fights without worrying whether he is going to die."

With a quick snap of the wrist, Juan threw the knife across the room sticking it neatly in a wooden pole. The twang of the knife vibrating could be heard in the silent tent.

Tito held his hand up to stop his men. He motioned them to leave the room. Checo eyed Juan with hatred.

"I propose we move into position so we are ready," Tito said. "If everything looks favorable, we attack, and if not, we monitor the town and the valley for another day."

"We can learn much in a day," Juan replied.

"If something is wrong, we will slip back into the jungle and wait it out," Tito said.

"Just like before," countered Juan.

"Just like before we knew we could win," Tito said.

"You must go outside and wait on Mono," Juan said. "The men are little jumpy after the three helicopters came swooping in today."

"My feelings exactly. The men may believe that Mono's helicopter is fair game," Tito replied.

"It won't do to blow him up before the attack," Juan said.

"I'll set out the smoke and flares," Tito said.

Juan watched from the cover of the tree line as Tito and his men set up the flares. His sixth sense told him to be wary. He saw Tito's top two lieutenants look over in his direction and lean close to Tito's ears.

"I'm tired of that fucking Jefe and his mind games," Checo breathed in Tito's ear.

"Now is not the time to speak of this," Tito said.

"He almost slashed my head off," Checo said. "What if he had, would then had been the time to stand up to El Jefe?"

"He's not the enemy," Tito said. "He brings us our matériel."

"We have the American now," Checo replied.

"He doesn't have the contacts for such things," Tito replied.

"We need to throw in our lot with Mono, and leave El Jefe to stew up here on his own," Checo added.

The rhythmic *chop chop* of the helicopter blades stopped their conversation. The helicopter came in fast over the trees, whirled in a tight circle to lose speed, and landed beside the smoke flares. Juan watched from afar as he nodded his head at the pilot's skill.

"That would be one tough pilot to shoot down," Juan said to himself.

Manuel Apostata, nicknamed "Mono", jumped out of the helicopter, followed by six of his men. He resembled more gorilla than man: bushy black hair everywhere, large, muscular torso and massive arms. Mono controlled the largest rebel group. His camouflage khaki uniform was neatly pressed with sharp creases along the arms.

The pilot kept the turbines at full cycle. Juan saw Mono look up and carefully survey the entire area. Juan did not move, watching without moving as Mono ran hunched over to where Tito was waiting outside of the blade wash of the helicopter rotors.

Mono embraced Tito and kissed him forcefully on both cheeks.

"How is El Jefe?" Mono asked. I see that he has many new men and much equipment. How much new matériel have you acquired?"

"Ask him yourself," Tito replied. "He is awaiting us."

Tito led Mono and his men towards Juan.

"You looked well-rested and ready for another fight," Mono called out in a loud voice to be heard above the whine of the two jet engines.

"I'm always ready for a fight," Juan replied.

"Tito tells me you have a plan to stop the Colombia military in their tracks here and now," Mono said.

"You can shut down your helicopter," Juan said.

"I can't stay long," Mono replied with a smile. "The pilot is scared he won't be able to start the turbines again. It's brand new."

Juan looked again at the helicopter. It glinted in the last rays of the setting sun. Astride its belly, two long arms extended laden with missiles, mini-Gatling guns and rocket pods.

Juan gritted his teeth; he knew such things were expensive, very expensive.

"Nice bird," Juan said. "Who gave it to you?"

"You're not the only one with foreign contacts," Mono replied tersely.

Juan shrugged his shoulders at Mono's non-answer. Such was the life he had chosen to lead after he had left his home country, sometimes he felt on an island, surrounded by well-trained brutes who had too much money and power for their intellect and who failed to grasp the significance of the struggle, not for helicopters and land, but for liberation.

"Come," Tito said, "Let's go to Juan's tent and show you our plans."

Juan let them go ahead while he looked over at the helicopter. He wondered if it was worth what Mono pledged to obtain it.

As he entered the tent, Tito was in the middle of explaining the attack. When he finished, Tito looked over at Juan.

"Does that cover it?" Tito asked.

"Pretty much," Juan said. "I like to keep it simple."

"What do you need me for?" Mono asked. "It looks like you have the valley sewn up."

"The government can give up land all day," Juan said. "Whether they control this part of Colombia or that part of Colombia doesn't concern them, as long as one group does not control more than they."

"They want us to play tug of war against ourselves," Mono replied.

"Yes," Juan said quietly, waiting for Mono to speak.

"They play this game against us all the time," Mono continued.

"Only if we allow them to play it," Juan said.

"You and I are not so different. Different countries but the same goals," Mono said.

"We all want peace," Tito broke in.

"Peace, yes, peace, blessed are the peacemakers," Mono said.

"For they are few in number," Juan added.

"Your plan will bring us peace?" Mono asked.

"With a united revolutionary front, we will control more of Colombia than any group ever has in recent past. We can stop this civil war now, and change the social structure," Juan said.

Mono looked at him. He furrowed his brow.

"What do you expect me to do?" Mono asked.

"Nothing," Juan said.

Mono eyed Juan carefully, weighing his response.

"We need your air support and to protect my flank, in case they bring reinforcements," Tito added.

"They won't," Mono replied. "They are abandoning this sector."

"The military is pulling out of the town?" Tito repeated.

"You're making it too hot to hold," Mono said.

"So you say," Juan replied.

"Yes," Mono replied.

"Who's stepping in to control it?" Juan asked.

Mono looked at him but said nothing.

"We're pushing forward with the attack," Tito said.

"When?"

"In three days," Tito said. "Wednesday early morning."

"I don't know if I can bring my men up in time," Mono said, looking directly at Juan.

"We need to know," Tito said.

"I will speak with my commanders," Mono replied. "I will let you know by Tuesday morning."

"O.k.," breathed Tito heavily, "I would like to know sooner. I don't want to be exposed if you cannot move into position."

"You have more men since the last time I saw you," Mono said to Juan.

"Many boys have joined us; they have heard of our victories," Juan replied, "and that I don't use men like cannon fodder."

Juan watched Mono tighten his jaw and grind his teeth.

"How many men do you have now?" Mono asked.

"Enough to take this valley," Juan replied.

"Where is the American?"

Juan shrugged his shoulders.

Checo began to speak; Tito looked at him crossly.

"Are you going to be ready?" Juan asked.

"Let's sit down and have a drink now that the talking is done," Tito said.

"I wish I could," Mono said, breaking out his usual smile and clapping Tito on the back. "I promise you, when this thing is over, we will drink many cups of whiskey."

"Like we used to do in the old days," Tito said. "I'm an old man now."

"You can still drink," Mono said with a laugh.

"When the occasion calls for it," Tito said.

"Juan, it's good to see you again," Mono said, shaking his hand.

Juan watched Tito and Mono leave the tent and walk back towards the helicopter. Juan called a couple of his men forward and ordered them to take the rocket launcher and conceal themselves in the bunker. Juan's lead adjutant, a wiry, dark-faced man with a trim beard and mustache, came and stood beside him. Willy, as he was called, watched with distrustful eyes.

As Mono and Tito walked towards the helicopter, they talked.

"I sensed tension," Mono said. "Are you two not in love anymore?"

"We have no problems," Tito replied.

"I told you not to trust him. He is not our paisano, not our countryman. The American is the one you need. Americans have the finest weapons."

"Mono, listen to me," Tito said. "Forget about weapons."

"Weapons make the warrior," Mono replied.

"Mono, this is a momentum changing battle, think about it."

"Yes, whoever comes out of this one alive will control Colombia's future," Mono replied.

"Are you in?"

"Of course," Mono yelled above the sound of whining jet engine.

Tito gave a thumbs-up sign as the helicopter lifted off.

From the cover of the trees, Juan watched the helicopter lift off and accelerate. As far as Juan could see, the helicopter descended straight down into the valley below. Juan waited, hoping he would hear the approach of other helicopters hot on the tail of Mono's bird. It was dead quiet.

"No one followed Mono in," Willy said quietly to Juan, "His pilot must have dodged the radar."

"He must have," Juan replied

Chapter Three – Sunday Evening

"Anthony," Sofia said softly.

Anthony attempted to rise off the small table. Sofia gently laid her hand on his chest. She pulled up the stool and sat next to him.

"You're young, too," she said.

"Not as young as I used to be," he replied.

"We cope, but the war is hardest on us. That's why I talk crazy and say words I shouldn't, saying things I've no right to say. I'm sorry if I offended you, Anthony. I know you're not a killer. I'm not sure what you are. I'm not sure what I am."

Anthony nodded, feeling too lost and nauseous to trust a response.

"How does your arm feel?" Sofia asked.

"Sore," he replied.

"My mother was sorry that she had to clean your wound the way she did. It is very difficult to buy supplies. If they have them, they can't send it because the delivery service is closed down. If delivery is possible, then they don't have the supplies."

"I survived."

"When she is most desperate, she sends me down to the coast to buy them. It takes two days. The roads are bad, and too dangerous to drive at night."

"You have a car?" Anthony asked.

"Of course," she replied. "I know how to drive it. I don't take it because the bus, although crowded, lets me look out, and it takes about the same amount of time."

"Next time they send me somewhere, give me a list and I'll pick up what your mother needs."

"She would appreciate that. Thank you."

"It's the only way I can repay her for fixing up my arm," he replied.

"This is better talking like this. We should stay here and not leave," she said.

"I would like that," Anthony said.

"Captain Anthony Wyatt," Sofia said with a serious face. "My name is Sofia Matifino; it pleases me to make your acquaintance."

She extended him her hand, which he took and shook lightly.

"Ms. Matifino, it pleases me to make your acquaintance," he replied.

Anthony rose to kiss her lightly on her cheek, but either the light was bad, and he mistook, where she was or she turned her face slightly to him, and he kissed her on the lips. Neither of them moved. They heard footsteps in the hallway. Sofia broke away and stood up. Before she opened up the door, she turned around and looked at him.

"Rest for a little while longer, I'm making us something to eat before we have to leave."

She slipped out and closed the door behind her. He heard her talking to someone in the hallway. His arm hurt, but he could not rest. He sat up and flipped the light switch. The sharp fluorescent light filled the room. He looked at his arm. The bandage was clean and neat.

Damn these small planes. If he'd had a helicopter, they never would have got him. Helicopters he could fly, fly well too. It was the ground that was dangerous. He had not even heard the shots, only the plinking noises as the bullets hit the plane's aluminum and then felt the pain as one hit his arm.

Bad luck, like the first time when someone had shot at him. He had heard nothing that time, either. He saw the cockpit explode beside him, and the co-pilot was messed up bad. He had to grab him to keep him from falling out while slamming the controls back and forth. Something had broken. He had heard the firing then. And it pursued him, no matter how much he swerved and swooped, causing him to plummet, almost biting it in the trees. But they had stopped shooting, and he had learned. It had to be that way, you had to be shot at and not lose your nerve.

Anthony had to return. It was late. He walked out of the room, flicking off the light as he left.

"Anthony," she looked up from the sink, where she was washing her hands. "I've made something to eat."

She looked at him.

"Is something wrong?" she asked.

"No, I need to get back," he said.

"My mother wanted to look at your wound when you woke up. She had to leave, but she'll be back soon. There was some kind of accident. You look hungry. Please sit down," Sofia said all in a rush, not wanting him to leave.

The small table in the kitchen was set for the two of them. The multicolored ceramic plates had already been served with food. Anthony could see the steam rising off the white rice, and next to it lay black, creamy beans and cooked ground beef swimming in tomatoes and peppers.

Sofia was holding the soap out to him. He took it and washed his face and hands. He sat across from her; she bowed her head and whispered a short prayer.

"Please go ahead," she rose from the table. "I forgot the arepas."

His mouth watered as he picked up his fork and smelled the rich aroma rising from his plates. He hadn't eaten well in a long time.

"You're hungry," she said to him as she returned to the table, placing a plate of hot arepas in front of him. He looked down. He had finished half his plate and his mouth was full. He nodded.

"My mother always says that she likes watching a man eat. Now, I know what she is talking about. It is very satisfying to watch someone enjoy your food so much. Don't stop. You have plenty of time to talk when you finish."

When Anthony had cleaned his plate, Sofia, without asking, filled it with more food. She ate slowly and looked at him. She had stopped talking, realizing that he felt obliged to say something in return. After his third plate, he stopped her from filling it again. Something in his background usually stopped him for eating so much at someone else's house, but he was hungry, and she kept smiling at him and serving him.

"Thank you," he said as he pushed back away from the table. "The food was very good."

"I'm glad you enjoyed it, she said, standing up and clearing the table. "I'm making some coffee to keep us awake for the long walk back."

He turned his chair and looked at her. She set the plates in the sink and pulled down a small espresso maker off the shelf above the stove. He watched as she packed the metal filter with coffee, filled the small pot with water and screwed them together. The blue flame shot up as she turned on the burner and placed the pot over the fire.

"You don't have to come back with me. I can find my way."

"I like walking at night," she said. "Carlos is coming. He will meet us along the trail. I won't be going all the way up."

Black liquid started coming out of the top of the coffee maker. She stirred in two heaping spoons of sugar and put the top on. She let it finish brewing, while she set the table with two small cups and saucers.

"I hope you like coffee tinto. It's like espresso, and it's all we drink here."

Anthony nodded. He had heard of espresso coffee, but he had never drunk it. The first time he had drunk coffee was in the mess tent. It tasted like burnt, dirty water.

She poured the coffee into the two small cups and sat down across from him. While she was making the coffee and clearing the dishes, he could watch her intently. As she sat in front on him, he became self-conscious. He looked down at the coffee.

"Try it," she encouraged him.

He drank the strong, sweet coffee. It was good.

"I said you would like it."

"You told me to try it."

"You liked it," Sofia replied. "You should always listen to me. How many girlfriends have you had?"

Anthony wasn't sure how to take her playfulness.

"Not many," he said.

"I don't believe you," she said with a smile. "I know boys are more experienced in such things, particularly handsome ones." She smiled beautifully.

"We had better go," Anthony said, changing the subject. "It's late.

"Give my mother a few more minutes to return, and then we'll go. I won't tease you anymore. I don't have much experience with boys. I liked a boy very much, but ..." she trailed off.

"What happened?" Anthony asked tentatively. "Was he killed in the war?"

"I don't know," Sofia responded. "The last time I saw him I was riding on a bus home from University. It was Christmas vacation. During the break, I wanted to see my family so I took a bus from Bogotá. Have you been there?"

"Yes, when I first came, I arrived in Bogotá. I spent several weeks there at a language school improving my Spanish."

"I wondered where you received your Colombian accent from," she replied. "You speak Spanish very well."

"Thank you," he said. "I know you are being kind, but you say it so sincerely."

"You do speak well. Americans don't take the time to learn our culture," she said. "Besides, you speak it better than I speak English."

"I will have to teach you English," Anthony said. "We can start now. Repeat after me, 'How do you do?'"

"Oh that's easy," she said. She repeated the phrase. "It makes my nose itch."

He rubbed her nose with the tips of his fingers. She giggled.

"Say something else," Sofia said.

"What do you want me to say?" Anthony asked.

"Tell me how beautiful I am. No," she paused. "I'm kidding. Teach me something important."

"Where is the bathroom?" he asked in English.

"That's important, but not very serious. Besides, I know that one already," she said. "Where is the bathroom?" she repeated in English.

Her accent had a sweet lyrical quality.

"Ask me something more serious," she said.

"Where did you go to University?" he asked again in English.

"Bogotá," she replied in Spanish. "That's a better question."

"I thought I was going to try to teach you English," he said.

"Ask me questions in English, and I will answer you in Spanish. We can learn from one another."

"Okay," he replied. "Do you like me?" he asked.

"That's not very serious," she laughed.

"To me it is," Anthony said.

"I didn't mean it wasn't important, and the answer is 'yes," she replied.

"You have to respond with a longer answer than 'yes," Anthony replied. "How will I improve my Spanish?"

"Give me another chance," she said, "Ask me another question."

"Do you have a boyfriend?" he asked.

She wrinkled her nose at him and shook her head no.

"I'm sorry," she said. "I'm not playing the game well. You have me confused."

"Don't blame me. I'm asking the questions."

"Ask me another question," she said.

"What happened when you were with the boy?" Anthony asked in English.

"What do you mean? I have never been with a man before," she replied embarrassedly in Spanish.

"No. I didn't mean like that," Anthony switched to Spanish to explain. You were telling me about a boy you were riding on a bus with."

"When was this?" she asked.

"Just now."

"Oh, when I was returning from university on the bus? No, he wasn't with me. I was taking the bus back here. At the time the route was fairly safe; the government controlled most of the roads. We passed through Monteria, and we stopped because some barrels and trees were blocking the road. An unofficial road block."

"Someone had blocked the road?" Anthony asked.

"Yes. When the bus stopped, several armed thugs entered the bus and told us to dump our valuables into some dirty cloth sacks they were holding. My arms were shaking so hard, not from fear, but from being robbed by my countrymen. I could not remove my bracelets. They were cheap gold bracelets I had bought from a street vendor. I started to panic. The men with the pistols were moving through the bus and coming closer and closer, screaming and shouting that they would shoot anybody who didn't cooperate. I put the bracelets against the window ledge trying to force them off my wrists when I saw the boy I knew walking along the side of the bus. He had a bandana on, but I recognized him by the way he walked. He was the leader of this gang of thieves. Before he could look at me, I put my head down in my lap holding my arms above my head with my purse in them. When the thief came by I felt him snatch the purse and grab my wrist and I thought he was trying to drag me out of my seat when I felt the bracelets slide off my hand."

She laid her shaking hands purposefully on the table. Anthony gently covered them with his hands. She looked up at him.

"The man, or boy, I saw went to University with me," she said quietly. "We studied English together in the evenings. He used to call me, "sister." Do you think that would have saved me if he saw me?"

Anthony shook his head no.

"It is a strange thing to remember something so terrible. I had shut it away and vowed never to relive it. They didn't shoot anybody that day. At the time, I wasn't worried about dying. I guess you don't think about dying when you are about to," Sofia said.

"You don't," Anthony replied. "You think about surviving. I imagine you think about surviving until the very end, that way the end doesn't scare you because you don't know it is coming."

"I wasn't thinking about being shot," she said. "I was thinking about my father. I wondered what he was thinking about just before the bus blew up. I wondered if he heard or saw or felt something, anything."

"He probably did. Time slows down to nothing. It's a shame really, when we have no time left we finally realize how precious it is so we slow it down and experience every millisecond. I've tried to slow time down and perceive every second, but I can't."

"I know. I've done that too," Sofia said. "I try hard to experience everything. I lose my focus and daydream, then I wake up later and wonder where the time went."

"What type of man was your father?" Anthony asked in English.

"I like that question," Sofia said smiling. "I like talking about my father. My father was a good man. He originally came from Italy. His parents sent him here to live and work with his brothers who ran a bakery."

Anthony laughed.

"I know it sounds very cliché, an Italian bakery. Clichés originate from somewhere," Sofia said. "He was youngest and the favorite. He was encouraged to attend school where he studied law. He did very well. He became an attorney for the state and then a judge."

"Was that why he was blown up?" Anthony asked.

"The police said that he was in the wrong place at the wrong time."

"You don't believe it?"

"My father was a very structured, disciplined man," Sofia replied. "He went to work at the same time every day. He ate lunch at the same time. He took the same bus home every day. He never stepped away from a case, no matter how dangerous the criminals were. They like to kill judges."

"I've never understood why," Anthony said. "Killing the judge doesn't solve your problem. The state will simply assign another judge to try the case. There are always plenty of judges. The state is the most powerful thing out there, and judges protect us from the state."

"My father was known as a fair judge," Sofia said proudly.

"If there were no judges, it would be a police state. The state would kill anybody who stepped out of line, disagreed or wasn't liked."

"You've just described Colombia," she replied. "Only anonymous judges now and secret trials."

"Your father was a brave man," Anthony said.

"My father is dead, and nothing will bring him back," she said. Her eyes were wet.

"If your father worked in the city," Anthony asked, "why does your mother live here?"

"After my father was killed, my mother came back here," Sofia replied. "She grew up in the adjacent valley. My grandmother moved with her."

"Your grandmother's here?" Anthony queried. "I haven't seen her."

"She has seen you," Sofia said, a smile coming back to her face. "You don't think my mother would have left me here alone, unchaperoned, with a man?"

"We are being watched?" Anthony asked with a grin.

"You haven't noticed?" Sofia replied. "What type of spy are you?"

"I'm not a spy," Anthony said. "Besides, I thought I was on friendly territory."

"You are on friendly territory. They don't want you too friendly, so you're being watched."

"I'm not going to do anything," Anthony said.

"It's not what you are going to do," Sofia said teasingly. "It is what we might do, which concerns my grandmother."

Anthony suppressed a laugh. "I didn't know that I was doing so well."

"You're tall, good-looking, and a man," Sofia responded. "That is all my grandmother knows."

"When I return, I'll wear a bandana and then she won't know it's me," he replied.

"You'll have to wear one over your head like a washing woman," she replied. "Otherwise, she'll recognize your blond hair. Did your father have blond hair?"

"My father?" Anthony said, reflecting back on what his father looked like. His father had gray hair. In his grandmother's house, he remembered a picture where he had blonde hair. "As a kid, I think he had blonde hair. I never asked him."

"You told me he died when you were young?" Sofia asked.

"Yes," Anthony replied.

"I'm sorry," Sofia said.

"He died a long time ago," Anthony said. "He couldn't handle life in Montana."

"You're from Montana," Sofia said. "I've heard of it. It's big and wide open."

"Yes," Anthony said, "the land of the big sky."

A clock chimed in the distance.

"It is late," she said. "My mother will probably be out all night. It happens sometimes. When these farmers have an accident, they are scared to come to the hospital. She has to treat them in their house as best she can."

"They are scared they can't pay for it," Anthony asked.

"No," Sofia said. "If they don't have the money, the government pays. They are simple people with simple beliefs. They don't believe in medicine and hospitals. They trust my mother because she is kind and good."

"I had hoped to see your mother before I left," Anthony said, "to thank her for my arm."

"She will need to check your wound tomorrow," Sofia said. "You can thank her then."

"I might not be able to return tomorrow," Anthony replied. He looked at his watch. "I have to return," he said without conviction.

"I know," she replied. "Put your coat on inside out and I'll find you a cap to wear."

He saw his jacket lying by the door. He reversed it and put it on. She had returned with a dark blue sailor's cap in her hand.

"It's my father's," she said. "He talked about sailing to Italy, but he never did it. The cap will pull down close over your ears and cover your hair. Your hair makes you stand out."

"You've told me," he said as he pulled on the cap. He passed a mirror as he walked to the back door. He didn't look at his reflection; he probably looked like a goof.

She pulled on a jacket and led them out the rear door, locking it behind her. She listened at the back fence. She pulled open the heavy wood door and went into the street.

The street was damp. It must have misted because Anthony had not heard the rain. Anthony had been listening for the rain. Juan was worried about the rain coming too early and ruining the attack. They were due for some heavy rains; it had not rained for several weeks.

Sofia linked her arm within his and pulled close. Anthony felt the hardness of his pistol against his hip and smelled the sweet cleanliness that comes after a light rain. Sofia was warm and supple on his arm, and the breeze cooled him, over-dressed as he was on this warm night with the cap and jacket. A horn sounded off in the distance, alerting him that he was on unfriendly ground.

She talked quietly to him. He didn't respond, fearing his voice and accent would betray him to unseen ears. Several vehicles passed them as they walked quickly along the streets. Sofia was taking him on a different route back. Instead of passing the many shanties and street shops, they were walking in front of solid, stone homes with large railings. They were approaching a road where steady traffic flowed.

"We have to walk up this road and cross the bridge. On the other side of the bridge, there is a walking trail which follows the river," she said.

"Why didn't we take the same way back?" Anthony asked.

"This way is quicker, and at night, the army patrols don't stop anybody. They are home in their beds."

Her eyes flashed excitement.

He didn't like it. It was an unwarranted risk. He told her so.

"Carlos comes this way," she said to him.

"Carlos is from these mountains," he replied. He should not have let her lead. Everything was screwed up.

"I know these mountains and town. I have walked along here countless times," she said.

"Yes, but you didn't have a foreign mercenary with you," he said. "No matter what I wear, I look and move differently. I have to be more careful."

He moved closer to the busy road and looked down. The cars were lined up further down the road.

"Do they ever put check points on this road?" he asked.

"Sometimes. There is a small gate house on each side of the bridge," she responded.

Christ, he thought, things can go from going so good to screwed up in about two seconds. He needed to return quickly, but he didn't want to make a foolish mistake. He didn't want to be paranoid either. It was late.

"Stay here," he commanded. "I'm going forward to check it out. If I don't return, I made it across. Go home."

"You can't find your way up the mountain at night. The trail is unmarked."

"I'll go first then. If I have any problems, you can go and tell Juan."

"Anthony, listen to me," she said. "I didn't bring you this way to be caught. If you want, we can go back the other way, but I'm telling you that will take much longer."

"Much longer?" Anthony asked.

"We won't arrive before daybreak. You saw how long it took us to run down. I showing you a shorter way. Stay with me and we'll walk down the road and across the bridge like we've done it a hundred times before."

Anthony looked up the road. The cars, which were lined up, had moved on, they probably had slowed to let an old dog cross. He had always trusted his own instincts and found it hard to rely on others. He pulled out his pistol, clicked off the safety and tucked the hand clutching the pistol inside his jacket. He nodded to her. She looped her arm around his free arm; they walked out along the road.

As they approached the bridge, Anthony saw that the guard house was lit. He pulled the brim of his cap down to his eyebrows. A soldier was sitting in a chair in front of the guard house watching the traffic stream by. The other was leaning on the long pole they used to stop traffic in front of the guard house. Anthony could hear them talking loudly to one another; a radio was playing inside the building.

Sofia pulled her arm away and grabbed his free arm with one hand on his elbow and the other hand in his to lead him along. She led him directly towards the guard house to pass in front of it.

"Hello, gentlemen," she called out in a strong voice.

Anthony's grip tightened around the gun. It was difficult to see without lifting his face up. He heard two voices greet her; he looked to see if a third one was inside the building.

She kept walking and talking, guiding Anthony around the gate and to the side of the bridge where a narrow cement walk ran.

The guard leaning against the gate came from around the building and called out to her.

"*Senorita, todo esta bien?*"

"Yes, everything is fine," Sofia responded. She saw him shift his hands on his rifle.

"*Y El Senor?*" the guard asked.

"Oh, you didn't recognize him. I'm taking Manuolo back. He has been at my mother's this evening."

"*Oh, esta bien,*" the guard responded. His shoulders slouched and he let his rifle fall to his side. He waved a good-bye at Sofia and went back to the front of the guard house.

Sofia walked quickly across the bridge, pushing Anthony along. She furtively glanced back at the guardhouse. Nobody watched. At the end of the bridge, she pushed Anthony down a steep slope and pulled him along a dark trail, which led back under the bridge beside the fast running river.

"Wait a second," he said quietly. He pulled his gun out from under his coat, clicked the safety on and stuck the gun back into his waistband. "I don't want the gun to go off after we made it safely across."

He grinned at her. They had made it. Relief flooded over him. He scooped her up in his arms and held her. Damn this world, he thought. She pushed away from him and pulled on his arm to follow her. She scurried through the dense bush; Anthony had to keep both hands in front of him to stop the branches from scratching his face. The trail rose steeply. They climbed quickly arriving at a high ledge where they could look down and see the dim lights of the town. The bridge had disappeared from view.

They were breathing hard. Anthony pulled off the cap and jacket. His shirt was soaked.

"You were right," Anthony said. "We will return faster, running up the mountain."

"I was worried," she responded. "When I lie, it makes me nervous. I didn't realize how fast we climbed until I reached here. We don't have far to go."

"Who's Manuel?" Anthony asked.

"Manuolo," Sofia replied. "Manuolo lost his eyesight when he was playing with some explosives left behind by the military. He visits my mother and helps her out around the clinic. I thought Manuolo was going to come across the bridge and expose my lie. Tomorrow I will go and see him and invite him to our house."

"I told you it was dangerous to cross the bridge. You shouldn't take such unnecessary risks."

"We are here," she said. "Do you want to stay here or do you want me to lead you back?"

"Go ahead," Anthony said.

She trotted quickly up the trail. Anthony struggled to stay with her. He was going on his second night with no sleep. Between being with her and crossing the bridge, his adrenaline pushed him hard onward. As the town shrank below him, he relaxed, captivated by the night sounds of the forest masking their soft footfalls up the trail, and even more captivated by her graceful movements in front of him. He resolved to concentrate on his duties, and more resolved that her beauty and affection belonged to someone more worthy than a bandana from Montana.

"Sofia," Anthony whispered urgently.

She turned quickly, as if expecting him to call her. He moved up close to her.

"Let me lead. We are close to the camp. There are sentries posted along all the trails. I don't want you shot by an itchy finger."

"That would not be a good end to the very pleasant day," she responded.

He looked at her and decided to tell her how he felt, but the sound of feet scuffing along the trail silenced him. He grabbed her, pulled her behind a thick bush and jerked out his pistol. He waited as the footsteps came closer. He stepped out from behind the bush.

"Carlos," he said with a relief. "You make as much noise as an elephant coming down the trail."

"Since you know there are no elephants here on the mountain, you will not shoot me," he replied, looking down at Anthony's unholstered weapon.

"You are right, my friend," Anthony said. "It is good that you make such noise."

"Carlos," Sofia said, as she stepped out from behind the bush and embraced him.

"I am sorry Senorita to make you walk all the way back here. El Jefe had me busy, and I am now just coming down," Carlos replied. "You should have waited for me. It is very dangerous at night."

"He wanted to return, and I brought him back," she said.

"You should have waited for me," he said again. "I will guide you back."

He turned up the trail. Every so often he stopped and hooted. In answer to his call, a hoot echoed out of the woods. They joined back with the main trail leading to camp, which Anthony recognized. Carlos led them to Anthony's tent.

"El Jefe is not here. He has gone," Carlos said without explaining further.

"Are you hungry, Señor?" Carlos asked.

"No," Anthony said. "I ate already."

"Then you are not hungry either, Señorita?"

"No, thank you Carlos, but I am thirsty."

Carlos left the tent.

"Thank you for bringing me back here," Anthony said. "You know these mountains."

"You're welcome. I've spent my summers here," she replied.

"I would like to see you again," Anthony said.

"I'd like that also," she answered.

"Can you stay with me tonight?" he asked.

"No, I can't stay here. It's not proper," she said.

Carlos returned with a jug of water.

She drank directly from the jug and turned to Carlos.

"I need to return. I don't want my mother to worry. I didn't tell her that

I was leaving," she said.

"It's too late to walk back alone tonight," Carlos replied, "I will walk back with you."

"You're tired, old man," she responded gently. "I know how hard Juan has been pushing you."

"I will not let you walk back alone. I will accompany you," he replied.

"Then Carlos, I will stay with you tonight and go back in the morning," she said.

"That is better, Señorita. You may have my bed, and you will sleep well," Carlos said.

"Anthony, I will see you in the morning," she said.

She embraced Anthony and left the tent. Carlos followed. Anthony lay down and looked at the tent ceiling. He was very tired, and he could not help but think about her. Her perfume lingered on his clothes. He wanted to go to Carlos' tent and tell her how he felt. It was only a short distance away. It was not proper. He had never heard such words before. *Proper*, he thought. What was proper here in the jungle in the middle of war? He fell asleep.

Gregory Arthur Solsrud

Chapter Four – Monday Morning

Anthony awoke and saw the first glow in the east through his tent flaps. The morning air was already hot and damp. He filled his lungs with deep breaths. He had slept restlessly; her scent still hung in his nostrils. He had to see her again. He felt his bandage. It was tight and secure. He looked at the tape around the bandage. If he pulled at it, just a bit, it'd come loose. Loose bandages needed to be redone; he would have to return with her to the doctor. He pulled on the tape. The adhesive held fast. He pulled harder, feeling the adhesive slowly give away. The bandage dangled off his arm. He dressed quickly, combed his hair and ran to Carlos' tent, hoping she was awake.

Carlos looked up, saw him and waved.

"Good morning, Señor," Carlos greeted him. "I am not used to seeing you so soon in the morning."

"Good morning Carlos," Anthony said. "Is Sofia awake?"

"Awake? She has already left. She wanted to return before the village woke up. She didn't want to be seen returning in the morning."

"I missed her?" Anthony asked.

"She said to say good-bye," Carlos said.

Anthony felt tired. He sat on a log.

"Damn," Anthony said to himself.

"I'm glad you didn't see her and go with her," Carlos said. "El Jefe wants to see you."

"Where?"

"Further along the ridge," Carlos replied. "Tito is preparing his men to move. We are to meet up with them there."

Carlos pointed to a vague point further along the mountain.

"You lead and I will follow," Anthony said.

Carlos nodded.

After they had walked a good distance, Carlos sat down on a small outcropping of rocks and pulled a small flask out of his pack. He drank and offered the flask to Anthony.

Anthony held up his canteen and said, "No, thank you, Carlos, I will stick to water."

"*Chicha* is better than water, Senor," Carlos replied. "It keeps you moving fast."

"If I need to go faster, I will find a car."

Carlos laughed, showing his yellowed teeth. "A car won't help you up here, maybe a mule and this." He held up his flask and drank again. "You are young and can recover your power quickly. If your arm hurts, you need to return for some doctoring."

"I need some," Anthony said. "My bandage has come loose."

Carlos, reading his thoughts answered quickly. "After this, we will return to the doctor and have her redo it."

"Where is Juan?" Anthony asked.

"Not far," Carlos said. "He is probably on the point, watching the town."

"Why don't we go and meet him?" Anthony asked.

"He will come here on this trail. I don't want to come through the jungle to meet them. They might shoot us by mistake."

"That would be a shame," Anthony said. "I already have one extra hole in my body. I do not need two."

"With two holes, you could spend more time at the doctor's house," Carlos said.

"That would not be all bad," Anthony replied.

"We are early, would you like some coffee?" Carlos asked.

"I had coffee with her last night, and it was good," Anthony said. "How are you going to make coffee here?"

Carlos fished inside his bag and pulled up a small café tin and a bag of ground coffee. He packed the metal filter with coffee. He fumbled through the bushes and picked up several small sticks. Within a few minutes, he had a fire going. He set the café tin on the fire and sat back. Coffee boiled up.

"I didn't bring a cup," Carlos said. "You can drink it straight from this. Careful you don't burn your lips."

Anthony sipped the coffee from the café tin. It was hot and black.

"You didn't sleep much," Carlos replied. "This coffee will wake you up. You will need to be awake; we have a full day, and Sofia said she would see us when you returned to have your wound checked."

"She did?" Anthony looked up. He grinned while he drank his coffee. "That's fine then."

Diego came running up.

"El Jefe isn't here yet," Anthony said, anticipating Diego's question.

"Good. I came to talk to you, *Capitan*."

"About what?"

"El Jefe has us running up and down these damnable hills and now we are not even going to attack," Diego said.

"Who told you this?"

"My brother spoke with Checo, Tito's man," Diego replied.

"I know Checo," Anthony replied.

"Checo said that Tito trusted you," Diego said. "All of us want to follow Tito, but he is not going to be here. If you lead us, I will follow and so will the rest of us."

"I have not spoken with El Jefe yet," Anthony replied.

"He will not attack. He has gone scared."

"He is not scared."

"It happens to all men, *Capitan*."

"And to you," Anthony replied.

"Not to me. For I do not fear death."

"You don't wish for it either?"

"No."

"Be careful with whom you speak about such things," Anthony said slowly.

"I can trust you. You are Tito's man."

"You can trust me. I am my own man. I will talk with El Jefe and make my own decision about the attack."

"*Si, Capitan*, but know that we are anxious," Diego saluted stiffly and ran off.

Anthony finished the coffee as Juan approached. He was flanked by Willy and three others.

"Carlos, Anthony," Juan spoke softly. "I am glad you are ready. It is time to go. Carlos, find Tito and bring him to the point."

"Yes, Jefe," Carlos replied. "I will find Tito."

"Good," Juan said. "Anthony, "Follow me close."

Juan told the others to join in behind Anthony. Juan moved quickly through the jungle. Part of the way, he followed narrow trails, other times he ordered the soldiers to cut a path through the jungle with machetes. Juan's men were masters of the machete, adroitly carving tunnels among the web-like vines or cleaving entire tree trunks in a single blow. They stopped occasionally to deftly cut small bamboo shoots and drink the droplets of water hidden inside.

Juan was extremely cautious when he was on the offensive. Juan lived by ambush and cunning, moving catlike through the bush and minimizing the size of trail he needed. He constantly moved and rarely slept in the same place two nights consecutively.

They climbed a steep incline and looked carefully out onto the valley. Juan pointed out the large flat rock below them. It provided an excellent lookout over the town; however, as he whispered to Anthony, he explained that if one can see, one can be seen.

"There is movement in the town, more than yesterday," Juan began. He put his binoculars up to his eyes. "We will need to descend closer for a more accurate count of the vehicles, but I believe they now know we are here."

They climbed down the incline. Juan told the other soldiers to take a smoke break further down the trail. They sat some distance away into the jungle.

Juan rolled a cigarette, gave it to Anthony and rolled one for himself.

"You are only united with your comrades if you are fighting the same enemy," Juan said in English.

He rarely talked in English. He spoke well with an American accent. He dragged on his cigarette and slowly exhaled, enjoying the slow trickle of smoke through his mouth.

"The problem is," he continued, "I know what enemy I am fighting, I don't always know what enemy my comrades are fighting." He waved his arm haphazardly around, motioning to the entire valley but nothing in particular. "I hope they are fighting the same ones I am."

Juan looked focused, as if he was trying to formulate his thoughts. Anthony said nothing.

"You know I like you Anthony," Juan said slowly.

"Yes," Anthony replied.

"The men like you and look up to you," he said. "You have an excellent mind."

Anthony's face reddened. He was not sure where this was leading.

"Are you going to take over?" Juan said.

Anthony started to speak. Juan held up his hand to stop him.

"I have been very lucky to have lived long. I know I cannot continue forever. It is a very dangerous business that we are in."

"Peace is around the corner," Anthony replied.

"Yes, but if it doesn't, these men need a leader," Juan said. "Tito has been talking to you?"

"Tito has been talking."

"When you first came to me, did you know how to live in these mountains?"

"No," Anthony replied.

"Did you know how to launch a coordinated attack?" Juan asked.

"No," Anthony replied.

"Did you know who to trust and who to avoid?" Juan asked.

Anthony shook his head.

"You have learned quickly, and you have more to learn. Do you think you will be greater than I?"

Anthony looked down at the ground. He knew Juan had spent much time with him. He did not know what to say.

"Allegiance is a tricky thing in a guerilla war. To lead means to give up normal relationships. Every day, you must lead men to their deaths." Juan said.

"I know."

"Be careful what you reach for, Anthony, it might blow your hand off."

"We should attack and attack now," Anthony said.

"Anthony, you don't have a blood commitment to one side or the other. You fight for your ideals. It makes you harder to manipulate, but not impossible."

"You think I'm being manipulated?" Anthony asked.

"Everyone is in this pestilent civil war."

"You are still here, Juan," Anthony said.

"Yes, by the grace of God," he replied, kissing the medallion of St. Jude which hung on his chest. "I wanted to speak with you about such things so you make the right decision when the time comes."

"That time will be a ways off," Anthony said.

"From your lips to God's ears," Juan said, kissing St. Jude again.

Juan field-dressed his cigarette and burned the paper. Juan looked at his watch.

"We are foreigners here. Never forget that," Juan said quietly in English.

He turned quickly and called out to the soldiers. They ran up quickly.

Moments later, Carlos appeared with Tito. Juan led them back up the incline.

"Over there, Tito" Juan said as he pointed to an adjoining peak, "I ran a small ruse along the ridge. About thirty boys ran back and forth all night as if a battalion was entering the valley. From below, they saw them, and in response, I believe they are pulling out. We will watch them closely today."

"I need to be at the mouth of this valley. Down there," Tito said, pointing far down the valley.

"Yes," Juan replied. "If we attack."

"If we march the backside of the ridge, we will move without being seen. It will be longer but safer for our plans," Tito said.

"We should wait until we know they are pulling out, if not, you will be exposed when you leave the ridge," Juan responded.

"Let me worry about keeping my ass covered," Tito said, rubbing his chin.

"You have to stay covered, in case we call off the attack."

"We can be in position by tomorrow."

"Tomorrow?" Juan replied skeptically.

"Yes," Tito replied.

"It is a long distance, through heavy brush," Juan said.

"If I tell them to run, they will run," Tito said confidently.

"I don't know," Juan replied. "We will not know if the army is pulling out or setting up better defenses."

"Do you have your artillery in place?" Tito asked.

"It doesn't matter, Juan replied tensely. "They have radar in place."

"I thought you destroyed it."

"They set up a new one."

"I can find it and destroy it," Anthony spoke up.

Juan looked at him.

"Did you hear that?" Tito said. "The radar will be destroyed."

"It hasn't been yet," Juan said. "Carlos and Anthony still need to find the radar and destroy it. If they cannot find it, we do not attack."

"I will find it," Anthony replied.

"Anthony said he will find it, he will find it. You can shell the colonel and his men to speed them along," Tito said.

"They might stay," Juan said.

"If they stay," Tito replied, "we'll crawl back up and over the ridge and slip into our dark jungle, safe and sound."

"Jefe," Carlos stated. "It's Shrove Tuesday tomorrow."

"It is?" Juan responded. "I didn't remember."

"We'll attack before daybreak on Wednesday," Tito responded enthusiastically. "After the fight, we will rub ashes on our foreheads in the beautiful cathedral of Santa Angelia."

"After carnival night, the *federales* won't have any fight in them," Carlos interjected.

"It is a solid plan with excellent timing," Tito replied. "We will penance the *federales*."

Tito laughed out loud. He had a large booming laugh.

Juan scanned the town. He pointed to a large group gathered in the central part.

"From here, I can't see well enough to determine what they are doing."

"I see them," Tito responded.

"We need to go down and to verify what exactly is being moved," Juan said calmly. "Carlos, take Tito to the spot we went to the other day."

"The flat rock in front of the flowering bushes?" Carlos asked.

"I don't think we need a closer look," Tito said.

"If not for you, then for Anthony," replied Juan.

Tito looked at Juan carefully. They stared at one another, but neither said anything further. Juan turned to Carlos.

"Stay low on the rock. I don't want us to be seen, in case they have their snipers out."

"I understand, Jefe," Carlos replied. "We will meet you there."

"Anthony," Juan said. "Follow Tito."

Tito and the others watched Juan disappear in the jungle. Within seconds, he disappeared from view; within a minute, they no longer heard the swish of the trampled bush.

Carlos directed them to go down to the right. Tito held his hand up to stop him.

"The jungle is a mysterious place. The low-lying cover snags your feet; the middle bushes whack you in the eyes, and the canopy trees darken your path," Tito said.

Anthony thought he heard the cracking of a branch behind him. Tito pointed Carlos forward. Carlos led them down along a steep trail; it cut sharply to the left. Anthony swung from one branch to another to descend. Tito stopped and listened. Checo and Miguel, his two lieutenants, appeared soundlessly behind him. Anthony only saw those two when Tito was planning his attack. Anthony stepped back, his hand instinctively going to his gun. Tito held his finger to his lips. He motioned Anthony to a spot where the trail leveled.

Have I taught you how to live off this tough land?" Tito whispered.

"Yes," Anthony responded quietly.

"Have I told you that we must suffer much to gain victory?"

"Yes."

"With machetes and saws, we have built industrious camps from nothing and, as quickly, disbanded them, leaving nothing to trace," Tito said.

"Yes." Anthony said, thinking on the many camps they had moved to and from. Tito and his men resourcefully used every plant, rock and tree to hew out a living in this savage undergrowth. Their honed skills showed how long they had been hiding and resisting in this heavily forested jungle.

"We. . . I have wreaked havoc on Colombia," Tito whispered fervently.

The hair on Anthony's neck rose. Tito was acting strange. He took a deep breath, held his tongue and waited.

"Now is the time," Tito said. "To come out of the shadows and take what is rightfully ours."

"We can win," Anthony replied.

"I feel it too. We have the advantage," Tito whispered.

His face was so close to Anthony's he could feel the heat of his breath.

"You know I like you Anthony," Tito whispered slowly. "And trust you."

Anthony felt someone move in close behind him. He mentally stopped himself from pulling out his gun.

"We need that artillery barrage to force the army from the town," Tito said. "You have my support."

"Kill the bastard," Anthony heard Checo hiss behind him. Checo crawled forward and squatted next to them. "We don't need him anymore." Checo breathed heavily.

"I told you we are not doing it that way," Tito said. Tito looked around; his words came out loud.

"We will not give ground now," Checo said. "We are close to victory. Mono is with us."

"El Jefe got us here," Tito whispered again, his emotions better in control. "Never forget that."

Anthony looked down. It was too soon. He could not go against Juan now.

"Listen, we must go now," Tito said. "Anthony, know that we are behind you."

Tito moved forward quickly; they came to several large flowering trees. Anthony wanted to ask what their name was, but Tito held his fingers to his lips.

Tito whistled. A whistle responded. Tito crouched down and crawled carefully out from the trees and onto the top of a flat ledge. The edge of the rock rose up creating a natural wall. Juan was sitting at the edge of the rock, his back against the rock. He motioned them forward.

Tito motioned his men to stay put and keep a lookout; he moved forward to Juan, followed by Anthony.

"I will look over the edge and check for spotters," Juan said.

He unslung his binoculars, turned and looked over the rock wall. Anthony followed his movements as he slowly surveyed across the entire horizon. Juan looked at Anthony and nodded.

Anthony held his breath and looked over the wall. The valley spread out below. Large military cargo trucks were bringing in supplies. Juan pointed at the central plaza. While Juan counted the trucks and vehicles, Anthony watched a group of young recruits who were exercising. At such a distance, their movements synchronized, hands, arms and legs raising and falling as if pulled by a common string.

Juan pushed the binoculars at him; Anthony concentrated its power at the group. Up close, a fat soldier lagged ever so slightly behind the rest. His florid cheeks moved in and out quicker than his arms moved up and down. His feet barely left the ground, fluffing small dust clouds with every step. To his left and right, soldiers, faces identical with unfocused stares and impassive features, moved listlessly, their arms and legs never rising as high or as quickly as they should, mouths closed while silently breathing through the nose. The entire group stopped. Anthony scanned the plaza. A man with a large hat and closely-cropped beard was talking with the young squadron leader. With a curt nod, the man ended the conversation. As he turned to walk away, Anthony noticed silver colonel leaves on his tunic.

"How many trucks have you counted?" Juan whispered gruffly.

"I ...," Anthony moved the binoculars off the plaza and started scanning the small town. Dividing it into four sections, he quickly counted the military vehicles in one section and multiplied by four.

"96, approximately," Anthony added.

"Yes, around a hundred. Same as I have been counting for the past week," Juan replied. "They are leaving now."

Tito crawled up behind them. Behind him followed Checo and Miguel.

"Some fast moving jeeps are coming into the town square," Anthony said quickly. "They are stopping in front of the colonel. A man has jumped out and is talking with him."

"Give me the glasses," Tito said softly.

Anthony handed him the binoculars. Tito swore softly as he focused the central plaza into view.

"It's the fucking paramilitary," he swore.

"This confirms my suspicions," Juan said. "The government is asking the paramilitaries to help control this district."

"Why would the government do that?" Anthony asked, as he turned to Juan.

When Juan stayed silent, Tito responded quietly, "Sometimes, the government cannot attack us directly. Maybe the politicians say the costs are too high or maybe they are interested in negotiating peace or maybe they too are tired of the war. When that happens, either the army pulls out completely or doesn't leave its barracks."

"We need to attack before they set up in town," Checo added quickly.

"The paramilitaries can't be any tougher than the regular soldiers," Anthony replied.

"When the paramilitaries press the attack, usually they can't find us, so they shoot anyone they believe is helping us. We retaliate and shoot everyone who is helping them," Checo said. "This bloody tug of war continues until one side becomes strong enough to control the area or the army steps in again, always against us."

"With the paramilitaries here, the army is not interested in this district. If the colonel knows he has no reinforcement coming, the plan should work," Tito said.

"Tito, why don't you convince these paramilitaries to join our cause?" Anthony asked.

"*Antonio*, here, you fight against the side who killed your father, no matter what your political beliefs. The government jailed and then killed my father. I fight to overthrow the government. I don't know, but that *Cabron* down there probably thinks his father was killed by a band of leftists. Now, he wants to kill as many leftists as he can. If he shoots me, he will feel bad, but comforted that he has revenged his father."

"That's senseless," Anthony replied.

"Maybe. While you are fighting, you convince yourself you are liberating your motherland from oppression. Sometimes, you become very rich and powerful, like Mono, especially if you can tax the drug traffickers in your area."

"You still believe in the *'Gran Colombia?'*" Anthony asked.

"I have to," Tito responded, "Or else it makes me little more than a kidnapper and murderer. I know I am not one; the Gran Colombia must be attainable."

"When a government abuses its people, nature will rise up and overturn a corrupt political system," Juan said. "The powerless will have their day."

"When the battle is close at hand, I am glad you are on our side, Juan," Tito said.

"Thank you for your confidence, but I have an uneasy feeling," Juan replied.

"You will come out of this unscathed, like every fight we have," Tito replied. "It will be successful. I know it."

"I am worried about Mono. I don't like Mono's new helicopter and his evasive talk," Juan said. "He needs to commit and fight."

"I will speak with Mono," Tito replied.

"It is not like him, to stand back from a fight. When we win," Juan continued, "it will be better to say that a united revolutionary front defeated the government, and they will have to discuss peace seriously."

"When we win, Mono will join us immediately so he can take credit for the victory," Tito replied. "If he doesn't, you can take the full credit."

"I don't want credit, I want peace," Juan said. "I want to go home, watch my peppers grow in my small garden and watch the children play in the street."

"Don't start talking like this to the men, gentle words confuse them," Tito said, "Most of them, all they know are war and conflict."

"When should they learn about peace, when they are dead?" Juan answered.

"No, of course not. Talk about peace confuses them, particularly when it comes from you. The men think you are going to sell them out."

"Sell them out?! Everyday I give my life for them," Juan responded angrily.

"Never forget," Tito responded, "you are a foreigner here, like *Antonio*. Foreigners come and go."

"It is other Colombians who are killing them."

"I know, but it is easy to blame foreigners for the troubles. When you start talking about freedom and revolution, you scare people."

"This innuendo and jealousy behind my back... And they call me the sneaky one."

"It's only talk."

"Talk kills."

"Please, Juan. Just promise me that when we win, you keep your revolutionary fervor controlled," Tito pleaded.

"For you my friend, I will let my actions speak louder than my words," Juan said.

"I believe we will win," Tito said. "When you are animated, it animates the men and they believe they can defeat anyone."

"Which makes me more dangerous," Juan said interrupting Tito. "I have heard that before, and I am still alive. Now is not the time to fight with words. There will be time enough, if we push the army shark and its feared paramilitary lampreys back into the sea."

"Are we going to fight, Jefe?" Carlos asked.

"You have relatives in the village," Juan said.

"Yes, Jefe," Carlos said, "but I will do what you ask."

"I know you will, Carlos. I am always careful what I ask," Juan replied.

"It is unpleasant to be caught in a war against your brother," Tito said shaking his head. "When I first took up arms against my government, I was fed up with the corruption and duplicity."

"Did you serve in the Colombian Army?" Anthony asked.

"I was a captain in the special forces," he replied. "They sent me on many secret missions, some nice, some not."

"The bad missions made you leave?"

"No," Tito chuckled, "You inure to those. No, it was a simple mission; I was sent to check on the border defenses of Venezuela, our neighboring country. They gave me a camera, a military map and secret codes to write in and send messages back. I went across the bridge between the two countries as a tourist."

Tito drank from his canteen.

"I must not have been thinking good because as soon as I crossed, I started snapping pictures of all the military installations along the bridge and the other side of the river. I was so busy taking pictures I didn't even notice two soldiers come up to me. They had to tap me on my shoulder to attract my attention."

"Tito becomes very concentrated on what he is doing," Juan interjected.

"Yes, well, they got my attention and took me to a small office. Many lower ranking officers came into the office and talked to me. All I gave them was my name, rank and serial number. After awhile they let me alone until a colonel came in to speak with me. He kept after me until I finally got tired and told him what I was doing. He became extremely angry, yelling that I had committed high treason and should be shot."

"I didn't know what to say. I looked around the room, and inside the little office was a picture of Simon Bolivar, titled "Liberator of Venezuela.' I couldn't help but smile because in my colonel's office hung the same picture titled 'Liberator of Colombia.' I said to the Venezuelan colonel, 'We have the same chief and a little while ago we were in the same army."

"The colonel's attitude changed. He, too, dreamed of a united South America similar to that of Simon Bolivar. He led me out of the office and invited me to drink with him. Several bars and many hours later, we walked arm and arm across the bridge singing to a united South America."

"He simply let you go?" Anthony asked.

"Yes," Tito answered. "It started me questioning why the army was making war against its own people. I quit the army and began fighting for my country's freedom. Once we are free, we can look to join other countries in a grand alliance."

"An alliance of rebels," Juan said.

"Rebels cannot delay," Tito said vehemently. "The army is ready to pull out of this sector. We should be ready to fill the void before the paramilitaries hunker down."

"Without Mono, it would be foolish to attack on our own," Juan replied.

"If we attack and win, they will believe we are too strong to be beaten. The army will completely pull out of this sector. I have seen it happen in the south."

"I know. Mono controls a large area with very little trouble."

"Exactly, once they pull out we can move to the coast and control everything," Tito said. "Even the paramilitaries will not fight us."

"It is a gamble," Juan replied.

"When I go into town," Carlos said, "there is talk that Mono is already here and is coming to liberate the town."

"You see," Tito said, "Mono has already joined us in spirit."

"I wish his spirit would bring a few guns along," Juan rejoined.

"They won't know if Mono is or isn't with us," Tito replied quickly. "If the colonel retreats along the road, I'll have my men along the lower ridges to drop the hammer. Let's go. Checo. Miguel."

They disappeared through the flowering bushes.

"Anthony, you promised much," Juan said slowly. "If the radar is not destroyed, our artillery can do nothing against their planes and helicopters. It will be a slaughter."

"I understand," Anthony replied.

"Do you?" Juan asked.

Gregory Arthur Solsrud

Chapter Five – Monday Noon

Anthony quickly ran back to his tent, grabbing his gear bag. The thought of seeing Sofia excited him. He had observed this valley long enough he could triangulate the radar's position, then he would see her. The only problem was slipping into town during the day, he would figure that out when he got there. Maybe Carlos would give her a message, and she could meet him. What if she didn't want to see him again or was occupied? He shoved stuff into his back pack.

"You are leaving so quickly?" Carlos asked. Carlos had come into his tent.

"I ... Yes, it is a long way down, and we have much to do. We should leave."

"I told you she would make you feel like you were sixteen," Carlos said with a smile.

"You knew I wanted to see her again," Anthony said. "Is it that obvious?"

"All you can think about is how to be near her," Carlos said simply. "I had a girl."

"You did?"

"Yes, and I remember what it was like. Thinking about her all day and waiting for the pleasant nights."

"Where is she?" Anthony asked.

"If I stop to talk about her, we won't see yours," Carlos replied.

"I wasn't sure how to, I mean, how do I see Sofia in town. It's full daylight."

"In this country, there are many hidden cliffs. It is not safe to walk around unguided. Your guide will figure a way into town."

"My life will be in your hands."

"And mine in God's, so we should reach where we are going," Carlos said. Carlos looked up, he saw Tito coming towards them. He was alone.

"Anthony, you are ready to leave?"

"Yes, I will find the radar station," Anthony replied.

"With that news, we are on the march," Tito said satisfied. "The next time I will see you will be in Santa Angelia. Anthony, promise me one thing?"

"Name it," Anthony replied.

"No, I want you to hear it before you agree," Tito said.

"What is it?"

"Stay true to yourself and stay true to the cause," Tito said.

"That is a simple request," Anthony said.

"Possibly. Everyday I risk my life to punish the murderers and traitors of my Gran Colombia. I will probably die in battle," Tito continued. "The people who sell themselves out cheat themselves out of a life."

"I promise you," Anthony said. "I'll stay true."

"Remember, all it takes is one man who believes," Tito said. "We, Colombians, no longer believe we can change anything. We are too close to it. My countrymen need to reacquire the fervor through you, like I have."

Anthony looked at Tito.

"Can I ask you a question?" Anthony asked.

Tito nodded.

"Have you asked Juan the same thing?"

"Juan is the truest person I know. He fights for his ideas," Tito answered. "People in power don't trust him because they can't control him. His ideas threaten them."

"Juan will attack," Anthony said.

"I am not worried. You have my support. You know what to do," Tito said.

"You will be here when I return," Anthony said. "I will not be gone long."

"I will not be here. We are moving out now. I must lead my men. Miguel is staying behind."

Anthony thought on Tito's words before he spoke.

"You need Miguel," Anthony replied.

"We need that artillery barrage," Tito said. He smiled, shook Anthony's hand firmly and left.

Carlos and Anthony started down the main trail leading away from the camp. Along the trail were makeshift tents and covers, young men in dirty fatigues sat silently, chewing slowly on mangos and cleaning their automatic rifles. The trail was wide. They walked side by side.

"My girl and I were in love," Carlos said. "We got what comes out of love. Catholic girls do not believe in birth control. You had better be careful."

"We haven't gotten to that point," Anthony said defensively, "and I don't think we will."

"You will, it's a natural course of things," Carlos replied. "You could no more stop water running down a mountain."

"Where is your child?" Anthony asked.

"My daughter lives down on the coast. She works doing the books for a rich industrialist. She was born smart, like her mother. I'm not book smart," Carlos continued. "When I was twelve years old, I remember my father coming to school. The teacher wanted to speak with him. He told my father that it was waste of time for me to attend to school. My father took me home, and I worked with him every day. I liked it. I never understood much at school, and my father liked having me home. He had someone to help him and talk to during the day."

"Your father sounds like a very good man," Anthony said.

"He was," Carlos said. "When I started seeing my girl, he told me to be careful that I would find myself in trouble. He did not stop me. He only talked to me. I didn't listen. That's what love does to you. It makes you crazy."

"My father taught me to fly and shoot, but he never talked," Anthony said. "He was never very happy being stuck in the middle of a bunch of farmers. I guess he imagined himself as more in life."

"My wife's mother was like that. She was never happy we got married. When my wife died, she said I killed her."

"You raised your daughter?" Anthony asked.

"Yes, I see her as often as I can," Carlos said.

They walked in silence.

"Having a child is a wonderful thing," Carlos said. "You are the biggest thing in their life. They listen for your voice and come running to hug you no matter how bad you smell. All they want is your love."

"You make me feel ungrateful," Anthony replied. "I never thanked my parents for much. My father always said he worked hard so I could have a better life."

"You grow up," Carlos said. "Thank them by living your life as you want."

"I'm trying, that's why I came down here," Anthony replied. "All my dad wanted was to be a war hero, and I guessed he passed that dream onto me when I was a kid. I keep imagining myself going back to a big parade in my hometown where we stop in front of city hall and the mayor comes out and gives me a ribbon."

"It's a lot danger for a ribbon," Carlos said.

Anthony looked at Carlos. Sometimes, when Carlos responded, the choice of words was not what Anthony expected. This was one of those times.

"I'm not here for the ribbon," Anthony replied. "I like being part of something. I like saving people's lives. I guess I don't think what we do is that dangerous. At least when I'm with Juan, I don't feel any danger."

"He's not afraid to die," Carlos said. "Did you know he was a priest before?"

"I can't see him as a priest," Anthony replied.

"El Jefe doesn't talk about his past. I know these things."

"I won't bring it up. I wonder what it is like, being a priest?"

"Probably the same as being you or me, one has to live rightly with God."

"Getting right with God," Anthony chuckled. "Carlos, you ask the impossible."

"No, it is easy," Carlos replied seriously, "Eat well and lie down with your girl afterwards."

"If life were only that simple," Anthony said.

"It is," Carlos said, "you have to make it that way."

Carlos descended on an unfamiliar trail. Anthony tapped his shoulder and signaled for him to stop. Pulling off his pack, he reached into a side pocket and grabbed a small leather pouch, worn smooth and dark by use. He took out a small brass compass.

He held his father's compass steady. The army had given his father this compass, which had been given to Anthony when he was twelve. After marching his young son around for a summer in the large swamp close to their home, his father presented him with the compass telling him that he had received proper military training that is, repeating something over and over and over again until you are numb from thought. Only until he had completed the compass training would his father let him hunt by himself. One night, his father woke him up, dropped him off in the middle of the swamp, gave him a map and told him to find his gun and hunting gear, all by daybreak. Anthony now chuckled aloud, as he saw his father surprised face the next morning as Anthony padded down to the breakfast table in his bare feet and pajamas. His father looked up from his paper and morning coffee and said that he was preparing to go and look for him. His father asked if he had given up and come home to bed. Not responding at first, Anthony finished his breakfast, walked over to a folded blanket in the corner. Underneath it lay his gun and hunting gear. His father smiled and never asked again where he was going, understanding he always knew his way home.

He motioned for Carlos to continue, silently counting his paces as they trudged on. Every fifteen minutes, he stopped and wrote quickly on a small notebook, which he carried with him. After about an hour, they came upon a small stream. Following the stream, Anthony could see an opening in the thick trees. When they came to the opening, the stream fell over a cliff forming a small waterfall. From the top of the waterfall, they could see the town below them. The large church steeple rose above the small clay-roofed houses.

"Come let's move in a little closer," Anthony said.

"And let everyone know a gringo is tramping around Santa Angelia," Carlos replied. "Your presence would even make an army private suspicious. There might be patrols about."

"We need to find an antenna which sends the signals up to the radar station," Anthony replied. "We must climb higher to spot it."

They crawled up a hill. Anthony unbuckled his pack and pulled out a spotting scope. He leaned against a fallen tree and measured the various distances, jotting down figures in his book. He would ask Carlos to identify different features, while he slowly mapped out the coordinates. Anthony wanted to be accurate, measuring everything twice.

Below them, Anthony saw the creek flowing. Sofia had told him it merged into the river, which ran around the town. He looked out but could not see the river.

Anthony packed up his spotting scope and stood up.

"What do you want to see next," Carlos asked.

"We need to go down the valley," Anthony said.

"I don't think that is wise. Someone will notice us with that telescope," Carlos said. "There's a lot of traffic on the road today."

"Let see how close we can move," Anthony said.

Anthony walked straight down the hill. He heard the sound of vehicles in front of him. Carlos quickly put his finger to his lips and pointed ahead. Carlos suddenly dropped to his haunches. Anthony did the same.

Along the road, soldiers were marching. They must have marched out of town much earlier and were now returning. Anthony recognized the insignia on the uniforms; they were part of the Colombian Special Forces.

After they passed, Carlos led them away from the road.

"There are many soldiers out at this time," Carlos said. "It is safer for them to be out during the day."

"I should have followed your advice," Anthony said. "We need information to press the attack, but not at the risk of being caught. Let's return to the waterfall, so I can figure out what to do."

Carlos took out his machete and cut a trail straight up the hill through the jungle. They came out at the base of the falls. They climbed along its side until they reached the top.

"Since I cannot go into town," Anthony said. "you must. Do you have pen and paper?"

"No, Señor," Carlos replied.

Anthony ripped a sheet out of his notebook and took a pencil out of his backpack. He quickly drew a picture of a satellite dish. He turned the paper over and drew out an outline of the town.

"You need to walk around and find something that looks like this," Anthony explained. "Mark on this map where it is and in what direction it is facing."

"I can do that," Carlos said. "I will also make a little check for every tank I see."

"I don't think that is necessary," Anthony replied.

Carlos nodded.

"Can you try to count the number of soldiers you see?" Anthony asked.

"Yes, I can make an "x" for every ten I see," Carlos said.

"That should do it," Anthony said. "Be careful and return safely. I will wait for you here."

"If I see the Doctor's daughter, I will tell her that you are waiting for me here," Carlos said.

"I don't think anyone can find me here, it's pretty thick."

"She is from this valley," Carlos stated simply. He tipped his hat and descended through the brush. Anthony followed his retreating back as he made his way down the steep slope.

There were many more things that he would like to have known, but he didn't want to confuse Carlos. He had not seen any helicopters come into the town. This struck him as odd. Supplying a faraway post, there would be aerial activity. Even if they were pulling out, they would want to move certain things out with helicopters or bring in specialized personnel to help with the pullout. The road up the valley was very poor. It took a day to come up the whole valley by truck. The quiet was unusual. Maybe they had lost interest in this area and were no longer going to put the resources here. Maybe, it was only the quiet before the storm.

There is nothing to do but wait until Carlos returned. Anthony looked at his watch. They had taken longer than Anthony expected; now, with Carlos gone for several hours, and evening approaching, there would be no time to see Sofia. Anthony felt weary. He sat down on a rock, the warm sun heating his neck and back. The longer he sat the more noise the surrounding jungle made. He heard strange noises running through the underbrush. He stood up and looked for a more protected spot. He walked closer to the waterfalls and crawled under some large palm fronds. Pushing aside the large ferns and leaves, he sat down under a canopy of leaves. He could see neither the creek nor the town from this spot. He felt secluded. After a while, the insects found him. Hundreds of small bugs from biting no-seeums to large mosquitoes echoed the call throughout the jungle that lunch was to be found under the palm canopy. He pulled his shirt collar up close to his neck. They concentrated on his lips and eyelids. He could not last long; he had to move. He crawled back out of the underbrush and moved away from the stream. He found a small opening in the jungle where the sunlight shone bright. He sat with his back against a large broken palm tree, the intense sun closing his eyes. The insects were less fierce. He dozed off.

"Wake up," a soft voice whispered, jolting Anthony to attention.

He whirled his head around and saw Sofia's delicate, tan face staring at him. His eyes must have conveyed his alarm.

"I didn't mean to frighten you," she said softly.

"I wasn't expecting you and fell asleep."

"It's difficult sleeping nights all the way through. The humidity has been bad for days."

"Yes."

"When it doesn't rain but should, the air becomes soaked."

"Where is Carlos?" Anthony asked.

"I told Carlos I would take care of you."

Anthony pushed himself to his feet and stood next to her. She smelled fine. A fine layer of sweat covered her arms, which hung loosely at her sides. Her long black hair reflected the sun.

"I see you almost found it," she said casually.

"Found what?" he asked.

"My fern palace," she said simply.

She pushed back through a thick wall of tall wall of brush and an opening in the trees filled with ferns lay before her. Among the ferns, mango trees with low hanging branches thick with fruit stood like sentinels. She walked forward and picked a couple of mangos from the nearest tree.

"Here," she said, giving one to Anthony, "wild mango from Colombia, growing among the fern beds. I love touching these ferns, soft and supple. This is my own private fern and fruit garden; one can walk within ten feet of it and never see it."

"You have to know where to look for beauty," Anthony replied.

"Yes," she said, looking up, "yes, you do."

Anthony pulled his knife out and started skinning the mango.

"No," Sofia said, "like this."

With her teeth, she pulled the soft peel of the mango off in velvety strips. She sucked the mango, the juice running down her chin.

Anthony continued to peel the mango with his knife. He cut it into pieces and ate it like the apples back home.

"Are you afraid of dirtying your hands? Follow me I'll show you were there is plenty of running water to bathe," she said coquettishly.

She grabbed his hand and led him out of the fern garden and along a narrow path following the creek. As the path turned away from the direction of the creek, she carefully separated several large palm fronds and motioned him through the open space. She entered after him and picked her way carefully among the dense foliage. They descended a steep slope; the sound of crashing water became louder. The plants and ground were moist; a fine mist hung in the air.

Sofia came to the edge of the foliage where a rocky ledge began; the water fell heavily along the rocks.

"From here, be careful, the rocks are very slippery. Put your feet and hands exactly where I do. Don't fall."

Anthony nodded. She stepped slowly out on the ledge, letting Anthony put his hand and foot in the same spot from where she picked hers up. As they passed behind the falls, the spray changed from a mist to a heavy deluge. The ledge went sharply inward behind the cascading water where the small path led to a large cavern in which they could stand.

"My father showed me this many years ago. He was a mountaineer in Italy. He climbed up and down all of the nearby cliffs when he came here. He found this while he was climbing the falls, looking for a quicker way up to the pass."

"It's very private."

"I liked coming here while growing up. It gave me some place to think. I used to keep food and wood in the back. I'll bring some back later. Let's go now. I want you to practice coming in and out, so you can do it when I am not here."

After the third in and out, Anthony tried it on his own. He covered the slippery distance easily, the holds falling naturally where he put his feet. He came back to where she was waiting and watching him from the foliage.

"You're a natural climber," she said.

"I hiked a lot when I was kid growing up in Montana," Anthony said. "You climb better than I."

"I like heights. Climbing up these mountains doesn't bother me. I don't think I want fly in a plane. It's better to have ground underneath your feet."

"Once you fly above the treetops, you never want to come down. Walking around on the ground is more dangerous," he added, slapping at a buzzing mosquito.

"Especially out here in the jungle where everything bites or stings you," she laughed.

"I know," he said, involuntarily rubbing the bites on his neck. "I thought we had big mosquitoes back home. The ones here about carry me away."

"The insects don't bother much. It's the soldiers carrying rifles that scare me."

"If you believe Juan, they will soon be a thing of the past," he said with conviction.

"Thing of the past!" Sofia spat between her fingers. "Our past is what scares me. Everyone talks about the glorious past and our noble history. When it comes to revenge and laziness, your neighbor is quick to pull the trigger."

"The government is at fault for the war," Anthony replied.

"Don't blame the government for the war. The people receive the government they deserve."

"You can't blame the people for the war," Anthony replied.

"Those paramilitaries who you saw, where do you think they are from?"

"From Colombia?"

"Yes, and from right here. I recognize most of them and they recognize me. Do you think that makes me safe?" she asked.

Anthony shook his head no.

"That is the country in which I live. Those are my people."

She stood up and clenched her fists.

"What do I do? Spy on our country's soldiers so other soldiers can come and kill them." Sofia's words came out harsh.

"Am I not the same?" she continued.

"Did you ask to be in this war?"

"No."

"You are trying to survive, like everyone else."

"Survival, at what cost I ask myself."

"At the cost of your own life if you don't survive," Anthony replied.

"That's my point, there are things worth more than my own life," Sofia said. "To sacrifice such things to save my life is to debase myself."

"What is worth more than your own life?" Anthony asked.

"Your honor. Your country," Sofia replied quickly.

She fell silent for a moment.

"Do I confuse you?" she asked.

"Yes," he replied.

She looked at him hard with her dark eyes.

He continued, "You've made the war personal. Before I was involved for different reasons. Now, I want you to win."

"When can I tell you that I have won?"

"When you can climb along these cliffs and not worry about being ambushed by a gang with guns."

"I would like to see that day."

"You will. I am going to help you."

"The sun is going down," she said quickly. "We can return to the village."

"You want me to come with you into the village?"

"Yes."

"I should wait for Carlos."

"He will know where to find you."

"I don't know. It's risky."

"I don't want you to leave me yet," Sofia said quietly.

"I don't want to leave you yet either."

"I know how to cut through the alleys until we reach my mother's home. I want you to talk with her."

"She knows what you do?" Anthony asked.

"Yes. I have no secrets from her. She doesn't approve."

"No questions asked?" Anthony looked at her.

"No questions asked," Sofia replied

"I would like to see her again, and thank her for my arm," he added quickly. "It's too dangerous. We stumbled into a Special Forces patrol a little while ago."

"I know another way, through the storm pipe. I don't like to go that way because I'm scared of rats and everything else that lives under the ground in no light," Sofia said as she shuddered.

"Where does it start?" he asked.

"Along the edge of the river."

"Take me there, and I'll look at it."

They descended along the falls and followed the creek until it met the river. They scrambled along the river's edge staying in the shadows of the brush. It was nearly dark. They came to a large concrete pipe that was cracked and broken on the end. A trickle of water flowed along the bottom. Anthony reached into his pants pocket and pulled out a flashlight. He rotated the cover to red.

"We will go in a little ways before I turn on my light," he said. "Grab my hand, so you won't stumble."

Her hand was moist and warm. He switched the torch on when he could no longer see light at the entry of the tunnel. As they picked their way along the pipe, Anthony's heart raced every time he bumped against her. His breath came quickly.

"Do you wish to slow down?" he asked.

"No, I just. . .," she said slowly, willingly the words to come out.

He put his finger to her lips, "I know I feel it too."

"Since when?" she asked.

"Since I met you," he replied quietly.

She pushed against him and kissed him. His lips responded.

"We must keep going," she said.

"Don't let go of my hand," he replied.

"I won't."

She stopped when they crossed under another concrete pipe. Small metal bars ran vertically to the top.

"This leads out into an alleyway across from our house," Sofia said. "You can see out from the side, but you have to push the cover aside to exit."

Anthony started to crawl up. She pulled him back down.

"Your hair and skin are too light," she said. She turned to him, pulled his shirt collar up around his ears, pushed down his long sleeves, unfurled her scarf from around her neck, and put it on his head. "There that should help a bit."

They climbed out into the alley. When they heard voices, they pressed against the wall. When the voices drew close, she pressed against his body and turned his face towards her in an embrace, pulling her long, thick hair over his face and head. Even after the voices had long left, she stayed pressed against him.

"My mother's house is across the street," she panted.

They crossed quickly stopping at a small yellow door in the stone wall. She slipped a key out of her pocket and undid the lock. She stepped quickly inside pulling him after. She locked and bolted the heavy wooden door. She hugged him quickly, slipping away to run along the pathway, up the stairs and into the house. He followed a step behind her and ended up with her in the small kitchen.

Her grandmother was there preparing the evening meal. She introduced her to him calling her "Nana." Sofia reached behind the large kitchen door, took down a clean white apron and fastened it around herself. She looked over at Anthony.

"I need to help my Nana with dinner," she said. "Through there is my mother's library. She wouldn't mind if you used it."

"May I stay and talk with you, here in the kitchen?"

"Of course," she smiled continuing, "Nana, *Antonio* is going to sit here and watch us while we cook."

Nana clucked her tongue as she turned towards the stove.

"She approves of you," Sofia replied.

"Tell her I approve of you," Anthony said.

"She will not care. It is not your right to approve of me."

"I am the only one being tested?"

"Yes."

"Do I receive a prize if I pass?"

"We'll see. You haven't passed yet. You should think more about that than the prize."

"I will," Anthony said.

He leaned against the wood counter and watched her work. Her muscles rippled under her smooth skin as she kneaded dough. A faint line of sweat shined brightly under her nose. She pushed her hair back, leaving a flour mark along her red cheek and dark hair.

He pushed off from the counter and walked next to her. She looked at him. With the back of his hand, he brushed the flour from her hair, extending his finger; he wiped the sweat off her lip and with his wet finger cleaned the whiteness from her cheek. She blushed.

"You're distracting me," she said.

"Do you mind?"

"No."

Nana said something to her, which Anthony did not understand.

"She wants to know if you would like some red wine?"

"Yes."

Sofia spoke to Nana. Nana walked to the end of the kitchen and pulled a jug out of the pantry. She poured a glass and brought it to Anthony.

"To your health," Anthony said as he toasted to Nana.

"*Salud*," she responded.

"*Salud*," Sofia echoed.

The wine tasted warm and sweet. Anthony pulled out a large wood chair at the far end of the table and sat down. He watched Sofia as she prepared the food. As she moved pans on and off the gas stove, the smoke and stream rose quickly to the high ceiling. A large, slow fan stirred the hot, steamy air, the humidity escaping out a pair of long, rectangular windows devoid of glass and covered with black, iron bars. The ceiling stained by the smoke dully contrasted the pumpkin-colored clay walls patterned with hand-painted tiles. Nana worked at the other end of the table cutting the vegetables. When she finished, she carried plates and silverware through a swinging door into the other room.

"When may I be alone with you," Anthony asked.

"You're alone with me right now."

"Not for long enough."

"You're like the wild kittens that come to our window to drink the milk I put out," she replied. "I should not have spoiled you."

"Do you mind putting the milk out?"

"No."

Nana came back into the kitchen. She talked with Sofia.

"My mother has returned; she is changing. I'll show you where the bathroom is. You can wash up before dinner."

Anthony rose and walked over to the swinging door. Before Sofia came through, she turned around and talked with Nana. When she finished, she turned again and pushed Anthony gently through the swinging door. On the other side, she grabbed his hand and led him through the dining room into a small hallway. She opened a small door and pulled him into a small washroom. She pushed the door shut with her back and pulled his face to hers. After several moments, she gently pushed him away.

"Are you going to be like my wild kittens and run away after they have eaten?" she asked.

"Have you ever let the kittens stay?"

She smiled at him, flicked him on the stomach with her open hand and squeezed back out through the door, walking back into the kitchen.

"Nana, how did you know *Abuelo* was the one?"

"Child, you just know," she replied.

"How can you be sure, I mean, when you meet someone who is not like you at all? *Abuelo* and you were the same, so you could be sure. How can you be sure about someone who is different?"

"*Mi amor*, you think that your *Abuelo* and I were the same?"

"Yes, of course," she replied tentatively. "You never fought, and I never heard you whisper an ill word to him or treat him badly."

"Because I respected him, not because I thought like him," she replied.

"You both spoke Spanish and had the same history," Sofia said.

"Colombia and Spain are two nations divided by a common language and as a different as black and white. Your grandfather's family came from Catalan and if he had stayed, he would have been a mortal enemy of what my family believed," she replied. "What bind two people together is not their differences, whatever those perceived differences are, but their love for one another. Did I ever tell you that your grandfather kissed me the first day we met?"

"No. Impossible. That didn't happen back then," Sofia replied shocked. "Did you slap him?"

"Why?"

"Well, because he wasn't supposed to," Sofia said.

"We were married happily fifty one years," Nana replied with a smile. "Who was to say that wasn't the right thing to do?"

Sofia walked over and hugged her grandmother.

"Now, child, busy yourself and help me finish, your mother will be down soon, and we cannot keep the *Norteamericano* waiting," she said with a smile.

As Sofia and her grandmother talked, Anthony looked at himself in the mirror. His face was red; his eyes wild and unrecognizable to himself. He splashed his face with cold water, putting his head under the tap and letting the water run over his head. He shut the water off, resting his forehead against the cool, ceramic sink. Standing up, he dried his face and head with the small towel. He combed his hair and tried to straighten up his clothes. It was no use. He let himself out. Walking down the small hallway, he entered into the dining room, lit only with the small chandelier. Sofia's mother, Romona, was sitting opposite Sofia, as he entered the room she smiled at him and motioned him to sit at the head of the table.

"Welcome, *Capitan Antonio*," Romona said. Her voice sounded tired. "It is nice to have a man dining with us again."

Nana moved around the room and poured the glasses with a light, white wine.

"In your honor, I asked Nana to open up a special bottle of wine," Romona continued. "*Salud.*"

"*Salud*," Sofia and Anthony said in unison.

They ate in silence.

"You are quiet, my daughter. Has your day been that bad?" her mother asked.

Sofia blushed and smiled.

"No," she replied. "I was thinking about Papi. I wish he were here."

"Yes. He was never at a loss for words," Romona replied and smiled, more to herself, reflecting on a treasured memory. "In fact, *Capitan Antonio*, that is how he made me love him. He kept talking to me until I made him promise to be quiet. He promised to be quiet if I promised to marry him. I laughed and found myself married to him two months later."

"He sounds like a wonderful man," Anthony replied formally.

"Yes, he refused to accept this war. His family left Italy after the Second World War. He never saw the sense in the destruction. He said the same families ran Italy after the war as before the war. There was no improvement, just more dead and torn up people."

Anthony didn't know what to say. He looked down at his plate.

"Are you finished?" Romona asked.

"Yes," Anthony replied.

"You must have some dessert," Romona said. "Sofia, bring in the flan. I will cut it here at the table."

Sofia rose from the table, picked up the plates and went into the kitchen. Anthony heard the clink of plates being stacked.

"Have you ever had flan?" Romona asked. "I made it this morning. It is Sofia's favorite dessert."

Sofia returned with a metal tray and set it along with plates and forks in front of her mother. Romona cut several pieces, selecting a large one and handing it to Anthony.

"Enjoy," she said.

Anthony sliced off a corner with his fork. Romona watched him as he put the piece into his mouth and waited for his reaction. It was sweet and creamy. The top was burnt sugar. He had never tried anything like it before.

"Is it good?" Romona asked.

"Yes, it is," Anthony replied politely.

"Your commander Juan enjoys my flan very much," Romona said.

"He visits you?" Anthony asked.

"During the rainy season," Romona replied. "He says he cannot work when it rains. Work is his euphemism for fight. He has visited me quite often. We talk about many things. He is extremely well-educated."

"I didn't know," Anthony said.

"The rains will soon begin again," Romona continued. "I expect he will return, and we will talk again. That is unless he is killed."

"Juan said he was very lucky to have lived so long," Anthony said. "Without him, the movement will suffer."

"One should plan for one's demise," Romona said. "Although I can't see Juan being killed, he is elusive."

"He is very committed to having a government that fights for the people," Sofia said.

"He has explained to me many times about how the people must get so upset about the war that they'd develop the political will to change it. Until the people change, he cannot win," Anthony said. "It's difficult understanding what he means."

"It is necessary to turn political crisis into armed crisis by performing violent actions that will force those in power to transform the military situation into a political situation," Romona explained. "That will alienate the masses, who, from then on, will revolt against the army and the police and blame them for the state of things."

"He never says it quite so clearly," Anthony replied.

"I didn't say it. It's a quote from a Brazilian revolutionary," Romona replied. "I forget his name but not his words. Juan does not have time to think and read all day. It is a luxury of being an old woman."

"You are not old, Mami," Sofia said.

"A mother never changes in the eyes of her children, only in the eyes of the public," Romona replied, turning to Anthony. "I should like to continue to be friends with Commandander Juan. It is always good to be friends with the man who has a gun over you."

"He is not like that," Sofia interjected.

"He desires peace," Anthony said.

"We can only hope," Romona added sadly. "I keep reading and reading, trying to make sense out of this civil war, by understanding civil wars in the past."

"It is difficult being educated in the middle of a war," Anthony replied.

"Yes," she said. "One sees the suffering firsthand and from one's knowledge of history, one knows what will happen."

"What will happen?"

"More suffering. Happy is the mother of a level-headed daughter, sad the mother of a rebel. Take my advice, *Antonio*, leave this country while you can."

"We are winning," Anthony replied quickly.

"Next year you will be losing, and then winning, and then losing, until you are dead," she replied.

"The areas I go are not dangerous," Anthony answered.

"Not dangerous," she scoffed. "A bullet has no memory and no master, once it leaves a gun. What if the B-2 were to break down my door? What would you do then?"

"Army intelligence is not operating in this area," Anthony countered.

"Tell that to the family of Jose Xavier Peres. When we found him, his skin had been ripped from his skull and had bullet holes in it. His hands had been burned in a fire. The *campesinos* called me because his tied feet were not calloused, so he couldn't have been a laborer. Do you know who he was?"

Anthony shook his head.

"A doctor. Accused of collaborating with the *guerilleros*. And who are you? Which side are you on? Do you know who he was?"

Anthony looked away from her gaze and stared at the floor.

"My friend. A doctor who helped all who came to him. He had no political beliefs, only a belief that all sick and injured and tortured people deserved care."

"Mami, do you have to talk about him?"

"If I don't remember, who will? At least, we gave him a Christian burial, more than the thousands of others who are anonymously interred in our soil." Romona drank from her wine glass. "I can see in my daughter's eyes that she cares for you deeply. You are a good man. Take her out of here. Return to your country where you can live in peace."

"I am not leaving you, Mami," Sofia answered.

"I am an old woman," she replied. "I have had my life. You must live yours."

"The war will be over soon," Anthony stated.

"Even if it does, what will you have to offer your children," she said. "There are no schools; they have been blown up. There are no teachers; they have been shot. Only the old, the sick and the degenerates are left. No, it will take many years for us to recover."

"We have recovered, we are winning and a new order will prevail," Sofia said. "We will have freedom in the street and no more violence."

"No more violence. How quickly we forget. When I was a little girl growing up, I remember '*la violencia*.' People were stark raving mad and embarked on killing sprees against their neighbors. The Conservatives were in power on a popular vote. Gaitan, a popular liberal leader was killed; nobody knew who did it, but it didn't matter. The Liberals were mad and went out into the street in great crowds and looted and destroyed and killed randomly."

"Except in my mother's town," Sofia began.

"Which town was that?" Anthony asked.

Sofia gave him the name of the town.

"Sofia has heard part of the story, but not the whole part," Romona said. "I have only told her the good part that our town did not partake in these blood waves. The people knew one another and respected one another. But this respect is a fragile veneer, easily broken by the gentlest hand. I am telling you now so that you quit this fight before this country pulls you into its bloody whirlpool."

"Juan told me that this period was the start of the violence in Colombia," Anthony said.

"The start of the violence? It is only the start of people's memories," Romona replied. "The writers and scholars of this day are my age and can draw on memories from this period. Once we are dead, a new, later period will be the justification for the current killing. No, *Antonio*, our violence is deeply rooted. A cancer has grown onto the body politic over centuries and cannot be cut out without killing the patient. Have you seen the picture in my study?"

"I haven't been in your study."

"I will describe it to you. It is a picture of my mother's father sent to us at the start of the *la violencia*. He is standing in front of the Capital building with his *companeros liberales* cheering. He wrote a note on the back, "*Viva las Santanderistas!* When my mother saw the picture, she threw it away. I took it out of the garbage and hid it. It is the only picture I have of my maternal grandfather."

"He died in *la violencia*," Sofia said. "At least, we think he died, they never found his body."

"The bodies were piled up in the *Cementario Central* in Bogotá," Romona continued. "They had nowhere else to put them. Most went into a common grave. But look at the picture closely, he is standing there smiling, no, not simply smiling, but grinning. His hand held high, clutching a *machete*. His *companeros* are holding pikes and clubs aloft in celebration. Behind them, fire billows out the windows of the Capital building, and below them, lie the cadavers of the slain. Such is the history of politics in our family, but as I began, in the town where we lived, these vicissitudes never reached us, at least not yet.

The Conservatives had elected a new mayor and the town's commission. The Liberals who lived there were unhappy, because for years they controlled the town through their own mayor and commission. They felt entitled to anything they wanted. They feared the new mayor, not for anything he had done, but for things he might do to take away their rank and privilege. Bogotá, the capital, was on fire, and no troops were in our small town to maintain law and order. But as I told you, our town was the model of law and order.

On the night of the change of government, the new mayor threw a large party in the town's square. We had a beautiful party that night. Torches on bamboo poles lit the square with fire, making it seem like a faraway and fantasy island. There were only a few soldiers about. When fights broke out, most of the townspeople fled home. The drunk ones and the fanatical ones stayed. The leader of the Liberals stopped the new Conservative mayor and the town council from leaving. He wanted them to receive the cup. It was biannual tradition between mayors to pass the cup of the town. The cup had been a gift upon the founding of the town from the King of Spain. The new mayor did not want to do it, whether he was afraid or belligerent, I do not know. The townspeople seized the bamboo poles, which had torches on top of them and forced the mayor and the others to run through the square back to the center where the stage stood. The people would shake the poles at them, but it was very funny watching these men stumble and run along between the long rows of people. It reminded me of when they let the bulls run in the street and the people ran in front of them, but this time the bulls were the men. When they reached the stage, the game had nearly played itself out.

My father held the cup and was ready to give the new mayor the cup and end the evening. My father had not been the mayor, but the old mayor was not there, and everybody liked my father. He was kind and helped others. The crowd had stopped jeering and people's heads had begun to hurt. My father turned towards the crowd to tell them that the fun was done and that the cup would be returned to them in new elections in two years. The new mayor, Señor Francisco, called my father a filthy name out loud. He wanted the cup to be given to him by the old mayor, not his lap dog. Señor Francisco was an arrogant son of a bitch and swore at my father. I had never heard such words and I kept them in my head until I was older and I knew what he had said. The new mayor was rich. My father was the son of a poor immigrant. My father went over to Señor Francisco and cracked him on the head with the cup and told him he could have it. When the crowd saw the blood and heard the screams of the mayor for the justice and the police, they turned mean. The dirty and the drunk were left, and they were filled with the lust for blood.

Someone came forward and hit Señor Francisco with a bamboo stick. It made a satisfying whacking sound. The loud sound carried across the crowd and silenced them. I think that if the Señor Francisco would have called out and apologized, the crowd would have let him pass unharmed; they had, after all, come to celebrate his inauguration. But he cried that he didn't deserve this treatment at the hands of the people. He strutted through the long line of people swearing at each of them. Everyone hit him with the bamboo stick. And he fell to the stone floor. He died badly.

The other council members stood in front of the stage, huddled together. I can't remember any of their names, and I never asked my father. I remember their faces, pale and scared and trembling. The first people in the crowd saw those faces as I saw them and did not strike them. But the people behind, the ones who had let the blood of Señor Francisco pushed the crowd forward. The blood turned those people into great white man-eating sharks. As one is squeezed in a crowd, one fears for his own life and acts violently to save it, by shoving back with all his strength. This desperate shoving stimulated the emotion. A man who had not been in front and had not seen the faces broke through the crowd and whacked one of the council members on the head.

My father was pulling me back, but I was absorbed in the emotion that I had to see. I bit my father's hand and slid away from him. The man who had been hit was laughing. The crowd could hear the laughing but they could not see. There was so much pushing to see, but I was above it all on the stage and I could see it all. The man with the bamboo stick hit the laughing man again and again and again until his stick broke. The laughing man ran his hands through his hair matted with blood and looked at his hands. He stopped laughing. He jumped at the man with the stick and seized his throat with the bloody hands. The man with the stick fell back against the crowd who supported him and pushed him back. The man's bloody hands slipped from the neck, and he stumbled to the ground. The people pushed one another to the side to stomp on him.

The crowd struck at the others viciously as if the dam of reason had broken and insanity had drowned everyone. When they had finished, all that remained were battered pieces of meat on the ground, with bits of clothing attached to them. The people were shocked by what their frenzy had done. They threw their bamboo sticks into the river. I remember looking at them as they floated down the river, thinking that I could ride on them, a bamboo raft gliding away from the insanity to the safety."

"That was a long time ago, Mother," Sofia said softly.

"Tomorrow is promised to no one. One moment they are drinking to your health and long life and the next moment they are beating you to death with bamboo."

"Romona, what happened to your father?" Anthony asked.

"*Que va?* What happened is what one can expect. Then and now. The Conservatives called in the military to pacify the situation. Most of the people in the square and a few others disappeared. I was too young to know much about such things at the time, but I heard stories. My father fled to Italy. When he returned, he never went out much."

"*Senora Doctora, Senora Doctora*," a sharp voice cried at the door, "please open up. You are needed."

Stay here, the both of you," she said sternly under her breath. "I am going to see what is wrong."

She left the table, coming back quickly.

"There is an emergency. If I am gone for a long period of time, do not wait up for me."

"Mother, I'm going with you," Sofia replied.

"No, you must stay with him. I might need to send somebody back for more equipment or supplies, and I can't have him walking around my house in the middle of the night. His presence jeopardizes everything I have achieved here. I must go now."

Anthony and Sofia watched her carefully as she gathered her belongings, her small medical bag and a small sack of medical supplies. She left through the side door. They heard the large front gate swing open and swing shut. A large number of people had apparently gathered at the front gate of the house because they heard many voices greet the doctor, as she came through the front gate. They stayed at the window shutter until the voices had died down. Sofia walked away from the window, cleared the table and washed dishes in the cold water. Anthony came up beside her.

"What did she mean that I have jeopardized everything she is achieved?" said Anthony quietly.

"My mother is not part of this war. She is not part of anything. She only wants the dying, the suffering and the brutality to stop. People from both sides, or from all the sides, because it's not as simple as us versus them or one-sided versus another, the people from all sides come to her for help. She helps them all, without taking sides. She's Colombian first. My mother's side of the family has roots into the Colombian soil as wide as the banyan tree. Her great-grandfather, my great great-grandfather helped Simon Bolivar liberate "the *Gran Colombia*" from the Spanish. He wept as hard as Bolivar when the grand Colombia split into its various nation-states. My mother sees the same thing happening now, within Colombia. Each region wants to control its own destiny; each warlord wants to control his region; and no one wants to work together."

"I don't understand how I jeopardize things for her."

"You are from the United States. Your government is so closely aligned with our government, supplying the money and guns, that she cannot have you staying at her house without people believing that she works for the government," replied Sofia.

"I don't work for our government, stated Anthony flatly. "I don't work for anybody."

"People talk. My mother hardly lets revolutionary leaders into her house, much less the mayor or any other government official," Sofia said.

"In a war, everybody must take a side," Anthony replied.

"Why? So they can come around to kill your relatives when you're not here. No. My mother works very hard to stay neutral. And she has the respect of the people."

The grandmother came shuffling in and said something quickly to Sofia in a dialect that Anthony did not understand.

"There is somebody at the back door. I must go and see what they want." Sofia slipped out of the door leading from the back kitchen. Anthony heard her go down the back stairs and disappear silently into the night. He wanted to look out the back window, but was afraid he would be seen by the person at the back. She returned quickly and behind her followed Carlos.

Gregory Arthur Solsrud

Chapter Six – Monday Evening

"Carlos," Sofia said, "you frightened me. I didn't know you were coming here."

"The American told me to mark down things I saw," Carlos replied. "I'm here to report to him."

"I am happy to see you," Sofia replied. "You must be hungry."

"Not much," Carlos said. "I brought some bread along with me."

"Bread cannot sustain you for the whole day," Sofia said. "We cooked a fine meal. It will only take a few minutes to warm it up. Sit down."

Carlos sat down at the table in the kitchen. Anthony sat across from him.

"How did the day go?" Anthony asked.

"Good," Carlos replied. "I have your list."

"We can go over it while your food heats up. I glad you came when you did; it is unsafe if I stay here too long. I was ready to leave."

"El Jefe will be breaking camp and moving out," Carlos said.

"Yes, we are not going to return. We have something to do first," Anthony said.

"What is that?" Carlos asked.

"Before we speak about it, show me your list," Anthony said.

Carlos reached into his pocket and pulled out the folded piece of paper. He carefully unfolded it, pressing the corners flat on the hard wood table. Between several thick black lines, small marks had been carefully written.

"In this map section," Carlos said. "I wrote check marks for the places where I saw those large saucers."

Anthony looked at the paper.

"You have three marks," Anthony remarked.

"Yes, I saw three."

"They were mounted on wheels?" Anthony asked.

"Only one," Carlos replied.

"Which one?"

"This one."

"In what direction was the face of the saucer pointed?" Anthony asked.

"Up high, towards *El Pico de los Dientes*."

"That is where the radar unit is," Anthony stated flatly.

"The radar? Carlos repeated. "It is along the road in the valley. El Jefe destroyed it last week."

"Do you remember the helicopters yesterday?"

"Of course. El Jefe and you shot them down."

"They followed me," Anthony continued. "There is a mobile unit operating in the area. It has to be up high."

"On sides of the valley it is very high," Carlos replied.

"I thought of that," Anthony replied, "you couldn't pull a heavy trailer to the top of these mountains. It has to be a place where a road goes."

"There is only one road, and it goes through the middle of the valley," Carlos replied.

"I know of such a place," Sofia interjected. "It's called the head of St. Francis. You have heard of it Carlos?"

"Yes, it is a holy place," Carlos replied.

"It is beautiful, exceptional," Sofia continued. "They say that St. Francis of Assisi came to Colombia and built himself a home there. The seabirds come and flock in great numbers along the ridge, and all the birds of the valley nest in the trees."

Is there a road to San Francis?" Anthony asked.

"There was," Sofia replied. "It was an old monastery; the walls are tumbled down. I have not been there in years. I remember hiking up with my father. The trail was wide and level."

"It sounds like the perfect place. With an old road, they could easily drag and mount a temporary radar installation up there. If it commands a view of this town, it would be perfect."

"You can see the town clearly," Sofia said. "With a good imagination, you can see the ocean."

Anthony looked at the paper again.

"This section is blank," Anthony stated.

"Yes, you wanted me to make a mark for each tank," Carlos said.

"No tanks?" Anthony queried.

"No," Carlos said.

"In this section, you have marks all over," Anthony said.

"Yes, I tried to count the soldiers I saw," Carlos replied. "Every time I saw some, they came in groups and I couldn't count them quickly. Other times, I think I saw soldiers that I had already counted. I'm sorry I didn't count good."

"Carlos, it's fine," Anthony said. "I can use this information."

"Carlos," Sofia said, "wash your hands and face. The food is ready."

"Thank you, Señorita," Carlos replied, "you're very kind."

Carlos stood up and walked out into the hallway.

"You should not have Carlos write such things down. It is dangerous for him. The people of this town know that he cannot read or write. They will find it very strange that he is making notes on a piece of paper. It can mean only one thing."

"Carlos did it secretly," Anthony replied strongly. "He's not stupid."

"I didn't say he was stupid," Sofia responded. "He's not a spy."

Carlos came back and sat down.

"Carlos," Sofia began, "where did you take your notes?"

"I sat in the main square where all the traffic is," Carlos said, reaching for a piece of bread. "I didn't want to miss anything."

Sofia shot a look at Anthony.

"Did you make marks on your paper there or did you remember what you saw and mark it later?" Sofia asked.

"Senorita, of course, I wrote it immediately. My memory is not that good. The information is very important to El Jefe. I wanted it to be right."

"You might have well put a sign on his cap which read, 'Spy for the American soldier,'" Sofia spat. She turned to the stove, filled a plate with food, and set it in front of Carlos.

"I couldn't go into town," Anthony said humbly, "Juan asked us to do it."

"Senorita, don't blame the *Capitan*," Carlos said. "I should have been more careful. Thank you for the food. It smells good." Carlos ate.

"You should have known better," Sofia said, looking at Anthony. "You told me the other night that there are calculated risks and foolish risks. This was a foolish risk."

"When Carlos is finished, we will go out and look around," Anthony said.

"That is even more foolish," Sofia said, "the town is full of people tonight. Everyone is decorating the town for the celebration tomorrow night."

"Who's celebrating?" Anthony asked.

"Tomorrow is *Carnaval!*" Sofia exclaimed. "We have to eat all the fat and sugar we can because we can have none of it during Lent."

"And beer," Carlos said with a full mouth, "don't forget about drinking all the beer."

"Carnival is the best time of year," Sofia said smiling. "I love dressing up and having people guess who I am."

"Carnival," Anthony said. "Back in the states, we call it Mardi Gras. I've never much gotten into it."

"On Carnival night, you can do anything you want," Sofia said mischievously, "and God will forgive you. It's Carnival."

"This will be the first Carnival party I have missed," Carlos said. "Every year I wear the same costume. I had already taken it out and had it cleaned. The mask is cracked from when I tumbled down the stairs. The mask saved my nose."

"You're not coming?" Sofia asked.

"No," Carlos said. "We can't. El Jefe is planning something."

"The whole town walks around in costumes," Anthony asked, "and nobody knows who anybody is?"

"Yes," Sofia said. "Unless you tell them. My mother is very good. She guesses everybody."

"Carlos, we are going to Carnival," Anthony said. "I need to know what the military has here. Tomorrow night is the perfect opportunity. We can walk around town tomorrow night acting like a couple of drunks and observe everything."

"And I can help you," Sofia joined in.

"No, everyone will recognize you," Anthony said. "You cannot walk around with us tomorrow night."

"My mother and I were planning on going," Sofia said. "On Carnival night, you should go with someone you want to be with. It is a night for the unexpected."

"Carnival is a wild night," Carlos said with a satisfied smile. "The girls throw away their catechisms."

"It sounds as if everyone throws away the rules," Anthony replied. "It is a perfect night to collect information without being noticed."

"If a girl wants to go with you to Carnival, you are a fool not to go," Carlos said.

"We have dangerous work to do," Anthony said. "Sofia, it will be safer if you are with someone else."

"Safer for me or for you?" Sofia asked.

Anthony looked at her. The soft light shadowed her figure, visible under her tight, white blouse. He breathed deep, fighting his desire to go to her. He turned his head and stared at Carlos.

"Because the day after tomorrow, we attack, and we must destroy the radar station now," Anthony said. He looked at his pack. "I didn't bring many explosives. We will have to improvise when we find the place."

"We could roll it down the hill," Carlos said trying to help.

"Us, and twenty men," Anthony said. "We must scout it out first. If we cannot destroy it, we must tell Juan. We should leave right away."

"If you are going on foot, it will take you two days," Sofia said. "One day to walk there, and a day to walk back."

"We don't have two days," Anthony said. "Juan will call off the attack if it is not destroyed tonight."

"I can take you," Sofia offered.

"No, I can't risk it," Anthony said.

Anthony looked at Sofia. He was attached to her emotionally, and it clouded his judgment. Having her take them was logical, but it involved Sofia. He did not want to involve her anymore.

"If you want to reach it tonight, you have no choice," Sofia said. "It will only take a couple of hours to drive there and show you where the trail starts."

"There is much traffic tonight and no police checkpoints," Carlos said. "The police are very busy with carnival. You ride in the trunk where no one will see you. I will ride in front with Sofia. If we are stopped, we can say we are going to visit my daughter."

"I could put my mother's medical bag in the backseat, and say that I was delivering medical supplies," Sofia added.

Anthony wavered. It was a risky, but good plan.

"How soon can we leave?"

"I can clean up when I return," Sofia said. "Do you want to take anything to eat or drink, since you will be walking all night?"

"We can eat later," Anthony said.

They went out the back door and walked around the side of the house where there was a small garage. Anthony helped Sofia swing the old doors open. Inside the garage sat a small blue Renault. Sofia opened up the trunk. Anthony took his pistol out of the back pack and pushed the back pack to the back of the trunk. He crawled in. He barely fit. As Sofia went to push the trunk shut, Anthony held the lid.

"If they stop you and are about to search the trunk, blow your horn and talk loudly," Anthony said. "I will be ready."

"I understand," Sofia said.

He saw a look of fear pass across her face.

"Shut the lid," he commanded.

Sofia closed the trunk. Anthony heard the driver's door open and close. The car reversed slowly and bumped firmly against the gutter, which ran along the road. Sofia gunned the engine, and the car jolted into the street. The door slammed as Carlos jumped in.

They were off. Every time the car slowed down, Anthony strained his ears, listening for voices of guards at a checkpoint. The exhaust of the car choked him. He coughed. He thought that once they were out of the town, the relative wind produced by the car would take the exhaust away.

After starting and stopping several times, the car fell into a gentle rhythm as it cruised along the winding road. Anthony felt sleepy. He should not be sleepy. The car must be leaking carbon monoxide into the trunk. He could smell the exhaust; it was not overpowering, but he feared that his senses were being deadened. He could not keep his eyes open. He must open the trunk for air. He banged the trunk with his elbow. He was wedged so tightly that his elbow thumped ineffectually against the metal.

With his left hand, he felt the lock of the trunk. It was small and cheap. He thought of shooting the lock. If someone were following or along the side of the road, a shot would attract attention. He tried to pull the lock off the trunk lid. He could not tighten his grip to pull hard enough. He dropped his gun and ran his fingers over the lock. He poked the trunk latch with his finger where it inserted into the car frame. With a flat piece of metal, he could pry open the latch. He had a knife in his pocket. His head throbbed.

He did not know anything about carbon monoxide poisoning, but he felt sick. Something was not right. He laughed crazily to himself, he had traveled around half the world, been through firefight after firefight and had come out with barely a scratch. Now he would be poisoned while riding in a car driven by a woman whom he wanted to love and an old man whom he trusted with his life. Fate had a weird sense of humor.

Anthony shook his head to clear these thoughts. He was not going to die, not today. With his thumb and forefinger, he worked the knife out of his pocket, the tight squeeze forcing him to ease it out slowly. The knife dropped onto the trunk floor. He patted the floor and found the knife, picking it up with his hand. He unfolded the blade out of its casing.

He pushed the knife blade into the lock, but the car rocked, sliding the blade out of the lock. The ride had not seemed bumpy before, but now, every time Anthony inserted the blade in, a bump knocked it out.

He cupped the lock with his left hand and held the blade with the fingers of his right hand. Every jolt stabbed the blade into his fingers. After a particularly hard shake, the blade cut his finger, moistening the blade and lock with his blood. The blade was slippery. His head pounded. Anthony tried again. The car sensed his desperation and settled into a smooth glide. He pushed the blade into the narrow crack between the lock and the frame, touching the latch. He grasped the handle of the knife and levered the blade against the latch. The latched clicked free, popping the truck open. Air rushed in.

The wind blew on his face as he inhaled deeply. The fresh air revived him. His head throbbed with less intensity. With the wind passing over the trunk and the car banging off holes in the road, the lid bounced up and down. Anthony put his hand between the latch and the frame so the lid would not shut. With every bump, the latch smashed down on the back of his hand. It hurt.

Anthony pulled his sleeve over the back of his hand. The motion of the car gently rocked Anthony, which made his eyes close. He blinked hard and forced himself awake. He did not want to relax and have the trunk shut, sealing him in his final tomb. He thought of the common grave in the *Cementario* Central in Bogotá. He could be one of those bodies, slowly decomposing, unknown for an eternity. Who would miss him if he disappeared into one of those graves? That woman, Sofia's mother, could tell a story. She placed him in the middle of the square. He felt pinched in and claustrophobic from the maddening crowd. He could see those bloody hands slipping from the neck, the man staring up at the contorted faces as he fell. She should write that story down. She had a gift. If he escaped from this insanity, he would write the story down for her and send it to her. It would not be as good, but it would be something.

The car slowed. As the car stopped, he listened for sounds of a checkpoint. It was completely dark. He opened the lid turning on the trunk light as Sofia came from around the driver's side and looked at him.

"We forgot to shut the trunk," Sofia said. "You should have let us know. I hope the wind didn't bother you."

Anthony crawled out of the trunk. He picked up the pistol off the floor of the trunk and stuck it in his waistband. He threw the back pack over his shoulder.

"I opened the trunk. You have an exhaust leak, and I couldn't breathe," Anthony said.

"I'm sorry," Sofia said. "I didn't know."

"It's not your fault. You don't normally carry passengers in your trunk. Where is the trail?" Anthony asked.

The trail starts over there, at least I think it does," Sofia answered.

"Carlos can find it," Anthony said.

Carlos had left the road and was poking around the low-lying brush, looking for the trail. Anthony walked Sofia to her door. He pulled her close to him and kissed her. She stayed close to him.

"You had better leave, before someone drives by, or I don't let you leave."

"When will I see you again?" Sofia asked.

"Soon," Anthony said.

"Can I see you tomorrow?" Sofia said.

"I don't think it would be a good idea," Anthony said. "I don't want you hurt."

Sofia's face tightened.

"If you love me, return to me," Sofia said. "I will be waiting."

They kissed once more. She got in the car. Anthony shut the door. He watched Sofia turn around in the small road and drive back towards the town. Anthony walked over to Carlos.

"She will return safely," Carlos said. "There was no one on the road when we came down."

Carlos walked in ever-widening circles. He waved at Anthony. Carlos pointed to the ground. Anthony knelt down and ran his fingers along the ground. Huge tires had chewed up the vegetation and carved large ruts in the ground. The tire tracks led back out to the road in one direction and up through the brush in the other.

"Something very heavy was pulled up here," Anthony said. "We have solved our first challenge of finding the old trail up to St. Francis."

"Even a blind man could follow this trail at night," Carlos said smiling.

"Lead carefully old man. I don't think they would set up any mines or traps because they would have to return to check on the thing." Anthony said.

Carlos walked quickly. The old road was firm, wide and level, looping back and forth to gradually ascend the mountain. They stopped every so often and closely examined the tracks. The tracks were newly made. They could still see the sharp ridges of the tires embedded in the dirt. Anthony leaned close to Carlos.

"These mobile radar units are fully self-contained and can be operated remotely," Anthony whispered. "They probably have it guarded. If I were guarding it, I would watch the road. Can we cut through the brush, circle around and approach from above?"

Carlos stopped and looked straight up the hill. The moon shimmered off the thick, shiny leaves, illuminating the side of the mountain.

"The old monastery must have been on that promontory up there," Carlos said, pointing to the dark crag above them. "We passed a small trail which ran towards that peak. We could climb that and see where it leads."

"We should try. Walking up this trail straight to the radar truck is too easy," Anthony said.

Carlos descended until he found the small trail. It tracked across the mountain and under the crag and finally went straight up. It was hard going. Loose rocks made them stumble. Invisible branches sprang from nowhere and hit Anthony in the face. He kept his arm high across his face as a shield. The vines and ground bushes tripped them. Carlos did not take out his machete, fearing the loud whack would carry far on the quiet night air. They did not want to lose the only advantage they had, the element of surprise. As they climbed higher, Anthony thought he heard voices carried by the wind. They picked their way along the trail for what seemed hours to Anthony. They had lost sight of the dark peak, hidden from view by the tall trees.

Anthony thought Carlos was lost when Carlos stopped and turned to him. Anthony opened his mouth to speak. Carlos put his fingers to his lips and crept slowly forward. Anthony followed. They poked their head out through some bushes and looked over a small clearing. Anthony saw a dim outline of large box about one hundred feet in front of him. They had found the radar pod.

Anthony perked his ears listening for the slightest sound. He heard a cough. He saw the faintest light. It moved. He stared at it. It was the end of cigarette butt. Someone was sitting in front of the radar pod smoking a cigarette. He heard no talking. He looked for a second cigarette butt. Anthony tapped Carlos on the shoulder and held up one finger. Carlos nodded. Anthony pointed back. They noiselessly worked their way back from the clearing.

Anthony opened his back pack. He pulled out the parts of his rifle and snapped them together. He gave Carlos the back pack to put on. The first dull gray light appeared in the sky.

Anthony pushed the magazine soundlessly into the rifle's breech. He pulled the bolt back and slid a bullet into the chamber. The soft click of the bolt closing echoed into the jungle. He looked at Carlos who shook his head that the noise had not traveled far. Anthony crawled forward to the clearing and braced the barrel of the rifle on a low-lying branch. He looked down through the sights and placed the bead on the reclining figure.

The figure looked small and alone. Anthony looked up. He could wait. It was not full light. The target would be easier to hit with full light, and with full light he would need only one shot, and one shot was important in case others were close. Anthony glanced over his shoulder; Carlos had crept behind him. Carlos stared at the ground. His hands were folded. Anthony was not sure if he was asleep or preparing his soul for the shot.

The sky was brightening quickly. Anthony could see the figure; its head slumped heavily against its chest. The arms flung loosely along its side. Anthony pushed the butt firmly against his shoulder. He nuzzled the stock with his chin, closing his left eye and focusing his right eye down the barrel and aligning the small ball on the target.

"Breathe in deep. Exhale halfway," he whispered to himself.

He focused again on the resting figure, tranquil and peaceful in the morning's half-light. The birds sang to one another. He listened to the melodic whistling, which seemed to converge on him as if they were talking about him to one another.

"Look at the man prepared to do an unnatural deed. He shoots the sleeping man not for food or self-protection. A brutal act done on such a beautiful morning."

Anthony tried to push these thoughts from his mind, concentrating on his duty. He lifted his chin off the rifle. He could delay; he needed more light to see clearly. He gazed at the harmless figure. He could do this, he thought, he had to do this. He hated himself for having these doubts. He was not weak. He could not be weak. Nature was not kind to the weak.

The figure probably has children. I don't know if he has children, but if he doesn't have children, he has a girlfriend or wife who loves him, Anthony thought. Maybe he was the one who put the bomb on the bus, which killed Sofia's father. It is right that he should die. But if he wasn't the one, he doesn't deserve it anymore than her father. I must find out if he is the one.

Anthony sat up and cradled the gun. He tapped Carlos on the arm and directed him back. Noiselessly, they eased away from the clearing.

"Carlos, can you bring us closer? This shot is too far."

Carlos looked curiously at him.

"Señor, I will take you up to him so you can tap him on the shoulder. Is that close enough?" Carlos asked.

"Yes, it is," Anthony replied.

"Follow me," Carlos said.

Carlos stealthily snuck through the brush emerging into the clearing directly behind the radar pod. With hand signals, he directed Anthony to circle around one side of the box while he walked around the other. Anthony checked his rifle, clicking the safety to off.

As he stepped quietly around the radar pod, he laid his finger on the trigger. He raised his rifle to shoot and stepped around the last corner of the radar pod. The figure lay prone in front of him unaware of the peril pointing at him. Anthony looked up as Carlos carefully tip-toed out from the other side and waited beside him.

Anthony stared at the small body. The uniform hung loosely around his skinny appendages, and the dark, clear complexion evinced quiescence; it knew no evil.

"It's a boy," Carlos said.

A rifle lay alongside the boy. Anthony picked it up and gave it to Carlos.

"I am going to wake him up. Tell him to stay quiet, and we won't shoot him," Anthony said. "Point the rifle at him so he knows you're serious."

Anthony tapped the boy with his foot. The figure rustled and stretched. He opened his eyes. His eyes instantly drew in the two figures standing over him with pointed guns. The eyes widened with fear.

"Talk to him," Anthony said.

"We aren't going to hurt you," Carlos said.

The boy looked at Carlos then back at Anthony. He stayed silent and still.

"How old are you?" asked Anthony.

The boy said nothing.

"The man asked how old you are," Carlos repeated.

"Old enough," the boy relied.

Anthony smiled at his defiant attitude. He looked at Carlos. As he took his eyes off the boy, the boy leapt straight at Anthony.

Anthony sensed the motion and slammed the body of the rifle down on the springing boy. Metal clanged against the breech of the gun, and a knife fell out of the boy's hand onto the ground. Before the boy could react, Anthony swung the stock against the boy's head, sending him insensible to the ground.

"Jesus," Anthony swore. He knelt down and picked up the knife, handmade from a kitchen utensil.

"That little fellow could have stuck me with this one," Anthony said. He threw the knife far into the jungle. Carlos went towards the unconscious figure.

"Be careful, Carlos," Anthony said, "He might be faking."

Carlos shook the body with his hands. He checked the boy's pockets and found only a few coins and an extra bullet clip. He pulled a rope out of his pocket and tied his hands.

"Tie his feet," Anthony said.

As Carlos tied his feet, Anthony walked around the large metal radar pod.

"How are we going to destroy this thing?" Carlos asked when Anthony returned.

"I don't know. All I have with me are a couple of hand grenades. We will hardly dent the metal casing with those," Anthony said. "Take off the back pack and pull them out."

As Carlos took off the backpack, Anthony inspected the radar pod. Carlos laid the three explosive grenades on the ground. They blended in peacefully with the dark jungle foliage.

"We can disable it without blowing it up. See up there, it has a series of receiving antennae, which act as its eyes and ears," Anthony said. "They can repair those quicker than if we blew the whole thing up. But, if they don't see an explosion, they won't think anything is wrong."

"Should I put the grenades back?" Carlos asked.

"Yes," Anthony replied. "When you finish that, tie the boy to a tree. When he wakes up, he can't warn anyone. They'll find him when they come to check."

Anthony hoisted himself up on top of the unit. With his knife he was able to loosen the antennae to expose the wiring. He cut the wires. He wrenched off the small antennae and flung them into the thick brush. He hung off from the side of the unit and let himself drop to the ground.

"With no eyes, it can't see," he said to Carlos. "How's the boy?"

"He's breathing steady," Carlos said. "A bump on the head but no more.

You did the right thing Señor. It is a terrible thing to take a life from a boy. That is all he has."

Anthony picked up the boy's rifle and gave it to Carlos.

In the light of the morning, it was going to be easier to descend. Anthony felt pleased with himself. He had never seen so many birds in so many varieties. They sang in full voice as if trying to outshine one another.

Anthony unhooked his canteen and drank. In his pocket, he pulled out a small bag that Sofia had given him. Inside were three *roscones*, buttered rolls filled with guava marmalade and covered with sugar.

"Sit down and eat," Anthony said. "We haven't had breakfast yet."

"I am glad that she did not listen to you and packed us a small something to eat," Carlos said, sitting down and pulling a bag from his own pocket.

"It is pleasant to sit here," Anthony said. "I have never heard so many birds sing."

"We are on the edge of a national park. The park stretches across the mountain range until almost the ocean, though I have never been that far," Carlos said.

Anthony ate, wiping his mouth on his sleeve.

"How many roscones did Sofia pack for you?" Carlos asked with a full mouth.

"Three," Anthony replied.

"She packed me five. Now we know who is the special one," Carlos said with a wink.

"No," Anthony responded. "Now we know who the fat one is."

Carlos laughed.

Chapter Seven – Tuesday Morning

Carlos and Anthony finished eating the *roscones*.

"Carlos, how do we return quickly?" Anthony asked.

"We are walking," Carlos said. "Unless you can fly."

"Not without an airplane," replied Anthony. "I didn't think about the return. It will be dangerous to walk along the road during the day."

"I know, but there is no other road up the valley," Carlos said.

"Is there a trail or can we walk along the ridge?" Anthony asked.

"On the other side a valley, there is a nice trail which runs back to our camp," Carlos replied. "Do you see that flat part down there?" Carlos said as he pointed.

"Yes."

"That is where Tito will set his ambush."

"It's well protected and high. With the radar disabled, the attack can go forward. We must reach *El Jefe* this afternoon."

"It will take us until tomorrow to walk back."

"Isn't there another trail?"

"Many years ago, there was a railway that ran up the valley.

"They had a train here?" Anthony asked.

"Not a train for passengers. They used to mine silver in this valley, that's how the town was founded. They built a railroad to load the silver out," Carlos explained. "You've been landing the plane on the part of the rail bed which led to the mine."

"That explains why that dirt road is so straight and hard. I always thought some fat-assed donkeys had trod over that path. It's a good spot to land, and you can't see it from the air unless you are really looking for it, and even then it looks like an soft, bumpy dirt trail."

"You scare me every time you come down. The bushes grow quickly, even though we cut them," Carlos said. "The wings barely pass over them."

"My dad taught me to fly; he was a crop duster up in Montana. In crop dusting, coming down those rows of crops day after day, you can't be a foot off or the coverage isn't right, and you have to pass under power lines, around radio towers and between grain silos. It's like parking a car in a garage at one hundred twenty miles per hour."

"You are crazy. I'd rather walk down the old railway."

"Do you think you can find it?" Anthony asked.

"Yes, but it's probably overgrown and very slow to walk."

"We must return quickly," Anthony said.

"It will take us all day. *El Jefe* will have broken camp and moved."

"We need a vehicle," Anthony said.

"A vehicle?" Carlos said. "From where?"

"That's a good question," Anthony replied. "We need a ride from someone."

"Whoever picks us up will be very suspicious of you."

"Not of you, you can go back alone and tell the others what we have done," Anthony said. "I will walk to town and meet you at Sofia's."

"We cannot split up Señor," Carlos responded. "You can't walk back alone. It is too dangerous."

"El Jefe needs to know we destroyed the radar, or else he won't do anything," Anthony replied.

"I'm not leaving you unguided," Carlos said.

"I guess we are walking," Anthony said. He slipped on the backpack and shouldered the rifle.

"Let's go back down this old road. It's safe enough," Anthony said.

"We could ask the boy," Carlos suggested.

"Is he awake?" Anthony asked.

"I don't know," said Carlos. "I can check."

"No, we need to go," replied Anthony. "We have a long walk back."

Anthony gazed out before heading down. It was a beautiful view. The valley ran peacefully up to his right, with the river flowing full here at the mouth. Straight ahead in the distance, the flat fertile plains spread out. He thought he could almost see the ocean. The monks picked a perfect place for meditation and prayer. Tranquility lived here. Anthony saw the tumbledown ruins. He walked over to them.

When the military had cleared the area for the radar station, they cut the vegetation around the ruins. Anthony could distinguish several distinct foundations of the old monastery. It looked like three or four large buildings and a few smaller ones. As he walked on top of the crumbling walls, he saw a deep depression running along one of the smaller buildings. He picked his way among the larger stones to look down into the small hole to see if he could find something. He had loved trampling the woods and streams in Montana looking for Native American artifacts. He knelt down. The weeds and grass had grown thick, obscuring the ground. He would need a shovel. He did not have time; someday he would return.

He stood up and looked up the valley at the narrow blacktop road stretching far up to Santa Angelia. Way below him, he saw a speeding jeep, weaving across both lanes as it sped down the valley. It approached the spot where Sofia had dropped them all off. The jeep slowed, turned and drove up the old mountain road towards them.

"Carlos," Anthony shouted, "Come quick, someone is coming!"

Carlos ran over and looked to where Anthony was pointing. He saw the jeep coming up the old trail.

"We need leave now, Señor," Carlos said alarmed.

"We can't let them find the disabled radar station so soon," Anthony replied. "They will have time to repair it before the attack tomorrow. I only cut the wires."

"What do we do?" asked Carlos.

"How fast can they drive up here?" asked Anthony.

"Ten, maybe fifteen minutes," replied Carlos.

"There are two men in the jeep, a driver and a passenger," Anthony stated.

"Yes," said Carlos.

"Follow me. I have a solution," said Anthony.

Anthony ran over to the trail and started down. He ran about two hundred feet and stopped.

"Do you see that downed tree?" asked Anthony. "We need to pull it out and block the road."

"A roadblock," repeated Carlos. "That's a good idea. This tree will not work, because its roots are still in the ground, and we don't have a hatchet."

"Look for another tree," Anthony ordered.

"I can make a roadblock out of long branches," said Carlos. "Will that work?"

"Yes, all we need is for them to slow down so I can shoot them both," Anthony said.

Carlos grimaced. He pulled his machete from his waistband and chopped branches. As the branches dropped on the ground, Anthony piled them haphazardly across the trail. After several minutes, they made a large pile, which blocked the trail. Anthony looked at the rifle that they had taken from the boy. He loaded a bullet in the chamber and clicked off the safety.

"Hide yourself in the bushes over there," Anthony commanded. "The rifle is ready to fire. Just squeeze the trigger. Don't shoot until I shoot."

"I understand," Carlos said. He tramped into the bushes and hid himself. Anthony could not see him.

Anthony scampered into the bushes and hunched down. As he settled into position, the jeep came barreling up the trail. The driver slammed on his brakes to keep from hitting the brush pile.

Anthony heard the driver order the other soldier out to clear the brush off the trail. The soldier, no older than the first boy, jumped out and listlessly pulled at the branches on the top of the pile. He worked at it for some time, making little progress. The driver got down from the jeep.

As soon as the driver had grabbed the first branch, Anthony stepped into the open. He raised his weapon to his shoulder.

"'Hands up! Hands up! On the ground! We will shoot you," Carlos screamed at the soldiers while coming out of the brush with his weapon at fire ready.

The two soldiers looked at Carlos and Anthony and dropped face down to the ground immediately.

"Hold your gun on them," Carlos commanded authoritatively. "Don't move or he will shoot you both."

Carlos set his rifle inside the jeep. He pulled a rope from his pocket. He told the first one to put his hands behind his back. He tied his hands and feet together with the same rope. He quickly tied the other one in the same fashion. He turned to Anthony.

"That will hold them," Carlos said proudly. "What do we do with them?"

"Load them into the back of the jeep. We will put them next to the radar pod for someone to find them," Anthony replied.

They loaded up the two prisoners in the back of the jeep. They quickly cleared the brush from the road and drove up to the radar pod, where they dropped the two off.

"Get in, Carlos," Anthony said. "We have our ride back to town."

"Someone will see us," Carlos said as he hopped in.

"Good point," Anthony said.

He shut off the jeep, got back out and walked over to the two prisoners. He cut the rope off the first one. While he held his pistol on him, he told him to take off his clothes. The boy stripped.

"Tie him up and put on his clothes," Anthony said.

Carlos quickly tied the boy, while Anthony had the other one undress. Carlos tied up the second one.

"Good thing one size fits all," Anthony said as he slipped on the uniform shirt and pants over his clothes. "This one has sergeant stripes."

They jumped in the jeep and started down the trail. At several spots, Anthony did not think that the jeep would fit through the brush, but he knew that the jeep had come up this same trail.

"We should have taken the driver and had him drive us back down," Anthony said. "He was a good driver to have come up so fast."

"He was a crazy driver," said Carlos. "He's lucky he made it. Did you see where he nearly slid off the trail where it ran by the cliff?"

As the trail cut back and forth, Anthony swore that his tires hung in mid-air around a couple of the sharp curves. As they approached the main road, Anthony stopped.

"I want you to drive," Anthony said. "If you pass a military vehicle or come to a checkpoint, immediately drive off the road and run into the brush. I'll provide as much covering fire as I can. Do you understand?"

Carlos nodded and switched places with Anthony. He pushed the clutch in, raced the engine and took off. As they entered the main road, Anthony placed his gun at ready. He constantly scanned back to front for any signs of trouble. They met several vehicles, but with military presence so heavy in the area, no one gave them a second look. When the first car came up behind them, Anthony forced himself to look natural by turning to Carlos and talking. He observed the car. The driver, intent on passing them, never looked up at them. After several cars had overtaken them, Anthony told Carlos to speed up. Carlos drove a little faster for a couple of kilometers, but then settled into his old pace.

"I don't think we should drive into the town," Anthony said.

"I agree with you," Carlos said. "We were very lucky for this jeep. I'm afraid for when our luck runs out. I'm very nervous and want to get off the road. We are not far from town. We can cross the mountain on a different path to reach our camp."

"I don't want to tempt fate either," Anthony replied.

"I'll turn off the road," Carlos said. "We can walk from there."

Carlos drove the jeep onto the next dirt road. The road curved sharply twice. At the end of the second turn, Carlos slammed on the breaks, throwing Anthony into the dashboard and nearly ramming the rear of a military transport truck. Surprised soldiers inside the truck looked down at them.

"Back up quickly," Anthony uttered.

Carlos fumbled with the gears. Each time as he tried to put the jeep in reverse, he engaged a forward gear and bumped the truck. He ground the gears repeatedly looking for reverse. Inside the truck, the soldiers started laughing. Several of them shouted insults at Carlos.

"Push the clutch in," Anthony instructed, as he shoved Carlos's hand off the gear stick. Anthony shoved the gear stick over towards reverse and tried to slide it in. The jeep had been poorly maintained, and the clutch was misaligned. The gears ground loudly.

"Give me a little clutch," Anthony whispered. Anthony felt the mechanical grinding of the clutch against the gears and popped the jeep into reverse. It started backwards, but the engine died. Carlos had not given it enough gas.

The troops howled and called words out even louder. Anthony did not understand the slang. Carlos' face was blood red.

"Push in the clutch," Anthony yelled. It came out louder than he had intended.

As Carlos pushed in the clutch, Anthony reached over and turned the key. The jeep fired right up. Someone from the truck heard Anthony's accent and called out something about an American. Every soldier in the truck went silent.

Without being told, Carlos gunned the engine, reversed the jeep and backed the jeep down the road. Two soldiers had jumped out of the truck and were raising their rifles to fire. Carlos accelerated from the truck's view, wheeling backwards through the two sharp turns. Anthony heard the sound of intermittent gunfire. Carlos reversed all the way out to the asphalt and shot forward onto the road. Spinning the steering wheel, he lurched the jeep forward.

At the next turnout, Carlos flew the jeep down the dirt path some distance until it ended. He slammed on the brakes, bringing the jeep to an immediate halt. Carlos and Anthony sprang from the jeep and ran into the jungle. They ran steadily until Carlos stopped, kneeled over and gasped for breath. They caught their wind, while listening carefully for any pursuit. Carlos nodded to Anthony and tramped through the brush with Anthony right behind. They walked for over an hour before they stopped.

"They can't track us this far," Carlos said, taking a drink of water from his canteen. "We can rest."

"Carlos, you need to take some driving lessons," Anthony said. "You should have seen your face."

Carlos laughed, relieving the tension.

"I couldn't find reverse. I was so nervous. I thought our luck had run out and they were going to shoot us. They started laughing at my driving. I got mad and couldn't think."

"Our luck didn't run out, Carlos," Anthony replied. "I can still see their faces, especially at the end."

"We're very close to camp," Carlos said.

"I don't recognize anything here," Anthony said.

"We came a different way. And I walked very quickly."

"Walked? We were running up the hill. Wait till I tell Juan the story," Anthony said. "He will die laughing."

"Very funny," Carlos said. "You can tell him what you want. I'm happy that I was not shot."

Carlos rose and cut a new trail through the jungle. Anthony thought about her again. He wanted to see her. Carlos had gone some distance ahead. Anthony stood up and caught up quickly with Carlos, who made slow but steady progress. The vegetation grew thicker and the mountain steepened. They came onto a wide trail, which Anthony could see had been well used. They walked along this trail until Carlos motioned Anthony to stop. They stopped and listened. Carlos whistled. A repeating whistle echoed in the distance.

A group of soldiers came forward who Carlos greeted with enthusiasm.

Carlos introduced them as his cousins.

"Santo, have you seen El Jefe?" Carlos asked his cousin.

"He was on the observation point. We have been sighting in targets for the artillery," Santo replied.

"I need to speak with Tito," Anthony said.

"Tito has left. We are waiting to leave with Miguel," Santo said. "He is coming now."

They looked up the trail as Miguel strode forward.

"*Antonio*," Miguel said. "You are back already. You must have wings on your feet."

"The radar. It's destroyed," Anthony said.

"*Sí?*" Miguel queried.

Anthony nodded.

"The attack can go forward." Miguel shook his head and struck his palm with his fist. "Tito was right," Miguel said. "It is our time."

Miguel looked at Santo.

"Santo, send someone to tell Tito that the radar has been destroyed."

Santo nodded.

"And El Jefe?" Miguel continued.

"I have not spoken with him," Anthony replied.

"Will he attack?"

"I believe he will," Anthony said.

"If he doesn't, I must," Miguel said, seizing his arm. "I will tell him so."

"No," replied Anthony. "It is mine to do."

"Wait here," Carlos said. "I will bring El Jefe to you."

Anthony watched Carlos and Miguel disappear down the trail.

Are you hungry, American?" Santo asked.

"Yes, we have not eaten since this morning," Anthony replied.

Santo led him to a small clearing where a fire had been started.

When Sofia left Anthony and Carlos, she returned to her house without being followed. She slept fitfully. She awoke early, desiring to go after him and bring him to her, back to safety. She was preparing to leave when she heard the front bell ring. She called out to her mother. She did not respond so she went to the front window, moved the heavy curtain and looked out. The colonel was standing at the front door. She ran down into the vestibule, pulled the bolt back, and opened the heavy door.

"Colonel, how very unexpected, but pleasant to see you today," Sofia said.

"The pleasure is mine," the colonel replied with a slight bow. "I have wanted to visit you for some time, but I have been very busy."

"Please come in," Sofia said, as she stood back to allow him to pass through the door.

"Thank you," the colonel said. He called back to his driver and told him to wait.

Sofia led the colonel into the house and sat him in the living room, which looked out to the street.

"Would you like a coffee or something to drink?" Sofia asked politely.

"A glass of water, if it is no trouble," the colonel said.

"Of course, it is no trouble," Sofia replied. "Would you like anything in the water?"

"It is too early in the day," the colonel said smiling.

She went into the kitchen and brought him back in glass of water on a small metal tray covered with a napkin. She set it in front of him and sat across from him. The colonel drank.

"What has been keeping you so busy?" Sofia asked.

"We fear that the rebels may attack the town. We lost three helicopters a couple days ago close to the village. They were tracking a plane operated by the guerillas," the colonel said.

"I didn't realize it was dangerous here. I thought the war was taking place elsewhere," Sofia said, trying to sense what the colonel wanted.

"When I saw your mother yesterday, she said you like to walk in the mountains," the colonel began.

"Yes, I like to go and collect the wild coffee beans and fruit that grow on the hillsides," Sofia replied cautiously.

"I must warn you. It is not safe to walk alone up there," the colonel said. "Haven't you noticed anything unusual while you've been out?"

Sofia thought before answering the question, unsure whether this was a polite inquiry or someone had talked to him. There were many spies in the town.

"Unusual?" she looked at him innocently.

"Please forget I asked the question," the colonel responded sincerely. "It is difficult for me to separate from my work. I did wish to warn you about the danger though."

Sofia relaxed with his answer. He did not know of her activities.

"Have you been enjoying your posting here in Santa Angelia?" she asked.

"It's much quieter than where I was before," the colonel said.

"Where were you before?" Sofia asked.

"I was stationed at one of our bases in the valley of Calica," the colonel said with a grimace. "The air is fresher here."

The colonel looked uncomfortable. He drank again. Sofia looked at him without trying to make conversation. She was very curious now about why he had come.

"My mother is in her office," Sofia said graciously. "Let me go and tell her you are here."

"I came to speak with you about the carnival party tonight." the colonel said abruptly.

"The carnival party," Sofia laughed. She remembered no specific plans for carnival. "My mother and I usually go."

"Yes, that is why I came to talk to you," the colonel said. "I came to find out what time I should pick you up this evening?"

"This evening?" Sofia looked surprised.

"Yes, don't you remember? A couple weeks ago I asked you to go to the carnival ball with me."

"The carnival ball, yes, how silly of me. Now I remember," Sofia said. "I had been so busy lately that I had forgotten the date."

"I have thought about nothing else," the colonel said with feeling.

Sofia did not know how to respond. She had no feelings for the colonel, but she did not want to tell him no. He was a very powerful man in town. She should have foreseen his question. She will pay more attention in the future. When she did not answer immediately, the colonel believed it was his invitation to continue.

"The party will be great fun," the colonel said with more emotion. "The townspeople have put much energy into decorating the town. I have volunteered the use of my men. Music will play all night long."

"Is the town safe?" Sofia asked, hoping to change the subject.

"Oh yes, quite safe," the colonel responded. "In response to this threat, we have brought in a large number of troops. I keep them confined to their barracks, so that the true number of troops will not been known; in case, the rebels do attack. Well, what time should I pick you up tonight?"

"I don't know," said the Sofia.

"You do want to go?" the colonel asked. "You told me that you had a costume already made for the night."

"Yes I do," Sofia said.

Sofia's mind raced. Two weeks had changed everything. She had to go and tell Anthony immediately about all those troops. Yet, she could not simply leave. She had agreed to go with the colonel.

"Yes, I want to go. It does sound like fun," Sofia said, thinking of a response. "Unfortunately, I cannot accept because my mother does not like me to go out unchaperoned."

"Yes, of course," the colonel said smiling. "I expected nothing less. Your mother can accompany us. I've arranged a dance companion for her. Do you remember the sergeant who broke his arm?"

"Yes, he was very funny."

"I spoke with him and he, likewise, would be extremely honored to accompany your mother to the carnival party."

"My mother doesn't like surprises," Sofia said.

"She has already agreed," the colonel said. "I spoke with your mother about it yesterday."

"My mother did not say anything to me," Sofia replied.

"I told her that I wanted to speak to you personally to make sure that you didn't feel obligated to go because of some perceived need to be cordial with the Army colonel," the colonel said in a rush.

"Since you two have already talked, let me go and find out what time she wants to leave. Excuse me while I go and ask her," Sofia said.

"Ask me what?" Romona said, as she entered the room. The colonel stood and embraced Romona kissing her on one cheek.

"It is very nice to see you again," Romona said. "It has been what, two weeks since you last came over and had dinner with us?"

"It has been two weeks," the colonel said. "I was just apologizing to Sofia."

"The colonel was telling me that we are about to be attacked."

"I did not say that, Sofia," the colonel responded rapidly. "What I said was that headquarters has been monitoring an unusual amount of activity in this sector. They told me to keep an eye out for a potential attack."

"Quite exciting," Romona said.

"Maybe," the colonel said, "it is nothing for you to worry about. I came by to find out what time we may come and pick you up this evening."

"The carnival ball," Romona said with a sly smile. "I thought you had forgotten."

"No, I had not forgotten. As I was saying to Sofia, I have been looking forward to it. I have been so busy making sure that you're safe that I have not had time to come by."

"We should be ready at six," Romona said. "So you can be here at eight and then you'll only have to wait an hour."

"I will wait for as long as it takes Sofia to dress. Especially as beautiful as she looked last year in her costume," the colonel said smiling.

"You weren't here last year," Sofia said.

"Your mother showed me pictures," colonel replied. "You are a beautiful woman."

A loud knock echoed off the front door, relieving Sofia from responding. Sofia rose, walked through the vestibule and over to the front door to open it. A young lieutenant stood in the doorway.

"Sorry to disturb you, Señorita, but the colonel's driver said that he is inside."

"He is. Would you like to speak with him?"

"Yes," replied the lieutenant. "I do not wish to disturb you, but is very important."

Sofia let him pass and closed the door behind him. She led him into the formal living room and sat down on the couch across from the colonel.

The young lieutenant stiffly saluted the colonel and removed his hat.

"I'm sorry to disturb you colonel, but I have something important to tell you."

"Go ahead," the colonel said.

"Do you wish me to say it in front of the civilians?" the lieutenant asked.

"Was someone shot?" the colonel asked.

"No, it involves the sighting of the El Jefe and the American," the lieutenant said quickly.

"When?" the colonel asked, springing to his feet.

"He was spotted in a jeep with the American," the lieutenant responded. Sofia hung on every word.

"Go on," the colonel said.

"We were preparing our defensive positions, along the northern side of the road when a jeep came up on us."

"What do you mean came up on you?" asked the colonel.

"We had finished and the troops were loaded back in the truck. The truck was parked in the dirt road. The jeep came along the dirt road and couldn't pass because the truck blocked the road. The jeep reversed and escaped."

"Escaped?" asked the colonel, his temper rising. "Why didn't you pursue it?"

"It went back to the main road. They drove further, jumped out on some dirt road and fled into the jungle," the lieutenant explained. "We found the jeep abandoned."

"How do you know it was the American?" asked the colonel harshly, "and not a soldier going A.W.O.L.?"

"The men heard the passenger talking with an American accent," the colonel replied.

"If they heard him talking, why didn't they stop him or shoot him?" the colonel asked.

Sofia cringed with the word "shoot." The young lieutenant stayed silent.

"Why didn't you shoot him?" the colonel asked again.

"I didn't see him," said the lieutenant. "I was loading the troops into the other trucks. The soldiers, who saw them, swear that it was the American for whom who you told us to look."

"Damn," said the colonel slapping his fist in his other palm. "We had him in our grasp, and we missed him. It would have ended everything right there. That was brazen to steal a military vehicle and drive around in broad daylight. He will pay for it."

"Are we going to cancel the celebrations tonight?" the lieutenant asked. "They might be planning something."

"I know this El Jefe, *el revolutionario*. He would not attack a town where there would be overwhelming civilian casualties. It would ruin his reputation as the defender of the people. Post extra guards around the town, but nothing will be cancelled."

"Yes sir," the lieutenant saluted. As he turned to leave, the colonel spoke again.

"How do you know the jeep was stolen?" the colonel asked.

"I assumed. The jeep had our markings," lieutenant said. "They probably stole it from the street."

"Stole it from the street? I don't think so. What idiot leaves an unguarded jeep in the street? Find out where the jeep came from, and it might give us some clue as to what they are planning," the colonel said.

The lieutenant saluted again and left.

"I'm sorry for the disturbance," he said, sitting down again but holding his body erect. "We have been looking for El Jefe."

"I've heard people speak of him," Romona said. "He sounds like a mythological figure - part God, part hero, and part devil."

"He is the devil," the colonel said. "Make no mistake about that. He is the one that keeps this civil war going. We have the rest of the devils bought out."

"I'm surprised to find out that he is here" Sofia said. "Maybe your soldiers saw someone else?"

"The many people that feed the military its information said that he was working in this area. We have never been able to confirm it. He is here. I feel it. What he does not know is that this time, I will be ready for him."

"Ready for him? How?" Sofia asked.

"Napoleon once said that you cannot fight the same enemy or else he will learn your tricks," the colonel said. "I have faced him, and to my dishonor, he won. However, I have studied his tactics and have instructed myself on his tricks."

"Please Colonel," Romona said, "remember what I told you when I first met you. You are welcome in my house anytime as long you leave your colonel bars at the door."

"Yes, I remember well. I apologize deeply for this intrusion," the colonel said, rising and bowing low. "I promise on my honor, not as a colonel, but as a Colombian, it will never happen again."

"Eight o'clock then," Romona said.

"Eight o'clock," the colonel repeated. "Please do not mind if I arrive early, I will wait outside and will not ring the bell until eight o'clock."

"I am looking forward to attending the carnival party," Sofia said, smiling graciously.

"Excellent," the colonel replied. "You have made me very happy."

The colonel rose, thrusting out his hand. Sofia extended hers. They shook hands.

"Until tonight," the colonel said.

Sofia showed him out of the house and watched him drive off. She leaned against the rail.

Romona walked to her and led her back to inside. When she had shut the door, Sofia turned and looked at her.

"Do you think it is true?" Sofia asked. "That they almost caught Juan and Anthony together?"

"No," Romona responded confidently. "I don't know what they saw or thought they saw, but Juan is a very careful and cautious man and would not be gallivanting on the main road in an army jeep in broad daylight. Only the most foolish of all fools would behave like that. For your sake, I hope it was not your American in that jeep. I pray you are not behaving as recklessly."

"I am careful where I go."

"That is not what I meant," Romona replied. "you have spent much time with him."

"Mother, I am a virgin."

Her mother displayed an inscrutable expression.

"I have work to do," Romona said. "When I'm finished, I can help you with your costume."

"I will be in my room," Sofia said.

After her mother left, Sofia had much about which to reflect. She was extremely worried about Anthony. Where they found the jeep was exactly where was. She knew it. He had been foolish. Something must have gone wrong. She wanted to leave right away to go find him. But where would she go to find him, she thought? She could go to the cave. She must save him from himself. If only she could go now and find him, hold him, and protect him.

Gregory Arthur Solsrud

Chapter Eight – Tuesday Noon

"You're the American Carlos keeps telling us about. My name is Camilo. I'm Carlos' first cousin," a man sitting beside the fire spoke to Anthony.

"His first cousin?" Anthony repeated.

"Carlos doesn't talk much about his family, does he?"

"He talks about his daughter," said Anthony.

"He loves his daughter very much," replied Camilo. "It was a tragedy his wife died giving birth to her."

"You don't always know what life will hand you," Anthony said.

"The toughest things in life are bouncing back from your bad luck," Camilo said, "and your bad decisions."

"Carlos said to feed the American," Santo broke in.

"If there is time," Anthony replied. "the men are moving."

"We have broken main camp and are setting up positions closer to town," Santo replied. We will be staying here to bring more supplies and ammunition once the attack starts. Camilo, grab us some *alliyacas*."

Camilo reached into the fire and pulled out three stuffed banana leaves. He wrapped one in a rag and gave it to Anthony.

"Careful when you pull it apart," Camilo warned. "The banana leaf is very hot. Has Carlos made these for you?"

"Not served to me like this. I think he has cooked rice in these and given it to me."

"Santo, come take one," Camilo said.

When I come back, I have to send someone to Tito with the news," Santo replied. He turned and walked quickly down a different trail.

"This used to be slave food," said Camilo. "The slaves would take any food they could find, usually from their master's table and store it in banana leaves under the ground. When they were hungry, they would dig it up and cook it in the fire. It's a good meal when you don't have a proper kitchen."

Anthony watched Camilo as he pulled apart the banana leaves and shoved the rice into his mouth. Anthony's mouth watered. He tried to pull apart the banana leaves, but they were burning hot. He pulled them apart with the rag. The steam rolled off from the hot rice. He lifted it to his mouth and ate. When he finished, he drank from his canteen. He threw the empty banana leaves into the brush.

Camilo handed him a wine skin. He squeezed the skin, squirting the warm red wine into his mouth. He stuck the wine skin out towards Camilo to give it back to him, but Camilo motioned to him to take another drink. He squirted another gulp of wine into his mouth. The red liquid ran out the sides. He wiped his mouth with a shirtsleeve.

"Thank you," Anthony said. "I've not eaten."

As Anthony finished picking bits of rice from the rag, he watched a small bird hop around in front of him and peck at the ground. The ground had been trampled heavily; only a few blades of green stuck up here and there. With no cover, the insects must be exposed to the dirt, he thought. Bits of rice and other food left by the men might be covering the ground as well.

I don't know the name of this bird. The bird looks like a robin. Anthony looked over at Camilo who had his head down eating from the banana leaf. I could ask Camilo. He will tell me the general name for bird and be done with it. There are many birds and their names are all different. When I finish with this war, I will take up bird watching. Knowing all the birds' names would interest me.

Other birds flew into the same patch of ground and hopped around close to the first bird. There were six birds, some slightly smaller, and all the same coloring, not enough for a flock, so it must be a family of birds. The first one must be the mother bird, flying in and finding new feeding areas, and when she had fed for a while, without being eaten, the other birds followed her in. He noticed that when they came, she hopped closer to him. He, at first, thought it was to find better or more food, but she was moving closer to him to watch him more closely. If he made a sudden movement, she could warn the others.

He moved his arms. She flew away and the others followed. He could not see where they had flown in the trees. He stayed perfectly still. She came back and landed on the opposite side of the patch away from him. After awhile she hopped closer and the others flew in. Suddenly, all of the birds flew away.

Two soldiers ran by on the opposite side of the patch.

Camilo called out to them. They did not stop.

"Everybody is in a hurry today," Camilo said.

He offered Anthony the wineskin. Anthony took another drink and handed it back to him.

"I've heard El Jefe has promised us whisky after the battle," Camilo began again. "That is why everybody is in a hurry. We want to run down and kill so we can drink our whiskey."

Camilo laughed at his own joke.

"You might be killed for that whiskey," answered Santo from behind. He had returned by another trail.

"Getting killed for a good whisky is a good death," Camilo replied. "You too heard that we are getting whiskey?"

"Yes," Santo said, coming over and sitting in front of Anthony. "Whiskey in the belly is better than stones in the belly. It is all right for a man to die with whiskey in his belly."

"Anything is better than stones in the belly," Camilo said.

"Would you like to have stones in the belly?" Santo asked, looking at Anthony.

"No, they do not sit well," Anthony replied.

"No, they do not," Santo replied chuckled. "Lucky for me I can swim."

"Did you eat the stones?" Anthony asked.

"Did I eat the stones?" Santo repeated. He laughed aloud. "No. They were being served by the second army regiment down near Popayan."

"Serving stones to eat does not sound very tasty," Anthony replied.

"Someone had set fire to a military vehicle. They rounded up the young men in the area," Santo said with his gravelly voice. "They would torture them by cutting their stomachs open, filling them with rocks and throwing them in the river."

"Carlos said you were from the adjoining valley," Anthony said. "Were you fighting with a group down there?"

"No," Santo replied, "then I had no interest in fighting the government, I was just visiting friends. But when my turn to die came, I cried loudly and told them that I was not from there and that I did not know how to swim. The lieutenant was a sadistic bastard. He told the others to throw me in so they could watch me drown. He had never seen someone drown before. I tricked them. I ducked under the water and swam away, only surfacing quickly to breathe and diving before they could shoot me."

"You thought fast," Anthony said.

"You do when your life depends on it," Santo said. "After that, I promised I would kill as many soldiers as there were stones in Colombia."

"And he has," Camilo grunted.

Anthony had heard other stories of the barbarism that occurred. He had become immune to it, like most in Colombia. Why a certain person had survived baffled him more. It could not be God's way of letting the world know that such things went on, because enough people had survived such horrible tortures that whether it happened was no longer questioned. People questioned how it would stop. The stories never revealed that answer.

"You should rest a little," Camilo advised. "It will be a long night. Carlos will wake us when he returns with El Jefe."

Camilo took his own advice and rolled over on his side, covering his head with an arm. Anthony shifted off from the log onto the ground and leaned his head on the log as a pillow. He closed his eyes.

It was like riding on a Gravitron, the spinning fun ride Anthony Wyatt remembered as a kid. But this ride wasn't driven by a kindly old man who makes his living on the quarters pressed into his hands by the tow-headed kids blowing their last monies in their sprint to do everything once more before the dim lights finally faded at the county fair. The spinning ride matched their wildness to roam and dream and live one time in a long hot summer, helping them to escape the rising before sunset and tired itchy eyes and bleeding hands from de-tasseling corn and baling hay. The slow winding up of the large spinning machine detached the sugar and crumbs from the funnel cakes clinging to their red faces, and as the machine spun faster, loaned them the feeling of weightless, teasing them with the freedom of being astronauts in space.

No, it was not that kind of ride, although people waited, while the emaciated carnie with brown, cracked teeth extorted not only the fare but additional coins from the wide-eyed farmer kids taught to respect their elders, but devoid of the cunning to differentiate between the wise and the wicked. The powerful spinning machine cracked their necks as it lurched to retching speeds, dislodging their last loose change into the hidden cache below the wooden plank floor, and when at last the whirling walls came to rest, the last paper dollars, so laboriously earned, of the disorientated innocents are pick-pocketed by the long Fagin fingers of the operator.

He had been on both types of rides; the difference was not in the mechanics but in who operated the controls. Either way, it made him sick, it was only when he had aged and understood his desire for freedom and life had he understood what he was willing to do to have it, if only for a fleeting, fantastical moment. He did not want on again.

Anthony heard the sound of many footsteps approaching. He looked up and saw Juan walking up the trail with Carlos, Miguel and several others behind him. Anthony pushed himself to his feet, dusting off his pants.

"Anthony, you've caused a good bit of trouble already today," Juan shouted.

Anthony whirled as Juan approached quickly.

"I was doing what needed to be done," Anthony replied.

"We will cut off their retreat and surround them," Juan said quickly. "It will be a great victory."

Juan's enthusiasm spun Anthony Wyatt again. This was going to be a great victory.

"If they surrender en masse," Juan continued, "we will be able to capture their equipment. I will have a fighting force to contend with. I will be as strong as Mono. More men have joined me. I told Mono the other day of how many boys had been wandering into my camp, assured of our victories. Yes, I will have a commanding force of men and arms after this victory."

"Miguel, take your men and finish mounting the artillery. The attack can now go forward."

Miguel saluted him and ran off, followed by Santo and the others.

"Antonio, let us go to the ridge and count how many trucks and guns they have stockpiled in the valley."

Juan clapped Anthony on the back in great excitement and strode quickly toward the point looking over the town.

Anthony ran beside Juan to stay abreast with him. Juan kept talking in fast, clipped Spanish about the victory, the arms and the success. Anthony could only understand about half of what Juan said. He was more accustomed to the more leisurely speaking lilt of the peasant Colombians. It did not matter; Juan was happy, happier than Anthony had seen him in months. They quickly reached the ridge.

Juan threw himself to the ground, pulled out his binoculars and kept up his steady flow of excited Spanish. Anthony could make out that he was reciting many numbers as he scanned rapidly across the entire valley.

"Good. Good." Juan said through clenched teeth. "Tito should be close to the end of the valley, ready to move into position at first light. My men have moved most of the artillery into place and are ready to flood the valley on my command.

The colonel will surrender everything to save his own skin. His father is a senator, and he will always be rich."

"You are cutting off all means of his escape?" asked Anthony.

"That is the beauty of this plan. He believes strongly that victory is in his grasp and that he finally will have me encircled." Juan snorted. "He will realize too late that he is encircled. He cannot bring down El Jefe. Come we must go. We have much to do."

"And Mono?" Anthony asked.

"Mono will be in position."

"You spoke with Mono."

"Yes."

"Tomorrow," Anthony questioned, "we will attack?"

"Yes."

"How about Tito?" Anthony asked.

"Tito knows not to do anything until he hears me initiate the attack."

"Mono will be able to move his men in that quickly? When I saw him last, he was along the coast."

"When there is bounty, he can move very quickly. I do not want him too far into the valley to allow him to encircle all of my equipment and take it for his own. His value is his being with us. The mere fact that he is moving up against the colonel might scare him into surrender. Mono has a bad reputation as far as prisoner taking, particularly well-known ones."

Juan's tone dropped. He looked several minutes more across the wide valley. He scuttled back along the ridge on all fours, jumped up and started back to camp. Juan started talking again. He talked about how this would be the victory that would put their little ragtag outfit on the map. When peace talks resumed in the summer, they would be there. Like Simon Bolivar, he would have a say in how Colombia's future was decided.

"The key was that you blew up the radar. It will take a week to repair. We will capture the town before then."

"I didn't blow it up," Anthony replied. "I didn't have enough explosives."

"You didn't destroy it?"

"I disabled it."

"What did you do?"

"I cut the wires leading to the antennae."

"Cut the wires?"

"I cut them completely."

"That's it?"

"I destroyed the antennae."

"Did you kill the operator?"

"There was only a guard."

"Did you kill him?"

"No."

"No? Aren't we at war?"

"Yes."

"People die in war. Who do you want to die, us or them?"

"The radar is disabled."

"Was disabled. They are repairing it as we speak."

"You don't know that."

"If it is working when we attack, there will be a slaughter."

"There must be another way."

"If we shell them in their barracks," Juan said.

"You can't. You will destroy the town," Anthony said, thinking of Sofia and her mother; they must have many relatives and friends in town.

"We must destroy the town before it destroys us," Juan said.

"There are civilians," Anthony said.

"I have been too soft on them. It is their war, not mine."

"I will map the coordinates of every military target," Anthony said.

"I know about where they are, and I will eventually hit them."

"And destroy everything. There is a point right off from town, I will set myself up there and chart the targets."

"You cannot measure closer then I can up here," Juan replied.

"I will go into town and call in the artillery," Anthony said.

"You will not come back. Either the military or our own bombs will keep you there."

"Carlos and I can camouflage ourselves," Anthony continued. "On carnival night, everyone will be too drunk to care."

"You will throw your life away."

"The military will be occupied with the insanity of the carnival party," Anthony replied.

"You cannot take Carlos," Juan said.

"There is no danger for him in going. He will want to go."

Juan looked at him, unbelieving.

"From up here, we will bomb close, but not debilitate them," Anthony said. "With my front position guidance, we will annihilate their positions in the first salvo. The colonel's resistance will be finished."

"Have you talked to Carlos?" Juan asked.

"If it is as crazy in the town as everybody says it will be, I don't think anybody will notice us," Anthony replied.

"Carnival time is wild in Colombia," Juan said. "The year-round pent-up frustration of being Catholic releases itself on one glorious night."

"I won't get into trouble."

"You will be on your own," Juan said. "I won't help you, if you are caught."

"Yes," Anthony said.

Anthony returned to his tent, gathered up his personal belongings and shoved everything into his pack. When he finished and looked at the pack lying on the floor, he realized that he owned little in this world. It did not make him sad. There was a real freedom in not owning anything. He wondered what his mother had done with all his stuff back at his home in Montana. There was not much. He had a stamp collection from when he was a kid. His uncle had been in the Navy and had sent him postcards from all over the world. He remembered looking at the stamps and postmarks from faraway places and wishing that he was there. Now he was in a faraway place and wished that he was nowhere else. Maybe he would send a postcard to his uncle after this was all through.

Diego and a group of boys came running up to the tent.

"*Capitan*, can I speak with you?"

"Yes, Diego."

"We were talking about what we would do after the war and I was thinking the other day that I would go and do publicity. You know, I went to school for publicity, but I ran out of money and had to go leave and work to support my mother. I have many ideas."

"I did not know you had been to school."

"He did good in school. Listen, he has ideas to make money," another boy next to him interrupted.

"Shhh, let me tell," Diego said, "*Capitan*, you have American friends?"

"Yes, Diego," Anthony replied, "call me *Antonio*,"

"Thank you, and I will, *Capitan*," Diego replied.

"Tell him about your idea," another boy with bright eyes put in.

"They do publicity in New York. Do you have friends in New York?"

"I don't have any New York friends," Anthony replied.

"Do you like the coffee in Colombia?" Diego asked undaunted.

"Yes, Diego."

"We have the best coffee in the world. We have four types, *caturra*, *maragojipe*, *pajarito* and *borbon*. Only the ripest beans can be picked."

"You know a lot about coffee."

"We used to have a small farm, and my father grew coffee. He grew caturra. He used to go out every day and look at the beans because it is very important to pick the beans at exactly the right time. Immature beans have no flavor, and overripe beans are too soft."

"I am not sure if I understand what the idea is," Anthony said.

"Tell him the idea, you can tell him the history of coffee later," the boy with bright eyes said.

"I have to tell him how important it is that the beans are picked at the right time."

"Tell him that, and tell him your idea. He is important and is busy with other things," the other boy chimed him.

"You have to pick beans at exactly the right time. During one growing season, the time came for picking but a terrible storm came. The wind was blowing hard, so hard you could not stand up against it. My father was out there picking beans. I watched him and he had to hang onto the bushes to not blow away. He was wearing a long poncho, which fluttered like a large sail. With the tightness of his grip, his billowing poncho and the bushes, he looked like he was flying horizontally into the wind as he picked the beans. You understand?"

"Yes, I think so, Diego," Anthony said. He was not sure what the idea was but the young man's face looked so expectant and hopeful.

"I think it is a fine idea. Diego and I think it will sell many coffee beans."

"There's more," Diego said. "In the television, I saw hurricanes hit Florida and I thought you could have a fellow walking in the middle of a hurricane to go and buy a cup of coffee, and while he is drinking it, the wind could blow him horizontally. The commercial would show my father picking coffee beans horizontally in a windstorm saying we only pick coffee that is just right and then you can have an American like you, drinking coffee, saying that it is good enough to risk a hurricane."

"I'm not in the advertising business, but it sounds like a fine idea," Anthony said.

"Will you tell your American friends about it?"

"Yes, when I see them again."

"Will you tell them that I thought it up?"

"Of course, they will know that I did not come up with something so creative."

"You are very kind, *Señor Capitan.*"

"That is enough, Diego," his friend said. "The *Capitan* has to go."

He watched Diego and his friends leave; they were all skinny arms and legs as they ran off. Anthony could see Carlos walking around and looking into various tents. Anthony called out to him. Carlos came up quickly.

"The attack is going forward," replied Anthony.

"We are going into town?" Carlos asked.

"Yes, I need to warn Sofia. El Jefe is going to bomb the town."

"He will destroy it."

"Not if we relay exact coordinates of what he needs to hit."

"Still, people will die," Carlos said.

"Not the ones we are closest to," Anthony said. "We can save them."

"We should be close to everyone, Señor," Carlos replied.

"We only have a limited amount of time," Anthony said.

"We should go."

Carlos and Anthony started off down the trail to town. They walked quickly. Soon they were abreast of the waterfall. Carlos stopped behind him. He turned and whispered.

"I want to cut across this hillside to find out if we can see out to the town."

Anthony nodded in agreement. They climbed straight across the ridge, using the sinewy tough bushes as steps, until they came to a natural opening in the thick foliage.

They could see the town below them. They were directly above the small town square, which was busy with people decorating for the Carnival party. They seemed so close that Anthony instinctively squeezed back into the bushes to hide himself. He pulled out the map, made marks on the map and wrote corresponding marks in his book. When he closed his book and put away his pencil, Carlos took that as a signal to continue on closer to the town. Working their way down through the dense undergrowth was slow.

By the time they reached a road, it was near dark. They walked along the road for several hundred feet when Anthony heard the growl of a diesel engine. He grabbed Carlos by his jacket and pulled them both down into the thick weeds along the road. As the noise came closer, Anthony realized that it was not just one diesel but several. With his free right hand, he eased his pistol out of his holster and removed the safety. The trucks bore down on them, passing within several feet of them. They could hear the talking of the soldiers inside the trucks. Each of the trucks pulled a wagon or a small howitzer. Behind the trucks followed several jeeps and cars. Anthony could see that they, too, were filled with men; he could not recognize any rank or insignia.

After the last vehicle had passed, they arose and started walking quickly along the road. The mosquitoes bit them furiously. Anthony could not stop slapping at them. With his attention distracted, he did not hear the vehicle coming up behind him. More concerned with driving quickly into town, the black car beeped angrily at them, making them jump back off the road. It did not even slow down. Carlos crossed himself. Anthony swore softly, angry that he had not heard the car.

Anthony started to run, pulling Carlos along with him. After several minutes, they reached a few dilapidated shacks along the river. Anthony led Carlos along the shadow of the closest shack and squatted on his haunches. He looked out into the river trying to spot the pipe that led to Sofia's house.

"Rest," Anthony ordered, slipping his gun inside his clothes.

Carlos dutifully sat down and pulled a small flask from his clothes. He drank and offered it to Anthony. Anthony smiled, shaking his head no.

"This thing tomorrow," Carlos asked. "Is it a great thing?"

"The battle, yes, I think it is."

"We will kill many?" Carlos asked.

"Yes."

"Have you killed before?"

"Yes."

"And we will win?"

"We must win," Anthony replied.

"Good, then I can go back to hunting animals in these mountains. In the valley where it is always wet and where moist, large tubers grow," Carlos said. "The wild boars come down off the ridges, root up these sweet morsels and eat them. I wait in the bushes and when the biggest and fattest one comes, I shoot. It gives me great satisfaction."

"You like to hunt?"

"Yes," Carlos replied. "Everyone here likes to hunt. It gives us our meat."

"What else do you hunt?"

"Farther up in the mountains, the goats roam. You have to hold your hands very steady to hit one because they stand a long ways off and will not come any closer. They are not curious creatures. I cut the horns off from their heads and hung them in my home. Those horns give me great pride when I show them to others."

"Are they large horns?" Anthony asked.

"The largest here in the valley. When I think about the battle, I do not look forward to the killing, even though I know it must be done."

"You will be hunting men," Anthony said.

"Do not say such a thing," the old man said. "I do not like to kill men. Do you like the killing?"

"No. But it is necessary. I will kill during the battle. I do the killing because it is the only way I can survive. It is not easy to leave in the middle of a war. Someday, I will return to the land where I grew up. When I return there, I will not kill anymore, and I feel that I will not hunt anymore."

"After this war, I will hunt again. I think of the beautiful hide of the puma that hung on my wall and when it was cold, we would take it down and lie under it. Or I smell the stew cooking from the fresh meat of the roe that I had shot. I remember one deer that I shot had such unusual antlers. They were shaped like a perfect cross. I have never seen one the like before and never again. I cut the antlers off and gave them to the priest. He hung them up in the small chapel in the mountains."

"Where is the chapel?"

"It has been destroyed in the fighting. I would go to mass just to look at those horns. They reminded me of the real power of God to create anything he wanted on earth."

"And he created us to kill others," Anthony said.

"I believe so, too," Carlos said. "Otherwise it makes no sense. I believe that it is a sin to kill others, and we must atone for our sins."

"To win this war and to win tomorrow, we must kill," Anthony said.

"I understand that. As you say, it is necessary. I will do what is necessary," Carlos replied. "I am not a killer of men and the killing bothers me."

"At least, we do not hang up the heads on the walls as trophies," Anthony said.

"No, that would be barbaric, and it should be unthinkable."

"It happens here," Anthony said.

"Yes, I know. It is as if God looks in the other direction."

"God is not here. Only men are here. They have thrown out God, the Son, and The Holy Ghost so no one can see what they are doing."

"They still call on the name of God. I have heard them on the television. They liken us and those who fight like us to the devil," Carlos replied.

"May be we are. May be the devil has tricked us and we are fighting for him and we do not know it."

They were talking very quietly now, and it was completely dark.

"The devil is very smart, but a man must answer to himself," Carlos said.

"You think a man is responsible for his own killings?" Anthony asked.

"Yes, he is and I think he can forgive himself for his own killings. He has to forgive himself or one's Conscience will cease."

"I wish it were true," Anthony replied.

"It is true."

"I have seen too many men do many bad things to believe that we are given a Conscience, especially one that makes us behave."

"I must believe it, because I do not believe so strongly in God anymore. I must believe that there are some of us who do not like to kill."

"I do not like to kill, but I must," Anthony said. "There are those who like to kill and take pleasure in it, as you take pleasure in hunting."

"Yes, I have seen such men. They are best in a battle."

"Have you ever been in battle?" Anthony asked.

"Yes and no, I have been on the edges," Carlos replied. "One time near Boyaca before I joined up with El Jefe, the government had attacked our little group and we were beaten and we ran. We were in the valley and there was no cover and the *federales* could drive forward in their armored vehicles and shoot us. And they shot us as they desired, as if we were cattle running in the field. Do you think our battle will be like that?"

"There is a chance," Anthony replied.

"Well, then I fear that I may run as I did before," Carlos said. "I was a younger man and I was afraid. Now I am an old man."

"Stay close to me and I will look out for you," Anthony said.

"You have fought in many wars?" Carlos asked.

"Not in many wars, but in many battles," he replied. "they pretty much follow the same course."

"What course is that?"

"If your company holds together, you will win," he said. "Some will be shot and die, and the rest will survive."

"How do you know that your company will hold together?" Carlos asked.

"You don't. Each person in your company has instructions on how to do their job and if these instructions are good, because your commander is good and he has put you in a battle in which you can win, then it is your duty to follow those instructions, even if it means that you might die."

"I will follow your instructions when we fight," Carlos said. "I will not run."

Carlos said it so honestly and sincerely without any bravado or *machismo* that Anthony looked at him and believed him.

Anthony hoped the battle would go well. He knew he would play a small part in it, and he would perform it well. He must look at things like that in the future, as if they were all pieces of machinery designed to fit together in a precise way, responsible to the other pieces to do one's assignment so the entire machine would work well. He had let himself drift off into personal issues, when he should remember his duty and his assignment. He must think of other things now. He needed to move forward into the town to complete the mission, and although it was a small thing, it was important to the whole.

"From here, we'll split up," Anthony said. "You pick up your costume from your cousin. I will go to Sofia's and have her fix me up with a long cloak."

He saw the look of concern in Carlos' eyes.

"You need to warn your family. I will stay at her house and wait for you."

Carlos looked as though he was about to say something then merely nodded his assent. He again offered the flask to Anthony. Anthony accepted it, put the metal to his lips and let the liquid flow into his mouth. It burned going down his throat. He stifled a cough. Carlos smiled broadly.

"Look at the flask. It was a gift from my wife," Carlos said.

"It is beautiful," Anthony replied.

"Did you read the inscription?" he asked.

"No, it is too dark."

"I will tell it to you. "It reads *Fiel para siempre*" meaning "Faithful forever."

"I live by the motto," Anthony replied.

"I know you do," Carlos said. "That is why I shared it with you. I never stopped loving her, and I know I'm the only one she ever loved."

He stuck his hand out; Anthony shook it fully. Carlos disappeared into the darkness.

Anthony waited several minutes, listening for any sounds. As he took his first tentative steps out of the shadows, his feet scraped loudly on the gravel, the sound echoing across the road. He stopped. He consciously tried to pick up his feet and place them softly, heel first than the toes, one in front of the other. In the still night, the sound seemed to reverberate for miles. He moved as quickly as he dared in the dark along the river. Everything was black and strange.

The path along the river became more trodden and defined. The shacks changed into more sturdy stone homes. He kept out of the dim lights.

People danced and sang around the homes; they did not pay him any attention. He had missed the storm pipe; there were too many houses. He huddled under some bushes and thought about his next move. He could retrace his steps, but he might not be on the correct stream. There seemed to be several that flowed into the river around the town. He remembered a steep bank and a wall out of which the pipe stuck. He looked out at the water. He could not make out anything; it was too dark.

Fear crept into his heart. He scooped handfuls of mud and plastered his white skin and fair hair making it black. He pulled out his gun, clicked the safety to off and hid the gun under his arm. He got up and continued along the path. He hunched over as he walked. His spirits rose when he felt the bank inclining away from the river. He pushed on, expecting to see the pipe, but the trail led behind a tall cement wall, built as a dike to hold the river back when the torrential rains came. The trail led out into a stone street. He clung to the buildings along the street, hoping to find something he recognized.

He turned down an empty street with a broken stone wall on one side. He did not see any lights and could not tell what was behind the wall. It looked like a bunch of trees. If something came, he could be over the wall and hide in the shadows. He scurried along the wall when he heard loud laughing. He ran forward to a break in the wall and wedged his body back inside it. He was panting heavily. His hand made a scraping sound on the protruding rocks. He looked down. He was still clutching his pistol, safety off, in his right hand. He reset the safety, making a loud click. He looked up quickly, scanning both directions along the road. He slid the gun inside the holster, safely hidden under his clothes.

Anthony listened intently for more laughter. It was a woman's voice, somewhere off in front of him. He told himself to stay calm and walk normally along the street. Normal. There was nothing normal to him here, except the instinct to scream. He should not have left Carlos. He took three deep breaths and stepped out into the open street. He tried to imitate the walk of the young men he had seen in the capital city. After several paces, he gave up, knowing that a shuffling gait would attract more attention. He saw a car's headlights coming towards him. For a split second, he wanted to flee in the opposite direction; he willed himself forward. The car passed without breaking speed. He relaxed slightly. The street t-boned into another one lined with large houses with doors, which resembled hers.

A wild thought seized him: what if he could not find the doorway? He forced himself to breathe deep and to continue walking. He had been so certain he would recognize her door. He slowed his walk as he passed each doorway, looking for a mark that this was the one. Each successive doorway looked as uninviting as the last.

Another car was coming from behind; it was being driven slowly. Anthony tensed. He reached inside his clothes and cradled the gun. The car passed emitting heavy smoke from its tailpipe. Holding the gun calmed him. He had to find the alley. He had not walked very far before he spotted it, dark and inviting. He ran up the street along the parked cars and hid in its shadows. He breathed deeply and waited several minutes before he dared a look across the street. In the dull light from the street lamps he could see the yellow paint of her back door.

He ran across the street and pounded on the door. The dull thuds seemed to deaden three feet away from the door. No one would hear him. He could not yell; it would attract attention. The locals yelled for the doctor's attention, but his voice would always have that foreign ring to it. He could not risk it. He would have to go around front to ring the bell. As he was debating his options, the handle of the door moved. Nana opened the door. He stepped inside.

Anthony felt such relief that he scooped her up in his arms and hugged her. He set her down quickly when he felt how small her frame was. For a moment, he thought he had hurt her.

"Sorry," he mumbled. "I was happy you heard me."

In the light from the open back door, he could see her smiling. She grabbed him near the elbow and led him into the house.

He looked around. The entire house appeared dark except for this room. An opened bible lay on the small table. She told him that she was the only one home. Sofia and her mother had left together, and she did not know when either of them would return. They might be gone all night. All night? That was impossible. He had to start back in a few of hours; he wanted to see her, if only for a moment. He heard her ask him if he wanted something to eat. He did not remember answering, but she started to busy herself in the kitchen. He was not hungry.

A bell rang, startling him. He looked at her. She pointed to the front door. She must answer she said. He shook his head no. Somebody might need help, she insisted.

The bell rang again. A man's voice cried out. She must go to see, she said again. He agreed and asked her if she could speak through the door to find out who it was before she opened it. She said that beside the door there was a small window with an iron grate in front of it. He motioned for her to go and then followed close behind her. She moved very quickly for one so old, he thought, as they walked though the large house. He slipped his hand beneath his clothes again.

As she neared the doorway, the bell rang again. She opened the small window and told the person outside that she was an old woman and did not move so fast and that the person must have patience. A man's voice apologized and said he had a message for the colonel. She told the voice that she could take the message for him, but the colonel had already left. At first, the man seemed hesitant, but he told his message. He was the adjutant for the colonel. The colonel needed to contact him immediately. There was some trouble. He was very sorry to have disturbed her, but he did not know where to find the colonel; the whole town was in the street.

Jealously flared inside of Anthony. He wanted to rush out and beat this adjutant senseless for delivering the message. His head throbbed. He listened to the two of them exchange good-bye pleasantries. He had never met a people who took so long to say good-bye. As Nana closed the window, Anthony leaned heavily against the wall. She walked to the back of the house, leaving him in the small vestibule.

He had to talk to her. She was dining with the colonel; he told her to go with someone else tonight, but this was unexpected. He was going to find her.

He returned to the kitchen; Nana had a small supper laid out for him. He tried to ask her where Sofia had gone, but either she did not know or knew it would be too dangerous for him to wander around looking for her at this time of night. He eventually sat down, determined to eat quickly and leave. By the time he had finished eating, he had drunk several small glasses of wine, which had their prescribed effect of calming his nerves. Going out into the dark night into an unknown city filled with wandering patrols seemed absurd. Even if she had dined with a general tonight, she would still return home.

He yawned. The too-little sleep, the constant strain, and his injury closed his eyes unconsciously. Nana, seeing his weariness, brought a cleanly-pressed white sheet, a wool blanket and pillow out from a small closet. She led him into a small bedroom on the main floor. She quickly fixed the naked bed and helped him unlace his boots. He laid down telling her to wake him when Carlos came. She had no sooner tucked him in, when he fell into a fitful sleep.

While Anthony was searching for Sofia's house in the town, Tito looked out into the jungle blackness, slapping himself and cursing the flying insects. He waited for the rainy season. The rainy season brought cooler weather and rain, which drove these bloody thirsty parasites away, granting some peace. He scratched at bites over a week old. Velvety shafts of light from the full moon illuminated small areas, the contrast making the jungle darker and more mysterious.

The jungle was an elusive place. Evening ended quickly, beginning a long night where all the friendly day animals disappeared, hiding from the night creatures whose sharp shrieks and howls filled the air. In the final twilight, the insects became more vicious, knowing they had only one last meal before the end of that day. With a lifespan of a few days, the coming of each night was more precious than the last, understanding without the help of reason, the timeless struggle of not going gentle into that good night, and even more determined, as the light disappeared, to bite and eat on this day to reproduce and to survive.

They had stopped to rest. It was good solid trail, which ran along below the ridge. They had to ascend this ridge and cross over, which by Tito's reckoning would put them directly above their attack position. He looked up, trying to see if he could see Checo and the other men, but the undergrowth was too thick and tall.

He called his men together and started them moving. They walked for another hour, steadily climbing to the top of the peak. He was tired. As he stumbled forward, he heard Checo call out to him. His group had already arrived.

"Tito," Checo said, "you look tired."

"You are a sight for sore feet. My body didn't think it was going to make it."

"Our way was easier than I had remembered. We made good time. The ridge was level and easy to walk."

"Our trail was easy, only long," Tito said.

"I suggest we make camp on the other side of the ridge. There is a clear spot about a thousand meters further along," Checo said. "Before first light, we can descend the rest of the way down and be in position before the sun is above the horizon."

"Let it be done. It's too dark to descend down that steep slope. I don't want to lose any men over a cliff."

Checo walked among the men and told them where to camp. As they moved off, he went back to where Tito was sitting.

"You go ahead and make camp," Checo said. "The last group will need to pass by here. I will wait for them. Our spotters saw some men walking along the backside of the ridge. They should be here soon."

"After they come, find me so we can discuss the strategy for the morning," Tito said.

Tito trudged towards camp. His men hung shelters among the trees. Several of his men had started setting up his large command tent.

"It's very flat here," one of his men said. "I was going to set your tent up here."

"No tent tonight. We will sleep under the stars," Tito said. "We need to move out first thing in the morning."

"It is a beautiful night," his man replied. "Go and sit down, the food is almost cooked."

Several of his men had lit fires. One of the men pulled a log over next to the fire. Tito sat down. The men greeted him warmly. Someone put a plate filled with hot stew into his hands. He reached into his pocket and pulled out a spoon. He balanced the plate on his knees as he cleaned the spoon on his shirt. Checo came up and sat down close to him.

"I'm glad to see you, Checo," Tito said between mouthfuls, "no problems?"

"The men are excited now that we are here," Checo said. "They feel that luck is on our side."

"I agree," Tito said.

"I agree also," Checo said.

"Optimistic for once, Checo," Tito said. "That is not like you."

"Someone spoke with *El Capitan* before they left," Checo said.

"*El Capitan*," Tito said slowly with a smile, "that is a title of respect. He must have said something good to you."

Checo sat still, watching as the others quieted waiting for his words.

"He smashed the radar," Checo said.

A shout went up among the men.

"He has then," Tito said excitedly, "I knew I could rely on him. I am looking forward to tomorrow. We should route the *federales*."

"Have you set up some men around the perimeter?" Tito asked.

"Already done, Tito," Checo said.

"Good man," Tito said. He had good men.

Checo pulled out the map from his pocket and sat closer to Tito. Several soldiers crowded around them for a better look.

"We are camped here," Checo said, pointing to a heavily-lined area on the map. His finger left a smudge. He looked out his hands. They were dirty.

"Sorry, I didn't have time to wash up."

"None of us have had our showers tonight," Tito said with a laugh.

"See how the mountain cuts sharply down. That is a cliff which is over there," Checo said.

Checo indicated down the trail into the darkness.

"There are two paths down," he continued. "One that sweeps wide around the cliff, and the other one which drops along the right side."

"There is a third," a man named Raphael broke in. He was leading the third group in Miguel's place. "Directly over the cliff."

"If you are a bird," Checo replied.

"No," he replied. "With ropes."

"Can the mules make it down the steep trail?" Tito asked.

"Not as heavily loaded as they are," Checo responded.

"How long does the winding trail take?"

"About two hours?"

"The other one?"

"About an hour if you are sure-footed. The trail is loose and steep."

"Raphael, you lead the mules and the men carrying the munitions down the long trail," Tito decided. "You need to set-up before sunrise."

"Yes, I know the trail well and we can tie the mules together."

"At the base, it spreads out flat, doesn't it?" Tito asked.

"Yes, they used to plant sugar cane down there," Raphael said. "They farmed it too long, and the land went bad."

"How much cover is down there?" a tall soldier asked.

"Not much, they burned out all the vegetation to plant the cane, but there is wild cane growing down there," Raphael replied.

"That's not much cover," a man broke in.

"No," Tito said.

"There's no escape route, Tito" Checo said. "If El Jefe does not attack, we have no place to hide."

"You are worrying again," Tito said. "Remember *El Capitan* will be right next to him, he will not flinch."

"If they tried to attack us from the valley, they would have to come straight up at us. This flat area sits about several hundred meters above the valley," Raphael replied. "If we have a problem, I'll hold the ridge with a small group and a couple of pieces of artillery until everyone has moved back up the trails."

Raphael showed the retreat paths along the map.

"Except against an air strike," Checo said.

"Did you say Mono will provide air protection?" Raphael asked.

"Mono controls this area here," Tito replied. "I don't think they would risk an air strike."

"Have you talked to Mono?" Checo asked.

"I haven't tried," Tito replied. Tito stood up. "I'll try to radio him now."

After Tito left, the men huddled around Checo.

"I don't like it," a soldier with a long face said aloud.

"It's not yours to like," Checo growled. "If Tito wants us to go down there, we are going down."

"I've been with him as long as you," long face grunted. "And I'll follow him to hell if he asks, but I don't like it."

The men talked amongst themselves. Tito came back; he was whistling.

"Boys," cried Tito. "I just spoke with Mono."

"Is he out fighting or out whoring around?" someone shouted.

"He was leaving to go to a big party," Tito said. "He was in a very good mood."

"What did he say?"

"He is going to drink all night and meet us in the morning," Tito said.

"I promise you this, men," Tito said aloud. "Tomorrow, after we smash the *federales*, I will throw the biggest party for all of us. Bigger than any party Mono will visit tonight."

The men gathered around Tito; he walked slowly through the crowd, which parted to make a path for him. When he had reached the center, he stood up on a tall stump. A ray of moonlight had slid through a slit in the tall trees, illuminating his white hair, face and hands, the scene made more mysterious by the silence of the jungle animals.

"Men, I am here to ask for your help."

The entire group moved closer to listen.

"We can, as brothers, take back Colombia," Tito continued. "We have climbed up and down these mountains. Running down and sometimes being chased up these god-forsaken trails."

Several of the men shouted in agreement.

"We have been chased together and survived. We have starved together and survived. We have faced danger together and survived."

"Amen," shouted Raphael.

"Before us, we have our greatest opportunity and our greatest challenge. Before us stands the western battalion of the Colombia army."

Loud hisses could be heard throughout the crowd.

"And if the rains come, the army will catch us, trap us and kill us."

The men fell silent.

"They kill our families. They kill our friends," Tito said. "It does not stop us. We fight. We fight back. We fight for a united Colombia."

"Yes," the men shouted, cheering Tito.

"Do you love your country?" Tito shouted.

"We fight because we love Colombia!" shouted Checo from the crowd.

"Tomorrow is our day to fight. I ask you, now, as your commander, are you ready to fight for me?"

"Yes," replied the men in unison.

"As your brother, are you ready to fight with me?"

"Yes," the band of men shouted louder.

"I would be nowhere else, but here, among my brothers. If this is my time to die, then I will have died no better death than to have died here among my brothers. They will remember us, the few and the brave. They will talk about us. They will recite the national anthem in our name. Each one of you will be remembered for your acts of bravery. We will be remembered as the liberators of Colombia."

The men applauded and whistled, none louder than Checo.

"Tomorrow we win!" Tito yelled.

The men roared. The attack was turning out as planned. The coast was theirs.

Gregory Arthur Solsrud

Chapter Nine – Tuesday Evening - Carnaval

Anthony felt his shoulder being shaken. He ignored it. He wanted to sleep. He had been dreaming. It had been a nice dream, filled with pretty images and heroic deeds. His shoulder was shaken again. He squeezed his eyes shut and curled up into a ball.

"Señor?"

Anthony opened one eye.

"Carlos."

His voice came out rough and heavy.

"Señor, it is late. We must go, or we won't have enough time."

Time. Time was all he had. Time to get himself caught. He thought about Sofia. He would like to see her. He had been dreaming about her. He threw off the light sheet and spun around to a sitting position. His boots were neatly positioned by his bed. Nana was standing there. She was holding a small cup in her hands. She moved close to him and gave it to him. He noticed her hands shook. He took the cup and drank it. It was the black strong coffee, the same as Sofia had made him the other night.

"That will wake you up," Carlos said.

"Nana, when will Sofia return? I need to talk to her."

"She and her mother went into town to attend the festivities," she replied.

"We should wait for her here," Anthony said.

"Señor, we will be waiting some time. We must be going," Carlos responded.

"You can wait for her here, if you want," Nana said. "They won't come back until late.

"Señor, I am worried about you," Carlos said. "You sound different. Maybe we should stay here."

"No. I feel disorientated, but I'm fine. It happens when I am awakened."

"I didn't want to wake you. You told me we had to go out tonight."

"The coffee is clearing my head. I'm glad you woke me. We have to work tonight."

"The whole town is out tonight," Carlos said. "The town has not had a good party for a few years. I remember when they had these parties many years ago. We drank and sang. We had fun. It has been many years since I have attended a party. It's the only night of the year you can misbehave, because the next day you can atone for it."

Nana laughed.

"Did they go in their car?" Anthony asked Nana.

"No, the colonel came and picked them up. He was dressed in his uniform; he looked resplendent with all his medals."

Anthony looked at Nana.

"The colonel picked them up?" he asked.

"The colonel invited them to the party in town. My daughter felt that Sofia could not turn down the invitation," Nana replied.

"We must go into the town and find Sofia," Anthony said unexpectedly.

"Why?" Carlos asked. "We have a task to do."

"She can't be with the colonel on this night."

"She will be safe. There are many soldiers about. They are singing and dancing and . . ."

Carlos saw the look pass across Anthony's face and understood in an instant what he felt.

"If you wish, Señor, we can go into town, but we will look out of place without a costume. Do you have a costume?"

"No, of course not, Carlos. I didn't think to bring one with me."

"Señorita Sofia wore a beautiful, red costume with delicate black lace around here," Nana said. "She looked like a princess."

Anthony's face tightened.

"We need to go," Anthony said quietly.

"Everybody needs a costume, Señor," Carlos repeated. "You can't go without a costume."

"Anthony, I will find you something," Nana said. "First, you must shave. You can use the bathroom downstairs."

Anthony walked into the bathroom and was startled at how rough he looked. An unkempt bearded dirty man with bloodshot eyes stared back at him. His clothes, spattered with mud and blood, clung to him. He pulled them off and drew a bath. While the bath was filling, he found a razor under the sink. He stepped into the large tub. He lathered the soap in his hands and spread it on his beard. He shaved, careful not to cut his skin. He washed. He sat and let his muscles relax. The steamy water laved him. He stepped from the tub, took the towel from the hook, and dried himself. He looked down at the floor. His clothes were gone. On the wash basin, clean clothes were laid out. He put them on; they fit perfectly.

He wiped the steam from the mirror and combed his hair. He had not been this clean in many days. He felt good. He walked to the kitchen where he heard Carlos and Nana talking.

"Those clothes fit you well," Nana said. "I thought they would. My son-in-law was about your size."

"Where did my other clothes go?" Anthony asked.

"The maid is washing them. They will be clean when you return," Nana replied. "They were very dirty."

"Thank you," Anthony replied.

"You need a costume," Carlos said.

Nana brought out a long black robe and a mask with two eyeholes and no hole for the mouth. She explained that the costume was based on the local native legends. The ancient people who lived in this land before the Spaniards were called the *Muiscas*. They worshiped the sun god Sua and his wife, the moon goddess Chia. Chia became very lonely because she never saw her husband so she took on a human lover. Her husband found out and chased her lover during the day, and before he caught the lover to kill him, Chia came out and blocked Sua from seeing the earth. Night came to earth during the day, and the people were afraid. To appease his people and Chia, Sua promised not to kill her lover but demanded that her lover's tongue be cut out so he could not tell anyone of the affair. Once this was done, Chia moved aside, and Sua shone over the earth.

Anthony listened to the story as he slid the robe over his clothes. The mask was made of papier-mâché and long wool skirting which draped over his head and down his back. He set the mask on the table and went out to the hallway where his backpack stood. He untied it and reached in it, pulling out his nine millimeter pistol and three full clips. The Glock felt weighty and comforting in his hand. He snapped the clip in and slipped the loaded gun into his pocket putting the remaining clips in the other pocket. He returned to the kitchen.

"I thought you went and got a costume," Anthony said.

"I did," Carlos said. "It is easy to put on." Carlos slipped on a jacket and pants embroidered with yellow cloth. He showed Anthony his mask, which had a large beak and plumage of bright yellow feathers.

"You're Big Bird," Anthony joked.

"I don't understand," Carlos said.

"He is a cartoon character for children," Anthony explained.

"I don't know of him," Carlos said. "This costume is for the dances of the birds. It is a traditional dance for Carnival."

"You are going to be dancing. That I will definitely need to see,"

Anthony said.

"We will not have time for that dance," Carlos replied. "Where do we need to go?"

Anthony spread a large map on the kitchen table. Carlos bent over to look at it.

"This is going to be a bit difficult," Anthony began. "I will need my map."

"That's easy. I can hold the map," Carlos said, picking up the map.

"No, a bird and a mute do not walk around with a military map on Carnival night. We need to find a secluded spot where no one can see us while I take measurements. It could be inside a small courtyard or on top of a roof."

"Show me the map again. How many targets are there?" asked Carlos.

"Many."

"Show me the first two again," Carlos said.

"Here and here."

"I will take us to these two spots. When we finish, you can show me the next two. I will find us a place where no one can see what we're doing," Carlos said.

"As many times as we can, I want to pass through the central square," Anthony said.

"Why?" asked Carlos. "There will be many soldiers out."

"I don't care. I need to see Sofia," Anthony replied.

"Sofia loves you, Señor. You don't need to worry."

"I want to see her," Anthony said.

Nana led them out to the front. As she unlocked the front entrance, Anthony quickly put on his mask and stepped out into the street. The heavy door slammed behind them, the lock clacked loudly into place. Anthony could see well straight ahead, but he had no peripheral vision. He turned his head both ways. People were streaming down the street towards the square. Carlos walked and Anthony tried to stay abreast with him, but the partygoers jostled him. He kept losing track of Carlos. It seemed like the whole town had come out to party for this one special night. Many people were dressed up in fantastic costumes, unexpected in this city in the middle of the mountains where people had little money.

He followed directly behind Carlos. He felt extremely uneasy. He could not see to his side or behind him. He slid his right hand under the robe, pulled the gun out of his pocket and shoved it into his waistband. He caressed the butt of the gun.

Strangers hugged him and clapped him on his shoulders. They held out homemade wineskins. Carlos pulled him out of the fray, leading him away and down an empty alleyway. They crossed several more streets, ending up on a well-lit street.

Ahead, the entire street was flooded with lights. It was the main gate of the army barracks. They were walking on the opposite side of the street, passing in front of a park surrounded by tall railings. Anthony saw slides and swings for children glinting in the glare of the spotlights.

"We can go in here," Anthony whispered, pointing inside the small park. "I can triangulate the distances to the barracks."

The front gate was locked. They walked along the tall wrought iron fence until they saw a small gap and crawled through. They nervously looked around as Carlos unfolded the map. Anthony took out his measuring equipment and a small flashlight. With every night sound, they looked up, prepared to see guns pointing at them. Anthony finished and they moved to the next location. Each time they moved to a new location, Carlos dutifully walked them by the town square.

Every time, the square was filled with more and more people, but they did not see Sofia. They arrived at the last target. It was a tower filled with antennae and parabolic dishes. Carlos pulled out the map and unfolded it. Anthony measured and wrote numbers in his book, snapping it shut when he finished. He shoved the book and map into his waistband.

"Señor, I think I should carry them."

"If they stop you with it, you will be in trouble. If they stop me, I will already be in trouble. We are finished. Let's go back to the festival."

The night was bright with a full moon. The square was elaborately decorated. The large fountain in the middle of the square was lit with multicolored lights. The square had been cordoned off; people walked, danced and moved all about. Along one side, stone archways fronted the square.

The restaurants that normally operated under the stone archways had requisitioned more tables, filling one entire side. The tables were draped with cloths and covered with bouquets of flowers. Serious waiters in black pants and long white coats hustled between the tables and the inside of the restaurant, carrying trays laden with drinks and food. Every table was filled with people singing, dancing, and eating. In front of the old municipal building, the town had erected a large stage.

An eleven-piece band was onstage, three women in long tight Spanish dresses twirled and spun while singing backup vocals for a man clad in a beautiful black suit with a large flamboyant red tie and large fedora. He sang beautifully, stretching vocally from the highest notes Anthony had ever heard to the low growls of the saddest Spanish love songs. They had two trumpet players, two guitarists, a bass guitar, a drummer and a piano player. They enthralled the crowd.

The square had become filled with people, Anthony was bumped constantly. The great numbers of people relaxed him as if he were wearing a cloak of invisibility over him. He started to move to the music, when an unknown woman grabbed him and started twirling him around singing at the top of her voice. It was Carnival.

He slipped his gun into his pocket and clapped with the music. Someone handed him a cold bottle of beer. He drank it, prying his mask up with the bottle, and it tasted strong and sweet. Then he was arm and arm with other people swinging around and around. Cold beers would end up in his hand. He drank them. He swung as wildly around as they, and he felt the notebook and map slip from his waistband. The notebook splayed its pages over the ground and the map half-unfolded. Fear jerked him to action. He scrambled around and shoved the papers under his robe. Carlos was next to him.

"Give me them. I will put them in order." Carlos said.

Anthony gave him the map, which Carlos slipped under his costume. Anthony shuffled the pages of the notebook together and handed the pile to Carlos.

"I'll be back after I have put these away," Carlos said quickly, and then he was gone.

Anthony again was in a sea of unfamiliar, smiling faces. A girl grabbed his arms and swung him around; another beer bottle was pressed into his hand. He had never been to such a party. At every other party he had known, people stood around bored in small groups of two or three talking. Talking was not a party and here it was party and here it was living and here everybody was his friend celebrating and the fear and the tension were gone and there was Sofia. And he saw her. She radiated beauty.

She was dancing with the colonel who held her stiffly and turned measuredly around the square. It had to be the colonel whom he had never seen; he wore a pressed uniform adorned with tiny medals. Now they were arm in arm walking away from him. Rage flamed in Anthony. He walked after the colonel determined to tear each medal from the uniform and shove them down his throat and hang onto his throat until the colonel's face went from red to purple to white.

Carlos was in front of him and talked to him quickly as the words bounced out of Anthony's deafened ears until the neocortex heard the words that worked: that Sofia had to be here and it was her duty and look at her and she will be hurt if you do what you are going to do.

"They were only dancing, Señor, and not that well," Carlos continued without pause. "She is sitting down now next to her mother and across the table and she is not looking at him. She is looking around."

Carlos kept talking quickly until Anthony stopped.

People danced and walked in front of him cutting off his view of her.

She sat there elegant and beautiful and alive and he had to keep watching and he felt blood flow to his brain again. She was striking and beautiful and sensual. He would go over and talk to her. He feared nothing.

He heard a woman's voice call out the name Carlos. He half turned his head and recognized Doctor Romona.

"Carlos, you are part of the dancing troupe who will be entertaining us later this evening?" Romona called to him.

"No, Señora Romona, I cannot dance," he replied.

"I have been watching you," Romona replied. "You have been moving along quite nicely."

"How did you recognize me?"

"I recognize *El Novio*," Romona said. "The costume is familiar."

"Yes, Doña Louisa gave it to him."

"He looks very striking in it, particularly when he dances," she said. "Please dance with me, Anthony."

Anthony looked at Romona. She smiled pleasantly at him. They danced; she turned well and before long, he was smiling and relaxed inside. Her champagned-colored dress sparkled in the light and her teeth gleamed white and he knew where Sofia got her smile.

"That's better," Romona said. "I thought you would find trouble that you would not escape. Mind you, my daughter has not behaved much better. Dance with me awhile longer."

Anthony listened carefully. He concentrated on the beat, letting it move his feet. The next song increased the pace and they moved quickly around the square, in time with the pounding of the drums. With his limited range of vision, he ignored everything else for a moment. He twirled her away from him and their hands separated and he reached out without looking and grasped onto her hand again and pulled her back to him and he looked down to apologize and saw her face, and it was Sofia.

"Sofia," he uttered. The blood rushing to his heart and to his inner core.

She radiated at him, smiling as if she had never smiled in her life. She slipped inside his arms and hugged him tightly telling him softly that she missed him so much and she was scared he would not return. He encircled her in his arms.

Sofia grabbed Anthony's hand, pulled him quickly through the crowds and led him across the square towards the bridge, which went across the river. At the foot of the bridge, a small staircase ran down along the side to the river. She leaped down the stairs and followed the small path, pulling him back under the bridge, which encapsulated them in a dark shadow created by the bright lights of the party. They were completely alone.

She reached up, taking off his mask with two hands and pressed and kissed him. They entwined passionately as if the world did not exist and they were the last two alive. They stayed close together.

"Sofia, I want to be with you."

"I want to be with you, Anthony."

"Where?"

"I don't care where. Anthony, you are mine, and I am yours."

Anthony cuddled her in his fierce embrace, releasing the primeval jealously.

"Sofia. Sofia. Sofia," he uttered repeatedly.

"Anthony, I have been so worried."

She crushed him with an intensity he had never felt.

"Worried?" Anthony said.

"I thought you might be dead,"

"Dead tired but not dead "dead"," Anthony replied.

"One of the colonel's men came and told him about seeing the American, and the colonel left. I slipped out right after him to find out more, and in the street, I heard about someone being shot. When I saw the colonel again, I tried to ask him several times but he refused to say anything. Soldiers have been coming and going from our table the entire night. At one point, the colonel sat with such a smug expression I thought you were gone from me. I was frantic to know."

"Look at me, I haven't been shot," Anthony said.

"No, my love, come closer and let me feel that you are fine so that I will believe. Please don't leave, I want you to stay here."

"I'm not leaving," Anthony said.

Sofia pulled him along the small pathway and up the river away from the party. Anthony stopped.

"We should go back and tell your mother. She will worry."

"My mother knows I am with you, and I am safe. She is enjoying herself tonight," Sofia said. "Come on. I want to be with you." She kissed Anthony again.

"Your mother and the colonel?" Anthony asked.

"What about them?"

"I know it is strange coming from me, but you need to go back, no, we need to tell him and your mother, too, that you are leaving," Anthony said.

"It will only put you at risk," Sofia said.

"That's the point. If you weren't with me, but with someone from here, you would go back and tell your mother you were leaving. It's something your mother said. We must act normal."

"What's normal about us?" Sofia whispered.

"Nothing, that's what makes it crazy, but you have to go back and say your goodbyes, and I will come with you."

Sofia nodded. She walked back up to the stairs. She tied her lacing and pressed the creases out of her dress. She walked slowly up the stairs.

"Señorita!"

Sofia saw Carlos.

"Señorita, please talk to Anthony and tell him that we must go. It is very dangerous for him here and El Jefe entrusted us with a very serious mission. I have been waiting for the right moment to pull him away, but he has been out of his head all night."

Sofia's arm had slipped under Anthony's costume; she could feel his sweat and his strong pulse, which surged through his entire body. She had to be with him, but at what cost? She slid her arm away and turned to Anthony.

"Anthony, I think," she began tentatively.

"*Mi amor*," Anthony whispered quietly in her ear, "shhh."

Anthony turned to Carlos.

"It's our riskiest move yet, coming into town," Anthony said quietly to Carlos.

"Si, Señor," he replied. "I have been worried all night long for your sake."

"Do I look happy now?" Anthony asked.

"Very, Señor."

"Then only a few moments more," Anthony said.

"It is too dangerous," Carlos stated.

Anthony bent down and whispered in Carlos' ear.

Carlos looked at him curiously, grinned and then laughed out loud.

"You are now Spanish, Señor."

Carlos slipped back into the crowd.

Anthony put his finger to her lips to silence Sofia's questions and motioned that she should return to the table where her mother was. Anthony followed her.

As they approached the table, they saw that Romona and the colonel were engaged in an animated conversation. Neither of them looked up as Sofia sat down. Anthony stood next to her.

"As I look around," Romona began, "and I see all the broken down structures that need repair, I think about how much money we spend on this war when all this wants fixing."

"I agree," the colonel responded. "This city is beautiful. It is easy to destroy treasures such as these. People will vote to give you ammunition to destroy them, but they will not pay for restoring such wondrous architecture. Guns and bullets make the public feel safe, but it brings no future value, only waste."

"If the money spent in this awful war had been employed in rebuilding these public works, what beautiful old cities we would have," Romona replied invigorated. "We would have new bridges, roads, libraries, and incalculable improvements. What else have we lost or not obtained by spending those millions in doing good, which in the last war have been spent in doing mischief?"

"I studied agricultural engineering and in moments of weakness I think about what advances we could have made to agriculture, even to raising crops on the tops of our mountains, if only the money had been otherwise invested."

"Coming from the valley of Calica, you don't realize how old these buildings are. Some date back to when the Spaniards first came."

A staff sergeant came up unexpectedly and whispered in the colonel's ear. Agitated, the colonel pushed away the sergeant and focused directly on Romona.

"I am originally from Bogotá," the colonel replied in an attempt to sound casual and conciliatory. "There are many beautiful old buildings there. They are in sad disrepair as are many old structures around Colombia."

"Sofia, you're back," Romona observed. "She studied architecture at the university. Tell us how old these buildings are."

"The buildings are very old," Sofia replied. "Mother, I wanted . . ."

"You wanted to know if we were going out dancing," Romona interrupted her. "Colonel, how about another dance?"

"I would love to, but my leg is hurting me. Give it a moment to rest and I will be up."

"The Colonel was telling me about being stationed up in the valley of Calica. He was wounded there," Romona said.

"I did not know that," Sofia replied. "I am sorry to hear it."

The colonel looked up at Anthony and told Sofia to have her friend sit down -- that there were plenty of chairs. Anthony shook his head. The colonel insisted and wanted to meet local people of the area and show that the military was not above anyone. The colonel stood up, walked around the table and held a chair out for him. Anthony sat down. The colonel returned to his seat.

"What is your name?" the colonel asked Anthony.

Anthony looked at Sofia and pointed to the place where there was no mouth.

"Don't you recognize him?" Sofia asked.

"No. Should I?"

"He is "*El Novio*,"" Sofia replied.

"*El Novio*. The name is familiar," the colonel hesitated.

"*El Novio* was a beautiful young man with long eyelashes and a fair complexion. All the girls loved him."

"He sounds lucky, but why can't he speak?" the colonel asked.

"One night as he was returning home late, the moon goddess Chia came down to earth and seduced him. The next day Chia's husband found out and wanted to kill him, but Chia intervened and saved his life, but as punishment, his tongue was cut out."

"That is a tragic story," the colonel replied.

"The legend continues," Sofia said. "*El Novio* searches for his true love because when he finds her and kisses her, his tongue will grow back. Every so often Chia returns again to the day to watch out for him and foil his attempt to find his true love."

"Chia sounds a little vindictive," the colonel said.

"You don't mess with the gods," Sofia replied.

"Well, my friend, I hope you have an easier time of finding your true love and recovering your tongue," the colonel needled Anthony.

"*El Novio*, let us go and find you a girl," Sofia exclaimed.

Sofia attempted to rise from the table; her mother motioned her to sit down.

"With our modern times, maybe *El Novio* would prefer a man," the colonel laughed.

"Colonel, please excuse us," Sofia said.

"Unrequited love makes the best tragic stories, don't you think so, *El Novio*?" the colonel directed his question at Anthony.

"I love to hear such stories," Romona broke in. "Don't you have a fairytale story from your area? When I was young medical student, I traveled widely into the different areas, doctoring the people and administering medicines. I enjoyed their stories, which made up the folklore of their community. Some of the little villages had been there for hundreds, if not thousands, of years."

"My father was a very serious man, and he did not go in for stories," the colonel replied. "I remember when our nanny used to sing to my little brother to make him fall asleep. My father stopped that. He didn't want his sons growing up speaking street Spanish."

"We lived in the capital while my husband was alive," Romona said. "Bogotá is a wonderful city."

"Yes, there's so much culture, and things to do," the colonel replied excitedly. "While I lived there, I constantly went to the theater or the opera or a new show that came to the city."

"They have excellent restaurants," Romona said.

"They have the best restaurants in the world. The best restaurant of all on the Boulevard of the Liberator was *El Castillo del Rey*. Their seafood was the best."

"We went there," Romona replied. "I remember the food and the drinks being very good. Most of all I remember the waiters being very stiff and formal, and they wore such funny costumes."

"Yes, that is the place," the colonel cried. "There they knew how to serve someone. They modeled the uniforms after the court of Queen Isabella."

"Is that the truth?" Romona said. "That's very interesting."

The colonel explained in detail the size, the shape and the fabric of the hats, the aprons, and the uniforms. Sofia grew impatient. She stood up.

"Colonel, you promised my mother a dance once your leg was rested," Sofia said. "Where are your courtly manners?"

"Yes indeed," the colonel said. "May I have this dance?"

"I'd love to go and dance with you," Romona said graciously.

They went out into the square filled with people. A new song was starting up. Sofia grabbed Anthony's hand and led them out to dance. She pulled him close. Anthony felt her moving slowly beside him. He saw a faint bead of perspiration along her upper lip. He tipped up his mask and kissed her.

"You shouldn't do that," Sofia said. "I might have slapped you."

"I thought you were going to tell me, that somebody might see me," Anthony said.

"I don't care what people think tonight," Sofia said.

"Let me kiss you again," Anthony said.

"You can kiss me as many times as you like," Sofia replied.

"You are in a festive mood tonight," Anthony said. "What have you been drinking?"

"A little champagne," Sofia said.

"We need to find you more," Anthony said smiling.

"I'll do whatever you say," Sofia said.

She started to lean towards him to kiss him. Anthony felt a tap on the shoulder. Anthony turned; it was the Colonel.

"Excuse me," he was standing there calmly with Romona on his arm. She was smiling.

"You have the honor of dancing with the doctor, *El Novio*," the colonel said.

Romona removed her arm from the Colonel's and slipped it under Anthony's saying, "May I have the next dance with you? Do me the honor."

Anthony watched as the colonel led Sofia back to the table.

Anthony looked at Romona. She had a curious expression. The band had started a new song, a waltz.

"*Doña*," Anthony mouthed with a short bow, holding his left arm shoulder height and his right arm at waist level.

"*Don El Novio*," Romona responded. She slipped inside his arms. Anthony gently laid the back of his palm in the small of her back. The music began; Anthony started with a few tentative box steps and feeling more at ease, began to spin Romona around. She was a very good dancer. She was light on her feet, had perfect rhythm and followed Anthony's lead. Anthony returned to the box steps, increasing their pace with more confidence.

"You're an accomplished dancer Anthony," Romona said.

"When I was at the University, I took a course in ballroom dancing. It included waltzes."

"A very practical course. I didn't realize they taught such courses at the University."

"Neither did I. I didn't want to take it. I had a physical education requirement, and it was the only course that fit into my schedule. However, I enjoyed the instruction immensely, and it stands out as the most practical thing I learned."

"Dancing is fun," Romona said.

"I see where Sofia receives her beauty," Anthony said.

"You are a charmer," Romona replied.

"No, I only speak the truth," Anthony said.

He glanced over at the colonel and Sofia at the table; another officer was talking with the colonel. The colonel had a very tense expression. The soldier left abruptly. Anthony smiled.

"Maybe he should take some dancing lessons," Anthony said. "I would have expected him to dance more for all the restaurants and clubs that he has been to in Bogotá."

"Let's go to the bar. I would like a glass of wine," Romona said. She held his hand, and they walked over to the bar. She ordered two glasses of wine, which the bartender quickly set in front of them.

"*Salud,*" Romona said holding her glass up and clicking it with Anthony's, who held up his.

"*Salud,*" responded Anthony. "It is very good. Why didn't you order this at the table?"

"I was watching you," Romona said.

Anthony began to respond, but stopped when he saw the look on Romona's face that showed she wanted to explain herself.

"I was watching you as any mother might who worries about your happiness and safety. Sofia can choose whom she likes, but you're not free to behave as you like, wherever you like."

"We were very close," Anthony admitted.

"If your mask comes off Anthony, you will be in deadly trouble. The colonel has this square surrounded, expecting some sort of problem. I realize that you live daily with these dangers, but Sofia doesn't. You will put her in trouble. More trouble than you, because she has neither the experience nor the ability like you do, to flee such troubles."

"I didn't think. I wasn't thinking."

"I'm not mad at either of you. You are behaving like two young people in love, and there's nothing wrong with that. It's just that you can't behave like that here."

"You think anyone else noticed?"

"No. Whereas everyone only has normal vision, a mother has x-ray vision," Romona smiled. "When we return to the table, I will find some excuse for us to leave. I don't want anything to happen, particularly on such a lovely night."

"Do you want me to leave?" Anthony asked. "I will leave immediately."

"No, Sofia will think that I ran you off for the wrong reasons," Romona said. "She's happy now. I haven't seen her this happy in a long time."

While Romona and Anthony were dancing, a young lieutenant came up to the table to speak with the colonel. The same lieutenant had come to the house earlier that day. As the lieutenant spoke, the colonel wore a hard, aggravated expression.

"I'm sorry to disturb you again, Colonel. I've been looking for you everywhere. I'm glad that I found you."

"What do you want?"

"I have information regarding the situation," the lieutenant said.

"What is it?" the colonel asked.

The lieutenant looked around and began awkwardly.

"We found out, I mean, we discovered where the Jeep came from," the lieutenant said.

"Go on," the colonel replied, clenching his jaw.

"The Jeep was hijacked by the American and another Colombian rebel," the lieutenant continued. "A sergeant was transporting a new guard up to the radar trailer. He was stopped and ordered to surrender the Jeep to them."

"Did they shoot them?" the colonel demanded.

"No, they tied them up and left them by the radar trailer," the lieutenant said.

"Why didn't the sergeant shoot the rebels," the colonel replied heatedly. "That is what we are here for."

"The rebels sabotaged the radar trailer."

"Is it functional?"

"Not yet," the lieutenant said.

"Why not?"

"The American cut wires. I've ordered the technicians to examine it."

"Can it be fixed?" the colonel shouted.

"I don't know," the lieutenant replied.

"We must have it operational," the colonel said, slamming his hand on the table.

"They are working on it, Colonel," the lieutenant responded, placating the colonel's anger.

"I must leave to see what I can do to fix this mess," the colonel replied testily to the lieutenant.

The colonel turned to Sofia.

"I was truly enjoying this evening, Senorita Sofia," the colonel said. "You must excuse me, but again, duty calls. May I drive you home?"

"Carnival only comes once a year, Colonel," Sofia responded. "I will stay here and enjoy the music. My mother will ensure that I arrive home safely. Thank you for your kind consideration."

The colonel said goodbye and left, striding quickly out of the plaza, the lieutenant on his heels.

Romona and Anthony finished their drinks and walked back to the table. Sofia was sitting alone.

"There you are, mother," Sofia said. "I was wondering where you had gone off to."

"I wanted to show some friends of mine the beautiful costume *El Novio* is wearing," Romona answered. "Where is the colonel?"

"Duty called."

"That was lucky," Romona replied.

"Mother, did you want me to go home with you?" Sofia said.

"*Mi preciosa*, I'm having a very good time to night, and I intend to stay," said Romona. "You don't need to sit and watch over me. While I was in the bar, I did see some of my good friends. I will go in there and sit and spend the evening with them. You two enjoy yourselves. Go on and dance."

"This is one of my favorite songs," Sofia cried. "Come and dance with me."

She grabbed Anthony's hand. They found a spot on the square away from the table. Sofia twirled and glided around Anthony.

"This is much better than sitting at the table," Sofia shouted above the noise. "Are you having fun?"

"This is fantastic," Anthony replied. "I've never danced out underneath the stars before."

The band played a slow song. Sofia wrapped her arms around Anthony and laid her head on his chest; they slowly moved with the music. The song ended and an upbeat meringue played. They stayed together, moving to their own rhythm. Sofia looked up at Anthony. He slid up his mask and kissed her. They enfolded, closing the world off around them.

Sofia drew her head back and positioned Anthony's mask back over his face.

"You shouldn't do that," Sofia said softly. "Someone might see you and steal you from me."

"Can we go under the bridge again?" Anthony asked.

Sofia nodded and drew Anthony through the dense crowd. They crossed over to the bridge and ran down the stairs. Sofia kissed Anthony quickly and looked at him.

"Anthony Wyatt."

"Yes?"

"Follow me," Sofia said.

She snaked them along the path by the river, coming to another bridge. The staircase was finished with rough-cut stones. She walked up quickly, her heels clicking loudly on the rock. When they reached the top of the stairs, Sofia turned left. The street was lined with cars. As they crossed one of the side streets, a voice cried out.

"Where are you going?"

Together they spun towards the voice; Anthony reached inside his robe. He relaxed, when he saw who called them.

"Carlos" Anthony replied. "I thought you wandered off."

"No, Señor," Carlos replied. "I've been keeping my eye on you in case there was trouble with the colonel."

"You see, Sofia. My benefactor watches over me, making sure that I don't get into any scrapes."

"You need someone to look after you," Sofia said.

"I think he has found someone," Carlos said.

"Anthony said that he was tired," Sofia replied. "You kept him up all night."

Carlos laughed. "It was his idea. I had to come along to make sure that he found his way."

"We were going back to my house," Sofia said, "Are you coming?"

"I am enjoying the night. Carnival only comes around once a year. I think I will stay."

"Are you returning later?" Sofia asked.

"You will keep an eye on Anthony for me?" Carlos asked.

"Yes," Sofia said with a smile.

"Then I will see him later."

She embraced the old man and watched him shuffle quickly along the side street towards the town square. When he was out of view, she turned and linked arms with Anthony. They walked down several more blocks, turning and twisting through the crooked streets until they came onto a street that Anthony recognized. Down the street stood Sofia's house. Sofia stopped and pulled Anthony close to her.

"What did you say to Carlos?"

"Nothing," he said.

"No, seriously, when we first met tonight, he was very insistent on leaving and then he just dropped it. That is not his character."

"I repeated an expression to him that he had taught me," Anthony said.

"An expression in Spanish?" she queried. "Tell it to me."

"I . . . I . . ."

"Is it dirty? And involves a woman?"

She pushed away from him.

"No. Not at all. It's what I have learned here, from you."

"Now you must tell me," she said.

"*No se puede quitar lo bailado*," meaning, 'They can't take away that you have danced.' And I know that no matter what happens in the rest of my life, I will have danced with you," Anthony said.

Sofia reached for him, hugged him fiercely, and yanked him down the street towards her door.

Gregory Arthur Solsrud

Chapter Ten – Carnaval Night

Sofia led him to the rear gate. He waited while she felt under her dress for the key.

"Let me help you find it," Anthony said, as he caressed her hips.

"I think with your help, I've dropped the key."

"Knock on the door hard. Nana will wake up" Anthony said.

"If Nana wakes up, you are sleeping downstairs."

"I found it," she said.

She touched around and found the lock in the darkness; she inserted the key and pushed open the gate. She pulled him after her. Once inside the courtyard, the danger of the street disappeared. They grabbed at one another. Anthony pulled off his stifling mask and threw it down. He encircled her with his arms and kissed her passionately. She responded fervently.

She grabbed his right hand with hers and led him along the stone path up to the back door of the house. She turned the doorknob; the door was locked. She put her finger to her lip. She reached in her dress for the key.

"Damn," she swore softly.

Anthony looked at her; he had never heard her swear before. She put her hand over her mouth, looking guilty.

"I dropped the key by the back entrance," she said.

"Clumsy," he said as he pulled her to him.

"You made me drop it," she said.

Sofia dragged Anthony towards the back gate. Sofia knelt down and patted the stone threshold with her hands.

"It's very dark," Anthony said.

"I know it is," Sofia said. "Help me find it."

Anthony knelt beside her. He caressed her hands, impeding the search.

"We will never find it this way," Sofia said.

"I guess we will have to wake up Nana," he said.

He jumped up and ran for the back door. She ran after him, grabbing him from behind.

"Don't knock," she uttered softly.

She felt herself pulled into the house as he pushed open the door.

"What?" she mouthed, realizing they were inside.

"You left the key in the back gate. I took it out and kept it, figuring that we needed it to open this door," he replied softly.

She grabbed him with her arms and kissed him, almost toppling them to the floor. They clasped, moving their hands over each other until Sofia remembered where they were and gently pushed him back.

"Anthony, be gentle," she breathed heavily. "I. . . don't know what to expect."

At that moment, Anthony realized it. He was going to know her. He had never taken anything for granted with her.

"You're mine forever, my love," he said.

She closed the door quietly taking his hands in hers and led him up the stairs.

Each stair creaked and groaned louder than any flight of stairs Anthony had ever set his foot on. When they reached the second floor, Sofia turned and put her finger to her lips as they walked along a wide hallway. She pushed open a door, behind which ran another staircase. She pulled him up these stairs. They did not creak. At the top of the stairs, she pushed a door, which opened into a landing. She crossed the landing and swung open a large wooden door elaborately carved with figurines.

Anthony had never been in her bedroom. Wide and spacious, it encompassed half the top floor. Arched windows overlooked the whole town. A four-poster bed with a canopy stood silhouetted against the light streaming in from two large bay windows. She crossed to them and opened them. Music wafted through. They heard the passionate tenor voice pour out his heart. They had not left the party; it had followed them to this room. Anthony went to her. They kissed passionately.

Anthony fumbled with the small buttons along the side of Sofia's dress. In his excited nervousness, he could not undo a single button. She slipped open the top button. He watched her as she deftly unfastened the rest with one hand. She extended one arm showing buttons along her sleeve. She undid these buttons. She did the same with her other sleeve. She turned her back towards him, pulling the sleeves off her arms. Anthony, intuitively, lifted the dress over her head, dropping it to the floor. Sofia kicked off her high heels, then bent over and unbuttoned her stockings from her garters. She rolled her stockings carefully down her legs and slipped the garters off her thighs. In one smooth movement, she spun on her toes and snapped her head, whipping her hair luxuriantly around her. She faced him, dressed in only an intricately laced corset

She wrapped her arms around him and kissed him. She pulled the zipper down on the back side of his costume and pulled the outer garment from his body. He pulled his gun from his waistband and laid it on the window sill. He sat next to it to and unlaced his boots. He pushed them off with his toes and dropped them to the floor. Anthony pulled Sofia to his lap and undid the hooks of her corset, which ran up the back. She stood up. The corset dropped to the floor.

She stepped out of the corset, revealing a perfect body. Her skin was clear and olive-colored without blemish or wrinkle. It was more than how she looked that captivated him. She moved gracefully, her shoulders erect, arching her back while she effortlessly lifted her legs. Anthony stepped back from her, holding her hand while extending his arm. He looked at her. She looked at him.

"Is there something?" Sofia asked simply.

"I have never seen anything or anyone more beautiful," Anthony said.

"You make me blush," Sofia replied.

He had found a woman with whom he wanted to spend eternity. He was hers. He stood up, lifted her in his arms and carried her to her bed.

Anthony caressed and kissed her over all parts of her body. Her skin moistened with every kiss; her muscles tightened. She tasted like fresh berries. He moved to her mouth where she met him with a fury he had never encountered, making his body pulse and throb, stretching his very skin to keep such emotion in.

She felt desire for him and nothing else. It was like dancing; at first, waiting for the right partner to ask you and then exploring one another until you both gained confidence, gliding together. And with him, there was nothing neither forced nor contrived. They moved together as one, rolling around, holding one another, their lips and hands arousing their love for one another, skin to skin, building an internal frenzy towards mutual climax. She realized that he was inside. He rolled her over on top of him. It surprised her; she had been told it would hurt, but it happened naturally. She pushed her hips against him making herself moan and gasp. His body excited her, producing sensations, intimate and stimulating. She rocked against him again and again and again, until her head exploded. She heard him cry out. They lay holding each other.

His body was hot and steamy. She shook her long dark hair, covering them and creating their own private world. She rubbed her hand over his chest and stomach, arching her back and pushing herself against him. His hands ran along her spine, sending tickling sensations to her brain. His arms and chest were so muscular, yet he was so gentle and soft with her that the more he touched her, the more she wanted to feel his touch. They twisted around the bed, each angle opening up new horizons.

They did not notice that the party in the streets had died down. Only occasional laughter could be heard from the street below. Anthony rose from the bed and walked over to the window. People were still wandering along the street. He could see the large clock tower down at the square, but could not see its face. He did not want to see it. He did not want to know the time. He went back, held her tightly, and told her how good it felt to be next to her. He lay next to her for an eternity until he awoke with a jolt.

He looked back out the window. The noise in the street had completely died down. He knew he had to return. He had never walked away from anything in his life. The 'never give up' attitude had been inculcated in him ever since he was a boy. He must learn from his father's weakness. His father never ultimately coped with that terrible internal pressure of living up to other people's expectations. Anthony wanted to live his own life, and his life was with her. She slept, pushing close to him. She must be very tired after dancing wildly on the square. He looked forward to many more dances like that, with her. He was sleepy and struggled to keep awake. He never wanted to shut his eyes again, for fear that if he would close his eyes, she might disappear. A loud bang echoed through the window.

He rose from the bed and walked over to the window. He did not see the source of the noise. There were no cars in the street. His gun rested on the windowsill. He swore softly in frustration, pulled between the duty out there, and his love in here.

He looked over at her. Her eyes were wide open looking at him.

"Anthony, I'm still here," Sofia said quietly. "I will always be here for you."

"Will I be here for you? I have duties out there," Anthony replied, pointing his arm out the window. "I feel obligated to return."

"Those obligations can wait," Sofia said.

"Yes, now that I have found you. I must find Juan and explain that to him," Anthony said.

"Juan will understand. Night is not yet away. You don't have to leave anywhere yet. Come back to me," Sofia said.

He came back to her, pulling the sheet away. He drew in his breath, stunned at her beauty.

"Are you good?" he asked.

"Yes."

"It was your first time?" Anthony asked.

"Yes," replied Sofia. "I didn't think it would feel so good."

She looked at Anthony with a soft, amusing smile and said, "I don't expect it was your first time. Men are supposed to be experienced."

Anthony laughed.

"Why are you laughing, darling?"

"When will we marry?" Anthony asked.

"Not right away. We can wait a couple of months. My mother won't mind. It will take that long to plan a wedding. I had wanted to marry in the city, where I grew up. I must be practical. It will be easier to marry here."

"Do you think we should invite the Colonel?"

"If he is still stationed here, yes. He can be your best man. I will invite the whole town and have a big party, just like tonight. The mayor will marry us on the stage in the center square. Everybody will cheer."

"I don't think the mayor can marry me; I don't have proper status here," Anthony replied.

"Silly, you will be marrying me. I will grant you special status."

"To marry, you need a marriage license. The mayor will want to see it."

"I will talk to the priest," she replied.

"You can't make getting married easy; otherwise everyone will do it."

"I will talk to the priest. He will marry us. I know he will. He married a girl to this boy, and her parents did not want her to marry. When her parents found out, they said she wasn't married. Her parents went to the priest, and he said they were. Her father was very upset and went to the court, but the court said they were married. I will listen to you Anthony. You're more practical than I am. See, you know that a priest has to marry us. I will talk to the priest."

"Come here you," Anthony said, pulling her back onto the bed. "Are you always this silly or only with me?"

"Only with you. I feel safe with you."

"Marry me?," Anthony asked.

"Is that a proposal?" Sofia asked. She sat up, turned and looked at him.

"I guess it is," Anthony said.

"With no ring and you're not even on one knee," Sofia replied. "You will need to do better than that, if I accept you." She slapped Anthony on the thigh.

"Silly," Anthony said as he sat up and faced her. "You don't know what a prize you have."

"A prize? Half the people in this town are looking for you. Mind you, it's not the gentle half. The people you pissed off have guns, big guns."

"That's the way it looks now."

"And you're shot. I'm getting damaged goods."

"I will heal. Soon, me and my big tough friends will kick those mean people out of town, and then the whole town will love me. You will be married to a hero, who likes doing things to you."

Anthony caressed her. He gently picked her up and set her in his lap, holding her tight.

"Ignore me when I say crazy things," Sofia said quietly. "I'm scared for the future."

"Don't be scared. You have me now. I'm not leaving you. Until my last dying breath, I will make sure that you're safe. Don't be scared."

"When I'm with you, I'm not."

"Good."

"Do you have to leave?" asked Sofia.

"Now?"

"Yes," she replied.

"No, but soon," Anthony said.

"I will hold you until Juan tears you from my arms."

"Juan can see the future," Anthony said aloud.

"What makes you say that?" Sofia asked.

"Many of the men come up to Juan and ask him what I thought were strange things, like whether they were going to have a boy or girl, what lottery number they should pick or where they should build their house."

"We are very superstitious people. Juan is in a position of authority. His men look up to him. It's natural that they should ask him questions."

"I understand all that. It's more than that. They believe Juan can predict the future. It's strange, but I believe it, too. Why else would he allow me to come here tonight?"

"Common sense. You're coming down to see me," Sofia said. "What else could you think? The moment I saw you, I knew my reputation wasn't going to survive."

"No. He didn't know I was coming to see you. I came down to map targets," replied Anthony.

"Map targets? Don't you think Juan has this entire town already mapped out? He probably can tell you where every pothole is in town. That's why he's so good. He plans in minute detail, and he makes a backup plan for every scenario. The regular army officers aren't as experienced as he, aren't as smart as he, and are lazy. Every time that he comes up against them, he beats them. People, including his men, instead of praising his intellect and hard work, attribute his success to some ability to prophesy."

"He knew I wanted to see you and agreed to some plan so I could sneak into town?" asked Anthony.

"I don't think it was anything that direct. Juan understands people well. He knew you wanted to come to town, and he needed, most likely, to verify that the military had not moved anything around. That's one thing the military is very good at, moving stuff. It gives them something to do. He probably doesn't know anything about us. In fact, I don't think so. What he probably does think is that you have a wide-eyed, little senorita whose reputation you wanted to ruin."

"I do." He pushed her down on the bed and straddled her. "How can I have hurt your reputation?"

"You're a man, and I'm an unmarried girl. I don't mind. I'd rather have you than my reputation."

"I will marry you," Anthony said.

"I know you will," Sofia replied. "Let's not worry about that right now, tell me how much you love me."

"I love you."

"How much?"

"More than there are mountains in Colombia," Anthony responded.

"There are a lot of mountains in Colombia," Sofia said. "You must love me a lot."

"I do."

"Do you swear it?"

"I swear it." Anthony said, nuzzling her neck with his lips.

"What do you swear on?"

"What do you mean?"

"You have to swear on something for it to work," Sofia said.

"Something."

"What?"

"I am swearing on something," Anthony said. "Something."

"Is that the best you can do?"

"I swear on our children's future," Anthony said.

"I like that. That was good," Sofia replied. "You can continue."

"I hadn't stopped."

"No, you hadn't. I wanted to let you know it was okay."

"Do you like it?" Anthony asked.

"Yes."

Anthony felt her heart beat quickly. She breathed fast. Her hips moved hard against his. Her nails dug into his back. She arched and struggled against him, gasping, until her movements slowed. Anthony stayed on top of her.

"Sweetheart?"

"You've never called me 'Sweetheart' before," Sofia replied.

"I've never felt this close to anyone before," he said.

"Good. Stay this close."

"Sweetheart?" Anthony said softly in her ear.

"Yes?"

"I do love you."

"I know you do," Sofia replied.

They quietly in the still darkness.

"Anthony," she said.

"Yes."

"I love you."

"I know you do," he replied. "Don't worry, everything will be all right."

"Anthony?"

"Yes?"

"Do you have to go?"

"Tomorrow is an important day," he replied.

"I know. Do they need you tomorrow? Don't they have enough help?"

"They need me. It isn't like a regular job where I can call in sick."

"It would be nice if you were going to a regular job, and you could call in sick."

"I'll get a regular job. I can, you know, do other things."

"I know you can, darling," Sofia replied. "You can do anything you want."

"Remember when I told you that I was hired by a security firm?" Anthony asked.

"I remember well," Sofia said. "I called you a mercenary."

"Yes, and I have never forgotten it. I always wanted to explain myself to you."

"I judged you too quickly."

"I came down because I had been here," Anthony said. "I wanted to return."

"You wanted to return? When were you here?"

"When I was in the American military, they brought us down for training in Panamá, at least that was the excuse. The army had sent the 11th division to Colombia to help your military with its counter revolutionaries, but they were getting their asses kicked. We came down to help them and ended staying about six months."

"When I was in Bogotá, I saw many American soldiers," Sofia said.

"I could have been one of them. We headquartered there and went out on local missions with the Colombian military. While we were out searching for insurgents, they would destroy the coca fields. It wasn't at all like I expected. When people grow marijuana in the United States, they grow it in some obscure place where they don't even own the land, like in a national forest or a wildlife sanctuary. If the government finds the crop, it's destroyed, but the grower isn't caught. But here, we surrounded a small village. The farmers were out tending the fields. I spoke very little Spanish then, and hardly understood the local dialect. I remember a raggedy farmer pleading with the lieutenant colonel who led the expedition. The farmer had a baby in his arms and asked how he was going to feed his family. He came up to me and pulled on my uniform with tears in his eyes. They torched the field. The man was on his knees crying.

When I was a kid growing up in Montana, I remember a couple of men in suits coming out to our farm. I was old enough to understand that they were telling my dad they were going to take away his farm and his plane. My dad cried. I always thought my dad was the strongest man in the world. He never recovered from that. He kept sliding until he could slide no further.

Well, when I saw that man crying, I thought of my Dad. I thought of how he had suffered and been humiliated. I hated those men for making my father like that, for making him leave us. It was a child's hate, which cuts deep and stays with you the rest of your life. When I saw that farmer on his knees, I understood him. He needed it, and he suffered most when it was gone. I told the lieutenant colonel that what he was doing to these people wasn't right. He said it wasn't him but his orders. I told him that the government may have the guns and the power to destroy people's lives, but it doesn't make it right.

The lieutenant colonel didn't respond. I don't know whether he understood me in my broken Spanish. He must have. From the beginning, I tried to speak Spanish. When we got back to the Colombian military base, my colonel came up and talked to me, and told me that marines don't get involved in politics. I told him that I was trained to kill people, not burn fields, and that on the next sortie, he should order me to shoot the farmer. He shook his head in understanding, and we shipped out the next day, leaving the army there to figure out the mission.

Before we left, a Colombian soldier came up to me. He told me that if more people spoke and thought like I did, things would change. I told him that I could only say what I thought was right. He gave me his name and address and told me to visit him when I got out.

"When you got out of the military, you returned to Colombia to find him," Sofia said. "You keep surprising me, Anthony."

"I didn't come right away," Anthony replied. "I stayed in the States looking for a job. I had to move back in with my mom. I had been all over the world, been trained to operate the most complex, kick-ass machinery and was in phenomenal physical shape, and all I was qualified for was cutting open boxes and stacking shelves. One night, I was drinking at the local bar, and a biker group came in. They thought they were tough stuff and were hassling everybody. They called me a jarhead. I ignored them. But then I started thinking about how I had risked my life so they could act like a bunch of apes, it got me mad. I told them it was more my cussed county than theirs because I had fought for it.

A big slob tried to pull me off the bar stool. I decked him. He didn't have a chance. He was drunk, and I had been trained by the best. His buddies moved in, I got the first couple but about five came at me and I thought here comes the ass whopping. The guy who had come in with them had stayed quiet. He hollered at them. They broke it off and left the bar. I didn't know why his biker buddies listened to him. He was wiry and had a long skinny pony tail, and I didn't think that he could whip a fly. He came over to me and put out his right hand. I saw his tattoo on his forearm, and I shook his hand. He left the bar. I heard the bikes fire up and take off."

"What was on his forearm?"

"Same thing that is on the base of my neck."

Anthony turned around and showed Sofia.

"Semper fidelis," Sofia stated. "It's latin. Always faithful."

"It's the motto of the marines," Anthony said. "I realized what I had to do. I asked my mom to lend me the money, and I bought a plane ticket down here.

When I landed in Bogotá, it was different than I remembered. Everything looked forbidding and strange; I remember finding the street where my friend had lived, and walking up to his building, a multi-story apartment house. There were a bunch of call buttons by the door but only a few of them had names, and none with his. I followed an elderly lady in the front door. The address had an 11-C on it so I figured I try the third and the eleventh floor. I walked up the stairs. It wasn't the third floor because the apartments all had letters. When I reached the eleventh floor, I remember looking outside. The staircase had these slatted blocks to allow light in. It was getting dark. I didn't have any place to stay, and I couldn't speak the language that well. The hall felt a hundred miles long until I reached 11-C. I knocked on the door, and a woman answered.

I gibbered something so unintelligible in Spanish that I didn't even understand what I had said. She threw her arms around me, greeting me like a long-lost son. She hugged me around the waist and led me to the table. She set food in front of me. After I finished eating, she led me to the bath and gave me a towel. I ended up staying three months."

"When did your friend come back?" Sofia asked.

"Late that night. I think his mom and I were watching a Spanish soap opera. She had told me it was good for my Spanish. She had an unbelievable skill at making herself understood."

"Did she teach you Spanish?"

"Yeah, she had a real talent and a lot of patience. My friend got me enrolled in a Spanish course and introduced me to his closest friends. He had been drafted and was finished with the military. He didn't like being in, but it opened up his eyes and he told me. His friends and he were organizing to change things. Slowly as I understood more and more, I got pulled into the people's pain, as he called it. Every Colombian grooved on me when I showed them stuff I could do or told them stuff I had learned. The marines had trained me well, and I volunteered and registered for every bit of education or training they would give me. I loved learning it, and I learned well. Down here I felt unique; I was valuable. His friends introduced me to other friends until I met Juan."

"How did you meet Juan?" Sofia asked.

"I was drawn to him, like a moth to light. I had heard about his exploits and how passionately he believed in his men. When I met him, I told him I wanted to be the best. I feared that if I tell anybody that that boy introduced me to Juan, the boy's family and friends will disappear."

"Do ever see him?" asked Sofia.

"No, he was killed, at least that's what I heard."

"I'm glad you told me that," Sofia said. "It doesn't change how I feel about you. Those feelings I cannot change. Knowing how you came here makes me feel better about myself."

"That you didn't hitch up with a hired gun?"

"No, I fell in love with Anthony Wyatt." Sofia said. "Settle into my arms. You haven't slept all night. I don't want you to leave, and I know you must. I don't want you hurt because you're tired."

"Every since I've been a combat soldier, it didn't matter where I was or what was happening, I never worried about being shot or even killed. It wasn't that I was trying to be brave, I just didn't care," Anthony said. "Now I do care. Tomorrow I need to come back and see you."

"Tonight you must rest," Sofia said. "Tomorrow will come soon."

Anthony moved closer and snuggled in Sofia's arms. His ear lay against her breast. He felt the soft beating of her heart and fell asleep.

She listened as his breathing became deeper and more regular; she squeezed him tight. She sat looking at the window. He needed his rest before she would let him go. She carefully slipped her arm from under his sleeping figure. She eased out of the bed, rose ever so quietly and crossed to the window.

Sofia looked out to the open. No noise came from outside. The first light had not yet tinted the sky. Her enemy was the day. If night could thwart the day, just once, he could stay with her. The day would come and take him away. She pulled the pane in. She untied the heavy curtains, which hung stiffly around the frame. She would shut out the day. Night could stay.

"Sofia," Anthony called to her from the bed. He had reached out with his hand and felt no one.

"I'm here, Anthony."

"Is the day here?"

"No, my love. The night is not yet gone."

"Come back to bed," Anthony said. "I can't sleep, unless you're next to me."

"I'm coming," Sofia said.

Sofia walked across the room to the bathroom. Anthony heard the door open and shut. He heard water running, then footsteps padded across the floor. He felt her weight on the bed and felt her hand on his side.

"Are you thirsty?" Sofia asked. "I brought you a glass of water."

Anthony rolled over, sat up and faced her. The beer he had earlier drunk now made his mouth dry. He took a glass of water from her and drank it all. He handed the glass back to her and she set it on the table next to the bed. She fluffed the pillows, lay down and pulled his head back on top of her chest. Her skin was warm.

"I've slept alone my entire life, and now I can't sleep, unless you're next to me," Anthony said.

"That's how it should be. My grandmother tells me that she misses my grandfather very much. She says that the hardest part about falling asleep is not having him next to her."

"How long were they married?" Anthony asked.

"Fifty-one years," Sofia replied. "Stop talking. You need to sleep."

"She was married a long time," Anthony continued.

"Yes, she was," Sofia replied. "She thought she was never going to marry."

"Never get married. I thought all Catholic girls got married."

"Or became nuns," Sofia replied. "She grew up in a small town in northern Spain. She says it's smaller than here. I find it hard to believe that a town could be so small."

"I grew up in the country."

"It's a good thing you left. You might have ended up like an old spinster like my grandmother."

"I thought she was married?"

"She left Spain at twenty-five. Unmarried at that age made you a spinster."

"An old spinster at twenty-five," Anthony chuckled. "They married young back then."

"Yes, she comes from a different time. When she insists on chaperoning me and not having boys over late, I understand that she looks at the world differently than I do."

"She had better not find me here or I will be in trouble. I won't be able to come back," Anthony replied.

"She knows you are here," Sofia said. "She doesn't sleep much, and she has very good hearing."

"Won't she come and knock on the door?"

"I told her you were the one, like she knew that her husband was the one."

"She is very wise," Anthony said.

"Just in case, I locked the door," Sofia said. "I don't want her walking in on us. I would be more embarrassed than she would."

"That's one reason why I look forward to getting old," Anthony said. "Old people don't care what others think of them. They don't have the time for it."

"I don't think my grandmother worries about much, and she always knew she would meet him."

"They met in Spain?" Anthony asked.

"No. In her valley of Covadonga in northern Spain, there weren't many prospects."

"Covadonga?" Anthony said. "It sounds familiar."

"At Covadonga, the blessed Virgin appeared to the last Spaniards who were about to be vanquished by the Moors. She foretold of their victory. They defeated the Moors. My grandmother believed strongly in the Virgin and went there to pray for a husband."

"Your grandfather appeared?"

"No," Sofia said, slapping him. "Not directly. Her older brother, whom she had not seen in many years, came back from Colombia to show off his new wife and baby. He had left, worked hard and ran a little business in Bogotá. His wife needed help raising their child; he asked my grandmother to come back to Colombia with them. She accepted. She went everywhere with them. They often visited the wife's family who had an unmarried older brother. My grandmother fell in love with him. My grandmother was thirty-three; nobody thought she could have children. My grandmother had my mother, and my mother had me."

"Does your grandmother see the child who she helped raise?" Anthony asked.

"Only when she comes to Colombia and visits my family," Sofia said. "She married a wealthy Colombian because she was very beautiful. They grew tired of the violence and moved to Puerto Rico. They don't come back very often."

"Puerto Rico is beautiful," Anthony said. "I've been there."

"She asks my grandmother to come and visit her all the time, and tells her how beautiful it is. But my grandmother doesn't go," Sofia said. "She worries about my mother and me and doesn't wish to leave us alone."

"She takes very good care of you," Anthony said. "She must like me. When I came earlier this evening, she made me something to eat and made up the bed downstairs to lie down."

"You were here earlier this evening?" Sofia asked, then she caught herself. "Of course, you were, how else with the costume?"

"I felt foolish in the costume when I first put it on. Then I realized nobody knew who I was," Anthony said. "I think that's why I had such a good time tonight. I didn't feel like myself at all."

"That's carnival," Sofia said. "People act crazy."

"Look at you," Anthony said. "You brought a strange man home with you."

"You started strange, but I'm warming up to you. I might even keep you."

"I came here because I've no other place to sleep tonight," Anthony replied. "I didn't want to walk all the way back."

"I should charge you to stay here," Sofia replied, "like the little bed and breakfast on the square."

"I've already paid you," Anthony said with a grin. "You can charge me more. I don't mind paying."

"You haven't paid me," Sofia replied. "In fact quite the opposite, in addition to your room charge, you're going to receive a hefty bill for all the other services that have been provided."

"If you are running a bed and breakfast, what is for breakfast?"

"Nana makes the breakfast."

"As long as you serve it to me," Anthony said. "Right here."

"You spoiled," Sofia said. "You can't have breakfast without going to bed. You haven't slept in two days."

"It's almost time to get up," Anthony said. "You pulled the curtains shut. It's very dark in here."

"It's still the night. Go to sleep," Sofia said. "Wrap me in your arms and tell me that you love me."

Anthony held her tight and whispered that he loved her, letting his eyes close.

Sometime later, Anthony awoke in a cold sweat. He had pictured himself in a middle of a field, with Sofia beside him trusting him as to where to go, with mortars and bombs dropping everywhere.

It had been a nightmare. He touched the warm back of Sofia. She was sound asleep. He pushed the blankets aside and stood up. He went over to the window; it was still dark. He dressed quickly.

"Where are you going?" Sofia asked.

"To relay the artillery strikes," Anthony said.

"I'm going with you," she said.

"No," replied Anthony strongly. "Because of me, you have become directly involved, risking not only your own life, but your mother's as well."

"You're not going out there alone," Sofia said. "I will not let you."

"How are you to stop me?"

"I'm going to ask you not to go," Sofia replied.

"I need to go."

"I will go with you," replied Sofia.

Anthony opened his mouth to argue. He saw a determination set across Sofia's face against which he had neither the will nor the desire to cross. For selfish reasons, he wanted her with him. If she was next to him, he knew she was safe. He would not let anything happen to her.

"That's how it's going to be," Anthony said.

"That is the way it is going to be," she confirmed.

"We need to leave right away," he said.

Sofia told Anthony to wait in the room while she prepared them something to bring along to eat. He gave her five minutes. He wandered around her room. He picked up her hair brush and turned it over in his hands. Knowing that it was hers gave him pleasure in looking at it. He looked at the photos that were hung on the wall. Several contained a man with a trim mustache, fair hair and blue eyes.

Out the window, Anthony heard the heavy and familiar whump-whump of Blackhawk helicopters. He peeked his head between the shades and followed their lights as they flew over the town in tight formation, they slowed and hovered in the area of town Anthony guessed contained the army barracks. As they settled to the ground, the dark silhouettes of the buildings blocked his view.

The door opened behind him, Sofia came in with his heavy backpack on one shoulder, a bag and his clothes.

"I saw your backpack leaning against the wall in the hallway and brought it up," Sofia said.

"I'm glad you did," Anthony said, pulling the pack off her shoulder. "I need to bring it. You're stronger than you look." He caressed her bicep and shoulders.

"Is that your father in those pictures?" Anthony asked.

"Yes," she said. "He was very good-looking."

"I thought he came from Italy?"

"He did. He was from Mammola in Reggio Calabria."

"Calabria? In southern Italy? But he has blue eyes and light hair," Anthony said.

"Not all clichés are true. The Normans, the Christianized Vikings who had settled in France, invaded Sicily and southern Italy and established kingdoms. My father claimed this heritage by virtue of his blue eyes and fair hair."

"The Vikings went to Italy? I don't remember reading that in the history books, not that I paid that much attention," Anthony replied.

"If you stand in front of the royal palace in Naples," Sofia explained, "and look at the statues of the rulers of the city, Roger the Second, the Norman, is the first one. His rule began the modern history in Naples."

"That must have been strange for those ferocious warriors from the north coming down to a wild, hot land in southern Italy," Anthony said.

"My father greatly admired their own flexibility. They started out aggressive, asked no quarter and gave none. They conquered and united the south and blended the various cultures, languages and faiths. With their passionate intensity, Roger and his kinsman ruled by an aristocracy of talent with understanding and tolerance," she stated.

"All starting with ambition and a lust for adventure," Anthony replied. "When we settle down, I think I'll read up on the Norsemen of Italy," he replied. "I wonder why I never heard about them."

"They didn't live long enough to secure their place in history. Who knows what they could have been, if their line had not died out. I have several books," Sofia replied, as she watched him pull his belongings out and pile them on the floor.

"Here, you can put your clothes in one of my drawers," she said.

She slid open two large drawers in her dresser, taking out several blankets and carrying them over to her closet and putting them up on a shelf. She picked his clothes off the floor and folded them neatly into the drawer.

"Does this mean that we are moving in together?" Anthony asked.

"If you want to make my Nana cry," Sofia responded.

Anthony felt for his rifle. It was collapsed and in place along the bottom of the pack; the side pockets were filled with ammunition. He pulled out three clips for his pistol and slid them into his pocket.

"Give me the food sack," Anthony said. "I will put it in my backpack."

She brought the sack to him. He picked it up. It was heavy.

"This will keep us provisioned for days," Anthony said.

"Unless we have many mouths to feed," Sofia replied.

Anthony slung the backpack over his shoulders. He followed Sofia out of the room. Before she opened the door leading to the stairs, she turned towards Anthony. She kissed him and held him tight.

"My Nana has returned to her room to recite her prayers," Sofia said. "We can go straight down and out the rear entrance."

She put a hat on his head and pulled it down tight over his ears.

"Follow me close," Anthony said quietly. "I will cross to the alley and pull the cover open. You crawl down first and I will follow you in and close it. Understood?"

She nodded her assent. They trotted down the two flights of stairs across the hallway and went out the rear door through the kitchen. Before Sofia opened up the back door, she turned to look at Anthony. He had pulled his collar up close to his face. She saw that he had his hand inside his jacket. He nodded at her. She opened the door. They exited quickly, shutting the door firmly behind them. They crossed the street. They were inside the storm sewer without seeing anyone. He followed it out with Sofia behind. He stopped when he saw the light at the end of the tunnel; the matinal sun had lit the sky but not risen above the horizon. Sofia grabbed him.

"I know a place in the river where we can cross and save some time," she said.

"Okay, walk quickly, and don't run. If anybody tries to stop us, run like the wind. Don't stop for me. I will catch up with you."

"Is that a promise?" Sofia asked.

"I'm not leaving you."

"If we separate, can you find your way back to the cave?" asked Sofia.

"Easily."

"I will wait for you there," Sofia said.

Anthony followed her out of the large drainage pipe. She turned and followed the river upstream picking her way along a small path surrounded by needled bushes.

"Wait here," Sofia said. "There is an old rope bridge crossing the river up here. I've used it many times. I will see if anybody is around."

"I don't want you going alone."

"It's safer. If someone is there, I'll come back without talking with them."

Anthony waited impatiently. Several minutes later, Sofia came back.

"No one is around. We can cross."

They walked to the rope bridge. Two thick ropes were tied between two trees on opposite sides of the river, one high and one low.

"Sofia," Anthony said. "You cross first and hide in the bushes on the other side. Then I'll cross. If you see anyone, you know what to do."

She nodded and walked out to the ropes. She put her foot up on the first rope and jumped up grasping the top rope. Shuffling her hands and feet, she crossed quickly, the rope hardly swayed. When Anthony could no longer see her, he jumped out onto the ropes. Under his weight, the ropes swayed back and forth. He let the sway fade out and started to shuttle across the river. He used the same shuffling motion as Sofia, but the ropes swung as he moved his feet. Half way across the river, the ropes swayed hard, shifting the backpack on his shoulders and throwing off his center of balance. His feet slipped off the bottom rope.

With his entire weight pulling down the top rope, his boots dipped into the water. The bottom rope, free of all weight, vibrated at the level of his shoulders. He chinned himself to the top rope and exerted mightily to bring his chest to rest on the top rope. He balanced there for several seconds and slowly lifted his right leg up to catch the bottom rope with his foot. He hooked the bottom rope with the toe of his boot. He slowly transferred his weight to his foot, pushing down the bottom rope. He set both his feet on the bottom rope; it swayed. He stayed as still as possible and let the sway dissipate. He shuffled his feet and hands very slowly and steadily along the rope, minimizing any swing. He reached the other side and jumped down from the ropes.

He stumbled into the brush where Sofia was waiting. She was laughing.

"It wasn't funny," he said, massaging his biceps.

"Yes, it was," Sofia said. "At first I was worried because I thought you were going to fall into the river and drown. When I saw you were going to make it, I could have painted your determined look of concentration."

He pulled off his backpack and laid it on the ground next to him.

"Damn, I forgot my canteen."

"I saw it lying on the floor. In the hurry, I didn't think to pick it up."

Anthony went back to the river. He bent over and cupped water into his hands. He splashed water on his face. He brought a handful back and splashed it on Sofia.

"That's for laughing at my misery," he said. "We can go now. Maybe you can find a cliff to dangle me from."

"Stand next to the river so I can push you in," Sofia replied.

Anthony moved back next to the river. He beckoned her forward.

"Wait until we reach to the waterfall," Sofia said. "The water's deeper."

They walked steadily across the mountain. Every so often, Anthony could see through the dense foliage to the town. It was quiet. They came to the small creek that ran from the waterfall. They followed it upstream, wetting their feet. When they saw the waterfall, they scaled the trail along its side. Sofia climbed behind the rushing wall of water into the cave; Anthony followed.

Carlos sat beside a fire stirring the coals; the flames from the small fire danced eerily along the dark stone walls.

Chapter Eleven–Wednesday Early Dawn

Tito watched his men file singly past him.

He thought about the fresh air and blue colors of the ocean. He missed the ocean and the smell of the salt spray. Breathing in deeply, he felt the dense air of the close jungle fill his nostrils. He coughed. The stars twinkled in the sky. He looked at his watch. It was early, and he had not slept.

"Just a little farther," his commanding voice pressed them on. "Hurry now, we don't want to be caught with our pants down."

Tito felt inside his breast pocket for his small packet of cigarillos. He picked one out, examined it in the silvery light of the moon and pressed it to his nose. After he lit it, he let the gentle smoke fill his lungs, exhaling slowly through his nostrils. He smoothed his thick mustache and ran his hand through his wavy white hair.

Mono had called him on the radio. Maintain radio silence is what Mono had told him. The military was listening carefully in this area. Mono was to come up and protect Tito's flank with more men, anti-aircraft guns, and a couple tricks. Tito laughed out loud thinking of Mono; he was a true *paisano*, always a trick up his sleeve.

Since Tito joined up with El Jefe, they were becoming as famous as Mono. Tito's men had suffered three deaths and a few minor injuries unrelated to battle. The politicians and drug lords now called on Tito. The papers named him Colombia's most learned rebel leader. When they won here, Tito would have his own seat at the table when the government negotiated for peace; he would soon be wearing more gold than Mono.

Maybe there was something to the myth now growing up around El Jefe Juan. He definitely knew how to fight. At first, it was hard to trust him. He was different. It should not matter, Tito told himself; his ancestors were from Spain, like most Colombians. There were very few pure indigenous people left. They were all mixed people, Spanish, Indian, American, and European.

Checo, with several days growth of beard, stood off to the side, waiting on him. Tito had good men, he thought. To win, you needed good men. He blew out the last of the smoke from his lungs, field stripped the cigarette, and motioned him to come closer.

"Yes, Tito," Checo said quietly, after he walked over and stood directly next to Tito.

"A little farther and we will be at the reconnaissance point," Tito said. "I don't want everyone spread halfway across the fields. Group the men close so when I give the order to move, we all move together."

The tall soldier winced slightly, but said nothing.

"All right, Checo," said Tito, staring intently at Checo. "Tell me what you're thinking."

Checo thought carefully before he spoke. He had spent much time fighting with Tito. He respected his skill and his temper. Still, he had to say something.

"I don't like it," the tall soldier began slowly. His eyes darted around as if looking for the right words. "We're leaving the protection on this ridge. We've been swinging from bush to bush to get down," his voice stopped.

"We won't be going back up that way. Once we join up with Mono, we can drive with him down a regular road," Tito replied.

"Yes, but if something goes wrong, we're dead sons of bitches," Checo spat his words out.

"Nobody's going wrong now," Tito replied, catching himself. "I mean, nothing's going wrong now." He softened his voice, not to calm the tall soldier, his second-in-command, but to calm himself. "Our asses have been in tighter spots. We have the advantage, and it's time to push back the *federales* a bit. Besides, we have to stick our heads out of our holes every once in awhile." Tito tried to smile, but he felt tense. All he could muster was a friendly grimace.

"Get us through, Tito, just get us through." Checo looked at him intently for several seconds and trotted off quickly to reach the front of the line of the troops.

Tito gazed across the small plateau. It offered an excellent defensive position; a small ridge formed a lip along the perimeter of the plateau. The outcroppings of rock dotting the ridge shielded the artillery pieces within the natural stone enclaves. They could hold off the entire Colombian army from up here.

The area offered little covering vegetation, having been burned clean by the farmers. The new sugarcane crop was knee high. The men fanned out, moving quickly to the rocky ridge. As his men walked along the fields, their boots became black with the burned ash. He told his men to avoid tramping the sugarcane.

Back towards the cliffs, the first of Raphael's group and the slow, sure-footed mules lugged the heavy artillery through the sparse vegetation. They soon arrived at the edge of the plateau, looking over the mouth of the valley where the main road could easily be seen. The men, without instruction or fanfare, unpacked the mules and assembled the guns.

His men buzzed with the oncoming excitement of the fight. They could be down the slope and cut off all retreat down the valley. Tito set up a command post near a group of tall standing rocks, which reminded him of a ring of church spires. Tito was ready; he had his men in position. To the east, the sun started breaking the horizon.

"The main road is quiet," Raphael commented. "Not one vehicle since we've been here."

"The army slipped out under the cover of the night," another solider retorted, "and El Jefe and the others are in the town sleeping off the big party."

Tito laughed to ease the tension.

"The colonel probably moved out his troops as we slithered along the ridge," Tito said. "When the attack starts, the remnants will scurry along the road."

They watched the road in silence.

"What time was the attack?" Raphael asked.

"When we hear the bombardment start," Tito said.

Tito looked up the valley towards the town. The valley angled abruptly, cutting off a view of the town. He thought about radioing El Jefe, but remembered Mono's admonition about radio silence. The military monitored all the frequencies and could easily triangulate their position. He would wait.

"I wish something would start," Raphael said, "The waiting is killing me."

"The worst part of the attack is the wait before it begins," another soldier added.

"It will start soon enough and then you will not be able to wait for it to be over," Tito said.

Checo came running up to the command post, ducked between the rocks and stood next to Tito.

"We are in position," Checo said. "I don't see Mono."

"He will be here shortly," Tito replied.

"I don't see anything at all," Checo responded. "No soldiers, no vehicles, nothing."

"Mono is coming," Tito replied. "We are nervous."

"Yes, that is what I thought," Checo continued. "We haven't seen a single car come down the valley road since we've been here."

"That is odd," Tito said. "That is very odd."

"Yes, and I don't like it," Checo rejoined. "I think we should retreat immediately. Something is wrong."

"El Jefe will come through," Tito said. "I know you have your doubts about him, but he is a good man."

"I'm not worried about El Jefe," Checo said. "Our whole attack is hinged upon Mono's information that the colonel is moving his forces out. The army is not moving."

"You've seen nothing on the road?" Tito asked.

"Nothing. They must have set up a roadblock close to town. I keep thinking if they set up a roadblock to keep people in, it means they're not leaving. With no plans to leave, they must believe that they are being reinforced," Checo finished.

"Reinforcements mean they're planning an attack," Tito said. "So we sit here and wait for it."

"The Army only attacks when they know they can win. I keep thinking, why do they think they can beat us, when they don't know we are even here," Checo said.

"They still cannot attack us, unless we bring ourselves down off this ledge and into the unprotected valley, where we have no cover," Tito replied.

"We must break radio contact, and find out if El Jefe has moved out from his positions into the valley," Checo said.

"Even if the government has twice the amount of troops inside, it is still not enough," responded Tito.

"Unless they bring reinforcements up the valley," Checo replied.

"Reinforcements cannot arrive in time," Tito said. "We don't see any. We have an excellent defensive position. We will wait here, besides I need to speak with Mono before we move."

Checo signaled to a man standing nearby. A radioman came forward.

"You know my thoughts before I do," Tito said to Checo. He tried the radio, using different frequencies and codes. It was complete radio silence.

"Now that is strange," Tito said. "Mono always listens. It is very strange that he is not returning a radio call. Maybe he needs help or is surrounded," Tito said in desperation.

"We have heard nothing," Checo said. "If they are attacking him, we would see something, trucks going on the road, helicopters flying overhead and explosions across the plains. He would be on the radio calling you."

"Mono's not coming," Tito said.

"I did not want to say it because I know how much you love Mono,"

Checo replied. "We had the better protection until . . ."

"Until we came out onto this ledge and backed ourselves up against a steep cliff," Tito finished the sentence.

As Tito was about to give the order to retreat, he heard the rumble in the sky from heavy bombers. Tito looked straight up, the beautiful clear sky giving him excellent visibility. He saw them flying in a tight formation, wingtip to wingtip. Damn these clear skies, he thought, allowing him to watch his own personal destruction in slow motion, feeling the vibrations in the air as the two thousand pound bombs accelerated at twice the speed of sound towards him, the target of some thoughtless laser guided system.

"We've been sold out," Checo said.

"I swear to God," Raphael said, "if we survive, Mono will not breathe anymore."

"Then survive," Tito said. His eyes swept the fields. There was little cover, only nubs of sugar cane as far as he could see.

The bombs started to fall. They landed in front of them, below the edge of the plateau, throwing large chunks of the mountain on top of them. The noise deafened them. He shouted at his men to fall back. Many of them ran in circles disorganized and confused. The experienced or lucky ones crawled under whatever rock they could find. Tito cursed Mono at the top of his lungs. Someone had to survive. Someone had to tell.

As he ran, he stumbled over a body. It was Raphael. His shirt was stained red. His face was white. He bent down and cradled Raphael in his arms, trying to lift him.

"Tito," Raphael rasped.

"Raphael, we can make it," Tito pleaded. "Stand up."

"I can't stand," Raphael said.

"Yes, you can," Tito responded, "You must come with me."

"There is nothing left of me to save, Señor," Raphael wheezed. "Save yourself."

Raphael weakly pushed away Tito's arms. Tito gently let Raphael fall back to the ground.

The next wave of bombs fell, decimating another section of the plateau. Pieces of artillery, lined up perfectly for an offensive strike, vanished in the bombs' blasts. As if he were watching an approaching thunderstorm, destruction rained slowly towards him. The earth shook as his body was thrown high into the air.

He landed hard on a mound of dirt. His calf hurt, and he gasped for air. Over the plateau towards the mountain, he saw several of his men running as if the devil was chasing them. They had no backpacks and carried no weapons. Most of them were without helmets. He called out to them. They did not hear him.

He felt himself pulled up. He looked. Checo was carrying him over his shoulder, running towards the mountain.

"Checo," Tito called with all his strength. "Stop running."

"Tito, you're weak, I must carry you."

"No," said Tito, "set me down. That is an order."

Checo stood still, then reluctantly set Tito on the ground.

"Listen to me," Tito said. "Don't run. Stay here."

Tito coughed hard. He spat blood onto the ground.

"We've survived this wave," Tito rasped. "The next one will fall exactly to where you are running."

"I don't understand," Checo said.

"There is no time to explain," Tito said, "Follow me."

Checo looked at him.

"Move now," Tito screamed.

Checo jumped. Tito stumbled forward towards the old command post and threw his body behind the tall rocks.

The next wave of bombs fell, destroying the remaining part of the plateau. Instinctively, he covered his head with his arms as dirt and rock landed on him. He looked out over the plateau they had triumphantly crossed an hour earlier; no one was running. Bodies were strewn all over. Injured men moaned. Several men stumbled drunkenly around, miraculously surviving the bombardment but shocked into a walking unconsciousness.

He saw Checo stagger towards him.

"We've survived," Tito called out.

"What?" Checo shouted, pointing at his ears.

"Don't worry," Tito said, "Your hearing will come back."

Tito tried to rise to clap Checo on the back, but his body did not respond. Checo slid his arms under Tito and helped him to a sitting position.

"Stay calm, Tito," Checo shouted. "I'll carry you out of here."

Tito smiled. Checo always thought of others first. Checo's ear was close to his mouth.

"Check the other men," Tito yelled.

Checo grinned uncomprehendingly. At least, some on his men survived, thought Tito.

As he held onto Checo's arm and fought to breathe, he heard the high whine of jet engines coupled with the rhythmic throbbing of helicopter blades. A tight formation of three helicopters flew quickly towards the plateau. As efficient as crop dusters, they covered the open fields with automatic fire. The screaming pieces of metal tore apart the walking wounded and strafed the bodies of men who could feel no more. They circled the plateau three times and set down along the outside edge.

Tito watched from afar, as each helicopter disgorged its platoon of men.

The groups quickly assembled and moved through the destruction. Single shots rang out across the plateau.

This is my last stand, Tito thought, surrounded by church spires. No, from here, they looked like the statutes on Easter Island. He had been there many years ago when he was still in school. He was going to die with the ancients. No, the rocks looked like dildos or the spiky hair on his grandson's head. He laughed at the thoughts of watching him bumble around on the patio behind his house.

He looked over at the soldiers fanning across the craters and dirt. They walked too casually with their rifles held loosely, their short sleeves showing off their naked tanned forearms. Every so often, one would reach down and pull something off a body or take something out of a pocket. Stupid, Tito thought. They relied too much on their powerful weaponry. He turned and looked around for a rifle.

Tito heard moaning. He saw one of his men stirring. He pulled himself with his arms close to him. Blood trickled from his ears. Tito slapped his face; the eyes fluttered. He recognized the boy; his name was Kermin from the south near Pasto. He had told Tito that he had seen Galeras erupt. Tito was fifty-eight, and he had never seen a volcano erupt. He had had a long life and seen many things, but seeing a volcano erupt was not going to be one of them.

"*Hijo*," Tito said gently, "wake up."

The boy's eyes opened.

"*Mi Jefe*," he muttered.

"Pull yourself up and bring me those two rifles over there."

Tito pointed to two bodies that still had rifles strapped to their backs. The boy, Kermin, removed the rifles from the dead men and quickly loaded them, handing one to Tito.

He heard a scrapping noise behind him and looked over his shoulder. Checo was dragging a rocket launcher and a fifty-caliber machine gun through the rocks.

"Kermin, set that gun up," Tito said.

The boy crawled over, pulled apart the tripod stand and mounted the gun in the space to the right of Tito. Checo returned with ammunition. The boy helped Checo load the big gun.

"Kermin," Tito said quietly, "Lay yourself between those two rocks on my left and hold your fire until I shoot."

The boy nodded.

The first platoon had stopped and was drinking from their canteens. The sound of their voices carried to him, but he could not make out any of the words. Tito saw a young lieutenant come jogging back from one of the helicopters and shout at the men. They hooked their canteens back on their belts, shifted their guns to fire ready and moved forward en masse.

Tito looked at Checo who had lined up the automatic gun on the group. He tapped him on the shoulder and signaled that he was going to fire first and take out the lieutenant. Checo grinned in understanding.

Come on. Come a little closer to your uncle Tito, he said to himself. He would not be seeing any volcanoes but neither would they. This was the way to fight a war, face to face, bullet for bullet, instead of the unknowing bomb distributing death anonymously. He saw the round insignia over the left breast of the lieutenant, the name Perez in black, capital letters over three light green waves against a sea of black. He pulled the trigger.

The gun roared across the plateau.

With the bark of the Checo's big gun breaking his eardrums, Tito watched Perez stumble backwards and fall over unmoving. The first soldiers in line spun by the weight and speed of the heavy bullets tumbled like drunken partygoers to the scorched earth. The other soldiers, quicker and luckier, dropped and hugged the uneven ground.

Tito raised his gun and fired haphazardly at the platoons scattered in the distance. Without raising to his haunches, he couldn't tell whether he hit anything. Checo's gun stopped firing and the sound of the first return volley zinged off the rocks.

These stones formed a perfect bastion. Their obtuse angles giving Tito an excellent angle of fire and sight, while affording only the narrowest of gaps for a return shot, they could hold out as long as their ammunition did. He looked over and saw Checo had departed. Tito clicked the gun to single fire and pinged a few bullets in the dirt where the soldiers lay. That would keep their heads down. They should have more sense than to attack them directly. They would order up a trench mortar. It would be easy with a trench mortar.

Tito thought about the planes again and felt naked in between those rocks. Like the flayed animals on the spit that he had become accustomed to eating in the field, he was exposed as they. They loved their planes and their helicopters. If the helicopter comes, I will have an answer for that, he thought, feeling down and rubbing his left hand against the rocket launcher. He coughed, trying to clear the heaviness in his lungs. His coughs followed one after the other without being able to control them. His chest jerked in spasms until he felt a hand smack his back hard, arresting the seizures in his chest.

The lip of a canteen was being shoved in his mouth. The cool water soaked his dry mouth. He swallowed. The old ones who fought with him carried cut-up coca leaves in their pouches. When the trail grew steep, they slipped them in their mouths and chewed slowly. He could use a coca leaf. He sank his head onto the wet ground where the water spilled. The mud cooled his face. He breathed slowly.

"Tito?"

It was Checo's voice.

"I'm resting," Tito said. "Did you find much?"

"Do what?" Checo said. He brought his ear close to Tito's mouth.

"Did you find much?" Tito asked again.

"We can stay here for days," Checo said.

Tito laughed again. He controlled it so as not to send his body into spasms again. Days inside these dildos were more than he could stand or more than he had. He had hoped to see the sea once more before he died. He had grown up on the sea in that sprawling mess of a town, Barranquilla. There, they knew how to celebrate *Carnaval* with parades and *flotas* and dances. And the Caribbean women were the most beautiful in all of Colombia.

"Kermin, you are from the south. You have never been to Barranquilla. Promise me that you will go to Barranquilla."

"I will go, *Jefe*," the boy responded. "I have heard you talk of that city. Is it true that every woman there is more beautiful than Miss Colombia?"

"Yes, and when you tell them that Tito sends you, they will kiss you and want to take you home."

"That would be most pleasant, *Jefe*," the boy replied. "I would like to have a girlfriend."

"You will have many girlfriends in Barranquilla. I will make sure of that."

Checo fired. The repeating rifle echoed many times over within the rock walls.

"Save your bullets," Tito said.

"The whore-monger tried to crawl back," Checo said.

"Did you hit him?" Tito asked.

"No, the obscenity kept his ass low. I only kicked up dirt."

"*Jefe*," the boy asked.

"Yes," Tito asked.

"When will Mono come?"

"Mono?" Tito said. "*Que barbaro.* He will not be coming."

"But if we can stay here for days," the boy began. "He will have time to come."

"What talk," Tito said. "We will not be here to wait for him. He has lined his pockets with our deaths."

He heard the boy sobbing quietly. He lifted his face out of the mud and rolled over to his side facing the boy.

"*Hijo*," Tito said. "I could talk to you about honor and duty and patriotism, and they are all great things. You have heard me speak often of our fighting golden rule."

"*Si, Señor*," the boy said. "We can never submit."

He stopped speaking as there was a great hammering of fire against the rocks. They exploded several rifle grenades against the granite outcroppings, none breaking the protection within their sanctuary. The firing stopped.

"Kermin, do you believe in God," Tito asked.

"*Si, Señor*," the boy responded.

"Then it don't matter what you've done, there's only two kinds of people, saved and lost. You're part of the saved, you're going to a better place."

A voice shouted from across the way.

"*Rebeldes*," the voice came from just beyond where they had engaged the first platoon; the reserves must have moved up and supported them. "Throw out your weapons, or we will send the helicopters after you."

"What did he say?" Checo said.

"He said that he wants to date your mother," Tito said loudly.

"Bastard," Checo grunted and he let a burst of automatic go after the soldiers.

"You will pay for that, *rebeldes*," the voice shouted again.

"I wonder what he wants, and why they don't attack us," Kermin said.

"They are scared of you, my son, and they don't want to hurt themselves," Tito said. "They think they can call us out, and we will surrender."

"No, they want your head, Tito," Checo said.

"So you heard that," Tito said.

"Yes, the ringing stops every once in a while and I can hear again," Checo replied. "I saw them checking the faces, Tito. They are looking for you. A hundred million pesos for your head."

It was a dirty war, no, a grisly war, of taking heads and torture and reprisals and the slaughter of innocents, Tito thought. For years, he had lived by stealth and wits, rarely sleeping in the same place. The *federales* feared him. And what was it worth, a hundred million pesos, for his buddy Mono?

They did not deserve this beautiful land of the *indigenes*. Look at those beautiful trees, vines of flowers prospering among its branches and the sugar cane growing when no one watches it. We are truly in a garden of Eden, but instead of God sending a snake, he sent us. We are the snakes who poison the garden and corrupt the innocents.

"What does he mean, *Jefe*?" the boy Kermin asked.

"They do not want to waste more bullets on us," Tito replied. "We are not worth it. Keep your gun up and we will show them what a dear price comes with our lives."

"You've had your chance, *cobardes*," the voice called.

Tito saw a man scurrying back towards the helicopters, keeping himself low from crater to crater. He squeezed off a single shot in that direction, and the man disappeared. The obscenity of his mother must be crawling among the corpses, his nostrils filled with the stink of his deeds, obscenity himself, Tito thought. Those were my men, are my men, and today I will join them, but not before I bring more of these *hijos de putas* with me.

Lying here in the mud and the burnt dirt, Tito finally understood Juan and his power over the men. The government had their machines and fancy weapons and depended on them. It was not weapons that won, but what was inside, that was what you could not beat out of a man.

Tito thought about the little town of San Jose. They had been met on the outskirts and were asked to respect the pueblo's wishes and pass around the perimeter. In his arrogance, he said he would pass on the road through the middle of the town. As he walked through, he was humbled. All of the buildings, the play lot and the square were all named after dead martyrs, all killed by different warring factions, but the town struggled on -- more than struggled, it survived. He never passed by that town again, purposefully avoiding it in his campaigns to isolate it away from the struggles, and hoping that it would outlive them all as a symbol of what Colombia could be.

"What is that noise?" Checo asked.

Tito looked up. The long finger wings of the helicopter were initiating their spin. He was still fascinated by the plodding start of these fantastical machines. Soon enough, the blades were in full cycle, whirling faster than the eye could separate the four parts.

"The bird of prey is about to set down upon us," Tito said.

He heard the boy recite the Our Father and the Hail Mary in quick succession.

"Your uncle Tito still has a few tricks up his sleeve," Tito said to the boy. "The time for prayers will come later."

"Checo, move towards the middle and load the launcher," Tito commanded.

Checo obeyed.

"Don't fire until I tell you, no matter how much you feel it is right," Tito said.

"I will await your order, until this gun has more life it in than I," Checo said.

It came down to good men. Over there, the *cabron* could not order his men to follow him to insure their own self-preservation. Tito's *compadres* followed him until death.

"Stay low, and don't give those bastards a shot at you," Tito said.

He found it difficult to swing around and look at Checo. His upper body had tightened up. He wished for a coca leaf to give him some freedom.

The helicopter rose slowly off the ground and circled until it hovered, pointing straight at them.

Tito looked up at the granite spires. Hold you sons of dildos, he whispered.

The helicopter let loose its Gatling guns. The soft bullets plunked against the hard igneous rock. The metal that did not hit the outer surfaces zinged harmlessly skyward against the upward sloping inner contours. The sound reminded Tito of the sandblasters used to clean the cathedral of Cartagena in the Plaza Bolivar. What a fine sight that cathedral, with its thick fortress exterior and cool inside even on the hottest of days, it is no wonder that the early peoples, before air conditioning, loved to attend church. He himself would have been an avid churchgoer, maybe even a priest or a monk.

"Tito, look they are shooting their men," Checo exclaimed.

Tito propped himself up and looked out, the ricochets were carrying directly back onto the platoon's position, the metal flicked up the dirt like raindrops on a muddy puddle. Tito laughed, this was better than coca leaves. He laughed harder as he saw the men wiggling backwards to escape the death of their own fire. His chest seized as he laughed harder, he shoved his face into the mud to stop the spasms. This is too good, he thought. I must remember to thank God for his sense of humor.

The man who had called out to them was now on the radio to the pilot.

"For the love of Christ, stop the firing, you're killing us along with the rebels," the captain shouted into the radio.

"Shall I fire the rockets, *Capitan*?" the pilot replied.

"Hold your fire, I believe they are all dead inside."

Tito heard the guns stop. He told the others to shut their mouths and hold their fire.

On the other side, the second officer scrambled over next to the captain.

Tito saw someone scurry into the crater directly in front of him. You crawl very quickly little crab, he said to himself, but next time, I will be ready for you when you poke your head out of your little hole.

"You, soldier, advance forward and bring me the rebels," the captain ordered.

He addressed his order to the second officer. The second officer looked forward at the dead bodies of his comrades; the other dead lieutenant his friend Chente Perez, lay face up fifty meters in front of him, his uniform stained black red from where the bullets had ripped apart his chest.

"I do not think the rebels are dead," he said quietly, without looking at the captain.

"They are dead," the captain shouted. He shouted expletives at the second officer and ordered him to move forward.

"I will move forward under your direct order, but under protest, *Capitan*," the second officer replied. The second officer was a young lieutenant named Oliver Castellana.

"You," the captain directed his ire at the sharpshooter to the right of the lieutenant, "will you not move forward?"

The sharpshooter kept his gaze forward and said nothing.

"Can't you hear me?" the captain hollered, spewing forth spit and his face red.

"Yes, *Capitan*," the sharpshooter said.

"Move forward, then."

"I don't want to," the sharpshooter said.

"Do you want me to shoot you?" the captain shouted.

"No," the sharpshooter said quietly, staring at the ground.

I had better intervene, the Lieutenant Castellena thought. We have these rebels surrounded and now we will be shot by a captain full of himself and his medals. He had been with this captain before; the captain was extremely proud of his training with the Americans and the *Lanceros*; they had pinned many medals on his chest. He had cloth patches made to put on his khakis to display his prowess. It was easy to win medals when the people shooting at you weren't trying to kill you. He is going to kill us all, the lieutenant thought, unless I do something. He looked up at the captain who had pulled out his gun and was aiming it at the sharpshooter. The captain's face was blood red and he was swearing terribly.

It was bad enough that there had been so much blood shed on the first day of Lent. The lieutenant would have to tell the family of his friend Perez that he died, but he would have to lie about how he died. Instead of telling that he died looking for the head of a dead rebel leader, who now was holed up laughing at them and making life a literal hell, Castellana would have to invent some romantic story about how Chente sacrificed himself for the good of the corps. Why couldn't these rebels just give up and die easily? The captain only made it worse by shouting such blasphemies against the holy family. The young lieutenant was a devout Catholic and he crossed himself.

"*Capitan*," the young lieutenant said, "please don't shoot him. I will go forward."

"Finally, a soldier among the spineless," the captain yelled, swearing again.

"Yes, I am the only *Lancero* here," Lieutenant Castellana replied.

"What did you say?" the captain said.

"Nothing," the lieutenant replied.

"You don't think I have courage to go myself?" the captain said.

"I did not say that, *mi Capitan*," the lieutenant shouted.

The lieutenant knew that word *Lancero* would provoke the captain. Whenever the captain came back from special training, he complimented the soldiers by calling them *Lanceros* when they had done something stupid and courageous. Those that came back from special training loved to talk about killing, but to the lieutenant they seemed stupider on the battlefield. Their specialized training convinced them that they could not be killed by ordinary weapons, as if some superpower had been given them, making them immune. The lieutenant's friend Chente Perez was lying face-up in front of him as evidence that the rebels' bullets did indeed kill and would continue to hit them as long as they offered them targets.

The captain was now waving the gun at him and swearing, shit, maybe the lieutenant should walk out there, better to be shot by a rebel and earn a medal and a pension for his mother than to be shot in the back by superman *Capitan*. He probably put on his cape to get it hard for his mistress. The lieutenant turned his face away from the captain and smiled, the *Capitan* was probably impotent without his cape.

The captain was talking about *Lanceros* again, God he loved that word, but to the lieutenant it made him think of a half naked native running around with a spear. He would rather have his ass hunched down behind a rock with an automatic machine gun in his hand. Fuck himself and let the captain shoot him in the back, he was not going out there to be killed. Let the captain use his magic cape against the rebels' real bullets.

"All of you are cowards and have no right to wear the uniform," the captain said. "We have dead rebels surrounded and none of you have the *cojones* to move forward. I would not have you with me in a real firefight. When we return, I will report all of you."

The captain swore loudly and jumped up and called out.

"*Muertos! Rebeldes! Aqellos de chupa sangre de nosotros Patriotas,*" he said. "Dead ones! Rebels! To those who suck the blood from us Patriots."

Tito had to hold his mouth to keep from laughing aloud. How does one allow such a buffoon in the army? Such a load of garbage from this blueblood. The colonel screamed obscenities as he strutted forward. Tito almost felt sorry to end this spectacle. He gently squeezed the trigger, and a single shot escaped. It caught the captain in the middle of the forehead, and he dropped forward heavily, his raised right hand releasing his pistol, which bounced off the dirt and landed on top of the body of a dead rebel.

The platoon answered the single shot with a ferocity of fire not yet seen on such a small target. The lieutenant radioed the pilot who had remained hovering in a fire-ready position. The pilot lined up the unguided rockets through his fixed gun sight and in a smooth cadence, expended all of his rockets against the rebels' position. The geologic dike, standing alone for millions of years after the neighboring rocks had weathered away, stood firm against the human onslaught. Chips and chunks broke off in places where a natural seam, opened by centuries of rain, allowed the massive towers of rock to splinter. Lieutenant Castellana called a ceasefire. He radioed the helicopter pilot to fly over the target and shoot down into the rocks.

Tito lifted his head up and shook the dust and chunks of granite from his hair. His chest still hurt badly, but he felt no other pain. These rocks truly are dildos, Tito thought. And they have protected us better than dildos protected by condoms. This thought made Tito laugh. By nature, he was not vulgar man, but this war brought out vulgarity.

"Boy," Tito called out softly. "Speak to me if you are alive."

"I am, *mi Jefe*," the boy said proudly. "Do you want me to shoot back?"

"Nay, hold your fire. I am interested to see what these clowns do next," Tito said. "Checo? Are you still with me?"

"He is moving, Señor," the boy Kermin responded.

"I can't move so well," Tito said. "Go to him and make sure he is ready with the launcher. I see they are going to fly the helicopter at us."

"He sees the helicopter, *Jefe*, and he is ready," the boy said quietly.

The giant insect leaned forward with its nose pointed to the ground, inching its way closer to the rock towers. Tito rolled over on his side to look over at Checo and up towards the heavens. Tito saw the helicopter rotate its guns downward. As the Plexiglas nose of the helicopter cleared the front spires, Checo lifted the launcher skywards, sighted in quickly and pressed the trigger. Tito heard the hiss of the rocket and the loud explosion as the cockpit dissolved in fire. The great machine fluttered like a kite caught in the wind and spiraled towards the earth. Tito heard a loud noise but saw nothing as the helicopter crashed on the downside of the cliff, tumbling earthwards towards the jungle floor below.

"*Rebeldes*," Tito mimicked, shouting loudly, "come and join us now, or join us in death."

Tito laughed. What further death will they visit upon themselves today? They had their machines and fancy weapons and depended on them; they had lost many by their stupidness. A trench mortar would have been simple. He feared to let his laughter go, as bad as his chest hurt. He could not survive another spasm. He did not need any coca leaves. He sighted down his rifle, maybe he could pick off one more of these *gallenas* to take with him.

Lieutenant Castellana heard the laughter and had had enough. He ordered his platoon to fan out and surround the rebels' position and maintain constant fire to pin them down. They were not going kill any more soldiers and then slip into the jungle and disappear. He had called on the radio and ordered a helicopter to shuttle up a trench mortar and extra ammunition.

Tito heard the bullets tear off the rocks in every direction. So this was the end; they finally have someone who will finish it. He was relieved. His chest had stopped hurting him. He did not want to black out and force Checo to shoot him, although that would be the humane thing instead of letting them take him alive. Better a quick bullet in the head than a face to boot meeting with the army's counter-intelligence unit. How many years was he? Yes, Fifty-eight good years, he was ready to die.

"Kermin," Tito said. "Are you wounded?"

"No," the boy said.

"Then I want you to slip out between the rocks and escape down the cliff," Tito said.

"He cannot leave. They have circled around the back side," Checo said.

"Move your gun over, and I will provide cover from this side," Tito said.

"I will not leave you, Señor," the boy said. "It is better to die on your feet than live on your knees."

"We are going to die with our faces in the muck," Tito said. "It is better for a young man to live."

"You have taught me much. I am not afraid to die with you," the boy said.

A mortar exploded twenty meters in front on them. Tito screamed at them to blast away at the ones sending them to their deaths.

"In the name of the Father, The Son and the Holy Spirit, Amen," the boy Kermin whispered to himself while he fired. Another mortar exploded just in front of him. He concentrated hard on the Apostle's Creed, but could only reach 'conceived by the Holy Spirit' when a mortar blast evaporated his body from this earth.

The flash blinded Checo, making him seize the fifty caliber in a death grip, the torrent of bullets flying heaven bound as he slumped on the stock, pushing the muzzle up. Tito, whose face was stuck in the mud, fingered the cross and beads around his neck and repeated the comforting devotions over and over.

The men firing the mortar continued loading and sending the small "thumphs" towards the rock spires, but no one there knew it. Lieutenant Castellana ordered his men to shovel a shallow trench forward to where they could throw grenades inside the rocks. The first grenade bounced off and landed close to the thrower almost taking him to the same place as the rebels.

The lieutenant called a young soldier forward who was much known for his arm. He lobbed a grenade neatly inside the stone fort. Under orders from the lieutenant, he lobbed grenades until several soldiers crawled along the sides. These soldiers fired their automatic weapons into the mess of deformed bodies, broken rocks, and sulfur stinking, red-stained dirt, before the lieutenant would venture close and peek his head into the crest.

No one was recognizable in the sanctuary. Lieutenant Castellana would have no head to carry back to his superiors and Mono. They needed a head for the reward, with no head, no reward. There was going to be hell to pay on his return. He should cut off the head of the *Capitan* and bring that back.

He ordered his men to scoop up whatever parts they could wrap in plastic and load it all on the helicopters.

Castellana walked away from there, not wishing to see his orders carried out. He trudged over and knelt next to his friend Chente Perez, folding the now stiff arms across the torn-up chest and closing the eyelids over the sightless eyes. Castellana bowed his head.

"*Uno no se muere cuando debe, sino cuando puede,*" he said to himself, the words of his countryman, Gabriel Garcia Marquez, coming to him instead, of his sacred rosary: "A person doesn't die when he should but when he can."

Chapter Twelve-Wednesday Dawn

Inside the cave, Carlos rose and greeted them as they entered.

"I didn't expect to see you so early," Carlos said.

"Have you eaten, Carlos?" Sofia asked.

"Not yet," Carlos replied.

Sofia reached into the backpack and pulled out a sandwich wrapped in paper. She gave it to him.

"It is your favorite."

"It was thoughtful of you to think of me."

"We need to move into position before first light," Anthony stated.

"Yes."

"Did you warn your family?"

"Yes. They do not live in town; they will not be hit by the bombs."

"You are going to bomb the town?" Sofia exclaimed.

"El Jefe is going to strike military targets in town," Anthony replied. "Not the town, only certain parts of it."

"What if he misses?"

"I will direct him from close."

"What if people are walking through those parts?"

Anthony did not answer.

"I will go and talk to Juan," she replied.

"Sofia, we want the attack to go on. We can have victory," Anthony said.

"Innocent people will die."

"No, they won't. Carlos and I risked our lives so people will not die. I will be guiding the artillery."

"Senorita. *El Capitan* is right. We are not murderers. We did not kill the boy guarding the radar trailer."

"What does that have to do with bombing Santa Angelia?" Sofia asked.

"We disabled the radar but did not blow it up," Anthony said. "Juan wanted it destroyed."

"They discovered it had been sabotaged," Sofia replied, "and were repairing it last night," Sofia said.

"Last night? Why didn't you tell me?"

"I'm telling you now."

We must blow it up before the attack starts," Anthony replied.

"It is a long way across the valley," Carlos broke in. "They will have it guarded."

"We must try to do something," Anthony said.

They left the cave. The sun had just broken the morning horizon.

Loud explosions pummeled the air.

Anthony ran full speed towards the cliff to scan the open valley. Carlos and Sofia fell in beside him.

He needed to see. Anthony shielded his eyes against the glaring rays of the new sun and blinked as hard as he could to adjust his pupils to the brightness. The explosions cracked the still morning air with fierce sound waves. As his eyes slowly adjusted, he saw nothing in the town burning.

Anthony searched the skies for low-level fighters. High above he saw the silent bombers moving slowly against the deep blue of the new morning sky, a thin line of ice crystals trailing in their heavy wake. The explosions stopped.

"Has the attack started already?" Carlos asked.

"The bombs are coming from those jets," Anthony replied. "They are not ours."

"Smoke is coming from the end of the valley," Carlos said.

Anthony looked over the town towards the end of the valley where large columns of smoke stood like black stone pillars against the blue sky.

"They bombed Tito," Anthony replied flatly. He cursed softly as well.

"They bombed Tito?" a voice said from behind Carlos.

Miguel came out of the bushes with another man. Both were heavily armed.

"Who bombed him, *Capitan?*" Miguel asked harshly.

If Anthony could explain, Miguel, with his ferocious naivety, would not understand, lightning fast jets operating from floating islands of ships miles away, coordinating their drop with forward based radar systems, with a Colombian Air Force colonel communicating with his U.S. counterpart, informing him that the bombing raid had been efficient.

"Not Juan," is all Anthony could reply.

"It is at the very end of the valley," Miguel said. "Those must be big bombs if we can see the smoke from here,"

"Why is Tito down there?" Sofia asked.

"Tito was waiting at the end of the valley to attack the colonel when he pulled out his troops," Anthony said.

"The colonel? He is stationed here for a year," Sofia replied.

"Mono said he was pulling out."

"Manuel Apostata? The one they call Mono?" Sofia asked.

"Yes. Do you know him?" Anthony asked.

"By name, but not personally. I've seen his picture in the paper. He is the most famous of all the resistance groups fighting the government. I saw him last week."

"Where?" Anthony asked.

"In town," Sofia replied. "Do you remember the sergeant sitting at the table last night?"

"Yes. He talked less than I did."

"Last week, he broke his arm in an accident, and my mother was called to the military headquarters to set his arm. I went with her. While we were attending him, the door was ajar. I heard footsteps in the hallway. As I looked out, I saw the colonel pass by, walking with Manuel Apostata."

"Did he see you?" Anthony asked.

"No, I told my mother that I saw him."

"What did she say?"

"She said that if I wanted to help her. I should keep my eyes down and my mouth shut," Sofia said. "It was the only way to stay neutral."

"Jesus" Anthony cursed.

"I asked her if she had seen him here before," replied Sofia.

"Had she?"

"She had. Many times."

First, the botched radar station and now this, Anthony thought to himself. Why hadn't he asked Sofia earlier about Mono? Tito was dead.

"*Capitan*," Miguel said, "we need to go immediately to Tito."

"We must find El Jefe," Anthony replied.

"Tito needs our help," Miguel said.

"Your help? What help will you give against such bombs?" Carlos asked.

"The bombs are finished," Miguel said.

"Bombs are never finished. There are always more," Carlos said quietly.

"We must go now," Miguel said. "Tito needs help."

"Even if you left now, you will be too late," Carlos said. "If you make there, different bombs will have your names on them."

"Old man," Miguel said, "do not talk to me in frightened words. I am not afraid to die."

"Then go and die," Carlos said. "Because that is all you will do."

"No one is going without El Jefe's orders," Anthony said. "He will order help for Tito."

"*Capitan*, time is critical in an attack," Miguel said.

"El Jefe needs to be told what we have seen," Anthony replied.

"Won't Juan have seen the smoke?" asked Sofia.

"I don't know," Anthony replied. "He should have."

"The colonel has men all over this town waiting for El Jefe to attack," Sofia said.

"Carlos, find El Jefe," Anthony commanded. "Miguel, go with him."

Another wave of explosions erupted at the end of the valley; they watched in horror. Anthony gritted his teeth; Sofia brought her hands to her face; and Miguel swore loudly

"Go quickly," Anthony said. "The bombs still fall."

"Aren't you coming, *Capitan*?" Miguel asked.

"I am going to climb up higher to see more."

"Where should I meet you?" Carlos asked.

"Find me at the high look-out," Anthony replied quickly.

Anthony watched them disappear into the jungle.

"There is a peak above the canyon. We should not walk the main trail," Anthony said. "We don't know who's out there."

"I know these trails well," replied Sofia. "I can see someone else on the trail."

"You won't see an ambush or a booby-trap," said Anthony. "It's life in the jungle."

"I know a different trail. It is much steeper."

"Show me."

Sofia scampered off through the jungle, ducking branches and jumping over roots and fallen trees. Sofia stopped and hunched down. Anthony came up behind, breathing heavily.

"Jesus, you move through this jungle," Anthony said, as he bent on one knee beside her. "Wait a minute."

They rested several minutes. Sofia looked at Anthony, put her finger to her lips and jumped up. They ran at a break neck pace though an open area covered with loose rocks, entering a trail on the other side and tracking it across the mountain. As near as Anthony could tell, the trail followed the ridge above Santa Angelia. Sofia came to a cleared area, stretching narrow and flat along the steep mountain. Small stone houses with palm-leaved roofs dotted the clearing. Anthony started to walk out; Sofia grabbed his hand. She pointed below them, across from where they were hid.

Three troop transport trucks lined the small dirt road. The troops were milling around. Many were smoking.

Sofia, staying in the cover of the jungle, scrambled along the edge of the clearing until she came to another small trail, which led straight up. She bent down and looked at the soft ground.

"No new prints," she said. "We can take it."

Anthony hung onto the roots of the stringy bushes, which boxed in the trail. At certain passes, he used them as footholds and had to look straight up to see Sofia. She climbed effortlessly, continuously looking backward and speaking soft encouragements. The trail led out to an open cliff.

"Sofia," Anthony inhaled deeply. "We have no climbing ropes."

"We don't need any," she replied. "Except if you fall."

She kissed Anthony lightly on the cheek and latched onto a rock over her head. She lifted herself onto a small ledge and climbed up about thirty meters. Anthony watched carefully, remembering every niche where she placed her hand and every lip where she set her foot. The way up formed a natural vertical staircase; every place where Anthony needed a hold, there was a small crack. Sofia scaled the rest of the cliff quickly; Anthony followed. When they reached the top, Anthony stood up and looked out.

He could see over the entire town. The valley stretched out behind it. It looked peaceful. They were standing on a narrow precipice, which linked back to the main body on the mountain, forming a wide natural canyon. Anthony recognized the canyon immediately; below him laid the dirt road and his plane.

Anthony slid his pack off his shoulder and unpacked his spotting scope. He clicked it to high power and focused on the end of the valley. He could see the lingering smoke, but a dark ridge blocked his view of Tito's position. He swore softly.

"What's wrong?" Sofia asked.

"It's all smoke and fire on that plateau," Anthony replied. "They knew he was there."

"Did Tito survive?"

"Maybe," he lied.

He wiped down the scope and put it inside its case.

"To be up here, one feels so free," Anthony said. "Danger awaits us down there."

"If we were birds, we could soar away," Sofia said.

"With my plane, we could soar away," Anthony replied. "We could be free."

"I could never leave my mother or nana without them knowing," Sofia replied quickly. "They would think I had died."

"I don't want you to end up like Tito," he replied, "killed because of me."

"Anthony, I will leave with you," Sofia said. "If you are not here, there is nothing for me here."

"How would you like to live in Montana?" Anthony asked.

"They have mountains there?"

"Many of them."

"It is a long way?" she asked.

"Not if we are together," Anthony replied. "We have to go."

"Give me a minute to stretch."

Like a cat stretching in the midday sun, she stretched to relieve the stiffness in her cramping muscles. Something was different; her body was enervated. A climb like this did not tire her.

Anthony grabbed her hand as she tiptoed along the path, which ran along the lip of the narrow precipice. The jungle soon took over, and they no longer looked down the sheer cliff. The path cut sharply downward. When the path flattened and ran crossways to the slope, Sofia would leave the path and descend through the jungle brush. They reached level ground and walked easily for several minutes. Sofia signaled to Anthony. Directly in front of them lay the dirt road. They stayed in the shadows reaching the point where the tall trees began to cross over the top of the dirt strip. No one was around. The plane sat in front of them.

Anthony walked up to it.

He ran his hand tenderly along the wing as if caressing a baby. The plane comforted him.

"You love this plane," Sofia said, as she watched him.

"I love all planes. This one's not my favorite; it drives like an old Mack truck."

"What type is it?" she asked.

"Brazilian," Anthony replied. "My dad taught me to fly planes; the military taught me to fly helicopters.

"Are they easier to fly than planes?"

"No. You need more concentration and coordination."

Anthony slid the cargo door back. He pulled out a large duffel bag.

"Where did you fly the plane from?" Sofia asked.

"Good, I'm glad they threw this in here," Anthony said, while looking intently inside. He turned to her. "I'm sorry what did you say?"

"From where did you fly the plane?"

Anthony smiled.

"If I tell you that, I'd have to kill you. I don't fly back to the States every time we need something."

Sofia punched him in the stomach.

"You'd better not keep secrets from me," she exclaimed.

He grabbed and embraced her.

"Never. Help me cover the plane, please. If they fly over, I don't want them seeing it."

They pulled out the silky tarp patterned in jungle leaves and brush.

Together they spread the camouflage sheet over the plane.

"In the shadows, you don't notice the plane anymore. It looks like a bunch of bushes," Sofia remarked.

"It will be our way out of here," Anthony said.

"Won't they see us on radar?"

"If we stay low along the trees, they can't see us in the mountains," Anthony said. "Radar only covers the major cities, so we avoid them. Most of the radar equipment has been damaged, and if the equipment works, the electricity to it has been stolen,"

"In Bogotá, the poor people climb the power poles and hook onto the power for free. It's a problem," Sofia replied.

"It's the same for the radar. For maximum radar coverage, they are usually located far off the road on top of mountains where the locals can easily steal the electricity. I usually can see where the stations are by looking for a bunch of little shacks on top of a peak in the middle of nowhere. The government can come and fix it, but the next day the power is stolen again."

"You fly around undetected?"

"Pretty much, unless I give verbal position reports," Anthony said.

"How can a country run an air control system like that?"

"Remember what your mother and the colonel were discussing last night about the money this war siphons off, there isn't the money to keep things working," he replied.

They finished tying the cover on. Anthony looked at his watch.

"Come. We have to hurry to meet up with Juan," Anthony said.

They raced down the path, running until both of them gasped for breath. They slowed to a fast walk.

The moist ground muffled their movements through the underbrush. He looked back; she encouraged him with a curious smile. He pushed on. He thought of home.

Home. He stopped sharply as the word flittered through his head. Sofia came up quickly and slipped her arms around him. He put his arm on her shoulder. Home was where she was.

"It's not much farther, is it?" she mouthed.

"No," he whispered.

"How is the time?"

"Fine. How are you feeling?"

"Tired."

"Can you make it a little further before you must rest?"

"If you kiss me."

He kissed her deeply; her mouth was moist and warm.

"We can rest on the ridge."

He started forward, slowing to move the brush aside, careful not to let it swish back and hit her. The slope leveled. He stopped.

"We are nearing the ridge."

They climbed along the ridge until the thick foliage broke and he could see the town. This was a good sign.

"We are on the trail to the look-out."

Anthony saw movement coming down the trail. He pushed Sofia behind some bushes and pulled his gun free from his waistband, clicking the safety to off. He hunched down and, staying below the cover of the ground bushes, he moved up the trail and positioned himself where he could see. When he saw who was on the trail, he stood up and called out.

"Carlos," Anthony said.

When Sofia heard Anthony call out, she left the protection of the bushes.

"I was coming to find you," Carlos said.

"Did you tell El Jefe?" Anthony asked quickly.

"Yes," Carlos replied. "He has tried to radio Tito, but has received no response."

"He must not do that," Anthony said. "Tito is dead, and they will use the radio transmissions to find him."

"They can do that?" Carlos asked.

"Yes. Someday I'll explain it to you," Anthony said. "But right now, I need to speak with El Jefe. Do you know where he is?"

"Yes," Carlos answered. "He is not far. He climbed back up to see what happened. We will need to go very carefully. Everyone is very edgy. I don't want Sofia to be shot by mistake. When you follow, follow some distance behind. If they see me alone, they will recognize the way I walk. If there are three of us, they may mistake us for somebody else."

"We will keep you in sight," replied Anthony.

They followed Carlos at a distance. Carlos walked much slower than usual. He stopped often and whistled. He never walked down the main trail, choosing instead to stay on the narrower, less-used trails. After climbing a very steep slope, Carlos' whistles were answered. Carlos walked forward. Four men came out of the brush, fully armed, their guns leveled at Carlos. Anthony cursed himself for not having his rifle at ready. He could do nothing at such a distance with his pistol. With his rifle, he could save Carlos, squeezing out all four shots before the first man had hit the ground.

The men encircled Carlos and clapped him on the shoulders. Anthony breathed a sigh of relief. The young soldiers surrounding Juan must have already fired many errant shots. His drill sergeant had pounded it into him that the greatest discipline was holding your fire, especially when being fired upon.

Anthony saw Carlos look back towards them and wave them forward. As he walked up to the four men, he recognized one of them.

"Hello Diego," Anthony said.

"*Capitan*," Diego said gripping Anthony's arm tightly. "We are very happy to see you. What did you see?"

"I will need to discuss that with El Jefe," Anthony said. "It doesn't look good for Tito. I swear that whoever did it will pay."

The young men shook their fists in the air.

"I will take you to El Jefe," Diego said. "He is very close. We are standing guard for him."

Diego and another soldier walked in front, while the other two fell in behind Sofia. Diego walked very quickly. Anthony's mind worked over the bombing of Tito; the radar pod, functional or not, had not played a part, radar being for flying things. Tito represented everything good in the movement, being its and Anthony's moral compass. Tito's death must be avenged, victory being more important now that Tito must not have died in vain. Anthony wiped a tear from his cheek.

They came to the jutting promenade where Juan was standing, surrounded by his men. He looked up, and when he made eye contact with Anthony, he broke away from the group.

Gregory Arthur Solsrud

Chapter Thirteen-Wednesday Morning

"You're alive," Juan said.

"We must go to Tito," Anthony said immediately.

"I have seen the smoke, but I do not know," Juan said. "You went higher. What did you see?"

"It was a high altitude bombing," Anthony replied. "They knew where Tito was."

"Then that is the end of Tito," Juan replied softly.

"We don't know that," Anthony said. "We cannot abandon him."

"We all die alone," Juan replied.

"We need to find out if he is dead," Anthony insisted.

"It will take a day to move our troops over. They," Juan motioned toward the troops in town, "will have cleaned up Tito by then."

"Attack the main road," Anthony said.

"They have it blocked in both directions, and you know that," Juan said. "No traffic in or out of this valley without a fight. What's wrong with you?"

"We must fight," Anthony said.

"Fight? Fight to die," Juan replied. "They will be waiting for you."

"We must do something. We have been outnumbered before."

"Must we? We are a small group of men with limited firepower. We do not possess overwhelming force at the point of attack."

"They won't expect you to attack after this."

"Never forget your unwavering belief in your own folly," Juan replied. "The colonel is well aware of my aggressiveness, and Mono knows better than anyone how convinced I am that this battle in front of us will turn the tide of the war."

"Mono sacrificed Tito," Anthony countered. "Are you afraid of him?"

"You misunderstand my words. I am perfectly rational, and that is why I do not attack. There is a trap laid before us, begging the ignorant or those unschooled in history to walk into. Do you understand military history?" Juan asked.

"I'm not an expert, but I know more about history than Carlos."

"Don't flatter yourself," Juan said.

"No disrespect to Carlos," Anthony said quickly. "You asked whether I knew history."

"Carlos," Juan turned to him and asked, "What would you do?"

"Run for the mountains," he replied quickly. "I will do it, as soon as the two of you finish talking."

"Don't worry, Carlos. I will be running with you and Antonio here." Juan held up his hand to stop Anthony from arguing.

"As a general rule," Juan began again, "military leaders study history, but when it comes to planning a particular battle, they forget the one essential rule that has ruined more great armies."

"Which rule is that?" Anthony asked.

"Never underestimate the strength or intelligence of your enemy," Juan said.

"They have the same men and leader in the valley that you have defeated before," replied Anthony.

"Right now, we are protected by these mountains. We can attack or we can wait under these rocks, which have been here for millions of years and are not going anywhere. I want this valley; I want it so badly I can taste. When we move out into the valley, all we can do is fight. To fight, we give up our cover, which is our protection."

"We can use our artillery," Anthony argued.

"And give away our positions? Tito was annihilated. The same trap awaits us. Those planes are waiting to rain down upon us once we are out in the open. The military has been quiet today, too quiet. We don't pick up any radio chatter. They are holding their breath."

"You're retreating?" Anthony asked.

"No, I'm waiting for another day to fight," replied Juan. "If I don't move the men back up over the high pass that 'another day' will be today."

"You are a coward," Miguel said. He had been listening carefully off to the side.

"Coward?" Juan repeated. "No, respectful for my own life."

"And Tito's life?" Miguel asked.

"More deaths won't bring his life back," Juan replied.

"It will bring us victory," Miguel retorted.

"We need to go to Tito's aid," Anthony said.

"The bold Yanqui is going to lead us to victory," Juan said.

"It is better than cowering here in fear," Miguel replied aggressively.

"Any attack is suicide," Juan replied.

Miguel saw it clearly. Juan had gone soft. He has seen it in other leaders, the constant fear of their own lives, the constant butchery, a man's conscience can only take so much before it cracks, or turns psychotic like Santo's had.

Juan didn't move. He looked at Miguel intensely. He spat onto the ground.

"A leopard does not kill because he is cruel. He kills, because he is a leopard and needs to eat," Juan replied.

Miguel loosed his rifle, clicking off the safety. "Do something," he said quietly.

Anthony stepped in between the two of them.

He looked at Juan.

"Someone might still be alive and needs help."

"Fear destroys reason. Once reason is gone, killing can follow. Even an insane man has his motives." Juan said. He looked at Anthony.

"The bold Yanqui is going to lead you to victory," Juan said to Miguel.

"You've lost your nerve," Miguel said.

"Go then," Juan replied.

"We will take what we need," Miguel said. "Tito needs help."

Juan looked at him through slitted eyes. He held his hands loose at his sides.

"I will take them," Diego broke in. "We can ride mules along the top of the ridge. We can be there and back in a few hours."

"They will be watching the whole ridge," Juan said. "They will have helicopters circulating."

"I know it will be dangerous, Jefe," Diego said.

"Diego," Juan said, "bring me my mules back."

"Si, Jefe," Diego said.

"You go and avenge Tito's death," Juan said. "Make sure you don't pay too high of a price."

"Just be here when we get back," Anthony said.

"I will be here, although I expect I will be waiting for no one," Juan replied.

Anthony walked over to Sofia.

"I will return," Anthony said.

"Let me come with you," Sofia replied.

"I want to take you with me," replied Anthony. "If only to know that you're safe. It will be a long and difficult ride, which I know you would be able to do. I do not know what we will find. They may be waiting for us."

"What do you want me to do, wait until I hear that you are dead?"

"If Tito is dead, they cannot let any of us live. You must prepare to leave forever," Anthony said.

"I will," Sofia replied.

They kissed passionately, as if no one watched them.

"I must go," Anthony said.

"Señor," one of the young men came up to him and spoke, "Diego is with the mules. He sent me to find you."

"Take me to him," Anthony snapped.

The man jumped at Anthony's command and ran through the woods with Anthony close behind.

Sofia watched them run off.

"Go with God," she yelled after them.

Four mules with saddles stomped their feet and look nervously around. Diego was holding onto the reins. Miguel and another stood beside him.

"Diego," Anthony said.

"*Si, Capitan?*"

"Can you shoot well, Diego? Give me an honest answer. Our lives depend on it."

"I can shoot almost as well as you, *Capitan*. I will show you."

"No, Diego. I will trust your word on that."

"This one here," Miguel said, "is my brother Ferdinand. He is fiercer than I."

"Good," replied Anthony. "Listen carefully. Diego will lead, and I will follow. Miguel third, and Ferdinand fourth. We will ride together. If we see the enemy, we immediately split into pairs. Diego and I. Miguel and Ferdinand. We will not all stop. Two of us must get through. Understood?"

They all nodded their heads silently.

"They will be watching the trails and the open ridges with helicopters and long scope spotters. If you see a helicopter, hide. A mule cannot outrun a helicopter. Saddle up."

"*Capitan* Wyatt," Miguel said. "I speak for all of us. We are proud to serve under you. We will not fail you. You command, and we will obey."

"Ride like the wind," Anthony replied with conviction.

They settled on the mules and galloped off. Anthony had not ridden a horse in years. In his youth, he rode horses every day. The ungainly gallop of the mule threw him back and forth. As they crossed over loose sliding rock and down steep inclines, he was glad to have the mule's sturdy and nimble legs under him. Diego rode steadily, pushing his mule on as fast as it would go, only looking back occasionally to see that Anthony was behind. The other mules trailed instinctively. Anthony did not need to lead his mule, but only hang on to the lurching saddle.

Anthony thought about the scene with Juan. He should have taken over then, even if he had to shoot him. It would be better to be leading the entire force in rescue of Tito. He should not have backed down. Miguel would have supported him. The time was right. It was difficult to shoot a man who did not defend himself. Now they were chasing pell-mell along on open ridge in clear daylight. Anthony looked up in the sky. He saw nothing. The mules made too much noise to hear well. They would have to trust in providence to deliver them safely.

They rode hard and fast for three hours. Anthony ached. His injured arm was stiff, and he could straighten it no more. Diego stopped on the edge of a small clearing, filled with smoldering fire pits. They jumped down from their mules. Anthony's legs buckled under him. He stood up, stretching his legs. The others walked around, examining the ground.

"This was their camp last night," Ferdinand said. "See all the ashes and the broken bushes."

"You should have shot him," Miguel said. "We would have followed you."

"Yes," Ferdinand answered. "It would be better that we had more men."

"We must find Tito," Anthony said. "Are we at the mouth of the valley?"

"Yes. There are two trails down to the sugarcane fields."

"Sugarcane fields?"

"Below the cliff the farmers grew sugarcane. Tito was setting up there," Miguel said.

"Can we look onto this field without being seen?" Anthony asked.

"Yes," Ferdinand replied.

"Prepare your weapons," Anthony commanded. "We go. Single file."

Anthony walked over to his mule and pulled down his backpack. He quickly removed his rifle, assembled it and loaded it. He shoved his pistol into his waistband. He slung a filled cartridge belt over his shoulder. The others were similarly armed. Anthony motioned to Miguel to lead them quietly forward. They walked through the abandoned camp and followed the trail several hundred meters. They veered off from the trail and pushed through dense brush. Anthony crouched down and trod, step by step, towards a rocky ledge. As he approached the ledge, he dropped to his belly and slid forward. The others joined him.

Anthony's eyes could not believe the devastation. Bodies were flung haphazardly in and around large craters. Sugarcane smoldered and burned. Anthony laid his forehead on his arm.

"*Capitan*, what do you want us to do?" Miguel asked.

"I want you to burn this into your memory," Anthony said. "Move back." They crawled back into the jungle.

"Ferdinand, you and Miguel ride back and tell everyone exactly what you saw. Diego and I will go down into the fields to see if anyone survived. I don't think so, but we owe Tito that much."

"There must be survivors," Miguel said passionately. "We have had the hell bombed out of us before with very little cover."

"Helicopters came and finished the job, Miguel," Anthony replied. "We will check because that is our duty, but there is no hope."

"Let us go with you, *Capitan*, and look," Ferdinand said. "Diego can carry the message back."

"*El Jefe* must be warned."

"Diego will return safely. It is a very good trail. You rode it yourself. Please let me come down with you," pleaded Ferdinand. I have cousins down there."

Anthony thought it over carefully. The trail was good. If there were survivors, they would need help.

"Diego will ride back alone," Anthony decided.

They watched Diego race off. Anthony did not envy his long trip back and the hard task of delivering the message of the destruction of Tito and his men.

"*Capitan*," Ferdinand began. "I will lead us down."

"Agreed," Anthony said. "Look out for any soldiers. They may be sweeping the area."

Ferdinand rode more wildly than Diego. He pushed his mule hard, its hooves slipping and sliding down the loose trail. They reached the bottom quickly. Ferdinand galloped towards the edge of the blackened soil. He jumped off from his mule when he came to the first groups of bodies. He turned several over looking for his lost cousins.

As Anthony trotted up, he noticed that the bodies had neither weapons nor ammunition. About half lay in long rows close to where they stood. He rode over to the field artillery, mangled by the bombs. No ammo cases were beside it. He scanned the plateau and saw no one. He returned quickly to Ferdinand and Miguel.

"Other soldiers have been here," Anthony said. "If there were any survivors, they either shot them or have taken them prisoner. They will be returning. We need to leave now."

Miguel and Ferdinand looked at him, their eyes red.

"You can't avenge anyone if you're dead, or a prisoner," Anthony shouted. "Mount up. We go now."

On the far side of the valley, Anthony thought he could make out where the monastery stood. Anthony's eyes followed the rolling contour down to the town below; his eyes perceived movement. He squinted. Tiny dots were flying quickly along the tops of the trees. Helicopters. They must be returning to pick up the rest of the weapons and ammunition. They would be here fast. He looked over the sugarcane fields. They would be completely exposed if they crossed the fields towards the trail. He leapt off from his mule.

"Ferdinand, Miguel, your lives depend on what I tell you. Helicopters are coming back. Make these mules lie down as if they are dead."

Miguel grabbed the ear of his mule and pulled him to the ground. He spoke into his ear and the mule stilled. He grabbed Anthony's mule and brought to the ground. Ferdinand had his mule on the ground.

"Follow me," Anthony commanded.

Anthony ran towards a wide crater. He stepped over a dead body, throwing himself down on the ground looking out towards the pile of guns.

"Lie next to me. Keep your head down so they don't see you. Don't shoot unless I shoot."

The helicopters zoomed up over the lip of the ridge. Two landed alongside the pile of guns. The helicopters shut down their turbines. The crews, including the two pilots, jumped out and began loading the helicopters with the captured guns. The third helicopter hovered and then landed between the guns and Anthony. Four soldiers jumped out the back. The pilot stayed with the aircraft, letting the jet engine cycle.

"Those are Mono's men," Miguel said.

"We must kill him," Ferdinand said.

"Who do you want to save, the dead or the living?"

They stared at Anthony.

"Mono didn't have these helicopters before," Anthony continued. "He can ferry men over to El Jefe and block his route over the pass. Then the army can move in from below. They will have everyone surrounded and can shoot them like chickens. If we don't destroy them, Jefe and everyone will be wiped out."

"There are only three of us," Miguel said. "Use my life wisely, it is yours."

"And mine," Ferdinand repeated.

They did not bring any rockets or mortars with them. If they started shooting, they might disable one or two, but not all. Anthony stared at cycling helicopter. Missiles were hanging from its belly.

"We must seize that helicopter and use it to blow up the other two."

"What do we do?" Miguel asked.

"One of you must come with me," Anthony said.

"I will go," Miguel said.

"We must kill the pilot. Do you see how they left the back door open? Jump through there. I will come up along the side where he is sitting."

"I understand," Miguel said.

"What do I do?" Ferdinand asked.

"Stop those soldiers," Anthony commanded.

"I understand," Ferdinand repeated. "I will move forward with you and find cover. My shots will not miss."

"If I crash or I'm shot down," Anthony said. "You will be on your own."

"Destroy those helicopters," Ferdinand exhorted.

Anthony looked towards the helicopters; men were busy loading the weapons. Anthony crabbed to the side of the crater. He lunged from one crater to the next, followed by Miguel and Ferdinand. They reached a shallow crater directly behind the idling machine. Ferdinand pointed to where he was going to set up. Anthony and Miguel ran towards the helicopter.

Anthony slipped directly behind the fuselage of the helicopter, ducking under the horizontal tail and rotor. He felt the heat of the jet engine blast above him. He pulled out his knife and wrenched opened the door. The pilot slumped out towards him. Miguel had gotten there first.

"Pull him out, *Capitan*. He's dead."

Anthony dragged the pilot from his seat and dropped him to the ground. He slid into the pilot seat, fastening the seat belt and scanning the controls. Miguel jumped from the helicopter and lay in the crater next to Ferdinand. Anthony slowly turned the accelerator to full throttle. The turbine whined, and the helicopter vibrated. He engaged the collective and the main rotor started to spin. He looked forward; Mono's men were waving at him, not recognizing Anthony through the glinting Plexiglas. Anthony rotated the cyclic; the helicopter hovered two feet off the ground.

One of the other pilots motioned to Anthony to set it down. The other ran for his helicopter. Anthony had been recognized; the game was on. He rotated the cyclic further, lifting the helicopter off the ground. He felt clumsy, but the sensation was returning, like riding a bicycle after a long absence. Every small movement to the control stick made the helicopter lurch. He eased the control stick forward, and the helicopter flew straight. He had no time to practice. Time to line up on the target and shoot the missiles.

He had not thought about how he was going to shoot the missiles. Every firing system was slightly different. He flew over the other helicopters. He mashed down with his right foot to turn the helicopter around, glancing at the control stick and seeing the fire button at his right thumb. He scanned the middle panel and saw the switch to arm the missile. Lucky for him, they had not translated anything into Spanish yet. He could not think of the Spanish word for missile.

He flipped the toggle switch, and a red light turned on. The rotors of the first helicopter were turning. Within a minute, it would be off the ground. The only thing Anthony thought of was to hover directly in front of the other helicopter and shoot directly at it. The feel of the controls was coming quickly back to him. He dropped his helicopter in front of the other one and hovered inches above the ground. Anthony pressed the fire button with his right thumb.

The helicopter exploded, sending a heat wave back at him. Debris hit his windshield. He rotated the cyclic and lifted out. He flew left and right to make sure he had not damaged his own rotors. The helicopter handled fine.

Anthony circled around and lined up on the other helicopter. Its blades were rotating. As Anthony dropped close to hover, his main rotors caught the blade wash of the other helicopter. His blades lost lift. Anthony's helicopter banged down onto the ground.

The other helicopter lifted off. Anthony yanked up the collective to fly airborne, and fired a second missile. The missile raced under the fuselage of the other helicopter and exploded into the pile of weapons, shredding them to bits. He saw soldiers on fire running wildly away from the inferno. Anthony flew straight along the ground, deciding to build speed rather than altitude. As he approached the edge of ridge, he banked hard left and then right to avoid the tall, blackened rocks sticking high into the air.

As his helicopter cleared the ridge, Anthony flew below and behind the other chopper, directly in his blind spot. The other pilot looped left and right to see what was behind him, banking steeply to his right; ammo boxes and salvaged rifles tumbled out the open doors. The other pilot was lightening the helicopter to gain precious knots in vertical speed.

As a patient hunter, Anthony breathed deep, and settled into a rhythmic motion, following the other chopper's banks and swoops. He studied the other pilot's quickness and evasive tactics, sometimes watching the other helicopter clip the tall trees in a valiant struggle to break free. Anthony looked at his control panel; it showed one missile left. He thought about Miguel and Ferdinand stranded behind, he had to put down the other helicopter.

The other pilot grew impatient and soared skywards. Anthony knew the other pilot had made a mistake. Anthony followed him upwards but not at such a reckless climb. He saw the other helicopter shudder as its spinning blades lost their lift in the steep climb. The other helicopter slowed to a dead stop in mid-air. Anthony lined up the gun sights and fired. The missile flew straight and true, disintegrating the other helicopter in the air. Anthony watched the debris fall.

Smiling, he spun the helicopter quickly around and headed back towards the cane fields. As he pressed back, he surveyed his instruments. Both low fuel indicator lights were on. The fuel gauge showed no pressure. He did not believe that the pilot would have flown the helicopter with such low fuel. The gauges must be broken.

Anthony climbed higher to reach the altitude of the plateau. Ahead a smoke pillar marked the spot of the destroyed helicopters. He circled. He did not see anybody moving, and no one shot at him.

He hovered near the spot where Miguel had jumped out. Miguel waved at him from inside a bomb crater. He set the helicopter on the ground. Miguel lurched forward, carrying his brother over his shoulder. He dumped his brother onto the rear deck and jumped in. His brother's face contorted in pain. The deafening whine of the twin turbines prevented all talking.

Fearing incoming small arms fire, Anthony lifted straight out and at maximum forward speed. He flew towards their camp in the canyon, calculating arrival in a few minutes. He thought about what mobility this helicopter would give them and a surprise advantage in an attack. He would be able to shuttle Juan's men out of the valley quicker than they could walk.

The turbines stopped whining. The silence was deafening. Adrenaline stopped time for him. He looked at the panel. His power gauges dropped to zero. He was out of fuel. His training took over. He scanned the overhead rotor; it was spinning. He changed the pitch of the blades while he searched for an area to crash land. Steep mountainsides laced with tall, thick trees stared up at him.

Anthony saw the valley road far to his right, he could fall off and land on the road, he had enough speed and altitude, he thought, but it would be dangerous, someone would spot them and the first ones on the scene would be the military. They would be on top of them before they could escape.

Miguel poked his head through to the front.

Anthony shouted orders at him.

"Miguel, look for a clear landing spot."

Miguel hopped over the middle console and pushed his head against the glass and peered down.

"*Capitan*, there is a ledge over here," Miguel called out.

"Are there trees?"

"No," he replied, pointing at the ten o'clock position.

Anthony leaned forward and looked. Miguel pointed at a small rocky ledge, cut into the side of the mountain, wide enough to land but no more. They were steadily losing precious altitude.

"Miguel buckle up. We're going in."

Miguel jumped back to Ferdinand and lifted him into a seat, fastening the harness around him. He crawled back to the front seat and buckled himself in.

"Can I do anything, *Capitan*?" Miguel asked.

"Fill the tanks with jet fuel," Anthony replied.

"*Que?*" Miguel said.

Anthony had said jet fuel with a Spanish accent.

"*Se acabo el combustible*," meaning, "We are out of fuel."

"*Que va*," Miguel said. "How can a big machine like this not have fuel?"

"I didn't talk to the pilot before I took off," Anthony said.

"*En serio*," Miguel said. "We are out of fuel."

"Yes."

Miguel crossed himself and muttered under his breath.

This monster has to fit neat and clean between the trees, Anthony thought, and cannot miss the ledge, or else it is a thousand feet of rolling end over end inside a shell of sharpened, crumpled metal. He kicked in a little left rudder to turn the helicopter parallel with the mountain and pitched the nose up slightly. He settled fast over the small rocky target. He fought the temptation to pull up early. A bounced landing would send them careening over the side of the cliff. Patience. Patience.

Anthony pulled sharply up on the collective. The spinning blades bit the air and decelerated the giant chopper. The vertical speed indicator leveled at zero. The rear tail wheel settled on the ground, followed immediately by the main gear. He pushed hard on the pedals to set the brakes; he was not going to roll off his perch.

Anthony let out a small whoop of success. He gave Miguel a thumbs-up.

"I thought we were going to die," Miguel said. "The trees were coming up so fast. I closed my eyes."

"I closed my eyes too," Anthony replied.

"You did not."

Anthony shook his head.

"Ferdinand, did you hear that? *El Capitan* landed with his eyes shut."

"I don't care how he landed," Ferdinand replied. "This is the last time I will ride in a helicopter."

"No," Miguel said. "A helicopter is very safe. I was always afraid what would happen if a helicopter went down. Now I know. It lands gently on the ground."

"We had better go," Anthony said, as he looked straight down the cliff through the bottom of the curved plexiglas. He turned to Miguel.

"Slide the rear door open on your side. We will unload over there."

"Yes, *Capitan*," Miguel responded.

He pulled the door opened as Anthony helped Ferdinand unbuckle. Ferdinand's face was white. His clothes were soaked with blood.

Anthony lifted him to a sitting position with his legs dangling out the side.

"Miguel, Ferdinand needs to see a doctor immediately."

"No, Miguel," Ferdinand said. "I'm good. I will recover and return to fight."

"Look at him, Miguel," Anthony said. He knew the ones that had fought in the back country who feared giving themselves up. "We need to take him to the doctor."

"No, I am not going into town," Ferdinand said. He made to rise but fell back on Anthony's arm.

"Miguel, from here we can descend into town," Anthony said.

"Ferdinand, listen to him, and listen to me," Miguel said urgently. "We go to the doctor. There's nothing I can do for you."

"If I die, I die."

Miguel looked at his brother. He had lost much blood and was irrational. Still he was older, and he must obey his wishes.

"If the doctor comes here?" Miguel asked.

Ferdinand nodded.

"*Capitan*, can you bring the doctor here?" Miguel asked.

Anthony looked at the two of them. It was hard to understand ignorant stubbornness in the face of no alternatives. Anthony jumped down, walked out to the front of the helicopter and looked out. The town lay down to the right. He could not see any trails leading towards town. A narrow trail tiptoed along this ledge until it ran out.

The sun was high in the sky. He was sweating. Very well, he thought, if Ferdinand will not go down, the doctor would have to make a house call. They needed a sheltered spot where Ferdinand could wait without being seen. They will go to the cave. There was clean water to drink and to wash his wounds. He had no idea how to start; every unknown trail always led to a blind canyon.

"Miguel."

"Yes?"

"When you went down to town, did you ever pass by a small waterfall?"

"Many times, *Capitan*," he replied. "I have filled my canteen in that stream."

"Can you reach there from here?"

Miguel looked out into the valley and followed it to his left.

"See that ridge up there," Miguel said pointing down the ledge to a crest beyond. "The waterfall is on the other side."

"Does this trail lead over there?"

"That I do not know. We can follow it for as long it helps us and from there, I will cut a trail over."

"You start and find the easiest path to go. I will follow with your brother. We need to move quickly. An army search party may be coming up from the base right now."

"Ferdinand, it is time to go," Anthony said.

Anthony put Ferdinand's arm around his neck. Ferdinand's legs buckled. Anthony bent over and slung him over his shoulders in a fireman's carry. He was surprised at how light he was. He followed Miguel along the narrow seam of the ledge, the ledge narrowing and forcing him to shuffle sideways to carry Ferdinand along. He refused to look down to his right over the thousand-foot ledge.

Anthony concentrated on other thoughts, thinking about the geological forces that would cause a rock lip to form along a vertical cliff, the great upheavals of molten rock groaning and squeezing their way through the existing mantel to squirt out into this small cleavage, and the many who had previously trod this high wire trail in their flight to freedom and a better life.

They reached an incline that led straight up through the foliage. He took one look back at the helicopter. It was in good shape, only lacking fuel, and very handy here in the mountains.

The sweat flowed heavily down his face as he struggled up the path. Miguel had stopped ahead. Dense brush surrounded them on both sides.

"*Capitan*, we need to cut over to reach the ridge," Miguel said. "Set my brother down and rest while I cut us a path."

Anthony lowered Ferdinand carefully to the ground. While he gave him water, he heard Miguel pounding on the vegetation. Anthony looked up.

His bent figure whacked the bases of the thick palms and course vines. He slashed his machete wildly, driven by sheer willpower. Through the cracks between the green, the sun highlighted his florid face. His jabbing strokes sprayed the leaves unevenly. He leaned heavily on the machete and seemed mesmerized by the insects circling around him.

Anthony stood up, walked over and took the long blade from him. He swung the blade in smooth clocklike movements. The machete soared high above his head as each chop landed in its predestined place. Anthony reached an open area with flowering bushes. He walked back. Miguel was knelling next to his brother, cradling him.

"Miguel, lead us out," Anthony commanded in a soft voice.

Miguel looked at him while Anthony shouldered Ferdinand. They moved down the trail, crossed the ridge and followed a trail to the waterfall. Anthony laid Ferdinand down and climbed to the opening in the foliage where he could see over the town. The sun was high and bright. Walking into town in broad daylight was not a good idea, but Ferdinand needed a doctor.

"Miguel," Anthony said, "Run back to camp and find Carlos. Tell him what happened, and that we need help."

"I can't leave my brother."

"Without help, your brother will bleed to death. I will stay here and stop the bleeding and do what I can."

Miguel nodded and ran off as fast as could.

For the first time in years, Anthony crossed himself and mumbled a prayer.

Gregory Arthur Solsrud

Chapter Fourteen-Wednesday Evening

Anthony knelt next to the small creek and washed the blood of Ferdinand from his fingers. Ferdinand was unconscious, feet propped up, lying on a blanket Anthony had found in the cave. The bleeding had stopped; nothing more could be done.

Anthony sat next to Ferdinand and watched his halting breaths. With his shirt off, his ribs looked exposed and weak, his belly empty. Anthony's thoughts wandered back to Sofia; he owed her the strongest duty. Do not entice her into his whirlpool of violence and viciousness.

He rose to walk away from his thoughts. I shouldn't sit here under the bushes, he thought. Thinking only gets me in trouble. Action is what I need. He could not think right when he was around Sofia, such a beautiful woman; his hormones got in the way. He was away from her now and could think more clearly.

He did want to stay with her, but what would he do, teach English? He'd never been a teacher. All he had known and all he been trained to do was conflict and war. What does a warrior do when he retires? A warrior can try to return to his hometown. But he knows what he will find there after his long journey back. He will knock on the door, a strange face will come to the door, and the strange face will look at his awesome and terrifying presence. There is something about a man who lives by killing; his pores exude a poison. The strange face will shut the door, bolting it quickly to talk to him through the protection of locks and steel.

"What do you want?" the voice will ask.

"I'm looking for someone."

"Who?"

"I am looking for my mother."

"She is not here."

"Do you know where she went?"

"I do not know your mother."

"Please open the door and let me talk to you."

"Go away."

"Please help me."

"I'm calling the police. Go away."

The voice no longer talks at the door.

Is this the fate I want? And what do I trade for it, the only true family I have known. Abandon El Jefe in his most dire hour of need, and who will lead Miguel and Carlos and everyone?

Anthony heard brush breaking up the trail. He looked up and saw Sofia running towards him.

"You're safe!" she cried, as she flew into his arms.

"Yes," he replied as he hugged her in return.

She was more beautiful than he remembered. Her sun-kissed tanned body was wet with perspiration.

"Miguel said you had been injured."

"No -- his brother Ferdinand. He is badly wounded."

Carlos came up from behind, followed by Miguel.

"My brother," he sobbed. He knelt down next to Ferdinand and kissed his cheek.

"Has he said anything?" Miguel asked.

"He keeps talking, but doesn't make any sense."

"Ferdinand, listen, El Jefe said you will live," Miguel called into his brother's ear.

"When did speak with El Jefe?" Anthony asked.

"Right after I saw Carlos," Miguel replied. "He told me they saw the helicopter go down and thought it might be us."

"El Jefe doesn't know whether your brother will live."

Miguel looked at him. The *Capitan* had said something that didn't follow reason. El Jefe knew everything. Anthony looked at Carlos. Carlos looked away.

I was afraid to move him and have him bleed more," Anthony said to Sofia.

"I will bring the Doctor. She will heal him," she said to Miguel.

Miguel nodded.

"Ferdinand, hear, the doctor is coming," Miguel spoke loudly into his brother's ear.

"Sofia, I cannot go with you; it is daylight."

"Senorita Sofia, I will accompany you to the town," Carlos said. "There are many soldiers around."

"No. Carlos. You stay here, next to him," pointing at Anthony. "He moves, you move; he walks, you walk; he runs, you run. Understood. When I come back, you will know where he is." She turned to Miguel, "Keep Ferdinand quiet. Don't move him until the Doctor comes."

She left quickly, disappearing quietly in the dark bush.

Shortly after she left, Juan came out of the jungle. He was alone. He came and looked at Ferdinand. His brother Miguel cradled his head and held a damp rag against it.

"Ferdinand has lost a lot of blood. He will need blood," Juan said.

"Jefe," Anthony said, he wanted to say something meaningful to him. "The doctor is coming."

"That is good. She will know what to do."

They sat in silence for several minutes.

"We saw your helicopter fall but did not see any smoke," Juan started. "Miguel, told me about your landing on the ledge. I know that ledge; it is barely big enough for a man to stand on."

"I created my own emergency. I saw that the helicopter was out of fuel, but thought the gauges were wrong."

"You handled yourself well, Anthony. I know I can rely on you. The men are strung out all over this valley and are extremely anxious. I have instructed them to begin moving back up the mountain. I will need your help to lead them out safely.

"I wanted to talk with you about that," Anthony said.

Anthony decided to tell Juan that he was through. He looked at Juan's face. He looked tired. His shirt had flecks of blood on it.

"With some jet fuel, I could fly the helicopter back to our camp. We could use the fuel from the plane," Anthony said.

"A helicopter's the thing," Miguel said. "In minutes, we covered what took us three hours with mules."

"Or all day by foot," Juan replied. "Helicopters are fast, but they need fuel, a lot of it. They need parts, which are hard to come by, trained mechanics, and a clean place to work on them."

"It would be a nice thing to have," Miguel said.

"Juan, I am only suggesting we use it to shuttle everybody out of this valley as quick as we can," Anthony said. "We can carry fuel to it."

"Fuel is very difficult to transport over this terrain," Juan replied.

"We have stockpiled several barrels of jet fuel," Carlos said from across the cave. "The mules could carry them to the helicopter."

"And the steep ledge? Fuel barrels do not fly; they roll," Juan replied.

"I can take it there, Jefe," Miguel said. "I can lead a mule anywhere in these mountains."

Anthony had to make him understand. He had to grab Sofia and pull her from this madness. The ride was starting up again; he had to jump off before it was too late. He wanted to phrase his feelings correctly in front of Juan.

"Juan," Anthony said. "About the helicopter."

"We don't need the helicopter. Tomorrow, you have all day to move the men over the pass."

"I'm getting off the ride. I don't want on any longer."

"It will be more difficult without Tito, but we haven't lost yet. We bide our time and wait. Like we always have."

"No. I'm done. I'm offering to fly your men to safety then I'm through."

"You can't quit, Anthony. You love it too much, like I."

Anthony could see that his words were having no effect on Juan. Maybe that's what it was like when you became so involved in your own cause and in your convictions; everything was tangential to you. He would have to leave and not come back.

"Anthony, if you want to fly the helicopter. That is good. We will use the helicopter," Juan said. "Ferdinand, I mean Miguel, I have already sent someone to bring the three mules back. Tomorrow morning, take all of the fuel to the helicopter, and don't come back until you have done it."

"After that, I am done, Juan," Anthony said. "I know you don't understand it, but I am telling you so that you know."

"Now, I know," Juan replied. "Tomorrow, we will be like the flying cavalry of the United States army. You will be flying us, no?"

"Yes, I will fly for you one last time."

"Carlos, have you ever flown before?" Juan asked.

"No, Jefe, never."

"Well, tomorrow will be your chance. You don't even need a ticket."

"A ticket, Jefe, is it a ride?"

"Yes, it is a ride," Juan replied. "A ride you can never leave. No matter what you desire."

"But, I should like to get off," Carlos added with concern.

"Nay, not after you ride in a helicopter, Carlos," Juan said. "You will never want to walk again. You will sit on the ground and say, 'Fly me here' and 'Fly me there. My feet were not built to touch the ground; they are too old and slow. My desire is to move fast, like in a helicopter.' That's what you will say after your ride in a helicopter."

"I will ride in that helicopter, *Commandante*, but I do not think I will like it," Carlos said.

"You will like it, Carlos."

"I will ride, but I will not like it," Carlos repeated.

They heard whistling down the trail.

"It is Sofia," Carlos said immediately. He ran toward the inclined trail. Moments later, he returned with Sofia and Doctor Romona.

Romona went immediately to the boy. From her face, they could discern that things were not good.

"*Doctora?*" Carlos asked.

"Carry him into the cave, gently."

They picked him up with the blanket; he was light and easy to carry.

Juan's face was pensive and taut. As Juan looked at Romona, Anthony found it difficult to read his expression, a mixture of desire, agitation and relief. Romona nodded to Juan.

They watched as Romona quickly opened her medical bag, deftly inserted an intravenous needle in his arm, and attached a bag of plasma to it. Juan hung the bag on the rock wall above Ferdinand's head. Romona checked his injuries and said something to Juan, which the others could not hear.

"No, Romona, I am not going to attack the town," Juan replied.

"They expect an attack. I was barely able to pass by the defensive positions encircling Santa Angelia," she said. "The colonel has filled the streets with soldiers. Help me with the boy. He has metal in his belly. We must remove it, or it will infect him."

Juan knelt beside her.

"What do you want me to do?" Juan asked.

"I don't have any anesthetic. He's quiet now. I don't want him to jerk while I am inside picking out the shrapnel."

Juan motioned over to Miguel and Anthony. Anthony squatted over the legs to hold them immobilized. Juan and Miguel held onto each shoulder and arm. Romona poked into the bloody flesh. Anthony turned his head away. Ferdinand jerked violently; his eyes opened.

"Ferdinand," Miguel cried out. "Hold still. We are helping you."

Ferdinand flailed around and tried to throw them off. Juan called over to Carlos.

"Carlos, bring me the rum."

Carlos brought over a swollen skin.

Juan leaned over Ferdinand's face and looked into his eyes.

"Ferdinand," Juan said loudly. "Ferdinand. *Hijo.*"

Ferdinand's eyes cleared. He stared at Juan.

"I want you to drink this rum. It will help with the pain."

He squirted a long draught into Ferdinand's mouth. He swallowed and coughed. He squirted again. Ferdinand swallowed and coughed. Juan tried to squirt more, but Ferdinand held his mouth closed.

"Ferdinand," he said close to his face. "Drink again."

Ferdinand drank more rum and coughed.

"Good, Ferdinand you're doing well, here take some more," Juan encouraged.

Ferdinand drank again. This time he did not cough.

"I feel sick," he said.

"That is rum," Juan said, "at first, it makes you feel sick, then it makes you feel good, real good."

"Feeling sick is good," Romona said. "It means he is feeling something."

"Can't we give him something to eat? It will make his stomach handle the rum," Miguel said.

"Not until I finish taking the metal out," Romona said. "Make him drink some more and then he can rest and let the rum work."

Juan made him drink several mouthfuls of rum. He whispered in the boy's ear and pulled a blanket over him. He stood and walked over to Carlos who had started a small fire at the mouth of the cave.

"The fire will take away the dampness from the cave, "Carlos said.

Romona squeezed Ferdinand's hand. She signaled to the others to hold him down as she probed around his stomach. The rum had quieted him. He did not move. She finished quickly, pulling out several fragments. She sewed him up, gently washed his wounds and applied sterile dressings. She turned to Miguel.

"He should go back to town with me. He has lost a lot of blood and should be watched," she said slowly, trying to let her words sink in.

"I promised him we would go when you finished," Miguel said. "Were you able to take everything out?"

"I don't know. The only way is an x-ray."

"When he wakes up, we must go. I will honor his wishes."

"Even if he wishes to die? That is what could happen without proper care," she said.

"He will live," Miguel said.

"Juan, talk to Miguel. If his brother stayed with me for only one day for observation, the worst danger will have passed. If he begins to bleed up here, he will bleed to death."

"Ferdinand made a decision about what will be. I, too, will honor that decision," Juan replied.

"He does not understand things as you do. You must guide him in his decisions."

"That is where you and I differ. You assume because he is young, he cannot decide what to do with his own life."

"You talk as if he has the wisdom and life experience to make that decision."

"You will decide his life?" Juan asked.

"I or some other responsible person, yes," she replied.

"I know you use your skills every day to buy away death, but some of us aren't afraid to die. For some us, it is our destiny to die today."

"There's a difference between death and doing stupid things to increase the likelihood of death. I understand that at some future point, death will come to us all. It is our duty today to push that day off far into the future."

"One way, you may die sooner than the other. If you don't make those decisions, your own life is not yours. If it is not your life, you have no right to it."

"From our discussions, *Commandante*, I've always believed that you cared for your men as if they were your children?" Romona asked.

"Yes," Juan replied.

"As your children, you have the moral responsibility to help them make good decisions regarding their lives."

"Yes."

"With Ferdinand, you refuse to give that guidance," she said.

"You have your understanding on responsibility, and I have mine," he replied. "You would like to tell him what they must do. It is safer if he goes with you, but you cannot stop him from dying if he starts bleeding badly. You talk about probabilities of outcomes; in reality, you cannot predict what will happen. No more than I."

"I'm talking about a prudent course of behavior. Not throwing lives to the winds of chance."

"I teach my men how to make those decisions and let them know that their decision is right regarding themselves. You have told Miguel and Ferdinand about the consequences of their actions, and they're willing to accept those consequences. Ferdinand is not going to walk out of here and die, is he?"

"Probably not."

"It's as likely that he will recover," Juan stated.

"The bleeding has stopped. There is a chance it will start again."

"There is a chance of it," Juan countered. "We minimize our chances, we do not minimize death. We draw on medicine and technology to forestall death to the last possible moment. As Christians, Jews, Muslims, Buddhists, and Hindus, we proclaim the greatness of God and how he created us in his image and how he loves us, but yet, we exhaust every modern miracle to eke out life for one more second, one more minute, one more hour, one more week, one more month, one more year or one more something.

Instead of seeking to go back to Him in the shortest possible time, we prolong our time here. If we truly believe, we would throw out all modern medicine."

"Why don't you have your soldiers run down in the village and fight to the death? You will have your holy war!" she exclaimed.

"I did not use the term holy war," Juan replied. "Neither am I a fanatic. I grow tired of life, and people's insistence that we save life to the last possible moment. One who believes such rubbish is the strongest heretic and blasphemer who ever walked the earth."

"God put us on this earth for a purpose," Romona replied. "If he did not, where does that put us? Why should we put up with all this suffering and misery? I cannot accept that God is a great wonderful God and he puts you on this earth to go to ensure that they have the shortest lives possible. You kill your soldiers meaninglessly."

"I kill for duty. I have fired many shots with my rifle. I have fired many rounds on orders. I have thrown many hand grenades," Juan stopped.

He picked up the skin and squirted the liquid into his throat. He swallowed hard.

"Yet, when I look back over my many years of fighting, I feel little remorse," he said. He drank more. "When we cross over a battle field, bodies are strewn all over. I know my orders have killed them. When I order my soldiers to fire artillery, launch bombs and set up landmines, I kill. After the skirmish, I walk the ground and see the dead, made dead by my orders from my mouth.

Duty requires reasoning. I can give an order to go storm that village, and as a soldier he will kill to obey his orders. The soldier boldly goes because he believes in his duty to obey. No power on earth could force him to kill for me, unless he first accepted and believed in the duty."

"Duty is important to you. What about your duty to Ferdinand? When is he released from your all-powerful duty?"

"When he stops believing," Juan said.

"Believing in what?" Romona asked.

"What we all believe in. It is the common thread which binds us together," Juan said.

"What do you believe in that can keep you fighting for all these years?" she asked.

"I believe in the grand Colombia. I believe in a united South America. I believe in equality among all men. Corruption creates inequality and disenfranchisement. When men cannot pursue their happiness, because of the government, good men must fight back. I was educated, and I am intelligent.

From history books, I know what must happen. Corrupt men do not give up their power and entitlements easily. They rationalize, justify and ignore."

"People must be able to change, and they must be able to change voluntarily," Romona responded with emotion. "You can't force people to act. That is coercion. Coercion begets violence."

"To voluntarily act, corrupt men must believe that it will become extremely unpleasant for them, unless they act. Such belief is difficult, because you become immune to your own idiocy," Juan replied, his face red. A camel will sooner pass through the eye of a needle than for a rich man to act. War becomes the only remedy. The problem with war is that everyone, and I mean everyone, wants war, until the killing starts. Then nobody wants it. Killing does not discriminate.

Once the war starts, man's pride and fear blocks the way, making the cessation of the killing more difficult. Losing is unacceptable to man's pride until he has nothing left but his pride. Fear creeps in slowly, because war may be bad, but the vanquished pay a heavier price, so war continues."

"The war continues," Romona said. "That is the first thing you have said that I agree with. The war continues the needless pain, which makes it quicker to go back to your Creator where all things will be understood. How about the people who struggle daily to put food on their tables? They don't want the war to continue. They would be much better off if it simply stopped."

"No one wants the war," Juan replied. "It is a halfhearted civil war. No one wants to fight, because no one wants to die. Go and ask ten people in the street, and no one wants to die. Someone else can die, but that's the problem with war. War does not choose victims; it makes them. I came here to lead people to God.

I've been successful in this war, because I am willing to sacrifice all my men to survive. And what a glorious sacrifice. They don't want any of their men killed because it is politically inconvenient. They do not understand that death is the ultimate sacrifice, political, spiritual and fraternal.

If I survive and live to fight another day, I have not lost, so I have won. There is no way to defeat me, unless you kill all of my men and me. In attempting that, I will kill all of your men. That is why I kill, to live."

"What have we learned in fifty years? Nothing," Romona said. "You advocate overthrow of the government, but the government is never overthrown. There is always somebody in power collecting money. The first blow to law and order is a weak individual who lives his own foolish little life without the restraint of penalty for his actions. Remove that restraint and turn your citizenry into butchers and frenzied mobs seeking blood."

"What do you expect me to do?" Juan said harshly. "Sit back and watch the slaughter? You have a military with a bunch of hard-boiled janissaries beyond the reach of civilian authority. The military ideology is to complete missions successfully. The army has not changed its doctrines or its form of organization for fifty years.

The army is organized for conventional warfare. Casualties are an accepted and expected by-product of all military missions; the military lives by the sword and will die by the sword. Collateral damage is perfectly acceptable to military leaders as long as the mission is successfully fulfilled. The military 'controls' a troubled area by killing anybody they believe is against them."

"The government cannot use violence to resolve disagreements. When the government condones violence," Romona replied, "the public becomes immune to it. Killing becomes indiscriminate, organized crime and drug lords and any petty thief can use violence -- and society cannot differentiate. Explosives blow up and kill humble people in remote villages or in densely populated cities and no one knows if the deaths were ordered from a cold, bureaucratic desk, protected with guile, or from the hands of a thief trying to hustle money."

"Now, we are reaching common ground, Romona," Juan said. "If you ask any rebel leader who is fighting for his life, he will agree with you. We want a safe place to air our grievances. Leaders from all sides cannot condone violence of any sort and must use every effort to stop the killing, short of more killing. The army is an effective weapon to kill, but little else, it cannot negotiate because that is not its mandate, and it cannot judge because that is not its job."

"Lay down your weapons," Romona said. "Especially if you are unafraid to die, someone must go first. Use your impressive voice and overwhelming intellect to convince others."

"I know the end to that story," Juan scoffed. "The bravest man actually speaks out. Who is squashed first? Him and his free speech. Catching and disappearing somebody who speaks out is easy.

Catching and killing a man with a gun is very difficult, if not impossible. The man with the gun simply moves to another area until the army has killed everyone they wanted. He infiltrates again when the army leaves. And the cycle begins again. Who is left dead? The innocents. God put me here to protect the innocents, not to slaughter them."

"The violence continues with no let up," Romona spat.

Juan agitated, walked over to the fire and sat silently beside it.

"Enough already," Romona said, "quit thinking about the next heroic action you will do to injure or kill yourself."

Anthony walked over and knelt next to Romona. She turned away and tended to Ferdinand.

"Are you finished with the boy, Romona?" Anthony asked.

"Yes, he is resting peacefully. His bandages are dry. There is nothing more that I can do."

"It is very late; it's best if you go," Anthony said. "Carlos will accompany you back to the car."

"No, I know this wilderness. Sofia will be by me," she replied.

He helped Romona pack up her bag and the unused supplies.

"I want to check the boy one last time before I go. Wait for me outside," Romona said.

Anthony left the cave; Sofia followed. The sun was close to setting.

"Anthony Wyatt, you should counsel me about unnecessary risks," she said. "Flying a helicopter with no fuel?"

"That's why we need to leave. Are you ready?" he asked.

"Halfway," Sofia replied. "My mother alternates between letting me leave and imprisoning me in my room. When we walked up the trail, she was resigned to my leaving."

"Should I walk down with you or wait for you here?"

"Are you afraid of my mother?"

"Yes."

"You can have people shoot at you and fall out of the sky in a big piece of metal, and you don't want to face my mother?"

"Yes."

"Anthony, you never cease to amaze me."

"It's just that, your mother's opinion of me matters. Those people who shoot at me don't matter."

"If it will make you feel better, I will have my mother shoot at you. Although she will have to borrow your gun, she doesn't have one."

"She can shoot me. I deserve it."

"You do."

"Yes, for taking her only daughter away. I don't think I would let you go if I was her," Anthony replied.

"It's not her choice,"

"Your nana?"

"She left her home, with little hope of ever returning. She understands. A better life awaits me."

"Do you want to go to the United States?" he asked.

"It's safer," she replied tentatively.

"That's not what I asked."

"This is my country," she replied with conviction.

Anthony looked at the ground.

"Do you want to return?" she asked.

"I want you to be safe. I want to have babies with you and have them live out their natural lives."

"Shhh, my grandmother will hear," she whispered.

"It's what she wants, isn't it?" he asked.

"After we're married," she replied.

"Let's get married today," Anthony said suddenly.

"What's this all about?" Sofia asked.

"Tito's death hit me harder than any other," Anthony said. "I realized that I will die. Or worse, I realized that you will die. I don't want that. I'm quitting. When I return to Juan, I am going to tell him I'm quitting and taking you to the States."

"You are in a strange mood," Sofia replied. "Tito's death has unsettled you. Give yourself some time to reflect."

"I don't want you hurt," Anthony said, "because of me."

"I'm here for you," Sofia said. "Later, you must propose to me properly, not in the middle of the jungle."

"Yes, I will do it romantically," Anthony said. "Will your mother object?"

"Though I should say 'no' to my daughter," Romona said as she left the cave and heard the last of their conversation. "Well, *Capitan* Wyatt, you have made an impression since you have been here. We worried when we sent Sofia off to the University, that she would not return. Never did I think that I would lose her here in the little town of Santa Angelia. Embrace me, Antonio. For better or worse, you are part of the family now."

Romona hugged Anthony. He started to say something.

"No need to say anything," Romona said. "I sadly understand all too well."

Romona hugged him tightly and kissed both his cheeks. She pulled away from him; her eyes were wet. She gave the medical bag and supplies to Sofia and walked a short distance down the trail.

"I will come back later, under the cover of night," she said.

"I will wait for you," he replied. "I want to speak with Juan alone. I don't want to end it this way. I want him to understand, and tomorrow, there will be no time to talk."

"Go and talk with him. I will wait for you in my fern garden."

"Or I will wait for you," he said.

"I will return quickly."

"Sofia," he said urgently.

"Anthony," she replied.

"I love you," he said.

"And I, you," she said, and kissed him gently on the lips, turning to run to catch up with her mother.

He moved quickly through the brush, taking a different way back to the cave's entrance. Anthony came up directly behind Carlos, who was standing there waiting for him. Carlos jumped when he tapped him on the shoulder.

"Señor, it is a good thing I do not carry a weapon. I would have shot you."

"You shouldn't be so easy to sneak up on."

"I was listening to the katydids. Do you hear that fast chirping? Hear how they sing love songs to their mate. Even though I could crush them with my fingers, they sing out loud, defying me. Their long wings look like leaves, and I could no more catch them on this dark evening, than catch the wind."

"You might not be able to catch them, but I'm sure that there is something out there who eats them by the hundreds."

"The law of the jungle." Carlos said.

"Is El Jefe inside?"

"Yes," Carlos replied. "Ferdinand and Miguel left."

Anthony was surprised to hear this, but it was all right. He had wanted to speak to Juan alone.

"Was he walking?" Anthony asked. "Ferdinand, I mean?"

"Miguel half-carried him away. Color was returning to his cheeks. They didn't say much."

"Has El Jefe talked to you?"

"No," Carlos replied. "That is not his way."

"He talks all the time."

"Not about things on his heart. That he keeps closely hid."

"He knows I'm finished."

"He doesn't believe that."

"And you?"

"I will be waiting for you here. I will take you to her house."

"She is waiting for me."

"She is waiting for you," Carlos repeated.

"Yes."

"She should have stayed here."

"She is very headstrong," Anthony said.

Carlos smiled, his teeth made bright by the moonlight contrasting with the darkness of his skin.

"In the morning," Carlos asked, "should I come by and guide you?"

"No, I can find the helicopter. After all, I am the one who landed it."

"Jefe told me to take you to the helicopter. He doesn't want you falling off the ledge."

"Meet me here then," Anthony replied.

"Miguel told Juan that he would have all the barrels of fuel by the helicopter in the morning."

"All of them?" Anthony asked. "One barrel will be enough."

"I will go and tell Miguel that," Carlos replied. "*Señor*, are you going now?"

"Yes, in a minute. I want to hear the katydids sing."

"They are beautiful," Carlos replied, continuing, "You did not say good-bye."

"You know I am leaving," Anthony said.

"I knew it the first moment I saw you look at Sofia," Carlos said. "Now you have something to live for."

"I will come back to say good-bye," Anthony said.

"With love begins worry. I will wait for you in the morning," Carlos said.

"Thank you," Anthony said quietly.

Carlos turned and walked up the trail.

Anthony listened to Carlos' footfalls in the jungle until he could hear them no more. The katydids sounded like the crickets back home. Anthony turned down the path towards the waterfall and passed in behind the falling water.

Juan was kneeling with his hands folded in front of him. He rose and dusted off his knees when he heard Anthony enter the cave.

"Ferdinand is a child," Juan began, "mowed down like a tender shoot of wheat under a sickle. What do I do? I encourage him to rise in rebellion. Off he goes, ghastly pale with moribund eyes."

"He has no choice," Anthony replied. "He can fight and die or he can simply die."

"That is me talking. He has a choice. He can live. Instead, he looks at me with his dying eyes and desires to fight on. What will I do? I will dupe them. He will put his faith in me and I will follow my path eternally set down. And he will die, bloody and still."

"He will die as a man."

"A dead man has no value, except maybe to God."

"You believe in God?"

"It was my calling," Juan said. "But you did not return to talk with me about that."

"No. I came to make sure you understand that I am leaving."

"Then leave."

"I am."

"Why are you here?"

"I felt I owed you an explanation."

"You owe me nothing."

"I wanted to thank you."

"You owe me nothing. No thanks. No good-byes. Nothing."

Anthony stared at the stone floor. He had not run this scene out in his mind like this.

"What do you want me to say?" Juan asked. "Beg you to stay? Command you to fight? The eternal qualities of a warrior are irrational and iridescent, such as honor and duty and loyalty and resolution and courage and sacrifice of one's self. None of those qualities is in your head; they are in your heart. Your head thinks you want to quit?"

"I am quitting."

"What are you going to do?"

"Teach English," Anthony replied.

"Teach English? How long? Where?"

"I don't know."

"When that doesn't suit you, what will you do?" Juan asked.

"It will suit me," Anthony said. "The life I lead now is too dangerous for her."

"The real reason," Juan paused. "I told you that you cannot lead a normal life, have normal relationships and teach English when you choose this life."

"I am unchoosing it."

"The life chooses you in the end. It's something you cannot walk away from," Juan said. "When you came to me and told me that you wanted to be known as the greatest rebel fighter in the world, I thought you strange. I could not understand why you would risk your life here, fighting for a people you barely knew. Idealism works until the bullets fly.

War is the province of hardship and fear and suffering and death. Each of these brings out the best and worst in men. It has brought out the best in you. You are cut from a different cloth; you excel where the average man cowers and pisses his pants. You believe you can simply walk away?"

"I am in love."

"To love is good, for love is difficult," Juan replied. "For one human being to love another is the most difficult task. Love induces one to ripen, to strive to mature in the inner self, to manifest maturity in the outer world and to become that manifestation for the sake of another."

"We love one another deeply," Anthony said.

"Young people err because being beginners in love; they do not know how to love. Love does not have anything to do with arousal and mad coupling. True union cannot be built on uncertainty and immaturity. Young people throw themselves at each other when loves comes upon them. Is she waiting for you?"

Anthony stayed silent.

"I thought so. What of the future?" Juan asked. "Society perceives love as common public entertainment; it needs to be easily available, inexpensive, safe and reliable. Opening one's self, and surrendering, and every kind of communication are none of these things. You are willing to risk her life when true love would demand the opposite response."

"She understands the risks," Anthony replied.

"How can she understand the risks when you don't? You are going to go with her tonight when the entire fifth division of the Colombian army is out looking for you. Are you insane or merely in love?"

"I will be moving under the cover of night," Anthony said.

"What of Tito?" Juan asked.

This question cut Anthony to the core. He had been thinking of Tito ever since he first saw the plateau.

"Can you walk away from the memory that you were not good enough?" Juan asked.

"I didn't kill him," Anthony replied angrily.

"You could not save him," Juan replied, "like you couldn't save your father."

"I didn't kill him," Anthony said.

"No, he killed himself, believing that the best of his life was over," Juan replied. "Nothing better was going to happen to him."

"I was there. I should have been his hope."

"Guilt. Guilt created by the fear that one is not important enough to those we truly love."

"I'm leaving now with one I truly love," Anthony said. He stood up to leave.

"Anthony, I cannot command where there is no will to obey. I, too, am affected by Tito's death. I know that you believe you are in love, and you cannot measure up in the eyes of those who love you, your father, Tito, and now her, so you believe you can run away, even after investing years of your life in who you now are and building relationships with these men, with Tito, and with me."

"I'm not running away. I'm escaping."

"God has an inevitable plan for all of us. It is a mirage to believe that you can escape God's plan. Leaving for the safe white North might be the safest risk, but it does not guarantee the length of your life or the quality of it."

"What do you want me to do?" Anthony said. "Run out and kill Mono? I was too busy fighting for my own life."

"Tito wanted you to stay true to yourself," Juan replied. "You must figure out what that is."

"I will be back in the morning to help you lead the men out of the valley," Anthony replied, "I will be square to Tito, to you and to everybody."

"As you leave me tonight, understand that you are making a decision which will not sit with you."

Juan stood up. Anthony followed him out of the cave. Anthony looked after him. Juan had melted into the dark quiet of the jungle.

Anthony listened to the enveloping call of the katydids and slowly walked to the clearing among the ferns. In the opalescence of the silvery moon, he saw her walk towards him, the luminous beams radiating off her luxurious dark hair.

"I'm back sooner than I thought," she said. "I'm glad. Every night sound has put my entire body on edge. Look at me, I'm shaking."

She came to him. They held one another.

"I'm edgy, just like you. Juan thinks I am making a mistake," Anthony replied.

"You are tense. Let's go home. I can make it right for you."

"We should stay in the cave tonight," he said.

"We can take the pipe back," she replied. "There's no bed in the cave."

"How are you going to make it across the mountains?" he asked, squeezing her tightly.

"I will," she replied. "Only one last night in my bed."

"I want you to know that I will always fight for you, no matter what," Anthony said. "Although I'm a little afraid, aren't you?"

"I'm afraid of spider-filled, dark pipes."

"No, of death."

"We all will die; it's the living that most of us forget to do," Sofia said.

"The war ended too soon for my father," Anthony began tentatively, "and he ended up back in Montana, resenting every minute of his life. He always thought he was cut out to be a war hero. Living with smashed dreams kills you little by little 'til you end up killing yourself. There's nothing left for me up there."

"I will be your everything here," she said with brightened eyes.

"You are my everything; that's why I'm so confused," Anthony confided.

"We can make a great life here, fighting for a free Colombia," she said.

"I don't know," Anthony said. "I can't lose you."

"We will take it one day at a time, and you can change your mind as many times as you want," Sofia said. "I'm with you on the long road, not today, not tomorrow, but forever."

"I won't know what to tell Juan when I see him again," he said.

"Did he expect you to leave?" she asked.

"What do you think?" he asked her back.

"Juan knows everything," she replied.

"But he doesn't have everything," he said, encircling her close.

"No, he doesn't," she replied as she turned her mouth up to his.

Anthony slipped his hand under her light shirt and placed it on her hot stomach. His hand acted like a conduit, forming the contact between two power sources. Sexual energy raced between them; they kissed passionately, pulling each other's shirts off. Sofia pushed away from Anthony and ran wildly through the ferns. Anthony charged after her, catching her and releasing her, catching her and releasing her. Such was his excitement, his arm hurt no more. They fell into the soft, fresh ferns, Sofia clinging to Anthony's neck. The smell of his sweat and the sweet ferns mingled and lingered on her nose. He pulled off his pants and removed hers. He wanted her now. He did not know if he could hold himself back long enough.

He lay back on the blanket of ferns and pulled her on top of him. She straddled him and rubbed herself on him in slow circular motions until she felt him inside her and she kept spinning and spinning her hips against him until her entire body convulsed and sweat and shuddered. She cried loudly. The earth, moon and stars spun around her. And he didn't stop. She felt him lift her up and down with the strength of his hips; the tingling sensations vibrated her entire body; she wanted them to stop for fear of the unknown, for fear of a feeling she had never experienced in her life, and for fear of losing control. Tears fell freely from her eyes; she didn't want it to end.

They lay on the ferns catching their breaths. Through the opening in the trees, the stars sparkled; Anthony pointed out the constellations he knew. Tears continued to fall unwillingly from her eyes. She burrowed her face into his strong chest and hugged him tightly.

"What is the matter, Sofia?"

"I don't want this moment to end. I just want it to be you, me, under the moon, the stars, forever," she answered.

"We will. . ." he began.

She put her finger on his lips. She was his and he would last forever and tomorrow. Anthony sat up and cradled her in his arms. He rocked onto his feet and brought her up with him as he stood. He carried her around naked between the ferns. She clung to him tightly as he walked, feeling his strong, broad shoulders. He didn't set her down as he reached up into the low hanging branches and plucked two ripe mangos. They were thick and firm in his hand; he ripped the skin with his teeth; and, the rich juice oozed wet onto his palm. He fed her and let the juice drip over her neck and breasts. He licked the juice. Pleasure pumped through him.

Sofia pushed out of his arms and jumped to the ground, chasing him around the tree. He stayed just out of her reach in a mock game of tag. As the game intensified, she strained to grab him and he eluded her by a thread. She flung herself at him, and guessing her intention, he stood still and caught her full weight. He laid her to the ground; she could feel the fallen mangos on her back, giving her tingling sensations.

He stood over her. While he reached up and plucked several ripe mangos from the tree, she could see he was excited. She had never been this close to a man before and was curious, examining him closely, kissing and touching. She felt a cool velvety liquid on her skin. He was squeezing the mangos with his hands, the sweet drops falling all over her. She held her hands out and he squirted the juice into them, and she rubbed some on him as he stood in front of her. She tasted and licked and suckled, softly at first and increasing with intensity as he responded until she felt the salty surge of his warmth mingled with the sweet mango juice. She did not stop kissing and toying, excited at her power to create his intensity. He gently reclined her to the ground, kneeling beside her.

He squeezed several mangos on her breasts and other parts. He massaged her. She felt his excitement grow as he caressed and rubbed her skin. And then he was there, at the part she had always been told was hers and hers alone. She wanted to share it, and he knew that. Her breath quickened. His touch made her let go; she could no longer think or see, only feel. She grabbed his hair in her hands and held on.

It was a ride like no other. Private and close, twirling her body more than the colorful carousel which whirled in the park in the summers, twinkling with lights as the night intensified. His finger, lips, tongue and other soft parts were all over her, everywhere at once, like the whirling dervishes of her books, spinning her higher and higher. No wonder they said this should be avoided, because if they knew the sensations caused by such rides, no one would ever stop. As she bucked and moaned, she rode to ecstasy. God had sent him to her in her own private garden of Eden. Her romantic dreams had never reached such heights, involving her entire body and spirit, forcing loud screams from her lips and circulating fire in every nerve ending in her skin. The earth trembled. She shook her head wildly and clawed at the ground, rooting up large soft fronds, until she could feel no more.

She opened up her eyes. He was lying next to her, staring at her. Piles of pulled up fern plants lay strewn around them. She looked at her hands; dirt was under her fingernails.

"Is it supposed to feel this intense and out of control?" Sofia asked.

"Only with us," he replied.

"Bring me close," she trembled.

He entwined and protected her with his muscular arms, her essence accepting him, as a tailor-made glove envelopes one's hand. They stayed interlocked, fondling and stroking each other, writhing together as the sound of the jungle filled the night air. The world rotated a little bit more as they added another chapter to their own personal book of love.

Rolling to their feet, they collected their clothes and dressed. She cradled his face with her hands and kissed him fully on the lips.

"I should have brought a bag to carry mangos back in," she whispered.

"We can come back," he said.

"We can stay in the cave, if you want," she said.

"I've gone native," he said. "Nobody can catch me now."

"Let's go home, *mi amor*," she said.

She enfolded her arms in his and pulled him back along the creek. They did not speak anymore, moving step in step along the sandy ridges to the other side of the creek. Together, they ducked and crawled quickly through the pipe and out the other end, climbing up the small metal ladder together to shove over the heavy lid. They stopped in the alley, intertwined with each other and the fresh night air and the deep rumblings of a town asleep, exhausted by the previous night's revelry. They ran to the familiar yellow door. Sofia opened it and led him up to their hideaway on the third floor.

Sofia threw open the windows. They stood looking at the night sky filled with brilliant stars.

"Did you see it?" Anthony asked excited.

"Yes," Sofia replied.

"The shooting star lit up the whole sky."

"It was brighter than any star I've ever seen," Sofia replied.

"The star that burns brightest, burns the shortest."

"He eclipses all others," she replied. "Kiss me."

They kissed.

"That was for luck," she said quietly.

It was well past midnight before they fell asleep.

Chapter Fifteen-Thursday Dawn

He lay there quietly, listening to her breathe. He had to go. It would be light soon. He sat up. He had slept fitfully; his short night had been filled with dark dreams. He lay back down again.

"You must go," she said quietly.

"In a minute," he responded.

He did not want to go. He wanted to stay and hold onto this moment. It had never felt this way. He must leave; darkness protected him. Before she told him to go again, he rolled over and looked at her.

"Don't worry," he said softly. "I'm protected by your love."

"Lover, you must go. The rooster crows," she replied.

He put her finger to her lips and kissed her gently, pulling her on top of him. They moved together, grasping at each other in quiet, frenetic passion. Their movements stilled.

He rose and dressed quickly. He drank from the bottle of mineral water sitting on the bedside table. He sat beside her and caressed her stomach.

"You must go," she pleaded earnestly. "Pink is already showing on the horizon. The sun will meet you as you leave this house."

"Your love will cover me in an invisible cloak," he said.

Smiling, she pushed him off the bed, covered herself and walked him downstairs and out towards the back door. She pushed a key into his hand.

"What's this for?" he asked.

"It's your house," she said.

"My house?"

She smiled at him.

"It is good," she said simply. "May God go with you."

She opened the rear door and looked up and down the street. It was empty. She kissed him one last time and pushed him, fighting the urge to keep him safe inside her.

Once outside, he heard the door lock behind him. She was right, he thought, it was getting light. Still, it was dark enough, and safety was steps away. He pulled up his collar and pulled the black scarf over his head. He crossed the street and looked back up at her balcony. He could see her lithe figure standing away from the window, watching him. A diesel rumbled in the distance. He looked up one last time, turned and walked down the street, hugging close to the stone wall. Juan was wrong; no one was out looking for him; he would reach the jungle in minutes.

He started to think of her again. He smelled the remnants of her perfume. He recalled every line and shadow of her face. He had studied her face and body while she slept last night to imprint everything on his memory. He recalled the way her lips curved slightly and the way her lips parted as she breathed in her sleep. Her skin was without blemish, an even golden color across her whole body. Her legs were long and shapely.

A horn blew next to him.

"You there!" a harsh voice growled. "Where are you going?"

Out of reflex, Anthony looked up. A stocky man sat in the driver's seat. To his left, sat a young soldier armed with a rifle; he was not looking at Anthony but trying to stay awake. In the back of jeep, Anthony saw men who looked like they had just been picked up off the street. They wore no uniforms and had no weapons. As soon as his eyes met those of the man driving the jeep, he knew he had made a mistake.

"Come closer," the voice sounded harsher. "Quick!"

Anthony ran, scampering behind the jeep, crossing the street and entering a small alley. He heard the gears of the jeep grind, and the lights of the jeep silhouetted him down the alley. A car was parked in the alley. Anthony jumped up and over the car and outran the lights of the jeep. He heard the jeep's horn blowing.

Buildings lined both sides of the alley. The only way out was at the end. As he reached it, he stopped and looked out into the street. They had not circled around. He looked back and saw the outlines of several pursuers at the far end of the alley. He ran left, crossing the street and looking for some place to hide. Doors lined the street. In this early twilight, none looked inviting.

He had to scramble off this main street where they could catch up to him with the jeep. He turned off on a small street and followed it until it turned into dirt. He ran along several dirt streets not sure of which direction to head. He saw several small, dilapidated wood buildings on the other side of a wire fence. He jumped the fence and ran towards the buildings. The grass was shorn close to the ground. Small and medium-sized rocks lay everywhere.

When he reached the first wood shed, he hid himself on the other side and looked back. No one followed. He looked around; he had come to the edge of the town, but on the wrong side. The mountains and jungle were on far, uphill side. These fields opened into the valley. He had to try to circle the town under the cover of these fields. He crossed over to another wood shed closer to the field's edge. Along the edge ran a thick rambling fence of brush, which would hide his movements. He felt exposed as he moved from one wood shed to another.

He moved to a larger shed with a small, broken porch. As he passed the door, a small, mangy dog barked furiously at him. The dog startled him, almost knocking him off the sagging porch. The dog did not move from the doorway and continued to bark loudly. Anthony called to the dog to quiet it. Straight ahead, Anthony saw two large Rottweilers racing towards him, responding to the small dog's call. They were not barking. They raced out of the adjacent field, following the brush fence line to run him down. His only escape was back to the street.

Anthony turned and ran at an angle, reducing the distance to the wire fence. He risked a look back; the dogs had passed the first wooden shed without slackening speed. They were going to catch him from behind. He sprinted on his toes. The wire fence beckoned ahead. The fence was higher and more complete than from where he had entered. He leapt headfirst and rolled onto his feet on the other side.

The dogs pounded up to the other side of the face, their tongues panting over their sharp teeth, growling at the intruder on the other side. Although they could have easily jumped the fence, they paced up and down on their side, watching and waiting. The larger one perked his ears up and looked back at the brush wall.

On the far side of the brush fence, he saw a jeep moving slowly with several soldiers following behind. Anthony saw them and dropped flat to the ground. The small dog was barking again. Both large dogs spun in that direction, looked back at Anthony one last time and ran full speed for the brush fence. Anthony stayed low and slunk away, holding close to any cover he could find. Behind he heard gunshots and the shouts of men. Anthony followed the dirt path around until it came out into a street.

Anthony ran toward the buildings of the town. The street curved to the left. He came to a cross street and without breaking stride, looked both ways and ran left, keeping close to the side, where a wall ran along the edge of the street. As he ran along the wall, it dropped in height until the top was level with his shoulder. He looked back; no one had followed. He leapt over the wall. Landing and falling on the dirty ground, he pushed himself to his feet.

Large, leafy trees covered everywhere, causing an enveloping black stillness. He concentrated on breathing quietly and deeply to fill his lungs full to calm his racing heart.

He moved from tree to tree, stepping over different size stones. When he came to a knee-high stone, he saw an inscription. It was a tombstone; he had jumped into a cemetery. Not wishing to end up like the inhabitants, he kept moving diagonally across the tombstones, hoping it would lead to an easy way out. He saw the front gates; a chain looped in and out of the rails. He could stay here; but if they initiated a dragnet search, there was no place here to hide. He was not going back to her house and jeopardize Sofia. He had to slip into the jungle.

On either side of the gates, a tall-railed metal fence stretched along the street. He stayed hidden in the shadows as he followed the railing to the corner. He walked over some freshly dug soil and saw that someone had been digging a hole. It was shallow. Two shovels lay along the edges. The hole was not finished. For a split second, he thought of burying himself in the cemetery until nightfall, but he scowled at the morbidity of it.

At the corner, the railing fence joined the stone wall. The railing supports had pulled away from the stone, leaving enough room for him to slip through. He looked in the street. The first morning traffic was moving along. He needed to blend in and walk right out of town. He went back to the shallow grave and dirtied his jacket and face. A plastic sheet covered the mound of dirt. He rolled it up and cradled it close to his neck and face inside his arm. With his other hand, he slung a shovel over his shoulder. He squeezed through the slit between the stone wall and the railing. He walked down the street, hunching down to obscure his height.

He never looked up, only glancing quickly to steer clear of people and objects along the sidewalk. He did not know where he was. Along the walls, pasted ads for cigarettes and liquor hung faded. Metal sliding doors protected large openings in the building. Several had opened, revealing small businesses within. He was in a commercial area; he did not want to end up bumbling into the center of the town. At the next cross street, he turned left; it looked like a residential street.

He followed this street for several hundred feet; it seemed to swing around the town. He walked by house after house until behind the houses, the mountains rose in the distance. He had circled back around the town and was now within feet of slipping back into the protective jungle. Every house was encircled with either a metal railing with jagged spear tips or stone ramparts topped with broken glass, designed to keep strangers out of the courtyard and away from the house. Anthony walked quickly along the street looking for an alleyway or opening through a wall.

The sun shone brightly. The soft morning twilight had been replaced by full, hard daylight. Sweat stung his eyes. He wiped his face with his sleeves, and dirt fell into his eyes. He tried to clear it with the back of his hand but made it worse. He blinked hard. The pain in his eye was incredible. He tried to keep walking and looking with his other eye. He breathed heavily.

Anthony stopped in a small entry way built into a large masonry wall. He set down the shovel and plastic. He wiped his hands on his pants and pulled his shirttail out to clean his eye. He blinked rapidly as he rubbed his eye. His vision cleared. He knelt down to pick up his shovel and plastic. The reverberating echo of a diesel growled down the street. He peered around the corner and saw a military vehicle idling slowly towards him.

He shrank into the entryway. It must be a patrol out searching for him. He thought of donning the shovel and plastic and bluffing his way past, but he looked out of place in this neighborhood. He had nowhere to hide. He tried the latch. It turned. He pushed the door open and slipped inside. He gently shut the door behind him. He pressed his ear against the door and listened as the diesel rumbled past, never idling or slowing in any way.

After he heard the vehicle pass, he listened for other sounds of pursuit. The street was quiet. He turned his head and looked around the small yard. The weeds had overgrown the masonry footpath, and thick vines hung heavily on the tree branches. The stucco on the house walls had broken in several places revealing the red clay brick underneath. The windows were shuttered and barred. Paint peeled from both the windows and bars.

Anthony tried the front door. It was locked. He went around to the back door. It was locked. He sat down on the veranda with its broken bright tiles and looked out. The rear wall was higher than the front; beyond, Anthony could see the peaks of the jungle.

Escape was beyond that wall. He rose and examined the wall but saw no useful handholds to hoist himself up. He piled several pieces of broken block and stone along the wall. When he had carried all the loose stone from around the house, the pile was too short to climb over the wall. He needed a rope. He had to break into the house.

The windows were barred from the outside. He checked each of the windows until he found one where the bar wiggled. With one of the larger rocks, he pounded the bar loose, giving him space to break the shutter and window. As he raised the block to break through the shutter, a feeling of guilt came over him. He had never broken into someone's home before.

The old wooden shutters crushed easily under the heavy rock. He heard the glass shatter and fall on the stone floor inside the house. He banged on the shutters and glass until he cleared half the window away. He wedged his body feet first through the broken window. As he dropped onto the stone floor, his feet crunched noisily on the glass.

He walked to the rear door, unbolted it and pushed; it did not budge. With a mighty lunge with his shoulder, the door popped open, causing him to stumble onto the hard ground. He cursed as he sat up. The back door was now open, and the mountain lay beyond.

He dragged all the furniture out of the house to the base of the wall, building a makeshift pile to the top. He slowly eased his weight onto the pile, spreading it equally between his hands and feet. He crawled spiderlike until he reached the top of the wall. Iron struts stood up along the wall. Loose pieces of barbed wire hung from several of them.

Anthony clung to the two closest struts and pulled his head over the top of the wall. He looked down the other side. The wall seemed higher on that side, and below was a small ditch littered with sharp rocks. He could not jump without breaking his leg. He carefully worked his way back down the furniture to solid ground.

Anthony searched the house. He found nothing to make a rope. He went back outside and sat on the broken bright tiles, discouraged. He could not return to her, risking not only his capture, but hers as well. He had to risk going into the street again and finding another way into the jungle. When they did not find him, they would start a house to house search of the area. A large truck thundered down the street. He had to escape now.

Over the left wall, he could see the neighbor's roof. Close to that wall was a tall tree covered in thick, knotty vines. He could easily climb the tree with the help of the vines, but none of them reached over the common wall. The vines, of course, why hadn't he thought of that before? He could lace them together to form a makeshift rope.

Anthony climbed up onto the lower branches of the tree, pulled the vines away from the branches and let them fall to the ground. He grabbed vines until a pile was under the tree. He swung down to the ground and knelt next to the pile. He quickly braided several vines until he had made a long rope strong enough to bear twice his weight. He was going to make it out of here alive.

He slung the vine rope over a shoulder and climbed carefully up again; the furniture groaned and trembled. As he pushed his body onto the wall ledge, some of the furniture tumbled and smashed onto the ground below. There was only one way down. He wriggled onto the top of the wall and straddled the wall with his legs. He wrapped one end of the vine around the iron strut and let the remainder down the other side of the wall. The end of the vine rope reached the rocky ground. He quickly climbed hand over hand down the vine.

When he reached the bottom, he leaned his face against the cool block wall and rested. He looked back up the wall. The top of the wall soared above him. Disoriented, he decided to follow the rocky ditch until he found a trail leading up the mountain. It was safer to follow a trail than walk circles in the thick, jungle growth.

The ditch led away from the wall and followed along a grassy field filled with hard, spiny shrubs. He scanned the field and saw no movement as he followed the ditch. The ditch widened. Water pooled along the bottom. He guessed that he was following a creek bed, which would wind back into the mountains. He was making good time.

The bright sun was hot, and Anthony was sweating profusely. Flies bit his ears and flew into his eyes. The ditch had widened into a ravine filled with low-lying, sharp-needled bushes. Anthony concentrated on walking; the bushes leaned towards him, catching his fatigues or scratching the backs of his bare hands. As he tried to move quickly through the increasingly dense brush, he did not see the group of soldiers standing along the top of the ravine. Their shouts stopped him dead. His eyes focused on their silhouetted bodies against the hard blue sky.

Like a wild animal in flight, he broke into a run. The uneven footing and spiky shrubs made him feel as if he was running in slow motion. His ears perked, listening for the crack of the expected shot. It finally came, tossing up rocks a few feet in front of him. He kept running. Another shot came, tossing up rocks a foot in front of him.

Anthony kept running. He felt warmth in his right leg, and then heard the echo of the third shot. He tried to dodge around a large bush, but his right leg buckled. He fell heavily. He tried to push himself up onto his legs again but stopped, as three shots fired over his head. There was no escape. He rolled on to his back and looked up at the sky. It was a blinding blue.

He sat up. There was blood all over his pants, above the knee. He pulled his pants leg up. The bullet had scraped the skin off above his knee, but had not passed through the muscle. Christ, he was lucky, he thought, it looked like hell, but he could use his leg. From the bandana he carried, he fashioned a dressing to stop the bleeding. By the time he had finished, a group of young soldiers, no older than the ones led by Juan, drew close, their guns at ready, pointing at him. He rolled down his pants leg. He spoke to them in Spanish.

"You sure made a fine mess of my leg. Either carry me out of here or shoot me," the words came out harder than Anthony intended.

He did care whether they shot him. The adrenaline was wearing off. He did not want them looking too closely at his leg.

One of them told him to stand up. The young boy's voice carried no conviction. When Anthony did not answer, they looked at one another, trying to figure out what to do. The one who had spoken told two of them to run and bring the lieutenant. When they had marched off, the group fell silent. Anthony stared at the ground. He did not notice that a dark, thin man walked up to him.

"Can you walk?" the man asked.

"No. He shot me in the leg," Anthony replied through gritted teeth.

"You are the American," the man said, unable to hide his glee.

He ordered two of the soldiers to bring a gurney. They returned quickly and placed Anthony on the gurney. Six soldiers grabbed a handhold and carried him up the hill, struggling along the rocky incline. They came out onto a dirt road and followed it to where there was a large group of soldiers standing. They were waiting for them. Anthony could sense their excitement. The lieutenant ordered them to set Anthony down. Other soldiers replaced the original six, and they carried Anthony along the narrow, dirt road until they came to the main road.

At the main road, an army truck was waiting for them. Under orders, the men placed Anthony in the bed of the truck and sat on either side of him. The lieutenant crawled in to the back of the truck and sat at the end. He hollered a command at the driver, and the truck slowly started off. Nothing covered the back of the truck.

Anthony could see the buildings of the town coming closer. Soon, he recognized the town square. They circled around and headed inside the courtyard of one of the larger buildings on the square. Soldiers stood at attention aside the doorways. A short, fat officer came out of the doorway; he wore a major's gold oak leaf. He ordered the soldiers to carry Anthony upstairs. They lifted him out of the truck and carried him up the stairs to a small white-washed office.

The fat major followed behind. He told them to set Anthony in the chair. The fat one tightened steel handcuffs on his wrists. Anthony grimaced in pain as they set him on a small wooden chair. One of the soldiers returned with a large bottle of water and a glass and put it on the table. Anthony had had nothing to eat or drink all day.

"What now?" Anthony said flatly, looking at the fat one.

"We will wait for the colonel," he replied.

"What about my leg?"

"Someone went to find the doctor," he said. "You cannot die before the colonel arrives."

The fat major drank a glass of water. They sat there for several minutes without talking. A young soldier came in and whispered into the fat one's ear. He nodded, and the young soldier went out. Moments later, Anthony heard footsteps approach the door and a sharp rap on the door. The fat one said enter. Doctor Romona came in.

Her eyes narrowed when she saw Anthony. He could not read her expression. She came over to him, knelt in front of him and felt around the wound. She stood up, walked over to the fat one and looked down at him. Anthony had never realized how tall and imposing she was.

"I can do nothing for him here."

"I can't let him leave from here," the fat major replied, the smile fading from his face.

"You can't let him die here," she said. "The wound is still bleeding."

The fat one looked confused.

"He will bleed to death," Romona continued. "Or be dead in an hour from blood poisoning if the wound isn't cleaned properly."

The fat one's face sank. He raced out of the room. Anthony heard his voice, barking orders to the men outside. Anthony started to speak, but the doctor put her finger to her lips. The fat major returned.

"We will accompany you to your office. We will go now."

"Yes," Romona said curtly.

Four soldiers came in and carried Anthony onto the truck. The doctor climbed onto the rear of the truck and sat next to Anthony's head. The fat one looked like he was about to say something; instead, he pulled himself onto the back of the truck and sat at the end. They drove quickly through the streets.

The fat major struggled to hang onto the lurching truck. Anthony suppressed a smile. He could easily kick him off the back of the truck. They pulled in front of the house Anthony had left so happily only shortly before. He didn't like being held captive. The uncertainty unsettled him.

The four soldiers came up from the other jeep and carried Anthony into the exam room. He lay still on the metal table. The fat major had entered, leaving very little room for the doctor to move. Doctor Romona told him to leave. This time, his face appeared resolute, determined to triumph in this contest of wills. She did not move a muscle. He stared at her for several seconds. Finally, he shrugged his shoulders and walked out. The doctor closed the door behind him and ran water in the small wash basin.

"Sofia," Anthony mouthed her name.

She bent down close to his ear.

"She saw the soldiers call to you outside, and you ran. Someone came and told us that they were looking for the American soldier inside the town. Carlos came. They left, hoping to find you first."

Anthony started to rise.

"Lie down," she ordered. She unwrapped the bandana and cleaned around the wound.

"The bullet tore up the skin," she said. "It was a small caliber round. There isn't much damage. I need to clean and stitch inside the wound so it stays together properly."

Anthony winced in pain as she probed around the opening.

"Small wounds hurt as much as the serious ones," she said soothingly. "The small ones you recover from."

She turned and grabbed a syringe from the small surgical table. She filled it with clear liquid.

"There's not much of this left. I've been saving up for a special case."

"What is it?" Anthony asked.

"Anesthesia. It is the only way your body will let me work inside the wound."

Anthony felt tiny pricks around the wound and then the dull pressure of Romona cleaning the jagged edges of the opening. He consciously released the tension in his neck and focused his eyes on her face. She rapidly picked up instruments, used them, set them down and grabbed others. Her eyes reminded him of Sofia. He felt her prop his leg up and watched while she deftly bandaged his leg.

"Don't stop another bullet, and you will be fine," she said quietly with a smile.

He looked at her and hoped he would live through the next couple of days. For the first time in his life, he was scared of the future.

Reading his thoughts, she pushed the surgical table back into its corner and washed her hands in the sink. She moved close to him and stroked his face softly.

"You are very handsome," she said in a low voice. "I understand why my daughter is attracted to you."

"Don't jeopardize yourselves," Anthony said. "I cannot have that. I knew the risk I was taking."

"I know the colonel well. He has been stationed here for several months and has invited us to dinner on many occasions."

Anthony's body tightened. "No, I can't let you risk your own life."

"You're no good to Sofia dead," she replied.

"I'm not going to die," he said firmly. "It's not my time to die."

"No one knows when it is their time the die," she replied. "One only hopes that is not now."

Someone rapped sharply on the door. They heard someone try the door handle. The doctor called out and said that she was finishing up and the person should not disturb her.

"I can't hold you here any longer," she said.

"Tell Sofia that I love her," he said.

"She will do anything to set you free," Romona replied. "Anything. I know her."

"No. Stop her," he answered quickly. "She will listen to you."

"The colonel is very much infatuated with her," Romona replied.

"No, I won't have that. I would rather die."

"You are no good to her dead," she repeated.

"There are certain things I cannot live with," he replied.

"Like being dead," she said. "You can overcome anything except that."

She ran her fingers through his hair and looked at him.

A rap at the door came again. She leaned over and kissed him on the forehead.

"May God protect you," she said in his ear. "To help him, don't let anyone know how strong your leg is. The slight wound was your only luck today. Use that to your advantage."

She crossed to the door, turned the key and opened it. The fat one had his hand raised as if to knock again. He nodded curtly at her. Anthony moaned from the table.

"I don't recommend releasing him from my care. He has lost much blood. He is very weak. The wound is likely to open up again, and he will bleed to death. If he goes unconscious, rush him back here straight away."

The major ordered his soldiers to lift Anthony off from the table and onto the stretcher. While they were carrying him out to the truck, the fat one yelled at them several times to move him gently.

Down at the far end of the same street that ran in front of the house, Sofia and Carlos walked quickly. They stopped when they saw several military vehicles parked in front.

"Do you think they are looking for him in the house?" she asked Carlos quickly.

Carlos shrugged his shoulders.

"No, they don't know he has been there," she said to reassure herself, she half turned to Carlos, "Stay here until they are gone and then come in."

Several soldiers filed out of the house and jumped into the back of one of the larger trucks. A group of soldiers carried a stretcher out of the house. From this distance, Sofia could not see who was on it. She watched as more soldiers and several medallion-adorned officers came out of the house and jumped into the vehicles. The convoy drove quickly away.

She ran to the house and pushed all thoughts out of her mind. She had to find Anthony. She could face anything to know he was alive and well.

When she reached the front gate, Sofia looked back. Carlos was watching intently. She motioned him forward. Without waiting for him, she pushed open the front gate, scampered up the front steps and banged on the large door.

Her mother swung open the door and looked at her surprisedly.

"I thought the major had forgotten something," she said quickly, embracing her daughter. "I'm glad you're safe." She held her daughter again. She saw Carlos slip through the gate and close it behind him.

"Carlos," Romona called out to him. She motioned him inside and shut the door firmly.

"Do you know where he is?" Sofia asked.

"They just took him away," her mother said quietly.

"He came here?" Sofia asked.

"They didn't find him here. They brought him here. He was wounded."

Sofia's face whitened.

"A bullet passed straight through his leg," Romona added quickly. "They called me to examine him in that makeshift headquarters in town. I told them that I couldn't help him there."

"What happened? Was he hurt badly?" Sofia's questions came in a rush. "Where is he now?"

"The major who brought him said they shot him as he was escaping into the jungle."

"Why didn't you keep him here," Sofia interrupted her.

"That wasn't an option," she replied. "The colonel wanted to question him. Listen to me; he doesn't want you to follow him."

"How do you know?" she asked angrily.

"He told me," Romona said, staring intently into her daughter's unbelieving face. "While I cleaned his wound, I was able to speak with him. He was awake and coherent. He said that no one must come for him. No one. He repeated it three times."

"Where did they take him?" Sofia asked.

"Back into town," Romona responded.

"I know where they are at," Carlos joined in. "They have set themselves up in the old hotel."

"That is where they are keeping him," confirmed Romona.

"I am going down there to see if I can do something," Sofia said.

Carlos nodded. Romona put her hand on her daughter's arm.

"It's not what he wanted. It won't do any good. He's under heavy guard."

"I must try to do something," she replied. She pulled away and started to open the front door. Her mother caught her again.

"He didn't want you to do anything. He has a plan for escape," she lied.

"What plan?" Sofia asked.

"He didn't have time to tell me. He strongly insisted that you not do anything."

"Well, I'm going to," she replied. She pulled the door open and ran out.

"Carlos, go after her," Romona urged.

He was halfway down the steps and had to turn to reply.

"Yes, *Senora*."

"Carlos!"

"Yes, *Senora*?"

"Keep her safe."

Carlos nodded and ran through the front gate. After Carlos left, Romona sat down on a small stool in the front entrance. She crossed herself and prayed that her daughter would return safely. She stood up; even prayers needed help. The colonel came from a respectable family from northern Colombia. He would be reasonable. She will beseech the colonel.

Gregory Arthur Solsrud

Chapter Sixteen-Thursday Morning

"You are the first citizen from the United States I have met in my country," the colonel said.

"Your English is very good for never having met an American before," Anthony replied. "Although your accent sounds more British."

"I have been to England," the colonel said. "I didn't say I have never met someone from your country, just never in Colombia."

"You've been to the U.S. What part?"

"Georgia."

"Fort Benning?"

"Yes, how did you know?"

"I have heard of the American school."

They had been talking like this for several minutes. The colonel had been waiting for him in the interrogation room when they had brought him back. The colonel looked at Anthony, his face revealing nothing. He pursed his lips, looked down, and then looked at Anthony.

"Where are you from?" he asked.

"Montana."

"Helena?" asked the colonel.

"Very good. Few people know anything about Montana. I grew up in Sand Point."

"Sand Point, is that in the eastern part?"

"Northwest, in the mountains. Near the Canadian border."

"I see," the colonel replied with understanding. "That explains why you do well among the mountains here in Colombia. You're very difficult to track."

"I didn't know you tracked tourists."

"A tourist?" the colonel paused, "what tourist attraction are you visiting in this part of our country?"

"There's a very old church with great historical significance on the square. It's a passion of mine."

"The church? Are you Catholic?"

"No," replied Anthony.

"Are you an architect?"

"No."

"Why the interest?" asked the colonel.

Anthony felt like a fly who had a single leg stuck on a silvery strand of a large web. The large spider eyed him patiently waiting. A fly had only one opportunity to throw every muscle and sinew against the sticky bond and escape.

"Educational. Is a permit from the government or a dispensation from the Pope required to visit your church?" replied Anthony.

"It's not my church," the colonel said. "The church is not much, architecturally speaking. It is famous for the pilgrims who come to visit. The Society of Mary claim that the virgin appeared to a young peasant girl. It is interesting that a non-Catholic would be interested in a truly Catholic phenomenon."

"I know a few Catholics," replied Anthony. "Are you familiar with Covadonga?"

"In Spain?" the colonel said. "Of course."

"Yes," Anthony replied.

They stopped speaking, while they looked at one another.

"May I go now?" Anthony asked.

"To visit the church?" the colonel asked sarcastically.

"No. To visit what I like. Traveling around freely is still allowed, isn't it?"

"For those who are visitors, yes, but not for those who have broken the law," the colonel stated.

"You are not letting me leave?" asked Anthony.

"Not exactly. I am helping you seek proper medical attention for your injury. It is my duty to care for visitors and help them find proper medical attention. When there is a need."

"My leg is fine," replied Anthony.

The colonel walked over to Anthony and kicked his leg hard. Anthony rolled to the floor in pain. He felt the web catch hold and stick to him. He thought about striking back. Not yet, he thought; he would only enmesh himself more. Hold still. Bide your time.

Anthony fought back involuntary tears in his eyes and rolled to a sitting position.

"What did you do that for?"

"Don't act the innocent, Mr. Anthony Wyatt. You have been caught and will be dealt with summarily. We have concrete proof."

"If you have concrete proof, why are acting like a barbarian?"

Anthony's words made the colonel walk back to his chair and sit down.

"I'm not a barbarian. I protect the public. I do not kill innocents."

"You will kill those who want to walk around free," Anthony replied.

"Mr. Wyatt. Now you interest me. Freedom is such a relative concept. You want your freedom, Mr. Wyatt? Which freedom do you want most? The freedom to return to the States? The freedom to walk out of here? Or the freedom not to die a painful death?"

A sharp knock came at the door. The colonel strode over to the door and opened it. Anthony saw a young man with an old face and a silver lieutenant bar. He spoke rapidly with the colonel; Anthony could not overhear. If Anthony had been allowed to ask, he would have found out that the name of the lieutenant was Castellana. Lieutenant Castellana looked hard at the American and left the room.

Lieutenant Castellana had heard about the capture. He had not believed it at first, but then it fit. Someone other than an ignorant rebel had to have flown that helicopter. The American looked very young to be sitting there. He listened at the door. The colonel sounded like he was simply talking to the American.

Castellana knew torture went on in Colombia. He wanted no part of it. He believed in a free Colombia. Ever since they had been attached to that pig Mono, more soldiers had died foolishly. He was using the army for his own personal misdeeds. That whole fiasco of the rebels yesterday had unnerved him. He could have been the lead lieutenant looking for the head. It was no longer a war but a blood feud. Three helicopters had been lost, serving the colonel his own justice for rolling around in the mud with a pig, and more bodies of his men thrown in with it.

He spat on the stone floor in disgust. He listened at the door again, while wondering if the total value of all the rebels' guns equaled or even came close to the price of only one of those Blackhawk helicopters. He had heard that they cost millions of pesos. Inside, they were still talking. Maybe they would not torture this one. If they could torture an U.S. soldier in custody, what chance would he have, if they turned on him?

The colonel shut the door firmly and turned towards Anthony.

"Colonel, may I ask you a question?" Anthony asked.

"Yes," the colonel replied.

"How do you know who I am?"

"I have been looking for you," replied the colonel. "And I have found you."

Anthony thought quickly, could the colonel simply kill him here? He was American after all. Killing an U.S. citizen, especially by a senior Colombian military officer had to be a tricky business. He knew his passport was in order, including the resident visa and the entry stamps; he had paid dearly to have everything match.

"Why?"

"You are the link,"

"The link?"

"Yes. The link to Mr. De la Valle. Our government enemy number one."

"The link," Anthony repeated slowly.

"Don't insult your own intelligence, Mr. Wyatt. You have been cavorting around with Mr. De la Valle for some time now. We do not want you. You are only a means to an end."

"You believe that I am your link to this Mr. De la Valle."

"Yes, that is what I have been saying."

"So I've done nothing. You are holding me to find someone else."

"No," the colonel replied sharply. "I believe you have done much wrong against my country and mixed yourself in things which do not concern you. I do not believe in freedom fighters, or whatever romantic name you call yourselves. You are nothing more than terrorists against the people. As for Mr. De la Valle, he has been quite successful in confusing uneducated people in this country."

"People who do not believe what you believe are uneducated?"

"No, people who supply or take up arms against our government are criminals. I do not believe that you will deliver him to me. Your false sense of bravado will stop you from being a traitor to the cause. With you captured, I believe he will make a mistake, maybe even try to rescue you. So far he has eluded our ambushes, but everyone has a weakness."

"Educated people are listening because his message strikes sense. You can't muzzle a message."

"You twist the meaning of my words, even though my words are very plain. In this country, we have uneducated people who are easily swayed by rabble rousing talk. Or should I say, slain by rabble rousing talk, because such talk only leads to their death."

"In unsettled times, patriots flourish," Anthony said.

"Don't call such people patriots, they are nothing but killers, or mercenaries who place their own individual interests above those of the society. They are the dupes of statesmen. Yes, we know that some of the congressmen associate with your ilk," the colonel responded heatedly. "Worse in this country, they are the pawns of foreign governments who weaken our national government and the tools of conquerors who want to come in and control Colombia.

A leftist dictator, who has bought enough weapons and ammunition to outfit two armies, runs our neighbor Venezuela, and he hates your America and its meddling. We know where Mr. De la Valle obtains his matériel. Russian rifles and Brazilian aircraft."

"Oil money fighting superpower money," Anthony said. "An endless tug of war."

"With some drug money thrown to whomever will catch it. It is easily caught," the colonel said smugly.

"And the people caught in the middle," Anthony replied.

"It's where they should stay," the colonel said.

The colonel walked over to the window. The window looked over the river. Through this section of town, it was turbulent and fast. He unhooked the window and opened it, breathing in deeply. The stuffiness left the room. Anthony felt revived. He shifted slightly, carefully testing the web.

"Would you take off these hand cuffs?" Anthony asked.

The colonel looked at him skeptically.

"I give you my word, not as a gentleman, but as a soldier, I will not attack you. Your soldiers' messy shooting turned me into a cripple. Besides, what good would it do? Your men are right outside and surround the building."

The colonel, as if to prove he was unafraid of Anthony, walked over, removed the handcuffs, and placed them on the table. He sat down in the chair across the table from Anthony.

"You admit you are a soldier?"

Anthony bit his tongue, he was about to give a smart aleck answer, telling the colonel that he had never asked.

"I knew I could not hide it. A warrior always recognizes another warrior," Anthony replied.

"Indeed," the colonel replied flattered.

"The reports say you are quite a pilot."

"I was trained by the best, as were you."

"Yes, training separates the *Lanceros* from the grunts."

"Indeed. Are you from this area of Colombia?"

"No. Bogotá," the colonel replied.

"Are your parents Colombian?"

The colonel smiled, more personably this time.

"Yes. My grandparents were born in Spain."

"They were looking for a better life," Anthony replied.

"Yes. They left in the days of Franco."

Anthony smiled. People had told him that quite often here in Colombia. People left a repressive government to find a better life and freedom. Now people were leaving Colombia to have a better life away from the violence and injustice. How do you balance freedom with justice and when do you realize that you have lost?

"Maybe you can understand now, why I'm here," replied Anthony.

The colonel's face tightened for several seconds then softened with understanding.

"Speaking as if I were another person, I understand why you are here as well as what motivates Mr. De la Valle. Where we differ is how we effect our beliefs. I do not wish to discuss these things; such talk will only create ill will while we are relating so well."

This colonel talked in riddles; for a split second, Anthony felt the delicate web slipping.

"I want my conscience clear," the colonel resumed his hard expression.

The web snapped him back hard, and another limb was caught. Conscience clearing was not a good thing. He wondered whether his leg was strong enough to hold his weight while he wrestled the colonel to the ground. If he pivoted with his left foot around the table, he could reach the colonel before any significant weight went on his hurt leg. He could not have it buckle in his one and only attempt at life.

Lieutenant Castellana knocked and entered the room. He carried a plate of meat, cheese and bread. He set a pitcher of water and two metal cups on the table. The American was younger than what his first fleeting glance had showed him. The American looked up at him; Castellana walked quickly from the room.

Castellana had never participated directly in torture sessions. Torture was something that happened on someone else's watch. There were special places for it unless there was pressure for speed. Units from Intelligence and Counter Intelligence had always carried out the physical torture. One time Lieutenant Castellana had been ordered to stand guard.

They had wanted the subversive to sign a statement, but he refused to give his name or any information and only answered in obscenities, in contempt of the officer who had tied him to a chair and had half-killed him. They dragged him outside, and in a shallow, filthy puddle where the animals drank, they tossed him, bound to the chair. As he lay dying, he thrashed around in the water and muck unable to lift his face out, exhausted and wounded from the many beatings, his strength failed quickly. They left him there and led seven more past him inside the building. Castellana did not go in again, but walked to the other side of the barracks and smoked until he saw the Intelligence vehicles drive away.

The colonel watched the door close and lifted up his cup.

"To life," the colonel said.

"To life," Anthony replied. "Hopefully my own."

"We can work something out," the colonel said. "Please help yourself."

Anthony started to say no as a reflex reaction conditioned out of his Midwest upbringing, rejecting hospitality when it was first offered. True hospitality had to turn into a powerful struggle of who could deny oneself more, the offeror or the offeree. The absurdity of the situation hit him as well as how hungry he was.

Anthony tore off a large piece of bread, cut an ample piece of cheese and a couple of thick slices of sausage with the dull knife and fashioned himself a sandwich. The bread was stale, but the smoked cheese and spicy sausage made up for it, not quite up to his standards for his last meal but very passable to his empty stomach. The colonel cut a couple of pieces of cheese and sausage and sat chewing across from him. A sharp knock sounded and the lieutenant entered. He walked over to the colonel and spoke into his ear.

"Excuse me," the colonel said. "I will be back in a moment."

Castellana stayed in the room and stood with his back to the door, impassively staring ahead though still actively taking in Anthony, the open handcuffs piled on the table, the foodstuffs and the open window.

"How much cost a Blackhawk *helicoptero?*" the lieutenant said quickly in English.

"A blackhawk helicopter," repeated Anthony. He thought quickly. He had not expected the guard to speak to him. He observed his face and responded.

"A lot of money," he said slowly and distinctly in English.

"How much?"

"Ten Million dollars, U.S."

Anthony watched the lieutenant's lips calculate the amount of money that was.

"That is a lot of money," Castellana said.

"More than I will make in a lifetime, but those things are hell fun to fly," Anthony said in Spanish, smiling.

Lieutenant Castellana had been right, this was one who had flown the *helicoptero* and sliced up Mono's men. He smiled back.

"I thought so," Lieutenant Castellana said, answering him in Spanish.

Anthony felt the web give way, only his leg was stuck to a thread, one quick pull and he would be free.

"That is not all I have been trained to fly," Anthony said. He talked slowly and distinctly telling all that he had been taught and all the training he had received. The young lieutenant's unfocused gaze turned to direct looks to finally an awed, worshipping countenance. Anthony remembered these looks well, receiving them often from the first friends he had here in Colombia to the new rebel recruits, who in their questioning simplicity, were curious.

"I realized my time was done protecting my people so I sought out people who had no protector," Anthony finished.

Anthony saw that the young man was listening intently so he told him how he had first come here and worked with the Colombian army. Pain flashed across the Castellana's face when he told about the farmer holding his child.

"I'm proud of Colombia. I am for Colombia. That is why I am here to fight for Colombia," the lieutenant said.

"the corrupt government?"

"The government is the government. Nobody can change that," he replied.

"Except when the government wants to shred its paper files without emotion. Sometimes those paper files grow heads and arms and legs, and can scream and cry, and that's a terrible moment, isn't it? The victims have families and human motives to explain the sad little paper file and its make-believed sins."

"One girl didn't have a file. They didn't know who she was," Lieutenant Castellana said sadly.

"The government and *el pueblo*. The government is a dream, a symbol of nothing at all, an emptiness, a mind without a body, a game played with paper, without blood and dirt and screams and waste and loss and sadness."

"I love my pueblo," he responded with emotion.

"The government makes war, doesn't it, and imprisons *el pueblo*? To dream on paper, how clean, how easy to disappear a piece of paper, burn it with a single match, nothing left but a tidy pile of blow away ashes and a pleasant charcoal odor in the air, but not so with bodies," Anthony said.

"Not so with bodies," the lieutenant echoed.

"Am I being cleaned?"

"I don't know," he replied.

"Do you know who the government is most afraid of?"

"No."

"You," Anthony said.

"I'm not a threat." His eyes drew close and guarded.

"You're not? Your *Presidente*, the same one who dug you off some dirt street and trained you to be the best and gave you the perfect tools and the confidence, now fears that the dirt from the street of your mother never left your mouth and now you will use those tools against him to take back that dirt and that street that is yours by right and blood," Anthony said.

"I'm not a traitor."

"No, you're not. You're as well-trained and as mean and hungry and tough as I, and you know it. You don't have to take anybody's shit anymore, maybe when you were a dirty, scrawny kid who all he got from his father was a kick. Now, you can kick hard back, hard to the point of deadly."

The door opened quickly, banging hard into the back of the young lieutenant. Castellana turned angrily; his face set and blushed.

"Out of the way," the colonel shouted.

Anthony heard the colonel's clean, enunciated hard Spanish order him out. Lieutenant Castellana went instantly stiff and saluted. As he closed the door leaving the room, he glimpsed at Anthony's eyes. Castellana stayed outside the door listening.

Anthony had focused so completely on the lieutenant's face that he did not notice that Mono had walked in the room directly behind the colonel.

When Anthony saw Mono, his mind raced for understanding. He had met Mono and could not understand why he was here. Selling out another rebel leader for money was part of the price of being a rebel leader, keeping your friends close but your enemies closer. However, willingly and freely standing with a government army colonel ruptured the status quo of accepted behavior. But here he was.

"I believe you two have met?" the colonel said.

"Yes. How have you been, Anthony?" Mono said graciously.

Anthony mumbled a greeting, his mind confused. As his tongue and mouth exchanged pleasantries, his mind hammered at him that this was not the time. Mono spoke with his usual courtesy and flourish.

"How is your good *Jefe* Juan?" Mono asked.

"I do not know," Anthony replied.

In honesty he didn't, he could assume that Juan was up and over and through the mountain pass, unreachable and untouchable. Mono and the colonel looked at him unbelievingly.

"I came down to town without telling Juan," Anthony said. It was true to a point, he had come down to see Sofia. His thoughts stopped. He could not bring her into this; he needed an answer for why he was here. He prayed that they did not ask him anything until he had time to sort it out.

"You work for the government," Anthony said quickly. If he was asking questions, they couldn't, as long as they consented to answer.

"I work for myself," Mono said. "The government and I have the same interests right now."

It made sense. Mono had not had a military conflict with the government for several months, yet he had acquired a vast number of arms and military hardware. He understood why Juan had been so careful and cautious with Mono, realizing that Juan had already known.

"We are not interested in you," Mono said. "We need you to deliver us Juan."

"I cannot do that," Anthony said.

"It is either your life or his," Mono said. "Make that choice wisely. For your own sake or for the sake of your future children."

"What did you gain for murdering Tito?" Anthony said aloud.

"I didn't murder Tito. He was a casualty of war. He knew the risks. The government didn't give me anything."

"And the helicopter?"

"The government lent me helicopters to scout for them. They gave me one, which was stolen. The others were blown up by Juan's men."

"Juan blew up the first three himself."

"He did?" the colonel interrupted. "You're lying. He is an excellent tactician, but a soldier? He knows nothing about soldiering."

"I loaded the rockets and he fired them. The last one almost burned us as it crashed to the ground," Anthony said. "The other two I blew up alone."

"You blew them up?" Mono asked.

"Yes, with your helicopter," Anthony replied.

"You killed my men," the colonel and Mono said together.

"No," replied Anthony. He must watch his mouth. He did not want to be shot by both of them.

"They were strewn dead around the hulls of the helicopters," the colonel replied.

"They died, but not by my hand. All I did was blow up the helicopters. Their greed killed them in the midst of their plunder of the ill-gotten gain. While they pulled rifles out of the dead cold hands of the Tito's men, a couple of them jumped up and killed them. I was able to hop into the last helicopter and fly away."

"You fly helicopters?" Mono asked.

"I can do a lot of things," Anthony said.

"His file is full of achievements," the colonel said.

"You should come and kill for me," Mono said.

"I'm not a mercenary," Anthony replied.

"I'm short one helicopter pilot, thanks to you," Mono said, "think on it carefully, I can offer you food and a place to sleep and most importantly, your life, for awhile."

"I regret that I have but one life to give," Anthony said.

Anthony knew it was pointless to argue, but he had not seen his opening yet, his single attempt at wild thrashing to unloose himself from the web. He had to keep talking. Talking meant life, and they loved to talk here. They could talk you to death. Anthony smiled at his own play on words.

"If you're working for the government, what is your title?" Anthony asked quickly.

"Title," Mono said, thinking a moment and looking at the colonel. "I don't need a title."

"Mr. Apostata does not need a title. He is here at the bequest of his government," the colonel explained.

"Every government employee at every level, whether they are a lonely clerk in the department of the national parks or a high-ranking General, has a title. The colonel has a title."

"What is his title?" Mono asked.

"Colonel," Anthony replied.

"Colonel," Mono said with a laugh. "That is a good title for him. You may call me a civil servant."

"What level of civil servant are you? Every servant has a level."

"Well then, I'm not a civil servant. I am an independent contractor for the government," Mono replied with a flourish.

Anthony could see that he was enjoying this banter. What a crazy war, Anthony thought, shooting the shit with the guy who wants and will shoot me in the head sometime today. He sits, as if he has all the time in the world, probably because he does have all the time in the world. After he shoots me, he will feel badly, but then he will have to run around after someone else to shoot. I can see why he likes sitting here, to give himself a rest.

Mono wrestled around his breast pocket and pulled out a flask, took a deep swig and offered it to the two of them. They both refused. Mono shrugged his shoulders, took another deep drink and stuck it inside his breast pocket.

Anthony had smelled alcohol in the room. His father was a closet drinker. The raw smell of alcohol on the breath could never be covered, and the stink stayed in Anthony's nostrils to this day. He looked at Mono in contempt; the fat, drunken slob was filling up his liquid courage to shoot him. Anthony loathed him. He felt that cool rage fill his body. He slowed his quickening breaths.

"Save yourself some pain," Mono said fiercely, pounding on the table.

Someone knocked at the door. Mono didn't take his eyes off Anthony. The colonel crossed to the door and opened it. It was Lieutenant Castellana."

"Colonel, may I speak with you," the lieutenant said quickly. "In private."

"I'm busy," the colonel responded.

"It's urgent," the lieutenant insisted.

The colonel looked at his serious face and nodded.

"Don't do anything until I return," the colonel stated. He waited until Mono turned his head towards him and grunted. The colonel passed through the door; the lieutenant shut the door. The colonel walked into the empty room at the end of the hall.

"Yes, Lieutenant?"

"He is an American soldier," the lieutenant began tentatively.

"Maybe he was, but he no longer sports the colors."

"We should find out. The Geneva Convention has rules against such things."

"Against what things? A bunch of old men talking many years ago and thousands of miles away will not dictate how I solve our problems."

"It shouldn't end this way," the lieutenant began again. "Not for a soldier."

"He's not a soldier. The rules don't apply to him."

"Those rules protect all combatants, sir."

"Are you threatening me, Lieutenant?"

"No, sir. Not at all, sir. I . . .," the lieutenant fell silent.

"Lieutenant, guerillas are the nine-headed hydra monster. If you cut off a head, nine grow to replace it. You must burn the stub of the neck and set an example for the other heads, whose turn to burn will come."

"He is a soldier, sir."

"You are a soldier, and I am your Colonel. I have a job to do. And I will do it. The question you must ask yourself is what side are you on?"

"Sir, I always follow orders," the lieutenant said quickly.

"Good. And keep following them-- and leave the thinking to your superiors," the colonel said. "Besides, soldier or not, he's a mercenary; he's expendable."

Back in the room, after the colonel left, Anthony looked over at Mono.

"Why did you do it?" Anthony asked.

"Do what?" Mono replied. "Stop fighting the government, because the government stopped fighting me. Now I'm a peacemaker."

"No, betray Mono," Anthony said.

"You mean Tito," he replied.

"You betrayed yourself. No one will fight for you or trust you," Anthony said.

"No one knows what I do," Mono said. "No one will. I am very good at snipping off any loose ends."

"Like Juan?"

"Juan is not a loose end," replied Mono. "Juan is a threat to the government."

"You are a threat to the government," Anthony responded.

"I was a threat to the government," Mono said.

"Give Juan the same choice. Let him come in and be on the government payroll," Anthony said.

"He doesn't want to be."

"Have you asked him?"

"No," said Mono. "I know his answer. He has different sentiments."

"Is that what beliefs and friendships are?"

"Let me put it this way. There are many ways to change the current system. Juan chooses to take up arms against the government."

"You also do that."

"You keep mixing your tenses, Anthony. You must be tired," Mono replied. "I did, but no longer take up arms against the government. The government, after all, is democratically elected. I take up arms against those who take up arms against the government, sort of like a police officer for the greater good of the democracy."

"If you're a police officer, why don't you wear a badge and own a uniform from the government and tell people you're a police officer when you viciously murder for your own gain?"

"I can see that Juan has effectively brainwashed you," Mono replied, his face reddening. He swigged heavily from his flask.

"If you mean by brainwashing that I use my own eyes and ears to make my decisions."

"The communist El Jefe wraps you up with his tongue. Eh, comrade?"

"Comrade?" Anthony snorted. "I have few political beliefs and no faith in the words of politicians. Spare me your political lies."

"You offend me, *Señor*. I have honor, and I do not swerve from it. *El honor no se mueve de lado como los congrejos*" meaning, "One's honor does not move sidewise like a crab."

"Honor is the cloak of thieves, and your fat body needs the largest cloak."

Anthony spat viciously, and the gob landed directly on Mono's face. Mono jumped up.

"I'll kill you for that," Mono screamed, as he unbuckled his leather holster.

"I won't deliver Juan."

"I'll shoot you," he growled slowly. "I won't shoot you in your heart. I will shoot you every place where it will not kill you, until I run out of bullets, and then I'll go, reload, and shoot you some more, until you beg me to let you lead us to Juan."

The door opened suddenly. The colonel walked in.

The colonel placed his hand firmly on Mono's arm to stop him. They silently struggled for control. Mono tensed and appeared ready to the throw the colonel's hand to the side.

"Mr. Apostata!" the colonel said loudly.

With a tense face, Mono put his hands down along his sides.

"And Sofia's life?" the colonel asked.

The colonel's words drained every ounce of blood out of Anthony's head, arms and legs, coagulating it all in a large ball in his stomach.

"Sofia?"

"Yes, I know about Sofia and you. I was surprised to hear it. I actually thought she liked me. *Es la vida*," the colonel said, meaning, 'that's life."

"What would you trade for Sofia's life? What is that worth to you?" the colonel asked.

Anthony's head throbbed so hard he could barely hear the colonel. It sounded like he was yelling at him at the far end of a cave, the echoes reverberating and breaking up into a thousand miniature pieces, sharpened and deadly that they cut the drums of his ears as they entered. He raised his hands to his ear and felt inside to check to see if they were bleeding.

"I don't understand what you mean," he mumbled. "I don't know what you're talking about."

"It's simple," the colonel said. "I want the El Jefe Juan de la Valle, and I want him without useless bloodshed. We, or should I say I, do not want more soldiers being killed. It is not politically expedient to have the paper print that more soldiers were killed when you are trying to tell them that you are winning."

"The papers love to print about soldiers being killed," Mono said. "It is bad publicity. It makes people think that there is uncontrolled violence."

"The politicians and the rich tell the people what to think," the colonel spat out furiously, "it is better that the newspapers report that soldiers are not being killed because then the world hears that the insurgency is under control, which it is. I want Mr. De la Valle, and you can deliver him to me. I am willing to give you your own life in return. Since you do not value that, I am willing to throw in the girl's life."

"What is her life to me?" Anthony said in a weak attempt to bluff.

"Be wise, Mr. Wyatt," the colonel said. "Her mother just came to me, pleading for your life by telling me how much it was worth to Sofia and her. She crassly assumed that someone such as myself, coming from a honorable family and having such pride in family that I should understand her."

Anthony's thoughts froze; they knew about her.

"She misread me and my respect for family," the colonel continued. "A whore who sallies around with bastards and killers has no value to me. However, because of what you can give me, I will trade her life and yours."

Mono focused on Anthony's eyes, watching him with the shrewdness of an alley cat. He wasn't as drunk as he let on, or as brutish. He was more calculating than Anthony had assayed. Anthony unfocused his eyes and took in the whole room, estimating the weight of the table, the distance to the window, the quickness of Mono and the height of the colonel's throat. He could definitely kill one or the other, but not both before the other had a chance to shout, bringing help and the racket of automatic fire. It was not enough anymore to escape. With the open window and a leaping, headfirst jump, it had seemed so easy. Even with a broken leg or arm, he could have swum away and hid out until he got help. He had to break free and find her. Maybe he should offer up Juan as a casualty of war. As Mono absolved himself with Tito, he knows the risks.

The colonel was speaking to him again.

"What do you want me to do with you and your little girlfriend," the colonel said. "The little trollop was fun watching run around town with her false modesty. She has no shame. Her mother is good people, so sincere and level-headed, coming to the authorities with her problems. I will not disappoint her. I have offered a gentleman's solution to the problem."

"You want me to kill Juan," Anthony said.

"Save your girlfriend from a life of working the street. The easiest thing I suggest is that you go and shoot Mr. De la Valle. Knowing how well-trained you are, you should be able to be back here with the body in a couple of hours."

"How? I can't walk," Anthony replied, pointing at his leg. "Your men did a job on my leg."

He saw both men take in the information. Mono's shoulders relaxed. He put his hands on the table and leaned back in his chair. He took another drink, smiling.

"The doctor told me that," the colonel said, "and it gives me a plausible reason for detaining you. Now that I see your reaction, holding your girlfriend here while you hobble off and kill Mr. De la Valle for us, minimizes my risk. You will come back to me. If he shoots you, no loss to me. I have your little strumpet to console me.

"What if I bring in Juan voluntarily? Will he receive a fair trial?"

The question perplexed Mono and the colonel in its simplicity, as if the answer was child-like obvious.

"He will be shot like a traitor," Mono blurted out.

The colonel put his hand on Mono's arm to restrain him.

"He will be dealt with fairly," the colonel said.

"Fairly severely," Mono chuckled again.

Anthony looked out the open window and listened to the sound of the rushing water. It sounded fierce and forceful and fast.

"If I can't bring him back?"

"You know you can. He will not see it coming, will he?"

"What if I refuse?"

"It would be better if you cooperate," the colonel said. "I promise you not as a gentleman, but as a soldier that if you cooperate, you will be on the plane back to your home. Right away. You can leave. This is not your country. This is not your fight."

"If I don't cooperate?" asked Anthony again stubbornly. He had to be sure.

The colonel was silent.

"The government has me for political expediency," Mono said. "The Colombian government cannot kill an American soldier, even if you are working for the enemy. You are from the unruly and brutal north that despises us. It might come out that you are a spy under deep cover, or your daddy is a senator. Colombian heads will roll. However, because no one will find you or even a ransom note to know whether you are alive or dead, all they will know is that you are missing. The colonel will be contacted and asked to help search for you, the poor, missing American."

"I beg you, Mr. Wyatt. This is not your fight. You can leave it and be free."

"You need some encouragement," Mono said menacingly.

Mono reached for the butt of his gun inside his unbuckled holster. The colonel put his hand on Mono's arm to stop him.

"Colonel, don't touch my arm again," Mono said forcefully.

"I rule here," the colonel replied.

Anthony sensed his chance. Anthony tried to remember how the river looked the other night, as Sofia and he raced along it. He could not visualize the water; he had looked at only one thing that night. Rivers had water in them, and water broke falls, hopefully, four-story falls.

"No, Mono makes the rules," Anthony said loudly.

"No," the colonel replied, "I make the rules because I am with the Government. The Government makes the rules. Everybody votes and the people with the most votes rule and control the power. The Government gives me the power."

"Not in my pueblo," Mono responded. "The government controls the vote and the speech and retaliates against anyone who wants change, any type of change."

"Not here, Mr. Apotata," the colonel stated

"Why doesn't he have the right to speak his mind here? He has no right to speak it out there," Anthony replied, pointing at the door.

"Now is not the time to speak of such things," the colonel replied curtly.

"I understand why," Anthony continued, his mind raced, just keep talking, he didn't care what insults he hurled at them now. It was life or death. "Here a free expression of ideas merits a bullet in the head. It is no wonder that there is so much corruption."

"The guerrillas create the corruption," the colonel retorted.

"The government creates the system," Mono said heatedly, "When I started fighting the government, I chose a short life span. So I thought, if I only have a little time and there is so much risk, I need to be rewarded for my risk, so I stole, I built my nest egg to move my whole family into hiding or to another country to protect them, because you don't only kill me, but my entire family."

"Do not take up arms against the Army," the colonel said.

"You, as a military officer, were willing to sacrifice the lives of Supreme Court justices and anyone else to muzzle free speech," Mono replied.

"You cannot negotiate with terrorists," the colonel said.

"What defines a terrorist from a citizen?" Mono asked.

"When the citizen takes up arms against the state," the colonel replied.

"When do they do that?" Mono asked.

"When they are a terrorist," the colonel responded triumphantly.

"And Mono? When did he stop being a terrorist, and become a civil servant?" Anthony asked.

"We have never been heard," Mono said. "We seized a few judges to have our grievances heard in front of them, but the military shot every single one."

"As they should have," the colonel replied. "You cannot allow people to use violence to set up some sham court to cry about their problems; everyone would do it. Besides, there are legitimate ways to err your grievances."

"No, there are not," Mono said. "While the government was publicly broadcasting that it was dialoguing with us, the military was ruthless slaughtering us and anybody who openly helped us. Repeating a process well learned in history."

"The military has to maintain control," the colonel said.

Anthony made up his mind. This country loved to argue and fight. Look at these two he thought, partners in crime until one kills the other. He felt adrenaline begin to race his heart. He did not slow down his breathing.

"What does that mean," Mono asked. "Kill everyone?

"No, only those who take up arms against the government," the colonel replied.

"Every time the army labels a trouble spot, they talk about a military regime and re-conquest of an area as if it were an invasion of a foreign land of infidels. The military wants to impose public order on a region 'dominated by guerillas' or 'drug lords.' They talk about subduing the enemy and their accomplices, but who are they but ordinary citizens who got stripped of their nationality and labeled anti-patriotic agitators?"

"They are anti-patriotic agitators," the colonel contested vehemently.

"Then I am one," Mono said. "I took up arms because the military brutally murdered my family, and I said never again. I have the right to defend myself, my family, and my land."

"Mono, shut up!" the colonel said. He felt himself losing control. How could have he been so stupid to involve himself with this money-hungry gorilla? When this was finished, he would give this traitorous brute some of his own medicine.

"I speak because I have seen with my own eyes," Mono screamed. "The fighting for political power between the two parties while the country bleeds. What is your reaction to atrocities? Blame me. Do the politicians air these events? No, of course not, they want it hidden so they don't lose their slim control over the people. They don't want to dig in to the root causes of the insurrection because that doesn't give them any votes. The rhetoric attacks the government and individuals within the army, but not the army as an institution, because when a politician comes to power, he needs the army to maintain his control as much as the previous leader who just the fled the country."

Anthony looked at Mono's sweaty, excited face and the colonel's crimson neck and obdurate profile. Tears welled in his eyes, not from sadness or fear, but from strong overwhelming emotion, like the first time he had jumped from a plane. He set his hands loosely against the edge of the table, slowly rotating his weight onto the balls of his feet, and looked up at the two men. A tear ran down Anthony's cheek.

"I do not want to die, because I only have one life to live," he said quietly. He inhaled deeply and exhaled halfway, slowly gripping the smooth edge of the wooden table.

Anthony exploded into the table, catching Mono with the other edge under his rib cage and tipping him backwards onto the floor. He pivoted on his left foot, hunching down and like a shot putter, twirled and flung the table directly at the colonel's throat. The colonel had not even raised his hands to deflect the flying block of wood as the force collapsed his wind pipe, knocking him lifeless onto the floor.

The big man rolled through the fall, tumbling over his left shoulder and springing to his feet. He reached for his gun. Anthony leapt for his hand. Anthony's hand gripped Mono's right wrist as Mono grabbed the empty leather holster. Standing face to face, they looked down. Anthony saw it first. In the fall, the gun had spilled out, slid across the floor and rested against the leg of the dead colonel. Mono reacted first. Shifting his entire weight and stomping on Anthony's foot, he knocked Anthony backwards and off balance.

Like two tango dancers in perfect balance, their arms lifted together. Anthony fought to hang on to Mono's thick wrist. Anthony's backward momentum coupled with the force of gravity on his own weight pulled Mono towards him, as they both fell heavily to the floor. Mono's body pinned Anthony's legs. Mono flipped his right hand around and seized Anthony's left wrist, and his other meaty hand hung onto Anthony's right forearm. He shouted at the top of his lungs for help. He had a large, booming voice.

Anthony flailed violently against the web. His wings and legs buzzed and thrashed to escape. He was almost loose. He was up. He gave the web a violent kick and broke one leg free. He gave the web a final kick that his life depended on. The other leg broke free. Mono clutched his broken teeth and nose.

Lieutenant Castellana put his ear to the door when he heard the dull thud. He distinctly heard scuffling. They were beating the crap out of the American. He should step in and stop it. This was wrong. Not this way. And then what? He would find himself in a room like this, in the same place as the American and who would stop it then? He could not stop it without shooting the colonel or Mono. He heard loud shouts. It was Mono's voice. He looked down the hallway; no one was coming. No one else was answering the call for help. Castellana paused a moment, his hand gripping the doorknob.

Inside the room, Anthony jumped up and over Mono and looked out at the water directly below, turbulent and seething. The doorknob clicked. Anthony looked over at the door, expecting it to explode open and see bullets fly at him, tearing him apart. Anthony leapt though the window.

Lieutenant Castellana pushed open the door.

Anthony's eyes, with his head angled back in mid-air, met the clear, dark eyes of Lieutenant Castellana. A split-second later, Anthony felt the smart smack of the water on the top of his head. The water flipped him over, as he plummeted towards the bottom. He felt his legs hit the bottom. He pushed off the rocks and fought wildly for the surface.

Castellana stepped over the prone body of the colonel and looked out. He saw the American's head break the surface of the water of the raging waters. The head turned up to him. Castellana rose his arm to wave.

Anthony, one hundred feet downriver, saw the lieutenant's face at the window. Seeing the raised arm of the Lieutenant's, Anthony gulped air to dive, fearing rifle fire, but the lieutenant waved broadly. Anthony waved back.

The foamy waters spun Anthony against a large boulder. He raised his legs to absorb the force, smashing his knee into the rocks. The sharp shooting pains sent stars through his head.

Lieutenant Castellana leaned forward to see. Mono blundered into him, waving a small pistol to stick it out the window.

A boulder tumbled Anthony around, heading down the river backwards. He saw Mono's contorted red face at the window, but the lieutenant was in front of him, blocking him. A whirlpool twirled Anthony under the water.

"Shoot the bastard," Mono wheezed. "Shoot the bastard. He killed the colonel."

Lieutenant Castellana seized the gun out of Mono's hand, removed the magazine and clicked the bullet out of the chamber. He looked out. The American, fighting the heavy current, bobbed out of sight.

"Citizens can't be running around shooting off guns, can they?" Lieutenant Castellana replied.

Mono glowered at the Lieutenant.

"In this river, he will not survive," the Lieutenant said. "I will order my men to search for his body."

"I will ensure that he is dead," Mono said. "Give me your rifle."

He reached for the rifle slung over the shoulder of the young lieutenant.

"Stand down, civilian," Lieutenant Castellana ordered, pushing Mono away at arm's length. "You have no authority here. Your authority is crumpled on the floor below you."

"You have to get him back," Mono barked, glowering at the young lieutenant.

"The prisoner escaped while under your guard," the lieutenant shot back. "You have de Valle to think about."

"I will go and find him. Be prepared to send support troops and artillery."

"I will do my job," the lieutenant responded, "according to my chain of command. You are not in my chain of command."

"I will call your general directly."

"He won't be happy that you let the best chance of recovering Juan de La Valle fly out the window and drown in the river."

Mono stared up at the impassive face of the young soldier. It was hard and unyielding.

"You will see why they call me *El General*. I will personally bring back de Valle on a chain. I have more important things to finish than to see if I can piss farther than you," Mono replied.

As Mono turned to walk out, Lieutenant Castellana barked out orders. Two young soldiers flew into the room, pushing Mono aside. More soldiers filled the room behind them. Lieutenant Castellana ordered the men to carry the colonel. From a distance, Castellano followed Mono, watching him jump into his jeep with his brigade of men. Fervently, he resolved to protect his soldiers, each and every one from a wasted death, and more resolved to resist tyrannous brutes operating beyond the laws he swore to uphold. He will serve his county, and more importantly, his pueblo; no *paisana* will die without a file again.

Chapter Seventeen-Thursday Morning

At the moment Anthony was being taken prisoner, a small group of Juan's advance troops had witnessed the capture. They returned quickly to tell what they had seen.

"Willy," Juan called out to his lead commander.

"Si, El Jefe," he replied.

"What do you think? It's true or a trap?" Juan asked.

"I trust the men's information. The American has been captured. What we do next is your decision, Jefe."

Juan looked at Willy. They had been together much time and knew one another's thoughts.

"You think it is suicide," said Juan slowly.

"Suicide is strapping a bomb to your chest and having a trigger attached to a detonator in your hand," replied Willy

Juan laughed. It was good to have those surrounding you with a sense of humor for the hard moments in these times of struggle and war.

"Will you volunteer?" Juan asked.

"If it is your order," Willy replied sincerely. "I will go."

"Good. I will give you something more powerful than a bomb strapped your chest. Pick out eight men, arm them with 240s and hand cannons."

"We will make a hell of a mess."

"We might not stop them from killing the American. But they will not be alive to torture him."

"Nobody comes back from an interrogation," Willy replied.

"They should treat him differently; he is an American."

Now, Willy laughed.

"The day he aligned himself with us, he signed his Colombian death warrant," Willy replied. "Jefe, you have an optimism which is impossible to kill. Do you believe they would let you go free?"

"I know what future awaits me," Juan replied. "We move out in ten minutes."

Juan tried to force a smile at Willy, but inside, his heart hardened, hardening against those that would treat the American outside the conventional rules of warfare, hardening more against those sentiments of affection the American had created inside him, sentiment that undermined action, and hardening most against those that would use innocent lives, women, and children, to shield their misdeeds. Collateral damage would be high.

The word of Anthony's capture sped quickly among the troops. Juan knew in his heart that he would do something. Strict discipline and personal compassion intertwined in allegiance. Juan enforced harsh discipline among his troops, earning him a reputation for being ruthless. However, from the newest recruit to his top adjutant, they could recount personal stories of Juan risking life to liberate them, loyalty pardoning the necessity for ruthlessness. Although Juan never expressed it, love guided his actions, love for the man and woman next to him sharing the squalor and uncertainty of death or betrayal, love for its mere simplicity, like freedom, and love for those for whom he fought. Without it, he was no different than the sadistic paramilitaries. A rescue, no matter how insane, showed that a single soldier was more important to him than all the gold in Colombia.

Juan and his men raced quickly down the valley and approached the town from the north.

"Should I signal an artillery strike," asked Willy, "before we go?"

Juan shook his head no.

We don't want to let them know we are so close," Juan whispered. "There is always time to blow things up."

More importantly, Juan did not want them moving Anthony, in response to an attack. A helicopter put Anthony out of reach.

"We need someone to go into town," Juan said. "Where is Carlos?"

"He asked to go into town to help the American," Willy replied, "and I let him."

Juan grimaced. He needed eyes and ears inside the town. In these times, he felt extreme frustration. A simple telephone or radio call could organize and clarify action. They could attack with one blow. Carlos certainly knew where Anthony was being held; a simple call would do it. However, Juan had learned and had adapted. American ships anchored in the clear blue Pacific, constantly listened for all communications, across all frequencies.

Their sophisticated supercomputers, operated by a pock-faced eighteen year old, pinpointed their location in seconds. American planes, operating high overhead, jammed signals and distorted messages. Eavesdropping killed more guerillas than bullets.

Juan developed a simple old-fashioned countermeasure, detailed advanced tactical planning, visual signals and Morse code. However, in situations like these, where speed was priority, nothing could be planned. Modern technological war made them stumble around blind.

Sofia, Juan thought. She would know.

"Willy," Juan said. "I don't like the idea of ten armed men walking into a heavily fortified town in broad daylight. Only disaster will result."

"What's the plan?"

"Do you know where the doctor lives?"

"Yes."

"I'm going there to see if she knows where the American is being held."

"You want me to put a suicide bomb on your back as well?" Willy asked.

Juan smiled.

"I'll take Simeon with me. He knows the town. I will send him back with the location. Destroy it."

"Raze it to the ground?"

"Yes."

"I understand," Willy replied.

"I don't want you moving from this position," Juan said.

"Is that an order, Sir?"

"A request."

"Will you return with Simeon?"

"If I can," Juan replied. "Simeon, come with me."

Juan, with Simeon leading, skirted the town and entered the long, dark, drainage tunnel that Anthony had crossed only the night before. When they reached the end, Simeon turned to Juan.

"El Jefe, let me go up first to see if anyone answers the door."

Juan started to disagree.

"You are very well-known," Simeon replied quickly. "If someone should recognize you . . ."

Juan nodded. Simeon unshouldered his weapon and ammunition and gave them to Juan.

Juan watched Simeon climbed up and out of the dark tunnel. As he sat in the darkness, he thought of his children, growing up without the guiding influence of their own father. Yet, he didn't feel sad. Juan burned with a desire to show his children to live to their full purpose. He was a revolutionary, consumed with the fever to equal wrongs against the people, a fever so strong that he was willing to forsake clan, creature comfort, class and, even, country. Time would judge whether his life was a history of achievement or failure.

"Jefe," the voice of Simeon whispered, "come, it's clear."

Juan, laden with the extra weight, climbed slowly up the dark sewer pipe. As he exited, the sun blinded him. Simeon slipped his own gun and cartridges from Juan's shoulder, grabbing his arm to pull Juan quickly along.

They ran at full speed and slipped into the open door of the doctor's house. Doctor Romona was in the small anterior garden waiting for him.

"I assume that you didn't make this daytime visit to discuss politics," the Doctor asserted.

Juan bent down and kissed both of her cheeks formally.

"I don't see how the two of us could meet and not discuss politics."

"He is being held at headquarters," she replied immediately.

Juan looked at Simeon to see if he knew the place.

"It was the old hotel in the center of town," the Doctor said, addressing Simeon.

Juan motioned Simeon to go to relay the information.

"Before you send him, I need to know what you're going to do. I just came from there. I spoke with the colonel. He said that he would spare his life."

"Do you believe him?" Juan asked.

The question surprised the Doctor.

"He comes from a very fine family in Bogotá," she replied.

"Do you believe him?" Juan asked again.

The colonel would not lie to her, not about a young man's life; she could not accept it.

"He didn't say it directly," she replied. "However, I received the distinct impression that Anthony would be dealt with fairly."

"Summarily?" Juan asked.

Doctor Romona wavered.

"What to do?" she asked, feeling a shift of her basic understanding of human compassion and honesty. Anthony did not deserve to die, particularly with neither a hearing nor some tribunal; this was not her Colombia. She had sacrificed too much.

"No one comes back from interrogation," Juan said, repeating the words of Willy.

"He knows too much?" asked Doctor Romona.

Juan stayed silent for a moment, contemplating his answer.

"Yes, but I'm not doing it for that, I'm doing it for a more humanitarian reason. He prefers a quick, painless death."

She knew torture and summary executions happened in Colombia, the state's expediency to nasty, little problems.

"Are you going to try and rescue him?" she asked.

"If we attempt a rescue and miss, a helicopter will ferry him out beyond my reach. We are going to destroy the building. I'm sending Simeon back now with my orders."

"You cannot do that," she blurted excitedly.

"It's combat, Doctor. I know innocents will be killed. It does rest on my conscience."

"No, you cannot bomb that building," she cried, distraught. "My daughter Sofia is there. She went to headquarters to see if she could save him."

"I can give you twenty minutes, at most, to warn her."

The destruction of the building had now become personal, the curse of war. Destruction of other people and their property is clean, impersonal and acceptable.

The telephone rang deep inside the house. Several moments later, the grandmother came out.

"*El Americano ha escapado*," she said. "The American has escaped."

"Where is Sofia?"

"They didn't say. It wasn't her who called," the grandmother replied. "Wait, listen to me. They're coming to the house."

"When?"

"They didn't' say?"

"Doctora, I must leave," said Juan. "I will give you some time to ensure your daughter is out. We are still bombing, *por sia caso* -- 'just in case'"

"Juan!" she called out at him.

Juan had run out. Simeon, holding the rear door open and scanning the street, waved Juan passed him. Together they sprinted to the invisible shadows of the sewer pipe.

Inside the house, Doctora Romona had told her mother to see if anybody was outside the door.

"No one is there," Nana replied.

"I am going personally to the Colonel and bring Sofia back," Romona said.

"You didn't give me time to tell you. You can't," Nana replied.

"Why not? He must see me!" she retorted.

"He's dead."

"Dead. How?"

"They didn't say. He was interrogating the American, and the American escaped."

"Stay here. I need to go now."

Doctor Romona ran towards the garage at the rear of the house. She heard the loud rumble of a diesel. Her instinct warned her that the sound was not friendly. She ran to the front part of the house. Hearing more loud noise, she looked cautiously through a crack in the large heavy drapes covering the front window. A large drab green convoy truck stood in front; men were gathering at the front door. She heard a violent pounding on the door. Doctor Romona froze.

Juan and Simeon had just entered the sewer pipe when they heard the growl of a large diesel coming up the street. From the safe obscurity of the darkness, Juan watched the truck slow to a halt. Two men jumped from the back and started talking to a man in the front. Juan could not hear what they were saying.

"This is the house, but the front door is around the corner," said one of the men who had exited from the rear."

"You two, watch everything coming up this street and don't let anyone leave the house from the back," shouted the squat man sitting in the front.

The truck continued around the corner and stopped.

"Everyone out! Keep the truck running," the squat man commanded. "You, pound on the door with the butt of your rifle."

The heavy door absorbed the thuds.

"Open the door, or we will break it down!" the squat man shouted.

"Kick the door in," he commanded to his men.

They kicked in unison; the heavy door impassively stayed in place.

"We will have to blow it," a large man with heavy eyebrows said.

"Blow it," the squat man said. "Inside quickly. We want everyone alive as hostages. If you shoot a hostage, you answer directly to Mono!"

From the invisible darkness of the sewer pipe, Juan and Simeon could no longer see the truck or what was happening.

Mono's men," whispered Juan.

"*Coño!*," swore Simeon harshly. "We must leave, Jefe."

"What does he want here? He can't believe the American would return here."

"What does the *Cabron* always want? Hostages. Leverage."

Juan leaned against the dirty stone tiles. Remember what has made you successful, he thought. Live to fight another day had been his motto, his creed. Juan's thoughts at this moment rebelled against everything which had kept him alive these many years.

"Jefe, there are only two of us."

"We inspire by our example," Juan said forcefully, "Safety off and follow me!"

Before Juan could give himself a chance to doubt his actions, he leapt out of shadows and ran towards the doctor's house. The two men had their back to him. He sprinted past, trusting Simeon to take care of them. He had to catch the larger group by surprise; otherwise, it would be death. As he rounded the corner, he heard the burp of automatic fire from behind him.

Mono's men were caught completely by surprise. Juan fired in short bursts. They had grouped around the front door, like a little flock of chickens waiting to be fed. They tumbled in unison.

Juan saw the convoy truck being ripped apart by bullets; he looked to his left. Willy and two others had their guns held high. Willy motioned to the other two to check the downed men and the truck. The two soldiers moved forward quickly.

"Jefe, we have to leave immediately," Willy commanded.

"You left your position," Juan said.

"You have visited this doctor many times," Willy responded.

"A guerrilla fighter needs full help from the people of the area. This is an indispensable condition, "Juan replied.

"The pueblo needs full help from you, Jefe."

"I need to speak with the Doctor."

"Please be quick. If the army comes, from them there will be no escape."

Juan went to the back door. He knocked. Romona pulled the door opened. She looked in shock. She held the door, motioning with her head to enter.

"Romona, please come with me," Juan started. "It is very dangerous for you now."

She fell against him. He carried her to the kitchen and sat her on a chair. He found a cloth at the sink, wet it, and placed it on her forehead as he sat next to her. He gently held a glass of water to her lips. She refused it.

"I know it is not easy to take this all in," Juan said, "now is not the time for thinking. You must let me bring you to safety."

"Safety," she mumbled, "if I am not safe in my own house, where can I be?"

"You can return," Juan said. "It's only unsafe at this moment. Mono sent his men to abduct you."

"Today, Mono. Tomorrow, maybe you. A pawn in an endless chess game, easily sacrificed on the path to victory."

"Doctor, I know this does not make sense now, but you must survive. We must survive."

"Running and hiding from one place to another? The last cockroach surviving wins."

"You are in shock, Doctor. Please come with me for your own safety."

Juan felt a tap on his shoulder. It was Willy. They left the kitchen to talk.

"*Jefe*, we must go. We cleaned up outside and drove the truck with the bodies into an abandoned lot one street over."

"And the men?"

"Half are here inside with me," Willy said, pointing to the back garden. "The others are waiting my command, out of sight in the tunnel. Simeon told me that the American escaped."

"Nobody comes back from interrogation?" Juan replied.

"I'm glad to choke on my own words," Willy chuckled. "He escaped. We don't know if he is alive."

"I feel that he is alive."

"We must go," Willy repeated.

"I want to take the Doctor with us."

"Take her then."

"She is in shock."

"Do you need me to pick her up and carry her out?" Willy asked.

"No, I want her to go voluntarily."

"We don't have time. I don't know how much we do have, but I know we don't have much."

A knock at the front door signaled the end of their time.

Juan acted first, repeating the actions of Doctor Romona moments earlier, crossing to the front and peeking out the window.

"An army lieutenant is at the door," Juan whispered.

"Is he armed?" Willy asked, who had followed right behind.

"No," Juan replied. "He came in a jeep with only a driver and two armed guards in back. They are sitting there."

"Let him go away then," Willy replied.

Before they could react, Romona came and opened the front door wide. She ushered in the young army lieutenant, shutting the door behind him.

Romona walked into the room where Juan stood with Willy; the lieutenant following her, his view blocked by her body.

Juan pointed his pistol at the lieutenant. The lieutenant stopped.

"I don't want to kill you," Juan said softly, "and it is not my time to die."

Willy quickly disarmed the lieutenant and removed his radio.

Juan looked at his young face and his name over his pocket, "Castellano." The young lieutenant had no fear in his face.

"Lieutenant Castellano, I am Juan de la Valle, El Jefe."

Castellano's eyes narrowed. The stories were true; he did exist.

"Where does that leave us? You know my duty," the lieutenant replied.

"Your duty?" Juan asked. "Duty to whom? Duty to country? Duty to family? Duty to self?"

Castellano did not know how to respond. He stayed silent.

"Duty is used as a shield, not as an obligation anymore," Juan continued, "a shield to hide wrong actions."

"Juan, if you are going to kill him, kill him," Doctor Romona broke out in, "you are not going to convince him of the righteousness of your cause."

"Kill him?" Juan replied. "If I cannot convince him of the rightness of my position with words, I cannot with a gun." Men die. Ideas do not.

Lieutenant, have you been to the Doctor's clinic?"

Castellano shook his head no.

"It is a very tidy and appropriate clinic with a clean smell. However, when you look in the shelves, they are empty. They have no spare bandages, needles or medicines."

"We serve the poor," Doctor Romona responded.

"Who else lives here?" Juan replied quickly to give her no time to respond, "Yet, a couple of days ago, I blew up three *helicopteros americanos*? How much are they worth? No money for medicine for the pueblo, but plenty to blow it up, that's what I am fighting against."

"We need them to protect the pueblo from people like you," said Castellano.

"Maybe so. But I will tell you something, when I see the doctor's clinic filled with medicines and supplies, my job is done, and I am finished."

"From where do you come?" Castellano asked. "You have accent familiar, yet the lilt of your speech is different from mine."

"I am a patriot of Latin America," Juan replied. "For I come from everywhere and nowhere, I fight for people of all creeds, colors and countries."

"Who from here asked you to come and kill on their behalf?" Castellano responded with contempt.

"Lieutenant, a revolution is not a mango that falls when ripe. You have to make it fall."

"You talk about fruit when I speak about the *campesinos* who bleed when you make war here."

"Hunger starves the *campesinos*; their small food plots defoliated by the government."

"They should be growing vegetables and fruit, not coca to fund your war."

"Chemicals have not eyes and do not distinguish between mango and coca."

Despite his natural objection, Castellana found de la Valle to be an agreeable-looking man with a soft and ironic glance. While they conversed, it was difficult to look him in the eye; his gaze was unbearable, piercing, and so tranquil.

A knock sounded at the door. Doctor Romona looked out the curtain.

"It is the driver of the jeep," she said alarmed.

Before Juan could move, the lieutenant called out in a loud, commanding voice.

"Stay in the jeep! I will be out when I finish," Lieutenant Castellano shouted.

"The driver went back to the jeep," reported Doctor Romona.

"I am not afraid of you," Lieutenant Castellano said in a normal voice. His comment directed at Juan.

"Nor should you be. I am not your enemy."

"Mono told us your plan," replied Castellano. "To blow this town to bits if we didn't leave."

"Mono has his interpretation," Juan replied. "And his own morals."

Lieutenant Castellano looked at Juan with understanding.

"I was in Calica," responded Castellano.

"Calica was destroyed," Juan admitted. "I did not make the rules. We must carry the war into every corner the enemy happens to carry it, a total war. I planned to attack the colonel and his troops here, to make him feel like a cornered beast wherever he may move."

"The colonel is no longer alive to fight you."

"The government will send another and another and another, until the struggle is accomplished."

"The struggle?"

"The struggle every day so that this love for humanity becomes a reality," replied Juan.

"Love," scoffed Castellano. "The only love you have is for the love of war."

"To be honest, Lieutenant, it does become part of one during the struggle. My nostrils dilate while savoring the acrid odor of gunpowder and blood. Without it, I could not continue."

"It is the first honest thing you have said to me yet," Castellano replied.

"No. I have never lied. You, like others, want to hear and believe things about me to reinforce your distorted vision of me. I am a man who risks his skin for his platitudes. You wish not to believe or accept my platitudes because you do not understand how a man could risk his own life for a belief. To understand that is to understand me."

"I don't understand how you believe that violence achieves you victory," Castellano responded.

"Lieutenant, the exploited must use violence when the moment arrives. No, let me explain to you differently. Have you visited the school in this pueblo?"

The lieutenant shook his head no.

"The entrance in front, adequate, painted and a nice sign," Juan continued. "The part in back, where the students are -- dirt floors, no paint, and no desks. It is anti-pedagogical to expect *campesino* students to be educated there, while government officials drive Mercedes cars. That's what we are fighting against."

"Build a school."

"Yes, that is a wonderful idea. I place my hope in children and want to prepare them to take the banner from my hands. And there are many children and many schools to build."

Put down your weapon and build."

"Castellano, we have talked much about me. Tell me, what is your creed?"

"My creed? What is yours?"

Juan thought a moment.

"Love. And yours?"

Castellano, unsure of how to respond repeated the simple soldier's creed he had been taught in basic training. Juan stopped him when he got to the part of serving the Colombia citizen."

"Your duty, soldier," Juan commanded.

"To serve her," the lieutenant said.

"... through selfless service, putting her welfare before your own," Juan said.

"Yes," Lieutenant Castellana said.

"Lie down on the floor and place your hands behind your back," Juan ordered.

Lieutenant Castellana did as he was ordered. Juan crossed behind him and tied his hands. He ordered Romona to lie down. He tied her hands behind her back.

"I am taking the others in the house to guarantee my escape," Juan said. "Do not follow me. What would I have done to the hostages if you had not laid down your own life?"

"Shoot them," Lieutenant Castellana said. "You have a hatred which burns inside you."

"Lieutenant," Juan replied, pausing to reflect. "Hatred is an element of the struggle, an unrelenting hatred of the enemy, impelling us over and beyond our natural limitations. A guerilla without hatred cannot vanquish a brutal enemy. I will shoot them."

Juan turned to leave.

"Jefe," Lieutenant Castellana called out.

"Si," Juan replied, turning to face the lieutenant.

"You will die," Castellano said.

"In a revolution, one triumphs or dies," Juan replied.

Juan ran out the back door, leading Willy and the others. Juan did not take any hostages. As they scrambled back down the long tunnel, Willy called out to Juan.

"Do you think he will follow?"

"We have escaped the clutches of the dragon," Juan called out. "Run towards victory!"

Gregory Arthur Solsrud

Chapter Eighteen-Thursday Noon

Anthony swam hard for what he thought was the surface. His head popped into the air like a cork; he greedily gulped the air. The undertow swallowed him again. He relaxed his body and kept it loose to slide and roll off the large rocks. Whenever his face felt air, he inhaled frantically until the river sucked him down again. He was lightheaded, but under control. The river settled down, allowing his head longer above water. He splayed out his arms, using them as giant paddles to float in the deepest moving current. Looking back he could no longer see the building. Anthony, unable to see what lay ahead above the foamy water, attempted to swim for the bank. The current resisted strongly, pummeling him on submerged rocks, which banged his legs and ribs. Keeping his legs in front and arms spread out, he pushed his body out of the water to see down river. The river roared dead ahead, the flow increasing.

The vortex catapulted him violently. He fell freely over a thundering waterfall. With his eyes wide open, Anthony saw only massive rocks and spray, before smacking into the churning water below. The unrelenting force of the water pummeled him down. The ferocious underwater eddy held his body fast. Unable to swim up, Anthony pushed and clawed his way along the slippery boulders lining the bottom. He prayed that the maelstrom released him before his lungs ran out of oxygen. His head throbbed. Every sinew, fiber, and nerve commanded him to open his mouth and breathe in. He fought his own body for control. He fought the watery grave. He fought the desire to give in. Using his last molecules of life, he kicked frantically against the rocks, propelling his body to the surface.

His body surged out of the water. His arm banged into a fallen tree. He grasped its limbs for survival. He hung on, lifting his mouth above the foam to breathe the life-giving air.

He stayed there for several moments, the circling eddy pushing him neither up nor down river. The water could not trap him again. He would not survive the remaining rapids. He felt the limb, still green and strong. He had to pull himself out now. He reached up with his other hand. Hopefully, the limb will not break before he pulled out. The slipperiness of the wet wood made grabbing difficult. Hand over hand slowly, he climbed cautiously until he was against the dark slippery rock at the side of the river. The rock offered no handholds or crevices. With pure arm strength he pulled himself up the sinewy limb until reaching safety on top of the rock. It was dry and warm. He lay there for several moments recuperating. With his senses partially recovered, he looked back up at the waterfall. He could scarcely believe that he had survived the fall. The rest of the way down was a jumble of rocks and foamy water. He needed to find a way out He would do that later. Now was time for rest.

No. Sleep meant not moving. He had to keep moving. Movement meant not being caught. Movement meant life. Movement meant returning to her.

He was sure that they had started pursuit of him. He did not know what to do. If they knew the river, they would assume that no one could survive the fall. They would concentrate their search efforts above the waterfall assuming that he gotten out. His head throbbed. But if they assumed he didn't know the river, he wouldn't know about the waterfall and look for his body below the waterfall. I want out of here, he thought. The lack of oxygen is making me think poorly. If they didn't know the river, they would look for his body or him further down the river. That was most logical.

He shook his head vigorously. He could not think straight. His mind continued to roll in circles and probabilities if he should go back or down. He forced himself to breathe deep. He forced himself to concentrate. His mind returned to one thought: return to her. Return to her now.

The cold of the water had stopped the throbbing in his leg. He touched above his right knee. The bandage was in place. He scanned along the sides of the river. He saw no one. He listened for voices or shots; he heard nothing. Nothing, except the thunderous roar of the falls. The mountain rose sharply along the left side of the river. He spotted an opening in the thick underbrush, where there was a level, rocky spot. He climbed fast and hard to reach the rocks. He closed his eyes, exhausted. A sharp noise echoed down the river, and he forced himself to crawl to the safety of the thick jungle. He collapsed under the cover of several large palm fronds.

The wind blew across Anthony's cheek. He rolled over onto his elbow and pushed himself to a sitting position. His head ached. He gingerly probed the bandage above his right knee. The wound was tender, but the stitches were tight. It was not bleeding.

That was the difference between the good doctors and poor doctors, he thought. Good doctors went about their business with very little fanfare and little thanks. Afterwards you were fixed up. The doctor had done a good job on his leg. It was holding.

He looked around and could see nothing, neither buildings, nor broken shanties, nor trails. He scanned the river, looking for pursuers. He had to stand up and look around. They would be searching for him. He slowly put weight on his knee and stood up. He walked carefully, keeping his movements slow and controlled. The tightness gradually worked out of his leg. He crawled like a crab along the sharp rocks lining the river. The jungle verdure rose straight up along the side of the waterfall. He tried to swing up a branch along the steep slippery slope. The brush was too dense, forcing him to back down to find a passable route. He heaved himself from one steep, slippery rock to another until he came to an impassable vertical stone wall. The only route was down, swimming in the deadly river. He was trapped.

"Anthony!"

He heard a soft, whispered voice call out to him. It was her voice.

He looked up into the most beautiful face. It was Sofia. She hugged him fiercely and kissed him many times.

"When I heard you jumped from the window, I followed the river bank until the waterfall. When I did not see you above, I knew your body would be carried down here. I feared you had not survived," she cried.

She kissed him on his cheek and his other cheek and his forehead and on his brow, as if she had not seen him in many years. She could take away the pain that she saw in his face.

"I knew in my heart God would bring you back to me. I should not have let you leave."

"Sofia, I don't even know how you found me," Anthony began, "but we must leave immediately."

"Anthony, I do not know how you survived, but you did. God is with us."

"The colonel knows all about us. He bargained with your life for my help."

"Knows about us? My life? I don't understand."

"There is no time to explain. The time to leave is now. We have only a few minutes, if that."

"Calm down, Anthony. You're safe."

"No, we are not. They are coming here. We must run now."

Anthony jumped to his feet, pulling her. Sofia slipped her arm away from his grip.

"Anthony, calm yourself."

She put her hand softly on his chest.

"Please, Sofia," he pleaded. "This may be our only chance."

"Anthony. Stop." she said. "They are headed down the river to look for your body. I came from the headquarters. I spoke with a sergeant familiar to me, that's how I knew you escaped."

"Did he arrest you?"

"I'm still here, silly. You are blessed and fortunate that you did not die in the waterfall," she said. "Others have, and this is where we found them."

Anthony told her about Mono, about her mother's visit, and his escape from the colonel.

Sofia sat quietly for a while.

"I guess my mother was trying to do the right thing, in her own way."

"We must go and warn Juan," Anthony replied.

"The soldiers think you are drowned and will arrest you if they see you walking around. The colonel is dead. They will want answers. How insane are you?"

"The colonel is dead?"

"Yes."

If the colonel had not told anybody about the mother's visit, he had not told anyone about the interrogation. Only Mono knew what happened in that small room. Mono would be too occupied with catching Juan to worry about a local doctor and her daughter. There would be time later to clean up loose ends. Mono would be his loose end.

"We don't have to run and leave Colombia," Anthony exclaimed.

"I don't understand."

"You haven't done anything wrong. My passport is in order."

"Anthony you are not making sense. You need to rest. You have lost blood. Let me look at your wound," she said. She pulled at his pants.

"Not here," Anthony said.

"You're shy," she said.

"I don't like to have my pants off in broad daylight."

She pulled off his pants to examine his leg. A look of pain crossed her face as she fingered the dirty, red-stained bandage. She unwrapped the bandage. She pressed her fingers around the edges of the wound. The stitches held. His exertion had caused the wound to weep.

Anthony looked up at the torrent of water cascading over the rocks.

"How could you believe that I would survive?" he asked. "Am I alive or just dreaming?"

"You told me you were a good swimmer," she replied.

Her nonsensical answer made him smile. He did love her. He pulled her into his arms and held her tight.

"I wish we could stay here forever," he said softly. He held her a few minutes more, before he said, "We need to go."

"You are in no shape," Sofia replied. "And Mono?"

"Mono is finished. Juan has escaped from the valley and beat him. The other groups will hear about his treachery and not trust him. He will be a lion with no teeth. Tito had many friends here; some will hunt Mono down. We can stay here."

"You talk foolishness. It isn't that easy."

"Millions of people live daily lives here," Anthony said. "If we mind our business, why would anybody bother us?"

"It isn't safe for you. We need to run away from Colombia."

"Running away from this is ignoring it. We can stay here and work to change it."

"What would you do?"

"I could teach English," Anthony said.

"That doesn't pay much."

"You don't need much to live here," Anthony said. "Or with my military background, I could train the *Autodefensas* here."

"Train the paramilitaries to kill more people?"

"I was joking. I don't have much for family. My mom would miss me, but not like your family. I feel more at home here in two days than I have anywhere, at any time."

"You haven't been here much."

"I know. Here is where my heart is. Home is here."

"I don't know. We should be leaving this mess."

"There is no mess. Not yet."

"You don't know that. Don't say anything to my mother yet," Sofia said. "She was willing to let me go with you because she thought I was escaping to a better life."

"You are," he replied, "escaping with me."

"What -- an on-the-run foreign-born rebel?" she chided.

"No -- call me 'Anthony the Northman', today a rebel, tomorrow a leader."

"You have grand ideas," she said.

"I have a grand life now."

Anthony looked up at the waterfall. The water and spray thundered loudly, creating an intimate space where one could ignore the world, if only for a moment. He gently undid the buttons on her blouse.

"Oh, Anthony," Sofia cried.

He felt the energy of the world coursing through his veins. As he removed her clothes, Anthony no longer felt any pain in his leg. The world stopped momentarily for the two young lovers.

Sofia rose first, dressing quickly. She rewrapped the bandage on his leg. After he slipped on his pants, she laced up his boots.

"You tie them faster than I do," said Anthony quietly.

"Are you ready to climb?" she asked.

Anthony nodded. Sofia ducked under the canopy. She kept low, moving quickly below the large branches until she found a jumbled pile of green rocks covered in green vines. She climbed horizontally along the slimy rocks. The sound of the waterfall grew louder, but among the thick vines, Anthony could not see out. She climbed effortlessly, waiting for Anthony to catch up.

The vines thinned, and Anthony could see the spray from the falls. Here, the spray did not reach and wet the rocks, making the handholds more secure. They climbed straight up. Anthony dared not look down. They breached the edge of the cliff along where the waterfall cascaded down. They had made it safely; they were on top. Anthony stared at the plume of water, which had shot him out only a short time ago. He crossed himself; maybe he was blessed.

They walked very carefully now, even controlling their breaths, in fear of being too loud. They walked in sync, stepping heel-to-toe, not breaking a single branch or crunching a loose rock. The trail climbed steeply. It seemed to lead away from the river. It came to a level rise; the village spread out in front of them. They heard explosions. Anthony ducked down instinctively. Fearing someone would see them, they crept higher along the trail, glimpsing the spire of the church steeple and the roofs of the taller buildings. They crunched down and scampered forward for a better view.

They looked over the bridge that spanned the river, and down the street that went into the central square of the town. There was a smaller bridge further up river. *Campesinos* crossed the bridges covered in their brightly colored ponchos and dark hats. Their shuffling gait and blanketing wraps blurred the distinction between the men and the women.

"We need to cross the town," Sofia said silently.

"Not in broad daylight. You said I can't be caught. Can we go around?"

"The military is patrolling to the south of town. To the north it is a long way on foot. I have an idea," she replied. "Wait for me here."

She scuttled down through the brush and stealthily jumped over a stone fence and crept into a nearby thatch house. Inside, she found some peasant ponchos. She grabbed two, feeling a twinge of guilt for stealing the only possessions of this poor family, vowing to return to repay. She returned quickly, draped a poncho over Anthony's body and pulled a dark, wool hat far down over his head.

"Stoop low and shuffle," she commanded. She dug into the moist, black dirt and smeared its dark tint into his face, neck and arms.

She tossed the other bright poncho over her shoulders.

"Follow me and keep quiet."

The narrow streets on this side were lined with compact houses, covered with palm fronds and sheet metal. They reached a corner with a small open store and bakery. They scrambled along the dirt streets, avoiding the other peasants. With no gun, Anthony felt naked, desiring to flee deep into the jungle where they should be looking for him.

Ahead of them lay the small bridge crossing the creek; the other side laid freedom. Imitating the all familiar gait of the workers, broken and weary by many years of back-breaking toil, they blended in well, no one looking twice as they crossed.

They eased their way through the dense brush, staying off the main trail. They climbed quickly, without stopping. Sofia, scanning the trail ahead, saw movement and signaled to be still. They watched a small figure running down. It was Carlos. Anthony whistled loudly. Carlos stopped and peered into the bushes seeing Sofia and Anthony as they stepped from their cover. He came up and embraced both of them very hard, especially Anthony. When he released Anthony from his grasp, he had tears in his eyes.

"I thought you were lost," Carlos said quietly. "No one comes back from interrogation. I was very afraid. I blamed myself for not coming for you this morning."

Anthony rubbed Carlos' shoulder.

"No blame is needed. I have returned safe and sound and back to your care."

"*Gracias a Dios*," Carlos said. "El Jefe told me not to worry this morning. He said you had more lives than a cat."

"Tell me, what is the state of things?"

"El Jefe was in full retreat, but when he heard you were being held, he ordered everyone to congregate along the dirt road. He has left to rescue you."

Oh, Christ, Anthony thought, he had expected Juan to be up and out of this cursed valley by now. Why hadn't he gone straight to Juan? He had not been thinking straight. The entire group will be trapped and killed in a foolish attempt to save him.

"When is the attack?" Anthony asked.

"I don't know. He said they wouldn't expect an attack, so we might be able to free you."

"It's suicidal. They are waiting for him," Anthony replied. "He should have pulled everyone out already."

"Have you seen anyone coming?" Sofia asked.

"No, only you. There are many trails running through these mountains," Carlos said. "Antonio, I felt in my heart that you were all right, but I thought that it meant that God had taken you to be with him."

It was the first time Carlos had called him by his Christian name.

"Mono will be after him now," Anthony said.

"El Jefe is expecting that," Carlos said.

"Yes, but he has the support of the army," Anthony added.

"They need to reach the pass by night fall," Sofia said quickly. "In the dark, it is impossible to see and cross."

They climbed along the trail. Although the trail was easier, Anthony's leg was starting to stiffen up. Carlos looked back several times to watch Anthony.

Carlos stopped and waved them off the trail. Someone was coming slowly down the trail.

"Miguel?" Carlos called. The words died in his throat, as he saw Miguel dragging the dead body of his brother. "Are you hurt?"

"No, my brother took my bullet. He got the bastards, but they got him."

"What happened?" Anthony asked.

"Me and my brother were bringing the fuel," he began.

"Your brother? Ferdinand was badly injured," Sofia replied. "How could he carry fuel?"

"He could ride a mule. The doctor stitched him right good," Miguel replied. "We were on the mule trail, when my brother looked down and saw a group of Mono's men coming up. We waited for them."

"Miguel, we must go to El Jefe."

"I need to bury my brother. I don't want them to have his body."

Anthony looked at the quiet body of the brother. Miguel had looped a small rope around his ankles to drag him. Miguel's eyes pleaded with Anthony.

"We must work quickly," Anthony said.

Miguel nodded. Ferdinand had his gun still strapped to his shoulder. Anthony slid the gun off his shoulder and gave it to Carlos.

"Anthony, there is a small clearing up ahead," Sofia offered. "it is very peaceful."

Anthony nodded, lifting Ferdinand's body and carrying him like a small child in his arms. They walked to the small clearing.

"We can bury him here, Miguel," Sofia said.

Miguel fell over the body and cried.

Anthony worked with Miguel's knife and Carlos with his machete to make a shallow grave in the soft dirt. They lifted the body inside the hole.

"*Capitan*, can you say something?" Miguel asked.

Anthony had never been to a Spanish funeral and did not know a single prayer or mass. He looked at Miguel.

"I know some prayers, but only in English."

"Are they good prayers?"

"Yes, one is from Psalms, about the Lord being a shepherd," replied Anthony.

"I like that one. Please say it."

Anthony repeated the twenty-third Psalm. It was his grandfather's favorite. His grandfather had taught him to memorize it. The last time he had said it was at his grandfather's funeral. The words comforted Miguel who had stopped crying. Sofia repeated the rosary; Miguel joined in. Miguel threw loose dirt over his brother's body. He stood up.

"We can go now," Miguel stated.

Anthony felt hardness come into Miguel's voice, as if he'd given up on God and traded hope for revenge.

"Miguel, there are two ways to take dying, to stop living or to keep on. I can't tell you which way to take. You have to decide. I do know that if you pick to stop living, the person who died will have died in vain."

"I will live to kill Mono," Miguel spat furiously. "His men killed Ferdinand."

"Your brother died to save you, now what are you going to do with your life?"Sofia asked.

Miguel shrugged his shoulders.

"Ferdinand died to save you, to save us," Sofia continued. "Will you live to preserve his memory or die for his memory? Once you are gone, who will remember your brother?"

"No one. There are none of us left."

"You have to live on so your brother can live on," she said quietly.

Time was passing. Anthony had to find out how close Mono's men were.

"Miguel, I need you to find El Jefe," Anthony stated firmly.

"I know exactly where he went *Capitan*."

"I want you to tell Jefe that you saw me alive. He must not attack the town. Tell him to flee now!"

"Aren't you returning with me, *Capitan*?"

"No, I will follow your trail back to the ambush. I must make sure there are no more of Mono's men close."

"I will go with you," Miguel said.

"No, El Jefe needs to know that I am alive and that he must move everyone over the pass by tonight," Anthony said. "Do not fail me."

"I will not," Miguel said.

"I need Ferdinand's rifle."

Miguel handed it to him.

Anthony inspected it, opening the chamber and sighting down the barrel.

"This is a good gun. Ferdinand took good care of it. Miguel, do you have extra cartridges?"

Miguel gave him several.

"Avenge my brother," Miguel urged.

Anthony nodded gravely.

"Go now and go quickly. You have no time to lose," Anthony said.

Miguel ran off.

"Carlos, follow me. If you see anyone, call out."

Anthony followed the dragging marks the body left in the dirt. Where the dirt went hard, he followed the disturbed leaves and broken twigs. Miguel had dragged the body a long distance. Anthony saw a body lying askew off the side of the trail. He searched the trees for snipers. He saw no one. He approached the body; it was dressed in an irregular uniform, the insignia was Mono's own personal emblem.

Private armies running around like a regular one, no wonder this country is so dangerous, Anthony thought. He circled around and found eight more bodies grouped around where Ferdinand had set up an ambush. He had let them bunch up as they crawled up a steep section of trail, but the only way to kill them all put him in the direct path of their return fire. Nine was an odd number; someone was missing. Mono based his organization on the U.S. military. His squads had ten men and a leader. There were two others walking around.

He followed the trail and found red-stained ground, scraped up where someone was helping another person walk; one of them must have been shot. He turned to Carlos.

"Where does this trail lead?"

"To the town," he replied.

"They are too far ahead for us to catch up with them," Anthony said.

"May be not," Carlos replied. "This trail crosses back and forth. We use it with the mules, that is why it is so narrow and well-cut. There is a trail which drops straight down."

"Take me to it," Anthony said.

"Anthony, why do you have to pursue them alone? We must find the others," Sofia said.

"If we return for help, they will have made it to safety. There are only two of them and one of them is injured."

"How do you know?" Sofia asked.

Anthony did not have time to explain, but she needed to learn.

"Sofia, a squad sent out in advance is the eyes and ears of the main body of soldiers," Anthony said quickly. "If they don't return, the main body pushes forward slowly in fear of an ambush and of the unknown. They don't want to stumble into the enemy out of position. If we can cut off the last two members of the advance squad, we can gain at least an hour and maybe more to clear out of the valley. We have to find them now."

He tilted his head towards the trail as a sign to Carlos to move forward. Carlos ran through the brush. He did not need his machete. He came across the steep trail and started down. They descended quickly, slipping and sliding several hundred meters until the trail leveled.

"We can circle back to the mule trail," Carlos said.

Carlos angled off the trail and found the marked mule trail. Anthony examined the dirt. He did not see any blood or drag marks.

"Carlos, you stay here and wait until I come to you. If they come down the trail, you know what to do," Anthony said, looking at Carlos' rifle.

"Yes, *Señor*," Carlos responded.

"Sofia, come with me. We are going further down, in case they have already passed this point."

"Let me lead. I know my way back down better than you," she said.

She followed the trail down and forked off sharply as the trail bent back onto itself. They descended quickly. She turned off the trail into the jungle and returned to the mule trail. They were on a crest along a narrow ledge.

Anthony pulled out his binoculars. He scanned down the mountain, following the zigzag path of the trail. He dropped to one knee and pulled Sofia down after him. Sofia looked at him.

"I saw a long line of men working their way up. They have pieces of artillery slung on the back of mules," Anthony said.

"They are right below us?" Sofia asked.

Anthony nodded.

"The men we are looking for are already with them or above us," Anthony said.

He checked the rifle's magazine and loaded a bullet into the chamber.

"Stay behind me," he said. "We are going up the mule trail towards Carlos."

As Anthony was loading his rifle, Carlos was growing restless. He was accustomed to moving about, to leading men from this place or the other. This sitting and waiting was not his personality. What if the men did come, what would he do then? He had never shot any one before. The American had given him this rifle, but he had never used it. The day of reckoning was coming for all this killing. He knew God would make him answer for his part in it. He had never killed, but he had done nothing to stop it. Such things made him think, and his thoughts confused him.

He looked down the trail for the American and Sofia. Oh, they should come soon, and then if the men came down, the American could shoot them. The American didn't seem to mind the killing.

Carlos was a kind man and he did not like to think of killing, and he didn't think of killing when he was with others. He liked others to be around. He liked the American to be around. The American seemed very kind and sensitive too. He knew the American was not going to kill that boy by the monastery. That was a good thing. Killing a boy in a holy place like the monastery would have made a penance that would have lasted another generation.

He was not for the killing. That is why this civil war never stopped, they had to pay penance for all the killing their ancestors had done. He remembered learning in the school about the violent history of his own land. Even the great patriot Bolivar had killed. He didn't want to remember Bolivar for that; there were great things he did. He didn't want to be remembered for killing. He looked at the rifle in his hands. It was light. Much lighter than he thought a rifle should be. Something so deadly should be very heavy, to remind the man of its killing power.

When he was alone, this morality of killing returned to him, and he was alone now. It was immoral because it was against the commandments.

Carlos shooed the insects away from his face. He didn't like killing them; they were the smallest of God's creatures. He must move down and away from here. If he was not here, when the men came by, he could not shoot them. He probably could not shoot them anyways. He didn't know how the gun worked. He looked at the trigger. If I pull this here, he thought, the bullet will come out. He did not want to disappoint the American. He did not want to disappoint El Jefe. If killing these two men meant the others would be free, he should do it.

The American should not have left him here, *that he should come.* Miguel says they are Mono's men. Mono's men were *Foquistas*; they are ones who like the killing. El Jefe said that. They should like the killing so much that they sneak up the mountain to kill Ferdinand. Ferdinand was a brave boy. That he should kill so many Foquistas was an honor. I am confusing myself, Carlos thought, how can I say that it is an honor to kill another man? If I am able to endure this, then I have endured all an old man may hope to endure in such a war. *That the American should come.* The insects are biting me, and causing me to think ill thoughts. I cannot go home now, nay, I cannot return to my home until the war is done. I am on a list. El Jefe told me about the list. He cannot return either. We must win this war before we are allowed to return home.

He stomped his feet on the ground to shake the mud off his shoes. Then he leaned against the thick bush; its branches felt like a soft bed. The thought of killing these two men put a great sadness over him. He felt alone standing here in God's sunlight. He thought of saying prayers. He had not said prayers in a long time. In his happy days, he said prayers when he felt lonely. If he said prayers, God would see through him, knowing his heart was filled with killing two men whom he did not know, and if he did not say prayers, he might condemn his soul to hell.

He knelt down and lay prostrate on the ground, putting the gun to his side. I am sorry for the killing I am about to do. I know it is a sin, but I have to do it. There must be a dispensation from this commandment, and I ask for it now. I should have talked to the American before he left about it, maybe he knows about some relief. I can ask him about it when he returns, but then it will be too late for it. I ask this in your name, and I will not use your name, knowing that I am committed to doing something, which I know your name abhors.

As he lay on the ground, trying to pray, he heard the cracking of branches up the trail. He looked up and saw the two men. They were walking slowly side by side; one man was supporting the other who was grabbing his side as he walked. He recognized them as being with the band of Mono. The injured man was talking with the other, although Carlos could not hear what they were saying.

"Obscenity, this steep slope. I will be happy to return to my Guajira. I have told El General Mono that when I was shot one more time, that was the end. In Guajira, there is no slope higher than your knee. Obscenity, slow down, boy, if you can't obscenity slow down, leave me here and I will crawl on my own."

"I am sorry, but I slipped. The slope is very steep," the boy replied.

"It is steep and I have walked on steeper. What kind of country is this where they can make mountains so steep?" the injured man continued.

"The mountains are very tall here, but they are higher in the Cordillera Central. They are so high over there that you can touch the blue of the sky," the boy said.

"Have you ever seen the blue of the *el Mar Caribe*? That is a blue to behold, and you can walk along in the white sand with the cool water splashing on your feet."

"I have seen pictures. The north has many beautiful beaches. We are lucky it has not rained on us. When the rains start, I have seen it snow on the top of these mountains," the boy said.

"That I do not wish to see," the injured man responded. "We climbed very high today to be ambushed. That son of a whore must have been waiting for us the whole day in that spot."

"But you shot him," the boy said.

"Yes, but I did not hit the other. He is probably waiting for us in another ambush. When we find Mono, I will tell him that we can't squash those *cucarachas*. They scurry quickly into this jungle, and with only a few they can pin us down on these obscenity narrow paths."

"El General will not hear that willingly," the boy said.

"I don't care how he hears it; he will hear it from my lips. I did not take a bullet in my belly to keep my mouth shut."

This is how they were talking, as they walked up to the place where Carlos was lying prostrate along the trail and trying to pray.

Carlos watched them walk closer and closer. He brought the gun up on his shoulder and held it as he had been taught years ago in the army when he had been called up to serve. They had trained him with a long heavy gun that hurt his shoulder when it fired. You knew you were holding a killing machine when you held that gun, and the noise it made was enough to deafen you.

He pointed the gun at the injured soldier who looked like he was in much pain and it would be humane to shoot him, like one shoots a mule that has broken his leg. He pulled the trigger, but it did not move. He looked at the gun. The two were walking very close now, so close he could hear their words. He remembered El Jefe talking about keeping the safeties on so there would be no misfire. He looked at the gun and saw a small lever. He moved it over. It clicked loud. The men looked towards him. The men were coming towards him; they had their guns held level. They had not seen him yet.

The injured man heard Carlos click off the safety, bringing him to instant alert. He pushed away from the young boy and brought his rifle up to his shoulder in one smooth movement. He looked around, trying to focus his hearing on where the click came from. Maybe he was too paranoid after the ambush. Still, it was a distinctly metallic click. It was no stick breaking.

Carlos pulled the trigger.

The trigger clicked on the empty chamber. Carlos did not know what to do next. He put his head into the dirt. If he could not see them, maybe they would not see him.

The injured man heard a second, louder click directly in front of him. His eyes searched for movement. He saw a rifle lying on the ground under the bushes pointing at him. The injured man sprayed the brush with automatic fire.

The boy fell facedown beside him. The injured man whirled around; bullets caught him in the chest. He dropped to his knees. His last look was a tall man with light hair standing down the trail with his gun held high.

Anthony came running up to the two men. He checked; both were dead. He feared going into the bushes. He should not have left Carlos there. Why did he leave the old man there? Please God, don't let him be dead. Let him have run away and they were shooting at the wind. He saw the rifle lying on the ground. He crawled over and looked in the bushes.

Carlos was lying face down in the dirt.

"Oh Christ," Anthony moaned. "Oh Christ. Mother of Mary, why did you have to let this happen?"

Carlos looked up at him. He was surprised to see the American above him. It was a welcome surprise. The American had come. The American pulled him close and hugged him.

"Carlos, you do indeed walk with God," Anthony said.

"I'm sorry I didn't shoot them," Carlos said. "I tried. My gun didn't work."

Anthony picked up the rifle, saw the safety was off and the trigger was pulled. He snapped open the chamber. It was empty.

"Carlos, you didn't have a bullet in the chamber."

"I am sorry, *Señor*," Carlos said.

"Don't be sorry, Carlos," he replied. "It is my fault for leaving you here without knowing how to work this weapon. I should have stayed with you."

"I am glad you came," Carlos said. "I feared that my death was coming."

"Like hell your death was coming," Anthony said. "You are the protected one."

"Come, Sofia is down the trail," Anthony continued. "I didn't warn her that I was shooting. There was no time to think."

"My life thanks you for not thinking," Carlos said.

He liked the intimacy created between him and the American. No one had ever saved his life before. God would overlook this killing, he thought. A man about to kill another man is not doing God's work.

"I am glad I came in time," Anthony said, raising Carlos up to a standing position. "Listen, I'm glad you stayed here. You don't know what it is like to find somebody in this country stay in the same place as where you left them."

Anthony Wyatt was happy. A happiness that came rarely and spontaneously with this *rebelde* army, like the happiness of finding that you don't have to retreat back along the same ground that you've just won so bloodily. The Germans were right about good men, because it all came to down to one man. One man who stays and holds his position against all sanity. He had always thought it was training, but it wasn't training. It was having a good man. And this was a good man.

They turned and watched as Sofia came up the trail.

Carlos was happy he stayed in his position. It meant that Sofia would depart safely. Now that she was here, he could look at killing differently. Of course, if he had left, she would have understood. She was Colombian after all. It was our war. She chided him for putting himself at risk. His life was at not at risk now. He was feeling hungry.

They walked up the trail. The American led. He said he didn't want the two of them to get shot. The American was not afraid of being shot. He felt comfortable walking behind him.

As they came into the clearing where the dirt road ran, they saw a long line of men and machinery quickly making their way up along the canyon.

Chapter Nineteen-Thursday Afternoon

At the end of the long column of men and machinery, Anthony saw Juan. Juan came running towards them and hugged him fiercely, as if greeting a long-lost brother. He tousled Anthony's hair. He stepped back and looked at Anthony.

"You have no idea how happy I am to see you. You are my good luck charm, like a cat with infinite lives. When hope is lost in the world, the world returns you safely to me, my brother."

The effusive greetings pleased Anthony. He hugged him strongly in return.

"We were coming to free you," Juan said. "You came to us first."

"I had to make sure you were safely out of this valley," Anthony replied.

"See this men," Juan shouted, "They could not capture my greatest warrior!"

The men cheered and greeted Anthony.

"You must tell the other groups about Mono," Anthony replied.

"There will be time to discuss these things, let me look at you first, Jefe," Juan replied

"No, you are El Jefe. They shot my leg. I can't move like I used to."

"You look good for having been shot. They didn't harm your pretty face."

Juan threw his arms around Anthony again in a strong embrace.

"You've come back to me. I knew you would, and stronger than before," Juan continued, tapping Anthony's forehead indicating his mind. "You are El Jefe now."

"No one can replace you," Anthony replied.

"With you safe, we can all escape out of this forsaken canyon. While the men are moving out, I will wire explosives to blow up the excess matériel."

"I will help you," Anthony said.

"If you're strong enough to help me, you're strong enough to fly?" Juan responded.

Anthony looked at him curiously.

"You're free. Take your plane and escape with Sofia. Fly out of here," Juan said earnestly.

Anthony stared at Juan's face in silence. It was hard for him to realize his full significance. Free! Free of his duty to Tito. Free to learn how to love. He looked over at Sofia. He was conscious of Juan's eyes studying him with interest as if attempting to read his thoughts. After a long moment, he shook his head.

"Yesterday, I would have flown with wings on my feet," Anthony said in an unsteady voice. "Escaping is the safest way out, but I think it would be a mistake to abandon the men, you and Carlos."

Juan looked at Anthony seriously.

"This, too, we will discuss later," Juan said.

"I will blow up the munitions," Anthony said. "You go on ahead quickly."

"I will do it with you," Juan said.

"You need to stay with the men. There will be explosions. They won't know if they need to turn and fight or run like hell," Anthony replied.

"Depending on what's happening, they will do both," Juan replied.

"I don't think Mono will push up very fast. After the ambush and no scout returning," Anthony replied, "he will think you are waiting for him."

"Mono can be very determined. There is a reason why he controls much," Juan said.

"Leave me, Carlos, and a couple others. " Anthony said. "Sofia will stay with me."

"She can go on with me," Juan replied.

"My place is with Anthony," Sofia responded, removing all doubt.

"Watch yourselves and work quickly, "Juan said. "When we reach the pass, we will send off flares."

"When I see those, I will run like hell out of this canyon," Carlos added.

"You see," Anthony said, pointing to Carlos. "With Carlos with me, nothing can go wrong."

Anthony told the group about how Carlos escaped death.

"He is the anointed one," Juan said. "Carlos, take care of them."

"*Si, Jefe*," Carlos replied. "I know several trails out of here. We will beat you through the pass."

"I don't doubt it," Juan laughed. "If anyone knows these mountains, it is our Carlos."

Juan headed up the trailed followed by his officers.

"It is time to work," Anthony said. "The quicker we start, the quicker we leave."

"Anthony, shouldn't you leave the supplies here?" Sofia asked. "Mono and the other soldiers might never come."

"Juan never leaves behind extra supplies. He does not want to be killed by his own bullets. And he does not want the government to trace his sources."

"Can you leave the others to do it? Your leg is not strong."

"Somebody has to set those charges who won't blow up in the process."

A large stockpile of munitions remained in preparation for the attack. Juan and the men had carried off as much as they could. Anthony searched around the supplies and found plastic explosives. He explained to Sofia and Carlos where to put them and how to lace it together with wire. They worked from one end to the other. When they had finished placing the explosive, Anthony worked on the fuses. Carlos put extra explosives into a backpack.

"I'll set these to explode an hour after sunset, and we can watch the fireworks show. From on top, it should be quite a sight."

"What if someone comes before?" Sofia asked.

"I don't think the army can push along that fast," Anthony said.

"Don't worry about the army," Carlos broke in, "worry about Mono."

"He's finished," Anthony replied.

"Only if El Jefe escapes out of this valley," Carlos said.

"People are turning sides all the time in this blasted country," Anthony said. "Today's disillusioned guerrilla leaders are tomorrow's paramilitary leaders. One day they are fighting the government; the next day they are fighting for the government. Nobody has any loyalties here."

It showed what closeness they had to hear him talk badly about the country.

"Yes, but when you switch allegiances, you have to win," Sofia said. "If Mono cannot deliver El Jefe as promised, he will lose their support. His men look to his ability to command and to win. If he can't deliver El Jefe, his own men will switch their loyalty."

"He is finished. I don't see him pushing his men up this mountain quickly."

"You don't know Mono," Carlos said. "By betraying his *pueblo*, he is risking everything. He will not stop. He will have a plan. He is like El Jefe; he has a plan for everything."

"What plan can he have?" Anthony asked.

"I don't know," Carlos said. "I am not smart with such things. How would you stop El Jefe?"

"I would bring light artillery up here. The Yugoslavs make a good mountain gun, which can be broken down and transported easily. The Chinese have one also. I would set up here in the clearing and lob shells at them. When the shells burst on them, I would call in an air strike; an advance plane can laser in on the artillery hits and deliver an overwhelming pinpoint strike that would take out the entire pass and everything in it."

"That is what Mono will do," Carlos said.

"He would first need to carry his artillery up here, and he would need air force support."

"If it is possible, he will have planned it," Carlos said.

Anthony looked up and saw Miguel and Diego.

"Men," Anthony called out. "I'm glad you came back. I was trying to figure out how we were going to hold back Mono's entire army with only Carlos, Sofia and me."

"El Jefe asked us to go back. He said you would need the help. You could not do it alone."

"El Jefe thinks of a lot of things," Anthony said.

"*Señor*, El Jefe has a plan for everything. Even for plans that Mono has not thought of yet," Carlos said.

"Did he tell you what you should do?" Anthony asked.

"No," Miguel said.

"He said you would tell us what to do, that you are the next Jefe and we should listen to you," Diego said.

Juan knew how to subtly apply pressure to have men follow his will. Anthony had volunteered to lay a few charges and blow up the extra matériel. Now, he was commander of the rear guard with a force of four to stop he did not know how many. Anthony still had a lot to learn from El Jefe; Juan had earned that title. How did Mono look at the death of close friends, a casualty of war?

"Carlos, take them with you and bring back a fifty caliber machine gun, extra explosives and some mines," Anthony said.

"The big *maquina*, *Señor*?" Carlos asked.

"Yes, the big one," Anthony repeated.

Anthony mulled over escape routes to use if they were pursued. He looked at the high sides of the canyon at this point and the flat well-worn paths that crisscrossed the valley floor. We could push them over to one side, he thought, where we have stored the equipment, apparatus, and supplies from the aborted attack. We have already wired that to blow. If they are mixed in with it all, we will smash many of them and give us time to escape.

Anthony Wyatt pushed up the slope slowly, carefully looking for the right place for the big *maquina*. The big machine, he thought, it translated funny into English, maybe because it was not so big, compared to the other war machines.

Here was the spot. The jungle rose sharply to his left, cutting off all possibilities of attack from the left flank. To his right the jungle thinned, affording a superb range of fire. If he was leading the patrol, he would definitely move his company around and out of the way of the big *maquina*. He saw Carlos returning with the two who were laden with the supplies. He whistled at them.

"Miguel, set up the fifty caliber gun here and shield it well," Anthony said. "It will be protecting your life. Carlos and Diego, follow me."

He led them down the slope to the trails. He showed them where to bury the mines and the explosives along the trails, except for those, which led to the stored equipment. He crossed back through the jungle and climbed the trail, which led up to Miguel.

Miguel had set up the gun limiting his range to his right. He ordered him to pull the gun off its stand and to reposition it to where he had first showed him. Anthony explained what he was trying to do.

"Like water, you want them to take the path of least resistance," Anthony said, "Before they have a chance to surround you, you will be off and running to catch up with El Jefe."

Anthony cut several large palm fronds and crisscrossed them in front of the gun, hiding it from view. As he finished, Carlos and Diego walked up.

"Miguel and Diego, you stay here and work the big *maquina*. One can fire, and the other one can reload. When you are not reloading, you can shoot at them with your rifle."

"Where will you be, Capitan?" Diego asked.

"We will be behind you, supporting your right. When they come through over there," Anthony said as he pointed through trees to the opposite side of the narrow canyon, "we will blow the charges. Once I blow the charges, pull back into the jungle and by whatever path necessary, find your way back to El Jefe."

"We will not keep fighting them?" Miguel questioned.

"It is suicide," Anthony said. "We are only four. We only need to hold them a little."

Anthony watched them as they settled behind their makeshift fort. They laid their ammo alongside them. He waved at them, and started back through the green foliage. Sofia and Carlos followed. Anthony stopped where the ground rose slightly, making a mental note to know where to return. If you do well, he thought, and hold them even a little while or just get the officer leading the pursuit, it may make all the difference.

"Before we set up," Anthony said. "I have to wire the plane to explode."

"You are blowing up the plane?" Sofia asked.

"Only as a lost option. If they pursue us that far, we will need the diversion to disappear into the jungle," Anthony replied.

"Do you want to go back to the trail or cut through the jungle?" Carlos asked.

"You stay here and rest," he replied. "We will be back soon."

Anthony and Sofia plowed through the dense bush; woody spines tore at their clothes. Anthony mouthed curses as the thorns drew blood. They reached the dirt path leading to the plane Anthony had flown so often. Now it might help him escape again. They walked up to the plane. He slid the cargo door open.

"In the back, there are machine guns, ammunition, grenades and launchers."

Anthony found plastic explosive and packed it into a cloth sack. He showed it to Sofia, explaining what it was.

Anthony sat down inside the cargo door and looked up at the roof. The plane's reinforced ribbing encircled the belly of the plane. He felt along the upper side of the roof rib. There was an opening between the ribbing and the plane's outer skin. Out of the cloth sack, he pulled a rectangular block of plastic explosive and began squeezing it into a long gray snake.

"While I wedge this explosive in between the skin, load two backpacks with as much as you feel we can carry."

As he worked, he explained the different weapons to her. She loaded the packs quickly. He stepped and looked at his work, only an eighth of an inch of aluminum separated the explosive from the volatile jet fuel inside the wing.

They each grabbed a pack and exited the plane, their bodies dripping with sweat.

"The sun bakes the insides of these planes hotter than an oven," Anthony said.

"Handling that stuff would make me sweat more," she replied, pointing at the plastic explosive.

"Explosives take time to accustom," Anthony replied.

"I'm afraid that it will blow up in my hands," she said.

"Ever shot one of these?" Anthony asked, pointing to the rifle.

"No," she replied.

"I'll show you when we return to Carlos," Anthony replied. He should have asked her earlier.

Anthony picked up the long fuse and stuck one into the plastic explosive. He looked at Sofia. He did not want to risk both of their lives in case something went wrong.

"Take your pack and walk down the trail about two hundred meters. I'll be there as soon I wire this."

"It is dangerous?"

"You make me cautious. If it were Carlos, I'd have him do it."

"Let me do it."

"Next time."

"Okay. I will wait for you, this time."

He watched as she trudged down the road with the heavy pack. He will lighten it, allowing her to move fast if needed. She had much to learn. He stopped himself. In what was he involving her? This was not the life he wanted for them.

Concentrating on the task, he threw the cloth sack with the leftover explosives on the wing, walked inside the plane, shut the cargo door, crawled through to the cockpit and turned on the plane's electrical switch. He went back to the cargo door and looked at the light over the door. It was off. He pushed opened the door slightly; the light came on. He closed the door firmly, and the light went back off.

Anthony smashed the light with the back of his elbow and pulled out the two wires leading to the bulb socket. He laced the two wires into the other end of the fuse. Open the door and boom, he thought. He walked back up to the cockpit and wedged himself through the small side window, dropping onto the dusty ground. He walked up the trail to Sofia.

"No boom," she said smiling.

"No boom," he said embracing her spontaneously. "Not yet."

"See any movement?" Anthony asked.

"No," she replied. "It's quiet, and the birds are singing."

"The longer it takes them, the better for us," Anthony stated. "It can't be dark quick enough."

They walked back up the trail to Carlos.

"It is good to see you both," he said as he saw them approach. "I was starting to worry."

"Have you eaten anything, Carlos?' she asked.

He shook his head.

"Can we make a fire?" Sofia asked.

"Better not, in case someone comes. I don't want to give away our position."

He thought about what they would do if trouble came. Everything was suicide, with only five of them. When they retreated, they would have no one to lay down covering fire to allow them to slip into the jungle and regroup. They would be like Ferdinand, one heroic sacrifice and a hole in the ground. Anthony never wanted to end up in an unknown hole in the ground. He wanted a full military funeral with a flag draped over his casket, a twenty-one gun salute, and fighters passing overhead. They gave those to medal winners. Here, the only metal he was going to earn was going to be fired at him.

"All we have to do is wait and hope we don't see anyone," Anthony Wyatt said, more to himself.

Sofia handed him an *arepa* stuffed with something.

He took a huge bite, as he settled on the ground and stretched out his stiffening leg. He watched her prepare one for Carlos. He resolved to keep her safe; her life cannot mix up in this. Sitting on the hard ground, waiting for an unseen enemy, ambushing them, or them shooting you, the war made less and less sense.

"It's going to rain," Carlos said.

Anthony Wyatt looked up at the sky; dark clouds were building at the far end of the valley. He heard distant rumbling.

"When?"

Carlos shrugged his shoulders.

Anthony looked at his watch and at the sky. An hour, maybe two, that is all we want to get away. Life could send them some luck every so often, to everyone, not only to him. Luck was one thing you could universally share. Every one needed it and there was precious little to go around.

"Sofia, take the rifle out of your pack," Anthony said, "Before Carlos and I move into position, I'm going to show you how to use it."

Sofia took the rifle out and gave it to Anthony.

"Give me the magazine."

Sofia handed him a magazine.

"The magazine slides in, like this." Anthony snapped it in place. "To release it and put a new one in, push the button under here."

Anthony pushed the button releasing the magazine, which fell into his lap.

"You try."

Sofia pushed the magazine in and released it, handing the gun back to Anthony. Anthony put the magazine back into the gun, set the safety to on and gave the gun back to Sofia.

"When you want to shoot, flick this over," Anthony explained, pointing to the safety.

Anthony could not remember the Spanish word for safety. Sofia clicked the safety to off and then clicked it back on. She cradled the rifle carefully.

"Tomorrow, I'll show you how to fire it," he said. "I don't think you'll need it today."

"It's good to know how to shoot a gun," Carlos said.

"I've never handled one before," she replied.

"I used to go hunting over in the Valle Escondido," he said.

"That valley is beautiful," she replied with feeling.

"Yes, it has the largest roe bucks in Colombia," he replied.

Anthony listened as Carlos talked about hunting as a youth. It felt good to sit down. Anthony had not said anything about his leg. It was cramping more. The blood did not flow that well because of the wound. It didn't worry him. Next week they would be able to rest. It would be easiest to go to Bogotá. Anthony stared at Sofia's face and watched the beautiful way she formed her words. In the capital city, they could relax and mix themselves in with the eight million inhabitants. None would care who he was or what he had done.

They would first go to the *Estado Civil* and apply for a marriage license. Her grandmother would be happy if they did that; maybe getting married would not be all bad. She would look beautiful in white; for that matter, she looked beautiful in anything. She looked beautiful sitting there in her dark blouse, the fabric tight and sensual around her breasts. While they were waiting for the marriage papers; they would leave the capital city and go up to soak in the hot, thermal waters in Tabio. In the morning, after they had drunk their coffee, they would walk up to El Zipa for a bath and a massage. The afternoons would be theirs; he grew excited thinking about it. And the evenings, warm with a fragrant breeze blowing as you ate in an outdoor *cabaré*, lasted forever. He had dreamed of returning to that alluring, magical spot with someone. After all, what were dreams worth, if you had no one to share them with?

The fierce cough of the big *maquina* reverberated in the canyon. Anthony Wyatt jumped up. They were way out of position.

"Sofia, give me your gun," Anthony ordered.

Anthony loaded a round in the chamber and set it to single fire. He flicked off the safety.

"Point the gun like this at anyone that comes down this trail. Pull the trigger each time you want to shoot," Anthony said.

"Anyone?"

"Anyone coming down this trail will not be friendly," Anthony said.

He returned the gun to her and slung his pack over his shoulder. Carlos waited beside him; he signaled him to follow.

They ran at full speed towards Miguel and Diego. When the sound grew close, Anthony hunched over and scuttled through the jungle staying below the ground foliage. He reached the point where the trail straightened. He stopped.

He motioned to Carlos to cut off the trail and wait in the dense bush. He angled his way up a small rise coming to the spot he had picked out earlier. He pulled out his Zeiss 40 power scope and slowly spotted the woods. Figures moved slowly up both sides of the trail. The fifty-caliber machine kept up its steady firing. Mixed in with that sound were the single shots of a rifle.

The men sneaking through the forest did not return fire to give away their positions. Anthony had not heard a single mine blow. Miguel and Diego were spending ammunition. These men were well-trained; they would soon be close enough to shoot a rifle grenade directly at the big *maquina*.

Anthony slipped off his pack and loaded a rocket into his launcher. He watched several dark-uniformed soldiers group together. He fired directly into them. He ducked below the ground cover and hustled sideways forty meters. He set his rifle for automatic fire and released short bursts at anything that moved. He heard Carlos shoot. He listened to the echo. He heard shots echoing from where he had left Sofia.

With those shots came the boom of mines. Mono's men had retreated over the mines they had assiduously avoided in their push forward.

He traced his steps back and came out where he had left Carlos. Carlos was not there. Anthony Wyatt looked down the trail; he didn't see anyone. Carlos could be hidden among the large ferns lining both sides of the trail. He heard the first grenades explode in the jungle. They exploded down slope from where Miguel sat firing, but they would slowly move closer, until they stopped the big *maquina*. Anthony needed to blow the explosives to signal Miguel to leave the gun and hide.

The cache of equipment was directly across the small canyon, but to cross meant avoiding the mines and stealthy jungle fighters. His breath drew tight as he thought of being pinned down by an advancing company. He quietly withdrew back into the jungle and started to loop around.

He ran quietly, heel to toe and low to the ground. Off to his side, he heard the crashing of brush, the first of the soldiers must have broken through and was making a mad dash for the clearing. If he gave away his position with rifle fire, more would be on top of him before he could slip free.

Without breaking stride, he changed his rifle to his left hand, reached down, and pulled the knife from his sheath along his calf. As the other man drew closer, Anthony timed his leap through a clump of fan palms. He caught the other man, completely rolling him over and landing on his chest. He poised his knife.

"*Capitan*," Diego cried. "*Perdone mi vida!* -- Spare my life."

Anthony sheathed his knife and pulled Diego to the standing position.

"We ran out of ammunition so we ran," he replied breathlessly. "Miguel went one way with the gun, and I came this way."

"Follow me and move quietly," Anthony ordered.

Anthony ran straight over to the trail. He turned to Diego.

"Whistle for Carlos," he said.

Diego whistled. It was loud and melodic. An answering whistle came back.

"Whistle him here," Anthony said.

Diego continued to whistle until they saw Carlos creeping up towards them. He held his gun in his hand.

"I'm here," he called out. "I had to shoot twice to kill him."

"I slayed a bunch of them," Diego boasted. "They came at us like flies."

"We must kill them so we kill them," Carlos said. Carlos looked at the ground.

"Follow me and stay quiet," Anthony ordered.

Anthony Wyatt ran up the trail and cut across the jungle to the edge of the ammo depot. He pulled out two hand grenades from his pack and threw one in the midst of the equipment. It exploded with a loud bang. Nothing more exploded. He waited for more explosions. He threw another hand grenade ever farther into the equipment. The grenade exploded. Several rifles fired on his position, and a hand grenade erupted close. Diego and Carlos were hunkered down on the ground behind him.

"Diego, return up the trail. You're no good to me here," Anthony said.

Diego looked at him and opened his mouth to argue.

"Go now," Anthony said sharply.

Diego turned and ran.

Carlos saw Anthony move around to the backside of the equipment. He followed just behind him. He saw him take more *plastique* and wire out of his pack and run in and out of large containers looking for something. He saw him stop next to a barrel of fuel held in reserve for the machines. His blonde hair stuck out above the barrel. He was bent down close where Carlos could not see what he was doing.

The American ran backwards toward him, the automatic rifle swinging on his shoulder, as he placed the wire along the ground. He watched as Anthony cut the wires with his knife and attached them to an electric detonator. The large knife the American used reminded him of a hunting knife he used to kill the wild boars up in the mountains. When he had killed the wild boars, he felt exhilaration in bringing down the animal. When he had shot the man, it had made the opposite emotion in him.

The American had spoken right, to shoot a man was not like shooting an animal. He thought of the man's family, for not only must he reconcile for the man's death, if the man left children, he must pay for that as well. It is done, he told himself. He must think on it no more. The man had his rifle raised and would have shot him first, if he had seen Carlos soon enough, but he had not. He thought of Ferdinand, his body muddied after being dragged through the earth. His face looked peaceful. If he was to die, he wished to die quickly, to not have time to think about his death coming. The man saw his death coming and had shouted out vile expletives. That was not the way for a man to die. He hoped to die contented.

"Carlos," Anthony said. "Carlos, pay attention and grab this."

Anthony was handing him his pack and telling him to move away. Carlos shouldered the pack and ran back along the trail where he could see. The American hunched behind a large piece of equipment. The *plastique* exploded, sending a section of the equipment skywards. He watched the flames shoot higher than the trees. The American was running towards him, yelling at him to retreat.

As Anthony came by Carlos, he grabbed the strap of the backpack and pulled him along with him. He jumped over a large fallen tree, yanking Carlos along with him, and hunkered down in the mud.

The entire matériel depot erupted in flames. Anthony held his breath, knowing that the oxygen would be sucked out of the air around them as the inferno grew in size. Carlos coughed beside him. Anthony counted to sixty. Wind blew over him, as the fire created its own draft. He breathed in slowly. He reached his hand up above the log, feeling the intensive heat radiate from the fire.

"Carlos, we can clear out of here. There is nothing more we can do," Anthony said.

He took his pack from Carlos and crept backwards away from the log. He kept low to the ground until he could breathe easier. He turned and stopped, waiting for Carlos to catch up.

"Did you see Miguel?" Carlos asked.

"No, Diego said he left through the jungle," Anthony said. "We need to return to Sofia and leave."

Carlos moved out in front, leading them down the dirt trail to the heavily treaded trail out of this valley and over the ridge into safety. Carlos whistled loudly as they approached where Sofia was.

"Sofia," shouted Anthony. Hell, better to give away their position than to be shot by the woman he loved.

"Anthony!"

"We're coming up the trail. Don't shoot."

Sofia was standing erect. The AR15 held at her hip. She had a tight, emotionless gaze on her face.

"I saw something move so I shot."

It was her who had fired those shots.

"You were right to do so. You turned them back down the trail."

He did not say anything further. He shouldered the two packs and motioned Carlos to lead on.

It was a strange sensation to shoot a gun. It spat power. It created fear. Fear in her heart as she held this power, fear for those whom she shot, she knew that fear from personal experience, but it was the power that intoxicated her. She longed to shoot this gun again.

Anthony looked up along the trail; he thought he could see movement farther and higher up the trail. It must be the last of their column. They would wait to see if anymore came. With luck, darkness would fall before anyone came. Then they all would be safe.

After hard, fast climbing up the trail, Carlos veered off and climbed straight up the side of the mountain, backtracking through the underbrush. When they came out into a small rocky clearing, they could see the plane and the dirt road perfectly.

Anthony pulled his binoculars out of the outer pocket of his pack. He scanned the far end of the clearing and saw no movement. Sofia opened her canteen and offered it to Anthony. Anthony took a drink of the warm water. His leg was hurting after the long run. He felt extremely tired.

"Take these," Anthony said, handing the binoculars to Sofia, "look for any movement. If you see anything, wake me."

Anthony lay down and closed his eyes.

It felt as if he had just closed his eyes when he felt Sofia's hand pull on his wrist sharply. He rose very slowly and took the binoculars. He froze as the binoculars brought the clearing into view.

Two squads emerged out of the thick jungle undergrowth, fanning out on both sides on the far end of the road. More men were appearing behind them. They were not dressed in regular, dark army uniforms; they were dressed in mismatched clothing and parts of uniforms. Anthony brought the binoculars and hunched down below the safe covering of the bush.

This is not the government, he thought, paramilitaries. No. Paramilitaries would not pursue them up into the mountains. He looked again carefully with his binoculars. The men crept stealthily along each side of the road, carefully hugging the protection of the undergrowth cover. In no time, they would reach the airplane. He squatted down and turned to Carlos, handing him the binoculars.

"Who are they?" he asked, keeping his voice low.

"From Mono," Sofia whispered. "I recognize the uniforms."

Carlos looked through an opening in the bush with the binoculars. Anthony heard him swear softly. Carlos never swore.

"*Señor*, they are Mono's men," he stated.

"Mono's men? Christ, they move like the devil," Anthony said quickly, his voice revealing his fear. "I thought we had them pinned down and stopped."

"They must have come another way. I recognize the one in front. See that one there, he wears a cowboy hat. I've seen him with Mono. He brings him his cigars."

"Christ," Anthony swore.

They were right. He had seen the man when he was with Mono the first time. He joked to Mono about the cowboy hat. Mono said he was his most trusted. Anthony took the binoculars out of Carlos' hands and looked down.

The first squad had reached the airplane. The cloth sack with the leftover explosives sat like a warning flag on top of the wing. Christ, how had he forgotten it? Please don't let them see it, a little bit closer, Anthony mumbled. The cowboy's group had been moving more cautiously; they were about one hundred meters behind the first group. The first group had encircled the airplane.

Someone stepped out from the crowd and put his hands on the baggage door. They didn't see the cloth sack. Anthony tensed in anticipation of the coming explosion.

A loud voice shouted, echoing up the canyon towards them. The men around the plane dropped to the ground. Nobody moved. Anthony held his breath. The cowboy was hunched down, lined up with the plane on the opposite side of the road. The cowboy ran quickly to the plane. He looked carefully at the cloth sack, but didn't touch it. By the reactions on his men's faces, he was shouting orders to them. Every man, except for the one by the baggage door, moved away from the plane.

Anthony saw the cowboy walk up to the open pilot's window. He crawled inside. Several more minutes passed; Anthony strained his eyes and ears.

The baggage door opened up, and the cowboy jumped out holding something up. It was the fuse. The laughing and shouting carried all the way up to his ears. Several of the soldiers shot their rifles in celebration. The man who had approached the baggage door was being pushed around jovially by the other soldiers. Anthony looked again. The cowboy hadn't taken out the plastic explosive, and the sack was still on the wing.

He leaned over to Carlos and whispered, "Give me your gun."

Carlos fumbled around and handed him his rifle. Anthony checked the chamber; it was loaded. How far was the distance, twelve hundred yards? He dialed the scope up to full power and quick sighted on the sack.

"Sofia," he whispered. "I need you to follow me with the binoculars. Focus the binoculars on the plane. When I fire, tell me where the bullet lands."

She nodded.

Cautiously, they moved along the dusty rise on which they were hiding. The weeds thinned out further along the small ridge. Anthony crawled along on his belly until he had a clear view of the plane. He looked over; Sofia was beside him, peering through the binoculars.

The soldiers had congregated around the airplane. Several were tossing things out of the plane. The cowboy's hat was mixed in among them.

Anthony lined the crosshairs on the cloth sack. He breathed in deeply and exhaled half way. He gently squeezed the trigger. The noise reverberated across the valley. No explosion.

"You hit the ground twenty meters in front of the baggage door," Sofia murmured.

The soldiers all had dropped to the ground; some were scanning their location. Anthony adjusted aim. He breathed in deeply, gently squeezing the trigger after he exhaled half way.

A large explosion rocketed skyward. Large flames engulfed the plane and everything around it. Sofia hugged him fervently. Anthony looked at her and grinned; they had bought themselves some time.

They backed off the open ridge, grabbing their packs to run. Anthony turned to holler his excitement at Carlos, but Carlos was not there. Anthony stopped and turned.

Carlos was walking in circles along the open ridge. He yelled for Carlos to follow. Carlos did not look at him. Anthony yelled again. Carlos waved at him to go on.

"Run up this trail. I'll get Carlos. We will catch up. Don't stop."

Anthony ran back to Carlos.

"Come on Carlos," Anthony yelled. "They will be shooting at us any second."

"I lost my flask of *chicha*,"

"I'll buy you another. Come on!"

"I can't leave without that flask," Carlos said.

"I promise you, I'll come back and find it," Anthony shouted.

Carlos pushed aside a couple of bushes looking for his flask. Anthony heard zings of bullets fly past their heads. Anthony grabbed Carlos' arm and pulled him off the ridge.

They had barely turned down the small trail when fierce gunfire ripped up the small ridge. Bullets cut through the brush where they had been. Anthony heard the sharp whine of a mortar; he threw himself to the ground. Pieces of rock and dirt rained on him. He felt something heavy fall on the back of his legs.

He lifted his head off the ground, craned his neck to look with his right eye over his shoulder. He saw Carlos; his head was resting on the back of Anthony's leg. Anthony pulled his legs out from under Carlos, spun around, and lifted Carlos' head and shoulders carefully up close to his face.

"Carlos," he called softly. "Carlos. Say something."

Anthony shook his stubbly chin softly. Carlos opened his unfocused eyes.

"Carlos," he repeated.

Anthony heard the whine of another mortar; he covered Carlos with his arms and head. The mortar fell further up the ridge where he had taken the shot. Small pieces of dirt and rock fell at their feet.

"Carlos, we must go," he spoke gently to him as if to a child.

Carlos stirred; Anthony lifted him, pulling Carlos up to standing. With his left arm under his shoulders and right arm looped around his waist. Anthony dragged Carlos along the path. Carlos' eyes fluttered, and he moved his legs, supporting his own weight. Anthony's heart cheered. Indiscriminate bullets landed around them.

They were back on the main trail; Anthony pushed quickly forward, leaving the rifle fire and mortar blasts behind them. The trail climbed, and the brush thinned, soon they would be exposed. Carlos grunted something.

Anthony stopped. Carlos leaned his full weight back onto his legs; he pointed to the left with his free right hand. Anthony could not see any trail, only patchy brush leading up the side of the valley. Carlos pulled his left arm back. Without Anthony's support, he nearly fell over backwards before Anthony grabbed him.

It was Sofia coming towards them.

"Carlos is injured," she cried.

"Not badly," Anthony lied.

Carlos grimaced, his lips broke into a tight smile.

"We need to check him," she said.

"No time," Carlos exhaled hard.

"We have to keep moving. Don't turn and come back again. Speed is our savior."

"I can walk," Carlos wheezed.

Sofia nodded. She had walked these ridges; it was steep and treacherous.

"Give me your pack, Carlos," Anthony commanded; his tone left no room for argument.

Carlos slid his pack off his shoulders; it fell heavily onto the ground. Anthony could see that the motion had hurt Carlos. No time to check him now, they had to find cover. The soldiers would be moving up the trail. Anthony picked up the fallen pack and slid the straps over his shoulder, wearing the pack on his chest.

"Ready?" Sofia asked, looking at Carlos.

Carlos moved his head stiffly; Sofia turned and walked off the trail and up the steep incline. One hundred meters. Two hundred meters. Three hundred meters. They slowly crawled along, keeping behind the densest cover. Sofia led them down a small incline and back up the small depression it created. Anthony made out a small trail.

They walked another ten minutes; the bullets had ceased. Sofia climbed straight up. She stopped and motioned Anthony forward. She pantomimed to Anthony to take off the packs. Anthony obeyed and motioned to Carlos to wait for them. Sofia and Anthony crawled on all fours for about fifty meters. From behind some low bushes, they saw the clearing below, groups of soldiers assembled along the road; none had yet come up the trail. They were not yet being pursued.

"We need the binoculars," he whispered. They crawled back.

Anthony asked quietly for the binoculars. Carlos felt inside his jacket; his expression told Anthony everything. It had been lost in the explosion.

He sat down to calculate the risks. In this open valley, they needed the binoculars to spot their pursuers. It would only take minutes to run down and back. They had to go now, before Mono's men regrouped and headed up the trail. He felt Carlos stand beside him. Anthony grabbed the hem of his jacket.

Carlos turned towards him.

"I lost it, Señor. I'll go back down and find it."

"Sit down," Anthony said. "You're hurt."

He pulled Carlos down to a kneeling position and grabbed his pack. He pulled out a small first aid kit.

"Take off your jacket and shirt and clean your wound," Anthony commanded. "Be ready to move by the time we return."

Carlos started to argue, but a sharp stab of pain surged through his small body forcing him to fall to the ground. Anthony dragged him to a small tree and leaned him against it. Sofia ripped open the first aid pack and grabbed a bandage. Carlos took it from her and pointed down the trail.

"My flask," he said.

"If I have time, I'll look . . ."

"It's the only thing I have of her."

"I'll find it," Anthony said.

"May God go with you," he said hoarsely.

Sofia took off his canteen from his belt and set it beside Carlos.

"Clean up well, *viejo*," she smiled and rubbed his cheek. "We will dance when we come back."

Carlos smiled weakly. Anthony stood up, hoisting his rifle over his shoulder. As he followed Sofia back down the small incline, he took one quick look back at Carlos. Carlos was sitting still. When he saw Anthony looking at him, he raised his arm in salute.

Carlos watched Anthony turn and run down the incline. It was all calm and cool now. The sun had gone behind the clouds and made it pleasant to sit here in the open. He looked around and saw the steep sides of the canyon. He stretched his arms out to touch them.

Carlos thought about the man again and understood. Carlos did not shout out. He was not happy about it, but he was not lonely either. He was thirsty. The canteen sat beside him. All he had to do was lift his hand out of his lap, reach beside him, take hold of the canteen, turn the cap with his other hand, and put it to his lips. It seemed like a lot of work, and he was not that thirsty.

The American had told him to clean up. Carlos still had the bandage in his hand. The dirt from his hand had rubbed off on it and it was dirty. A dirty bandage wouldn't do; he might infect his wound. He needed another. The first aid pack lay at his feet. He would have to bend over to reach it. He would clean his wound with the bandage in his hand first; the side he hadn't touched wouldn't be dirty. He looked at the canteen again. He was thirsty.

Carlos reached into his shirt pocket and pulled out a small pink box. He opened it slowly. Inside was a folded, delicate white paper. He guardedly unfolded the paper. A small gold ring fell into his hand. On the paper was handwriting, even though he could not read, he knew what it said. Sofia had written it for him.

"*Hija*, I give you your mother's ring that you will wear it when you find someone you will love forever as I forever love your mother. *Papi.*"

Carlos wrapped it and carefully put back in his pocket. He needed to start climbing; he had to give this to her. *That the American should come.*

Carlos looked up; the clouds were very dark. It would rain soon. When it rained, he could turn his head up and drink the water falling from the sky. That would be better. He was tired and was going to save his strength for climbing up the steep side of the canyon. There was a path directly above them. I will need all my strength to crawl up it, he thought. He was looking forward to the American coming back. The American would find his flask and bring it to him, and the flask would take care of his thirst. He had never been so thirsty. He had worked with the American to wire the left over equipment. He had destroyed the radar with him. He did not feel lonely when he was with the American. He was unified with the gun and Anthony and the other men and the jeep. He was unified with the movement and all of Colombia.

Sofia and Anthony were back on the main trail, running flat out. If Mono's men had started up, they were dead. Sofia scampered up the narrow trail that led up to their earlier position. Without breaking stride, she headed up it. Anthony followed. The heat, the running and the excitement tired him. He was gasping for breath. He leaned over and vomited.

He wiped his mouth on the back of his sleeve. The taste in his mouth gagged him; he reached for his canteen; it was gone. He stood up and looked around. He saw Sofia looking in the brush; she let out a small yell.

She pulled the binoculars out of some loose dirt by their strap. As she walked to Anthony, she wiped the lenses and looked through them. The left side was cracked; the right was undamaged.

"You can see well on the right side," she whispered.

Anthony suppressed a small whoop of joy.

Anthony pointed to where they had early crawled on their bellies. They scuttled low along the bushes to the open ridge. He saw the flask, lying under a scraggly bush. He picked it up and looked at the inscription, "*Fiel para siempre.*"

Their sharpshooters were watching and waiting. Small arms fire tore up the ridge. Anthony dropped and hugged the ground. Pinned down by constant sniper fire, they could only crawl side to side. He listened while the mortar fire circled around them. Soon they would hit this position, and the end of the world would come.

Christ, why had he come back for the flask? He looked at Sofia. Her eyes were wide and expectant, waiting for his command. He would find a way out. She could not interpret the various sounds of war, and knew not that the end was close. He wondered what it would be like, dying. He stuck his head up and thought maybe they could run back towards the main trail and escape the ever-tightening ring of mortar fire. A bullet clipped the branch inches above their heads. He placed his cheek on her head and cuddled in tight behind a large rock. The mortar rounds tossed dirt on them.

"Hold me close, Sofia," Anthony whispered. "Soon it will be over."

"Don't talk like that, it scares me."

"I'm sorry. I don't want to scare you."

"Tell me that we will fly out of here."

"We will fly out of here."

"Tell me that you love me."

"I love you. I love you more than there are drops of water in the ocean."

"That's better. Now you're making sense."

A near explosion threw gravel and dead sticks on them. Anthony hugged Sofia intimately.

"I like it when you hug me like this."

If only I could hug her like this and shield her. God, save her; take me instead.

"Yes. I like it too."

"You're not leaving me."

"No, I cannot leave you now. You're mine for forever."

"Forever is a long time. Won't you tire of me?"

"For forever," Anthony repeated.

"Tell me again that you love me."

"I love you."

"I'm sorry I'm acting crazy. The noise is making me crazy. Can you make it stop?"

"Yes, it will stop."

"Soon?"

"Yes, very soon."

"Before it rains?"

"Before it rains."

"Hold me close and kiss me."

They embraced passionately, the ground trembling below them from the many mortars.

"The noise no longer bothers me. It reminds of watching fireworks in the Plaza Central."

"I'd like to see that with you."

"You will, my sweet. I will take you there."

"Do you promise?"

"Yes, I promise."

A large mortar landed on the other side of the rock protecting them; the blast shook the ground violently below them.

"Is this the end?"

"I think so."

"It's a good end."

"A very good end."

"A beautiful end. *Te quiero.*"

Chapter Twenty-Thursday Evening

Fierce machine gun and canon fire boomed above where Anthony and Sofia were lying.

The earth had stopped quaking. Gravel had stopped falling on them. A large machine gun kept it at bay. Rockets whooshed over their heads. Anthony risked sitting up to look up and over the large rock. His spirits soared; Mono's men were being blown to bits.

Anthony pulled Sofia up, grabbing her to sprint back up the trail.

Juan had come back for them. He could see him operating the big gun himself, raining fifty caliber bullets on Mono's men below.

He had to guide her to safety. He scrambled up the canyon wall towards Juan's position, holding her hand tightly. God had granted his wish. She will cross the pass and carry on.

"Anthony," Juan shouted.

Juan motioned to one of his men who replaced him on the big *maquina*.

"We came back to destroy the mountain gun," Juan continued. "My men have almost reached the pass."

Anthony looked and saw the destroyed artillery gun down along the dirt road.

"We must cross the pass before they can bring another one up," Juan said.

He waved at his men. They stopped firing the big *maquina*, jumped on two mules and took off up the trail

"Where is Carlos?" Juan asked.

"Over there," Anthony replied, pointing.

"We cannot go back for him," Juan said. "We must ride like the wind."

"I can't leave Carlos."

"He will find his way out."

"No, he's wounded badly."

"We must go. It will not take them long to start firing on us."

As if to accent that point, they heard an explosion down in the valley.

"We need to move now," Juan said.

"Take Sofia to safety," Anthony said. "I will find Carlos."

"Never leave a man behind," Juan said.

"He wouldn't leave me behind."

"I understand. Find him and follow us," Juan said. "We came down on mules. I will leave you one for him."

"Leave it tied up here, we will return by this path," Anthony replied.

"I'm going down with you," Sofia said.

"Go now, Sofia."

And leave you?"

"Yes."

"Promise me to come soon."

"I promise."

Anthony kissed her.

"Thanks for coming back and saving my life," he called out to Juan.

"It was my duty," Juan replied.

"Send the flare up, when you're safe," Anthony said.

"I will shoot it myself," she said.

"We must go," Juan grunted.

"Take care of her," Anthony said.

Juan waved and kicked the mule.

"I will stay with you," Sofia said.

"I'm asking you to go on with Juan and meet me at the top of the pass."

"When the bombs exploded so close, I was scared," Sofia said. "I didn't scream, but I felt like it. You held me and I knew it would be alright."

"I will be holding you soon. I will be right behind you," Anthony said. "With binoculars, you will be able to see me. I will not be in any danger. Mono will not follow us."

Sofia's eyes filled with uncertainty.

They kissed and held one another. Anthony broke their embrace; she turned, jumped on a mule to catch up with Juan.

He watched her gallop out of sight through the brush.

"Send the flare up," he screamed after her.

His right leg ached; his stomach was cramping. He forced himself across the incline towards Carlos. As he pushed on, he planned their next movements. He would patch Carlos up. The mule could carry Carlos to the top of the valley. If Mono's men moved up the main trail; Anthony would descend and rain rifle grenades and mortars on them. Mono's men would be forced to go after them, guaranteeing the others safety.

Anthony looked up the path and saw Carlos about fifty yards away.

Carlos was sitting where Anthony had left him; his head was slumped over his chest. Anthony hobbled close to him.

"Carlos, old man," Anthony spoke softly. "Wake up. You can sleep later."

He knelt on his left knee and caressed the old man's cheek. Carlos did not stir.

"Carlos," Anthony said louder, slapping Carlos' cheek. Carlos did not stir.

"Carlos," Anthony shouted, blinking back the tears; he pushed Carlos onto the ground and pounded on his chest. Carlos did not stir.

Anthony pushed his fingers hard against Carlos' jugular; no pulse. He started trying to resuscitate him. No response. He kept at it for several minutes. No response. He slumped over Carlos' lifeless body and cried.

Anthony carefully laid Carlos' body out on the ground. With his fingers, he combed his dappled white, curly hair. He brushed the dust off his jacket and pulled his sleeves down over his hands. He looked at Carlos' dirty wool pants, pocked with holes and patches. His shoes had worn-out soles.

Anthony looked at his own clothes; his shirt was filthy, stained with mud and blood and grease. His fingernails were black and the skin on his hands was scratched and red. His pants were shredded and his boots were torn along the arch. War was a dirty and slovenly business, fought by the ill clad and the hungry.

He looked in Carlos' pockets. Carlos had a few metal coins, some rope and a few bullets. Anthony took Carlos's flask out of his own pocket, held it up and shook it. The liquid swished around inside. He unscrewed the top and drained the contents into his throat. It burned all the way down. He coughed as he pushed the flask into Carlos' shirt breast pocket.

Tucked down in the pocket, Anthony felt something soft. He pulled it out; it was the small pink box he had brought to Carlos from his last trip. He wrapped it delicately in Carlos handkerchief and put it into his own shirt pocket.

Anthony clawed at the rocky ground with his hands to dig a shallow grave. His hands hurt and bled. He saw Carlos's machete lying askew inside his leather belt. He pulled out the machete and stabbed at the ground. The sweat ran down his forehead and stung his eyes; he looked up, expecting to see Mono's men. His fingers cramped from swinging the machete into the hard ground. He finished.

Anthony pulled Carlos into the small hole. He mumbled words, which came back to him from childhood prayers and bible recitations. He scooped up the loose dirt and piled it over the body. He stabbed the machete into the ground as a makeshift headstone. He stood there silently for several minutes.

Anthony picked up the two backpacks, carried them up the hill and dropped down on all fours to look out through the brush. Mono's troops had not pursued them; they were setting up two more pieces of artillery. A group of soldiers with spotting scopes scanned the valley. They stared directly at him. Anthony froze, scarcely breathing. They finally moved off his position, concentrating on the high pass where Juan was heading.

Anthony looked through his binoculars. He spotted Juan and the others moving up the scaling the final exposed trail below the pass. The artillery guns could reach Sofia.

Escaping into the undergrowth was his wisest self-preservative. Fear God, and offend not the State or its laws, he thought, and keep oneself out of the policeman's claws. Leave the lambs to their fate. He had done it on other missions. But before, they were someone else's lambs. He was ensnarled in this ancient pride and duty of husbandry. Juan had counseled him right, and he had not listened.

One can only learn from one who knows. Three nights ago, he was unfettered, and now he was responsible. He gazed through the dense bush; the goons were organizing, preparing to snip off loose ends from the thread he had owned, had used and had allowed to fray. And whenever any Form of Government becomes destructive of Life, Liberty, and the Pursuit of Happiness, it is the Right of the People to alter or to abolish it, and to institute new Government. And he had the skills and the confidence to shepherd them, and it is his Duty, to throw off such Government. Christ, the founding fathers created such high standards and obligations and burned them into one's collective consciousness.

Anthony mentally clicked off the distance between him and the large guns. His shots had to be accurate. He looked down at the spotters; only two remained, their long scopes aimed high over Anthony's head. Anthony rechecked his measurements.

He crawled back to the packs and pulled a launcher out of the pack. He calibrated the sights and loaded carefully. Small raindrops landed on the weapons. He looked up. The dark clouds had quickly moved up the valley; the leading edge was directly overhead. He carried the loaded launcher back to his position.

He cautiously pushed the brush aside and looked. The two gunnery teams had loaded the guns and were grouped around the back of each gun. Anthony lined up on the closest gun through the sights. He breathed in deeply and exhaled half way. He gently squeezed the trigger. He heard the sharp whoosh of the rocket speeding toward its target. The first artillery piece exploded.

Small arms fire clipped the brush below him. Mortars followed, sending up large chunks of rock. He slung the rocket launcher over his shoulder, turned and ran, grabbing the two backpacks as he crawled straight up the mountainside. As he twisted his way through the brush, the explosions expanded around his original position. He crawled behind a cropping of rocks. He had to climb quicker to fire another shot at the last gun.

He dug through the backpacks. he pulled out two ammo belts and clipped them around his waist. He put the two remaining rockets into one backpack, slinging it quickly on his shoulders. He shouldered the launcher and Carlos' rifle. As he rose to look below, bullets zinged off the rocks. He hunched down and listened as the deadly sounds moved around and then away from him.

He crept from bush to rock, warily keeping out of sight. When the deadly sounds came close, he hunkered behind the largest rock he could find until they moved away. He stealthily eased through the dense bush until he reached the backside of a small, long ridge. The ridge ran up and ended several hundred feet higher. Anthony guessed that the main trail ran parallel, but on the other side of the ridge. He could walk easier now, knowing that he was out of sight of the scopes.

He followed a narrow path cut along the backside of the ridge. The deadly firing had stopped. The smoke from the mortars drifted up the mountainside. The evening sun momentarily broke through the clouds creating a perfect rainbow against the curtain of light rain.

Anthony stumbled along a path, searching for a place to climb to the ridge. He spotted an opening where he could climb up the rocks. Anthony looked up the wall of rocks and dropped his ammo belts and the rifle. He stretched his arm and wedged his fingers into a small slit in the rocks. Pulling himself up, he reached out and found another handhold. He inched up the steep slope until he reached the top. He stuck his head around a rock to look.

They had moved the artillery piece behind some rocks along the edge of the road, shielding it from fire from his original position. He brought his binoculars slowly up to his eyes.

More soldiers had come. They wore regular army uniforms. They were lined up, kneeling behind any makeshift cover along the dirt road. Ahead and above them, Mono's men had begun crawling through the brush on both sides of the trail, rifles held ready, alert to an ambush. From up here, the long barrel of the artillery gun was exposed. Large leaves and thick vines hid the main body of the gun and its crew.

Through the canopy, Anthony could make out the movement of men, loading and preparing it for fire. He estimated the distance and slung the binoculars around his neck. He eased the pack off his back and took out a rocket. He loaded the launcher and aimed at a small gap in the foliage covering the gun. He squeezed the trigger. The trees erupted in flames around the gun.

Far up the mountain, Sofia looked back expecting to see Anthony. Carlos was with him. Nothing bad could happen. She lingered, waiting. The long column of men and mules were out of her sight. She waited a little while longer. Nothing. She started up the trail again. She easily caught up with the gray-eared mule and its driver, except the driver was no longer driving the mule but hanging onto its tail and letting the mule drag him forward.

They had double-timed marched up the canyon, never resting. The men with their heavy packs struggled to stay on their feet; the mules with their heavier packs seemed unfazed; they plodded on without complaint. Sofia saw up ahead a young man bending over and holding his side.

"Brother," she said, "let me carry your pack so you can catch your breath."

He looked up at her; his eyes filled with conflict.

"Thank you, Senorita, but I am not tired," his breath labored as he spoke.

He quickly shouldered his heavy pack and ran to catch up with the rest of his squad. She fell back in line again and walked.

As she struggled to climb a particularly steep stretch of trail, she stumbled, sliding down the incline when she felt a strong hand seize her arm. She marveled slightly, as she recognized Juan: He ubiquitously appeared, cursing slow-moving burros, exhorting his men, and reaching out to help the fallen; he never tired.

"Sorry, I wasn't watching my footing," Sofia said embarrassedly. She prided herself on her balance and endurance.

"It is a steep trail with many loose rocks," he replied sincerely.

She stood up and dusted herself off. She looked down the trail, watching the last of the men pass.

"I thought you were in front, leading us onto the right trail?" she asked.

"We have passed the gully of the seven trails. There is only one trail now, and it leads straight up the mountain. It is a hard trail, hard to lose our way and hard to climb up," he said with a smile.

"We haven't stopped moving," she said. "They obey well."

"Don't congratulate me," he said with a short laugh. He showed his teeth when he laughed. "No one wants to be last because of you."

"What?" she asked.

"Every time one of them falls behind you ask if you can help them," he stated.

"You are pushing them hard," she replied strongly.

"You push them harder. I could swear at them, and maybe even shoot a couple of them, but it would never be effective as denting their pride. Their *machismo* won't let them be carried by a lady," he said.

"I only want to help."

"You have. If they set up more artillery, they will destroy us. We are climbing in the open. No protection anywhere. The quicker we are up and over, the safer we will be."

He looked up the trail and saw that his men were out of sight. He beckoned her to lead the way. After leaving Anthony and Carlos, Commander Juan had pushed hard, determined not to lose any of his men, not a single one, nor any of his arsenal; more determined to reach the protection of the mountains beyond the grasp of the government and paramilitaries, and most determined to return, to kill, the revenge hardening his heart, signaling the end of his romantic illusions about struggle, sacrifice and scruples.

The trail steepened, cutting back and forth into the mountain. Juan and Sofia passed several groups of soldiers who had sat down to rest. As he passed each group, Juan shouted encouragement, calling out the names of many of the men. Juan never stopped climbing, willing his entire army to ascend the mountain as quickly as possible. The sweat dripped heavily off Sofia. She walked quickly, noticing that as she passed each bedraggled group, they slowly got to their feet and climbed on.

The trail leveled onto a flat plateau before it rose sharply upwards. Ugly storm clouds whisked swiftly towards them. Because of the narrow trail and steep incline, the men huddled close together, despite the heat. Some had their eyes shut; most stared at the ground and leaned wearily against their packs. She heard Juan shout something to the officers. They roused their units who, en masse, slowly rose and climbed up the last portion of the trail.

Sofia watched Juan command his men to move out quickly. Juan walked out to the edge of the small plateau, which commanded a clear view of the valley. He seemed to be waiting for something. He scanned the valley through his binoculars. His back stiffened. She walked over close to him and looked down into the valley.

She saw a ball of fire rise from below, the boom echoing up to her several seconds later. Too far to see any details with the naked eye, she looked at Juan for an explanation. He peered intently and said nothing. She could hear other explosions. Juan cursed harshly. It surprised her; she had never heard him utter an expletive.

"What happened?" Sofia pressed him.

"They have blown up the guns," Juan said without removing the binoculars from his eyes.

"They?" Sofia asked. "Who?"

"Carlos and Anthony," Juan replied.

"May I see?" Sofia asked.

Juan took the strap from around his neck and handed her the binoculars.

She stared into the binoculars, adjusting the focus until she could see the fire. Despite the power of the binoculars, the fire looked very far-off. The small explosions startled her. She tried to match the sounds with what she saw, but could only see smoke and confusion. She handed the binoculars back to Juan.

Juan turned and looked up towards the pass. Still, two or three directed hits and they could destroy the trail and trap them, able to shell them at their leisure and convenience, leaving nothing for even the crows to pick at. He cursed again.

The men had stopped, wanting to know the cause of the explosion. Juan needed them to climb quickly but did not want to cause panic.

"If you don't want your butts bitten by shrapnel, start moving," he shouted at the closest ones. "You can rest tomorrow."

Feeling the urgency in his voice, a murmur went through the troops and they began running up the steep gap. Juan trotted back to the edge and focused his binoculars below. Explosions encircled the American's position. He made the sign of the cross on his lips.

Anthony looked through the binoculars to check the damage to the gun. The trees were on fire and the gun had turned over, but it was not destroyed. The gunnery crew had surrounded the gun and were pushing and pulling it up right. He set the launcher carefully against the rock not wanting to bump the sights. While watching the crew, Anthony reached for his back pack holding the last rocket.

In his haste, he clumsily pushed the pack over and it slid. He scrambled after it, but it tumbled end over end down the steep slope. Anthony threw his hands over his head expecting an explosion. When none came, he leaned over as far as he could to look for the pack. He did not see it.

He unslung the binoculars, set them close to the launcher and jumped down the slope; it was steeper than he thought. Slipping, sliding and falling, he rolled over a couple of hard ledges. His momentum propelled him uncontrollably down, he landed hard. The pack lay several feet away. He sat up slowly, rubbing his leg. His pants leg was moist. His shoulder throbbed with pain.

Anthony crawled over and reached for the pack; his hand was covered in blood. He retrieved the fallen pack and hobbled over to the steep rampart. He tried to pull himself back up the rocky ledge, but his swollen hand could not strongly grasp the narrow cracks. He stumbled sideways through the thistly brush, desperately searching for a path to the top.

The slope lessened. Anthony charged up, but the dense brush and crumbling rock entangled his feet. Crawling forward, he would slide back down and gouge his legs and hands. Anthony finally ascended the ridge. Sprinting through thinner and less brutal bramble, he gambled and blindly crashed through the jungle towards the rocket launcher. Anthony struggled through the prickly vines, angered at leaving the rocket launcher; more angered at losing Carlos, the man whom he had grown to love and who had trusted him, and most angered at Mono, the vengeful blood coursing through his veins, replacing his reason and sense with pure killing hatred.

Anthony shielded his eyes with his arm and lunged forward; the pervasive prickles caught his clothing but did not stop his progress. He stumbled into an open area and looked out. The dirt road ran below him. Men were moving everywhere. He ran headlong along the ridge, determined to reach the launcher.

Several seconds passed before Anthony heard the first small arms fire, pinging off the rocks around him and spitting up small dust clouds. He hurtled forward, knowing he was close and hoping he would find the wall of rocks where he dropped the ammo belts and the rifle. He saw them. He stopped, gasping for breath. He looked up the steep slope above. He stretched his arm and began willing himself up the rocks, one handhold at a time. Finally , he reached the top. He stuck his head around a rock and saw the launcher resting peacefully against the rock. He swept it into his arms and kissed it.

Anthony reached into his pack, pulled out the last rocket and loaded the launcher. He fashioned the sling over his shoulder to steady his aim. He walked to the edge and dropped to one knee to aim directly down on the big gun. Sighting carefully, his eyes stared at the gun pointed directly at him. He squeezed the trigger, sending the rocket to its target.

In the very back of his brain, he saw a flame shoot out of the muzzle of the big gun and saw it recoil on its base. It had fired at him.

The world went quiet. He watched as the sky, the green brush, and dusty rocks circled around him. He knew he was falling. He landed hard, not being sure if he had lost consciousness; not moving in order to give his brain time to ask the other parts if they could move; and not feeling pain, feeling pain was a good signal from his body that he was not in shock from a severe injury. He rolled over on his stomach and pushed himself to his knees.

The launcher and backpack were gone. He stayed in this position for several moments and rose shakily to his feet. He walked dazedly through the prickly brush, not feeling it tear at his skin. He saw the ammo belts and Carlos' rifle. He knelt next to them and slung them over his shoulder. He put his hand on the ground to steady himself. He felt a great pressure on his chest. He could scarcely draw breath his chest hurt so.

If he could only delay them a bit more, he thought. He had to check to see if he had blown up that third gun. Surely, they must be over the pass now. The third gun had to be blown up.

He pushed himself off the dirt. He walked slowly. His lungs burned; blood came up his throat. He plodded up a path, moving determinedly. He heard steady fire strafe up and down the ridge. He saw an outcropping of rocks up along the trail. He lurched forward.

Anthony tried to jump up on top of a large flat rock, but his leg would not hold his weight. He sat down and leaned against the rock. They had been going pretty good until the plane. He knew in his heart he shouldn't have blown up the plane. The plane had been his escape route, his secret tunnel out of here, and he had destroyed it. Everything bad had happened after he had blown it up. Who was he talking to now? He needed to get on top of those rocks and look out. He sat still. His chest was hurting badly now. The pain in his leg bothered him. He hated pain. He pulled out his handgun.

I'll just do it now. It would be no different than swallowing that pill that you always carried with you. He was never going to be taken into custody again. He knew how that ended. *I guess I am no different than the ones who fight in the back country. Don't think about that. You have no time for that, you must see if the gun is blown up.*

He turned and pushed himself up quickly and jumped, clawing at the side of the rock. His weight came onto his right leg and it buckled. He crumpled to the ground. His forehead hurt. He touched it and brought his fingers in front of his face; they were wet with blood.

I am obscenity now. What did Juan say about not harming his pretty face? Well now it was harmed. He stared at his pistol in his hand. He had not lost it in the fall. The pistol would stay with him to the end and be his end.

No, he must think about her. Think about her crossing the pass and asking Juan for the flare gun. Think about Juan giving it to her and showing her how to shoot it. And her asking for another flare just to make sure he saw, and then a third.

Think about the flare. I can't. Think about heaven. I can't. Think about Bogotá and the warm thermal waters. All right, that is good to think about. Think about her in the waters with you. Even better. That is what it will be like. Bubbly warm waters and her holding you. Do you feel it? Yes. Then hold it and crawl up that rock.

He crawled from one rock to another. He made it to the top, lying on the flat rock and breathing heavily and waiting for the pain to pass. He dragged himself forward until he could see out. The third artillery gun was a mangled mess of metal.

"Do you see what you get when you mess with me," he yelled at the gun.

He coughed. He clinched his teeth tightly to hold back the blood that filled his mouth. Soldiers grouped along the edges of the road, but he did not see any movement along the trail. He spat out and away from the rock where he would not have to look at it.

All right, he said. And he rested quietly thinking about what his next move would be if he was down there. He had to think about something and work over a real problem in his mind in that his mind was slipping away from him, no different than the pain which had slipped away from him, like losing your sled on a steep, icy hill and watching it run all the way to the bottom without you.

Anthony screamed at himself and punched his right leg with his closed fist, which only sent a dull feeling into his body. He needed to do something, God if they could only come before I give out.

Anthony examined Carlos's gun. It was still loaded. He raised Carlos' rifle to his shoulder and sighted down the path. He stared at two large trees, which hung over the trail no more than a hundred meters away. He focused and waited until they would come. His arms cramped, forcing him to drop the gun. He held his head in his hands trying to control the pain.

He looked across the canyon. Thick, black clouds had come over his head and were sending large drops of water to him. He heard it splatter on the rocks. They were ugly clouds. Clouds made these dirt trails muddy and impassable. They were indeed cursed; the steep trace that slithered out of this canyon would be a whitewater stream within a few minutes in a torrential rain.

He pulled out his handgun and placed it beside him. Please give me strength, he prayed. Don't make me do it. Please God give me the strength. He cradled the handgun and clicked the safety off. God give me the strength, he repeated in a mantra. Please, God. Please God. Help me hang on. God, make the pain stop.

"No," he said fiercely, throwing the handgun down the slope in front of him. It stuck in the mud.

His luck was holding well at that particular moment. With the gun destroyed, the main group men had stopped, waiting on more reinforcements and supplies. A few had organized and started pushing up the trail on foot. Fierce rain clouds whipped the wind into a frenzy. Trees doubled over from the force of the rain hitting them.

Anthony looked down and saw soldiers climbing, slipping and sliding along the muddy trail. The narrow jungle trail morphed into a white water torrent. They looked like small ants clinging to the ground. He felt for the binoculars that had hung at his neck. They were not there. He felt around on the ground near where he lay; they must have fallen off during the explosion. The pain in his chest made his eyes water. He closed his eyes until the pain eased.

He was one with the rock. He breathed as easily as he could with his hands holding up his chin and his elbows on the rock. He was one with rain. The rain turned into a downpour, water pooling in the indentations of the rock. He touched the water. It felt soft. He opened his mouth and let the raindrops fill his mouth. He drank and his thirst was relieved.

He could see Sofia clearly. She was in the back of the long line of troops, lingering for him. He would run to catch her before she turned around and saw him. He would reach out and touch her. She would turn around, her eyes would be round with fear, until she recognized him, when her eyes would grow soft and full.

Men bobbed in and out of the brush, slowly coming closer. Mono led. Anthony recognized him, the stern face, reddened by the exertion, and his stubby torso, erect and rigid even as he walked quickly. He never looked back at his men. He kept going, determined and hard.

Anthony picked up Carlos' rifle, which lay at his side. He looped the sling around his left forearm and nestled the stock into his shoulder. He grasped the stock, feeling the indentations with the tips of his fingers. He set his elbow carefully and gently on the rock, keeping his muscles loose and relaxed. He laid his chin on the stock, rubbing his whiskers along the cool, wet steel.

Mono had stopped under the two large trees. A radioman stood next to him. Mono held the receiver and talked animatedly. He thrust the receiver back at his soldier and adjusted his poncho to protect himself from the jungle rain. Anthony slowly closed his left eye and with his right eye lined up the small ball on top of the rear site. Anthony waited.

Mono moved away from his men and the protecting trunk of the tree. Anthony breathed in deeply and exhaled half way. Mono turned and marched, shoulders squared, up the trail. Anthony slowly squeezed the trigger. Mono dropped facedown into the mud.

Light came to Anthony's eyes. The pain receded. He looked up, he thought he saw a halo, her halo, and everything was fine. His eyes focused and he saw a second halo and understood that it was a flare. A third flare exploded above him, creating a brief and fleeting rainbow encircling the light. They had crossed the pass.

She had made it. She was safe.

He smiled.

The pain was gone.

Gregory Solsrud lives in Atlanta, Georgia with his family including a son who Smites a lot, an iPhone with a daughter attached, some crazy redneck friends and a mailbox full of bills.

VISIT GREGORY SOLSRUD ON HIS WEBSITE

WWW.SOLSRUD.COM

CHECK OUT HIS OTHER WRITINGS

AND

THE SEQUEL TO *ANDEAN REBEL*

RISE UP REBEL

Made in the USA
Lexington, KY
14 March 2016